S

Sweet Tea and Secrets

Also by Nancy Naigle

Out of Focus
Inkblot (co-written with Phyllis Johnson)

Sweet Tea and Secrets

An Adams Grove Novel

NANCY NAIGLE

The characters and events portrayed in this book are fictitious. Any similarity to real persons, living or dead, is coincidental and not intended by the author.

Printed in the United States of America.

Published by Montlake Romance
P.O. Box 400818
Las Vegas, NV 89140

ISBN-13: 9781612185958
ISBN-10: 1612185959

Dedication

This book is for every woman who needs a break.
I've been there—done that.
It's OK to escape for a little while.

Sweet Tea and Secrets

Welcome to the small town of
Adams Grove, Virginia.

Chapter One

Jill Clemmons started each day with Grandma Pearl's favorite quote in mind: *Live your life in such a way that every single morning when your feet hit the floor Satan shudders and says, "Oh shit, she's awake!"*

Still in her jammies, Jill breezed into the kitchen after a perfect night's sleep, which was rare for a night not spent in her own bed. She'd probably still be asleep, but a spicy aroma had teased her awake. The closer she got to the kitchen, the better it smelled.

Aunt Milly stood in front of the stove, already coiffed right down to her red-orange lipstick, her signature color. Even with the frilled apron over her outfit, she looked way too thin for an active lady in her eighties.

"Good morning." Jill took an exaggerated whiff. "Now, that's home cooking." The smell had Jill's stomach growling a complaint for hurrying back home from Savannah to Virginia. She hadn't had anything to eat since lunch yesterday.

"Was that your stomach?" Milly spun toward the doorway and waved a metal spatula with an outdated avocado-green handle in the air. "Lordy goodness. You probably haven't had a good meal in way too long."

"I don't get much of this kind of cooking. That's for sure."

"'Bout time you got up. I thought you might miss out on breakfast. Are you living on a city clock these days?"

"I wish that were the case." Jill helped herself to a cup of coffee. "Bradley has an alarm set for everything from getting up in the morning to when to go to bed and everything in between. I never knew anyone so regimented."

"That man is a wee bit uptight, you know? You don't need alarm clocks if you're following the sun." Aunt Milly pushed the sausage around the well-worn cast-iron skillet. "Never knew Pearl to ever use a clock to tell her to get up. You either, before you up and left town."

"True." Jill leaned against the counter and took a sip of her coffee. It was hard to believe it'd been nearly a year since she'd packed all her stuff in Piggly Wiggly bags, loaded her little red pickup, and moved to Savannah for her job with the Kase Foundation. Until then, Jill had never thought she'd live anywhere but Adams Grove. Yet, on the rebound from Garrett Malloy, moving had become one of the biggest perks of the job. The only downside was being away from Pearl.

"I'm so glad you could make it back for the surprise party. I was worried with it being so close to your big shindig that you wouldn't come." Milly planted a lipstick kiss on Jill's cheek.

"I wouldn't miss this for the world." Jill stopped short of telling Aunt Milly about Bradley stomping around, mumbling complaints about her dropping everything to make the trip up and putting the Kase Foundation event at risk, even though she was in charge of the event time line. Aside from Bradley's foul mood, the Kase Foundation wouldn't suffer a bit by her being gone for one day. He hadn't been supportive. Not as a boss *or* boyfriend.

Jill pushed those thoughts aside and slid into one of the chrome-legged chairs around the orange-and-white Formica kitchen table. "Do you think we'll surprise Pearl today?"

"It's two weeks before her birthday. You'd think that would be surprise enough."

That had been Bradley's big heartburn. He didn't understand why she couldn't wait and celebrate Pearl's birthday on June 27, her real birthday.

"That grandmother of yours is near impossible to keep a secret from. It's the thought that counts, though." Aunt Milly cracked two eggs into the hot grease.

"So you think she knows?"

The eggs snapped and popped as they crisped in the hot grease. "I didn't say that. You never know with Pearl. That gal has her thumb on the pulse of this town."

"Always has." The thought of the calorie-laden breakfast worried Jill a little. She had to squeeze into the formfitting gown she'd picked out for the fund-raiser, but saying no to her tummy now would just be plain cruel. Plus, Aunt Milly had gone to a lot of trouble.

Milly slid a plate in front of Jill, then took off her apron and hung it on a hook next to the refrigerator. She glanced at her watch. "It's almost nine fifteen."

"I *was* a sleepyhead," Jill said.

"You probably needed this break. Pearl tells me about everything you're working on. I don't know how you do it all." Milly stretched out her arms for a hug, and Jill gave her a long squeeze.

"OK, sweetie, eat up. I've got to get my rear in gear to put on that Academy Award–winning act to get Pearl over to the church on time. Pearl wants to stop at the yarn shop on the way, and you know there's no rushing her once she's got her fingers in those bins. I can stall, but I can't rush her. If I rush her, she'll definitely get suspicious."

"You're so right. I'll lock up when I leave. Thanks for the lovely breakfast. You're too good to me."

"Of course I am. I'm your favorite aunt."

She was her *only* aunt—and not even a real aunt, at that. Milly had been Pearl's best friend for as many years as Jill could remember. "Good luck. I'll see you there."

Milly grabbed her purse off the hall table and headed for the door, waving a bony hand in the air as she slammed the door behind her.

Jill swept the last corner of her toast into the yolk and sausage grease on her plate. One quick pass over the kitchen and everything was back to normal. She washed and dried her dishes and put them back in the cabinet, then went to her room to get packed and ready to go.

She checked herself in the full-length mirror in Milly's bedroom, then gathered her tote bag and headed to the car. Her brand-new car was covered in dust from the drive down the dirt lane. Bradley would freak if he saw it today. He'd talked her into getting the fancy BMW to replace her truck. It wasn't important to her, but he hadn't been a big fan of her truck being parked in front of the house. Tired of hearing his complaints, she let him have his way. After all, you have to have some compromise in a relationship, and the kind of car she'd drive didn't seem one to go to the mat for.

Her sporty car hugged the tight curve on Old Horseshoe Road way better than her truck ever could. Honeysuckle grew high across the ditch bank, making the road feel isolated. As she neared the side entrance to the church, she couldn't see any other cars at the church building. *Maybe we* will *pull off the surprise.* Gravel crunched beneath her tires as she pulled into the back lot to park among the dozens of cars already there. Jill grabbed a bag from the passenger seat and headed for the door.

A pretty blonde girl Jill didn't recognize swung the door open as she approached and rushed her inside. "We're trying to be sure Pearl doesn't sneak up on us."

"Good thinking. Here's hoping for a miracle." Jill raised her crossed fingers, then turned her attention to a banner that read "Happy *Early* 85th Birthday, Pearl." Silver duct tape secured the sign to the wall above a long table filled with home-baked casseroles and desserts.

Bright balloons flanked the banner, and so many soared above the chair-of-honor that they threatened to lift it right off the floor. The thought of her tiny grandmother whizzing around the room above all the guests made Jill laugh.

A stove-sized box heaping full of nonperishables was set up near the cake. The food drive was Pearl's pet project for the community, and cans were the perfect gift from Jill. She hitched the bag up onto her hip to add the canned goods she'd brought to the pile, then set a brightly wrapped package next to the cake.

Mac's Bakery had outdone themselves. This cake had those food-show creations beat hands down. The three tiers together stood over two feet tall. The top layer looked just like one of Pearl's award-winning chocolate pecan pies; the bottom layer was a fondant woven basket full of colorfully frosted cupcakes that looked like yarn. Knitting needles rose high above them, both with a blue ribbon the size of a dinner plate attached. Just like the one Pearl had won last year. That honor would be up for grabs at the annual Festival Days Bake-Off on Fourth of July weekend. Everyone in the county vied for the coveted award, but Pearl's pie had won the last three years in a row.

The room buzzed with excitement. Jill took pictures and exchanged hellos with old friends she hadn't seen since she moved away.

"They're here!" someone shouted.

Suddenly, the room went dark and a hush settled.

Jill wondered how good an idea it was for fifty people to yell "surprise" at an eighty-five-year-old woman. But then, Pearl wasn't your average old lady, either.

Aunt Milly chatted loudly with Pearl in the kitchen. Everyone listened intently for the magic moment. Then, 3-2-1, the door swung open.

"Surprise!"

Pearl's mouth dropped wide.

"You little devils." Pearl wagged a crooked finger across the crowd of friends lined up in front of her. "You sure know how to scare the puddin' out of a gal."

Everyone cheered. Jill hung back, taking in the pleasure of seeing Pearl revel in everyone's delight. She still had her doubts that Pearl had been surprised, though.

"Oh my, is this…?" Pearl headed straight for the bin of food. "It is! You know the way right to my heart. This will feed so many." Her eyes twinkled as she turned around. "Thanks, y'all. All y'all." She swept a tear from the rim of her glasses. "So much." She scanned the large group of friends, and then her eyebrows shot straight up.

"Surprise." Jill opened her arms, enjoying the sparkle in Pearl's eyes.

Pearl marched over to Jill and kissed her on the cheek, leaving a bright-magenta smudge that Pearl quickly rubbed in with her thumb. Like always, she followed up with a kiss on the other cheek to make them match.

Jill hugged Pearl. "It's so good to see you."

"I knew it was going to be a perfect day today. There was only one contrail across the sky when we drove up."

"I didn't even notice, but that *is* good." Jill and Pearl had made it a practice to count the condensation trails behind the jets that soared across the sky. With Richmond, Norfolk, and Raleigh all being about the same distance from Adams Grove, it was a rare and lucky day when there were less than three or four. "Carolanne sends her best. She's in California on business; and from there, she's going to Hawaii with some friends from work. I told her you'd understand."

"Of course I do. She's such a thoughtful one. And such a dear friend to you. How long will you be staying?"

"I have to head back after the party."

Pearl raised a penciled brow and tsked. "My goodness. That's a quick trip, but I'm delighted you're here now."

Jill reached for Pearl's hand. "I miss you like crazy. I promise I'll be back once this fund-raiser is behind me. I can't wait to spend some time with you."

"I'd love that," Pearl said. "You coming back for a nice long visit—that's the best gift you could give me."

Jill lifted two plastic champagne cups of sweet tea from the table. She took a sip from one and handed the other to Pearl. "Not as good as yours," she whispered.

"That's because we know the secret." Pearl turned her attention to the voices blending into the best round of "Happy Birthday" ever. Only two candles stood tall on the cake. An eight and a five.

Pearl blew out the two candles. "I appreciate the consideration with the two candles. Eighty-five flames would likely set off the sprinkler system, and that'd be a mess." Everyone cheered as Pearl picked up the knife. "This cake is almost too pretty to cut."

"I've got pictures," Jill said, raising her camera. "Dig in."

"Don't have to tell me twice." Pearl cut the first slice, and everyone lined up to get a piece of cake. "You know how I love my sweets."

A loud knock from the fellowship hall door caused a pause in the festivities.

"We locked that so you wouldn't sneak in on us," someone shouted. "I'll get it."

Pearl plopped a piece of cake on a small plate. "That's probably Garrett. I asked him to come help move tables. I thought we were setting up for a reception."

Jill swung around to face Pearl. "That's not why you invited him, is it? You knew I was coming." Jill watched for a reaction, but Pearl busied herself with the cake, avoiding eye contact.

As Jill turned to walk away, Pearl grabbed her wrist.

"Oh, come on, dear," she pleaded. "It's my birthday. You two have to talk eventually. What better time than over cake? It's a party. Wait right here." Pearl scurried toward the door.

Jill knew surprising Pearl would be tricky, but she'd never considered that Pearl might be the one tricking her.

A warm rush heated Jill's cheeks. Maybe she was overreacting. Maybe it wasn't even him. Maybe it was just someone who was late. A singing telegram. A stripper. Anyone but Garrett.

She sucked in a breath as the door opened and hoped for the best.

All six-foot-something of Garrett Malloy filled the doorway. His hair was a little shorter than it had been a year ago. His skin was tan, and she knew he was going to tug off his sunglasses and tuck them into the neckline of his light-blue golf shirt before he even made the move. *Why does he have to look so good?*

Her heart pounded so hard the room began to swim. *Doggone him and that perfect smile.* She turned and hightailed it down the hall to the sanctuary without looking back until the door clicked behind her.

Out of breath, she stood clutching her chest.

She might have to talk to Garrett someday, but it wasn't going to be today. The sound of rustling fabric rescued her from the thought of him. When she looked up, a bleached blonde in an unfortunate red hoop-skirted bridesmaid dress stepped out of the choir room. A young man wearing a tuxedo T-shirt emerged behind her. Both froze when they saw her standing there.

"We just…We were getting something for the bride. She left something back here."

I bet. Like what? Your virginity? Jill rolled her eyes. "In church? Really?"

The two hurried out, slamming the door behind them.

Jill lowered herself onto the back pew and gazed at the huge white ribbons adorning the first few rows.

The wedding she'd always dreamed of in this beautiful church would never happen now. The day she and Garrett pinky swore their lifelong commitment under the monkey bars in the fourth grade, she'd started filling notebooks with wedding details. She'd even sketched out the fancy five-layer cake she'd have Mac create just for her. OK, so the plans gained a lot more class and dignity over the years, but it all started back then.

Delicate pink rosebuds and soft green buttercream vines would climb layers of shiny white fondant to a topper of double hearts made of sugar pearls. Her bridal bouquet would consist of long-stemmed flowers bundled by a flowing pink ribbon so light that the air would catch it and twirl it with each step she made down the aisle.

All those sugarplum dreams were history now. Just like her relationship with Garrett.

She squeezed her eyes closed and shifted her thoughts back to Bradley. He'd been dropping hints that something big was about to happen, and she was sure he was going to pop the question, but he'd made it clear that his wedding would be quick and simple, preferably on a beach. The dress she'd dreamed of for her wedding day wouldn't do well on a beach. Sand and salt water would ruin a beaded satin gown in a hurry; and she wasn't about to spend that kind of money and then ruin her dress, even if Bradley would.

A cool hand rested on her shoulder. She turned to see Pearl standing there.

"You missed him," Pearl said, sliding into the pew next to her.

Jill flattened her sweating palms against her pants. "I'm done missing him."

Pearl harrumphed. "I guess Milly was right."

"About Garrett? I'm glad someone finally believes it's over between the two of us."

"No. Not that. Milly says you're pigheaded."

"I am not," Jill said.

Pearl shrugged. "Yes, you are. Oh, don't go looking all offended. Sometimes that's good."

Jill sat back in the pew.

"Not good this time, but sometimes."

"I've moved on." *Is there anything that'll convince you it's over with Garrett?* "I think Bradley's going to propose."

Pearl let out a loud sigh. "Oh, honey, don't do something crazy. You don't want to marry Bradley Kase. I know I introduced the two of you, but he's not right for you as a husband. You're not in love with him. You're in love with the idea of being in love and married."

"Bradley is a good man, and the Kase Foundation does wonderful work."

"Love's kind of like sweet tea. The secret is all in having the patience to let it steep. Really, you barely know him."

"He's good to me," Jill said.

"Don't confuse material things for love, honey. I know you and Garrett went through some tough times. Trust me, I know about the challenges true love brings, but you two are meant to be." She tapped the top of Jill's hand in time with each syllable that followed. "Better to fight for what you really want than to be left wanting what you didn't fight for."

Jill laid her head on Pearl's shoulder. "Your matchmaker radar is off kilter when it comes to me and Garrett. He didn't want a partner. He wanted to plan his future down to the minute with a money-back guarantee before he would even think about taking one step forward. That's not what marriage is about." She couldn't tell Pearl what Bradley had told her about Garrett or about the accusations Garrett had made. There was no sense dragging Pearl into that drama. Especially not a year later.

"I seem to remember someone else wanting things her way, too."

"Was I supposed to wait forever?"

Pearl patted Jill's hand. "Here's the good thing about the future. It comes one day at a time. Follow your heart each day. You'll get where you're supposed to go."

"I love you, Grandma Pearl."

"Aw, honey. You haven't called me that in years."

"I know. I'm suddenly feeling like a little girl again." She'd been only seven when her parents died and Pearl added the role of parent to that of grandmother. Grandma Pearl was more special than a grandma could ever be. And Pearl was a precious treasure to most people in this town.

"Forgive me for the stunt with Garrett?" Pearl asked.

"You know I can never be mad at you."

"Good, and when you come back, I'll tell you the story of all love stories. You think you and Garrett had problems..." She ran her hand along Jill's cheek. Her voice softened. "Sometimes love requires great sacrifice, dear."

Stories. Pearl had a million of them, and Jill had a feeling Pearl made up most of them to suit her point, but it didn't matter. They were always spellbinding.

Jill stood. "Come on. Let's go back to your party."

They walked back to the fellowship hall and filled plates with homemade goodies before sitting at one of the tables with a crowd of friends gathered together to celebrate.

Aunt Milly rushed toward them with her camera. "There you two are. I need pictures."

Pearl tucked a raw broccoli floret behind her ear and leaned in with a huge smile.

Chapter Two

Jill was exhausted from the long hours she'd put in since she'd gotten back from Adams Grove two weeks ago, but seeing the grand ballroom of the Harbour Lady Hotel filled with the elite of Savannah, there to support the Fancy-a-Future Kase Foundation fund-raiser, was enough to keep her going.

"How's the best fund-raiser the Kase Foundation has ever had?" Bradley had stepped up behind her and whispered into her ear.

His breath tickled her neck. "I consider myself a primo project manager, thank you very much." Her business degree had helped, but more than that, she was thankful for the planning and communication skills that Pearl had taught her. "You're not biased, either, are you?" Jill leaned against him and scanned the room. "Can you believe this night?"

"You've exceeded my every hope." He spun her around to face him, then swept her into the crowd of dancing couples. "Tonight is perfect," he said, never breaking frame as he led her in a waltz under the beautiful chandeliers. "You are perfect. I couldn't have done this without you."

Her insides swirled in time with the fine layers of her gown that swept her ankles with each turn. She'd never felt so elegant or so proud.

"Still right on schedule, too." The silent-auction winners would be announced next—the finale. Then they'd call it a night. "I'm glad we're sharing this moment," she said.

"Oh, it's not over yet." Bradley's eyes held hers, the pull of his smile made his eyes twinkle and dance under the light.

Excitement flickered in her belly. *He's going to propose. Tonight.* She took in a deep breath to steady her trembling legs and keep pace with Bradley's smooth movements.

Bradley gave a nod of recognition to a tall man standing to the side of the dance floor. "Duty calls. I'll be back." He dropped a kiss in the nook of Jill's neck, and then he was gone—swept into the sea of black suits.

Jill zigzagged through the crowd. Her pride swelled at the thought of the funds she'd already helped raise, and the money continued to flow tonight. She watched as guests posed in their finest attire for the photographer. The enticement of getting their picture in front of the special silver background for donating over ten grand had seemed to push several donations up significantly as they kept one-upping each other with fat donations.

This ought to ruin the devil's day.

Tonight's event was a heck of a lot bigger than the chicken-barbecue fund-raisers she'd helped plan back in Virginia, but the same strategy had worked. Even the video montage was a big hit with this hoity-toity bunch of Savannah socialites. Seeing themselves on the screen, larger than life, fed their hungry egos and translated into an extra few digits in donations.

Genuine or for show, it didn't really matter because their donations would all go to the cause. The special camps the Kase Foundation funded were designed to position gifted youth, regardless of their families' income level, for great things. Planning this fund-raiser had taken a year of long hours, but tonight, the late nights and early mornings were paying off in dollars—*big* dollars—that far exceeded the foundation's goals to fund youth camps.

Jill accepted a glass of champagne from a passing waiter and eased into a seat at a corner table. Her work for the night was done. Someone else was in charge of the silent auction and closing tasks.

She smoothed her gown and lifted the glass to her lips. The bubbles tickled her nose, but the cool liquid relaxed her.

Pearl's comments about marrying Bradley played in her mind. Jill clutched the black onyx-and-pearl pendant on her necklace and slid it back and forth against its chain. The habit had broken more than its fair share of necklaces over the years, but the zipping sound had a soothing effect on her when she was in a crowd.

She scanned the room for Bradley. His height made him easy to spot, unlike her. She could get lost in a room of junior high students. Waving, she caught his attention, then tapped her wrist indicating it was time to close the event.

Bradley acknowledged her with a quick nod, then took the stage. His black tuxedo set off his soft blond hair and tan. He was easy on the eyes, but it was his commitment to children through this foundation that attracted her the most. If there was one thing Pearl had taught her, it was the importance of being an active part of the community, which was also why Pearl was so crazy about Garrett. He was a shining example of that.

Guests returned to their tables, and the room hushed as Bradley announced the winning bids.

Jill's phone vibrated, sending her silk clutch jitterbugging across the table. Her cheeks flushed as she swept her purse to her lap. She took refuge through the burgundy drapes that hung just behind her to answer the call.

She cupped her hand over the phone. "Hello?"

"Hey. Are you OK?"

Not recognizing the phone number or the voice, Jill responded with quiet emphasis. "You have the wrong number."

"Jill? Wait."

The sound of her name caused her body to stiffen. She lifted the phone back to ear. "Hello? Who is this?"

"It's me, Carolanne."

"It didn't sound like you. Hey, you're in Hawaii on vacation. Is everything OK there?"

"Here? Yes, but…"

"Can I call you back, then? I'm at the fund-raiser." Applause came from the ballroom.

Carolanne's pause set off Jill's internal alarms. Jill turned her back to the noise and pressed the phone closer to her ear. "Carolanne? Are you there?"

"Yes. I'm here." Carolanne paused again. "You don't know?"

"Don't know what?"

"Milly said she talked to Bradley early this afternoon. You—"

The champagne churned in her stomach. "Why would Milly talk to Bradley?"

"I don't know how to say this." Carolanne spoke in an odd, yet gentle, tone. "Pearl…She passed away. She's gone, Jill."

The sounds of the party vanished.

"I thought you knew. Bradley told Milly he'd tell you. I'm so sorry, Jill. I'm brokenhearted. I can just imagine what you're feeling."

Jill lowered the phone and clutched it to her chest. She swept the drapes back. Bradley stood at the podium, thanking everyone for coming. He made eye contact with her and flashed a smile as if things couldn't be better.

How could he?

It was like the oxygen had just been drained from her space. *Not Pearl.* She turned away from the curtain and lifted the phone to her ear. "No. She can't…"

"I can't believe it, either, and I can't believe he didn't tell you."

"No. He was..." *What? Too busy? Forgetful? Heartless?* There was no excuse. "How? When?"

"Milly found her." Carolanne's voice cracked. "She left a detailed message on my cell phone, but I didn't listen to it until just now. I just got in. I booked a flight and then called you. I'm so sad for you, for us. I hate that I'm so far away. It's only three o'clock in the afternoon here. I've got a seat on the five o'clock flight."

Carolanne loved Pearl, too. Who didn't? Jill swallowed and tried to catch her breath.

"Milly had spoken to her just a couple hours earlier, but when she got there..." Carolanne's voice cracked as she spoke. "It must have happened midafternoon your time. I know you must be reeling."

"This can't be happening. It just can't."

"My flight lands in Richmond noonish tomorrow. I'll be in Adams Grove by two o'clock. Should I meet you at Pearl's house? No, wait. I just booked a room at the hotel. Meet me there. Is there anything else I can do from here?"

That was just like Carolanne, always the stable one in a crisis. Jill swallowed hard. "I can't believe this is happening. I've got to get home."

"I'm getting ready to call Milly. I'll let her know we're both on our way."

Jill's heart seemed to shatter, stealing every bit of her strength. The black beaded gown she wore tonight suddenly felt like it weighed more than she did.

"I've got to get out of here. I'll see you tomorrow." Jill closed her eyes. "Thanks, Carolanne."

"I'm so sorry to have been the one to give you the news. I love you, girl."

Jill clung to her phone, praying that when she opened her eyes she'd realize it was all a bad dream. But Bradley's voice vibrated above the crowd, thanking guests, moving her way. His voice made her suddenly feel ill. He'd never been so thoughtless. She'd like to burst out there and demand an explanation, but she knew it wasn't the time or place for that. Instead, she slipped out of her strappy heels and ran out the rear exit.

When she reached her car, she tossed her shoes into the passenger seat, jumped behind the wheel, and sped away. No matter how loud she cranked up the radio, the volume couldn't drown out the news replaying in her head.

Pearl's gone. Gone. Gone.

Just a year ago, it had been Bradley's voice that soothed her when Garrett had broken her heart. Now Bradley had let her down, too.

Could he have thought this fund-raiser was more important than Pearl? His screwed-up family relations are no excuse. He knows what Pearl means to me. She's the only family I have.

Had.

Jill was driving so fast that she almost overshot the driveway of the house she shared with Bradley. Her hands shook as she parked and tugged the keys from the ignition.

Hiccup.

Stress had a way of bringing on the hiccups. Always had. She took in a deep breath and held it.

Hiccup.

That never works, she thought and exhaled loudly. At least the hiccups hadn't given her away at the hall. She had no desire to discuss this with Bradley right now.

She hurried into the house, pausing at the staircase to listen. The house was completely quiet. Annie must've gone out for the evening.

Thank goodness. She and Annie, Bradley's housekeeper, hadn't seen eye-to-eye since the first day Jill set foot in this house. That girl didn't have one Southern dish in her recipe box or a hospitable bone in her body. The only thing she and Annie had in common was that they were both short. But Bradley was nothing if not loyal to those who stuck by him, and she'd been with him for seven years. So Microwavin' Annie was here to stay.

Hiking up the skirt of her gown, Jill took the stairs two at a time in her bare feet. The smell of Bradley's aftershave still hung in the air. She dashed into the bedroom but paused at the sight of her image in the full-length mirror. There was no argument that her black gown was beautiful. But Pearl had always reserved black for funerals, so she had, too.

Until tonight.

When Bradley had surprised her with the fancy one-of-a-kind gown this morning, she'd had a bad feeling.

Always trust your intuition.

Jill pulled the bad-karma dress over her head and flung it across the room.

Her practical side forced her to cross the room, pick up the high-dollar pile off the floor, and smooth it before hanging it properly on a padded hanger on the back of the bathroom door.

Hiccup.

The beads on the designer dress sparkled, taunting her. She'd probably been slipping into it just as Pearl took her last breath.

She stepped into the adjoining closet, grabbed another hanger, and stretched to hook the handle of her suitcase on the top shelf of the closet. The hot-pink luggage fell to the floor in front of her. A Christmas gift from Bradley. The bright- and cheery-patterned suitcase had been a perfect present, but there wasn't anything bright or cheerful about today. She pulled down Bradley's smaller black suitcase instead, catching it midair.

Jill heaved the bag across the bed, tossed in the essentials, and then pulled the zipper closed. After a quick change into jeans and an old Virginia Tech T-shirt, she headed downstairs. The suitcase slammed against each step. It wasn't heavy. It just somehow felt liberating to do that to spite Bradley at the moment.

Following one good hiccup, the suitcase slipped from her hand, hit the next step at an angle, and tumbled the rest of the way down. She made her way to the bottom of the stairway and stood there in the foyer, contemplating. She ripped a sheet of paper from the notepad on the hall table and held the pen between her clenched fingers, waiting for something to come to her. Then she wrote:

How could you not tell me?
Going home. I'll use my vacation time.

Jill tossed the pen down on the table, but then picked it up again to write one more thing.

DON'T call me.

She underlined the word *don't* three times, then slid the paper next to the phone. She winced when she realized she'd written in such a fury that the words gouged the fine wooden table. It was a small price for him to pay for what he'd done.

With only one way in or out of the neighborhood, she prayed she'd get out of there before Bradley showed up. She headed to the car, tossed her suitcase in the back, and then accelerated down the driveway.

If he shows up now, he'll find out what an all-out Southern hissy fit looks like. And it's not gonna be pretty.

When Jill got to the I-95 ramp, she dialed Aunt Milly.

"Aunt Milly, it's me." Her chin quivered. "I just got the message." She couldn't even bring herself to say the words.

"I'd talked to her not an hour before. We were going to go to the market. Y'know, like we always do."

Milly's voice lacked its usual energy. "She said she didn't need anything, but I needed some milk and fruit so I stopped by her house, anyway. Doc said she must've taken one of her naps and never woke up. It's the way she would have wanted it. She looked peaceful."

Jill's fingers tingled from squeezing the steering wheel so tight. "I'm on my way now. I was going to wait until morning to call, but I needed to hear your voice." Despite the sadness in Aunt Milly's voice, her slow Southern drawl was like a warm hug that made Jill ache for home even more.

"Don't you rush, dear. It's the middle of the night, for goodness sake. You know how Pearl was about details. She had everything already planned. You should see the envelope she left with me. I've had it for years. We swapped them. Mine's in an old power bill envelope; hers is in a legal-sized manila envelope, and the darn thing is as thick as an old Sears Christmas Wish Book catalog. But it's fine, I'm not complaining. Besides, I've got the whole town to help me if I need it."

"No surprise there." *Pearl was the queen of lists and planning.* "What can I do?"

"Just be safe, honey," Milly said.

Jill could hear her shuffling through papers.

Milly rambled through the list of tasks. "Pearl'd already written her own obituary, so I'll drop that off at the paper in the morning. I already contacted the girls at the church with the songs Pearl had picked out. She even had Carolanne's phone numbers so I could contact her for you. I'm still going through it all. I'll let you know what's next."

"I can do some of that."

"Sweetie, at my age, I could whip together a good funeral with my eyes closed."

Jill choked back tears. Pearl had always said that those you'd share a family recipe or church bulletin with proved a family connection better than any swanky, scientific DNA test. Milly had been like part of the family for as far back as Jill could remember.

"I wish you wouldn't insist on driving in the middle of the night. You're just like Pearl, you know. Hardheaded. So I know there's no use me tryin' to talk you into goin' back and puttin' your head down on a pillow until daybreak. Be careful, dear."

"I will. I'll touch base with you in the morning." Jill closed the phone, then traced her top lip with her fingers. Whenever she cried, her lips swelled up like Angelina Jolie's, only not in a pretty way. Jill's hiccups finally subsided.

I'm so sorry I wasn't there, Pearl.

Chapter Three

Jill's phone rang again. She glanced at the caller ID. Bradley's name filled the screen. *What part of "don't call" don't you understand?* It was the fourth time Bradley had called, and each time his name popped up, it made her stomach churn, so she'd let all of his calls go to voice mail. This time she turned off the ringer and tossed the phone onto the passenger seat. She'd deal with him another time.

Memories weighed heavy on her heart and the gas pedal, too. She made the nearly six-hour drive from Savannah to Adams Grove in just over five.

At exactly three thirty in the morning, Jill took the exit off I-95 and turned down Main Street. The switch from interstate to twenty-five miles per hour felt like a crawl, but if it was one thing the locals knew, it was that you don't speed in this town. Usually, she took the back way home, but tonight, she needed to feel close to Adams Grove.

Someone had finally persuaded the town council to approve the purchase of pole banners to display down Main Street. The bannerscape of teal flags touted "Welcome to Adams Grove, est. 1897." The word *agriculture* scrolled up the side in a light shade of green like a watermark up the left of each flag.

Nice.

Floral & Hardy, the flower shop Teddy Hardy had opened right out of high school, had twinkle lights in the window. In the morning, she'd call Teddy and get him to make something special for Pearl.

Daisies for sure. Every type and color.

Jill's eyes misted.

The old pharmacy had a new sign. Sadly, Parker's Family Pharmacy was now a national chain.

Night-lights shone through the upstairs apartment windows over several storefronts. Those residents gave Main Street life, even though the businesses all flipped their signs from open to closed by six o'clock each evening and stayed closed on Sundays.

Just past the last shop, the streetlights ended and the road became inky black.

The blinker counted off the seconds to the lane that led to the house she'd grown up in. The tall pines were a welcome sight. Dirt kicked up behind the car into a rooster tail that glowed hazy red in her brake lights.

Tree branches hung across the path like a tunnel. Halfway to the house, she slowed to a stop, put the car in park, and lowered the windows. The humid night air rushed in. In a matter of seconds, her skin became sticky. The melodic hum from the wood's creatures filled the night. Closing her eyes, she lost herself in the deafening country quiet. The air conditioner dried her tears as quickly as they fell.

Unable to put it off any longer, she drove the rest of the way to the house. Jill walked across the long country porch and reached for the hide-a-key from the window box of geraniums that hung from the rail. The key was right where it had always been. She let herself in, set her bag down just inside, then flipped on the lights.

She took two steps into the still quiet. A tumble of confusing thoughts assailed her, and she wasn't sure which would win out. The sadness of her loss or the anger that she'd been away when it happened.

The pictures on the mantel were lined up perfectly, like they always were. A new one caught her attention. One of her with Garrett at the Pork Festival last summer. Tan and laughing, they held sticky barbecue spareribs and wore matching PIG OUT T-shirts. He had a red blotch on his cheek where she'd planted a barbecue kiss just moments before. That had been just days before the breakup. Pearl's smiling face touched her heart, and suddenly, she was too tired to do anything but sleep.

She went to Pearl's bedroom on the first floor and opened the second drawer of the tallboy dresser. Lifting a whole stack of neatly folded housecoats, Jill laid the stack on the bed and smoothed the fabric with her hand. Pearl's uniform.

A blue-and-white housecoat still hung from the bedpost. Jill held it to her face and inhaled the scent of coffee and spice. The wash-worn material was feathery soft, the tiny pearl snaps cool against her cheek. The sensations reminded her of carefree days under Pearl's watchful eye.

Always safe.

Jill slipped out of her clothes and into the blue-and-white housecoat, then curled up with the stack of housecoats in the center of the bed. Too tired to climb beneath the bedcovers, she hugged the housecoats and squeezed her eyes tight. Her eyes burned and her nose tingled as memories flooded her heart and mind.

In one blurred moment, she was seven years old, balancing on a wobbly stool in front of the kitchen counter, learning to make her first pie crust next to Pearl. She'd felt so grown-up pushing the pastry cutter through the dough and stretching it out to size with the rolling pin. Despite the flour that covered her from head to toe, that crust had turned out golden, light, and crispy. She'd earned the right to the family's secret recipe that afternoon.

She drifted asleep in a puddle of tears.

❖

A loud rumble jarred Jill awake. She squinted against the morning sun that streaked across her face like a laser.

"What the...?" Jill kicked out from the pile of housecoats and stumbled to the window. One tug sent the old shade whirling to the top of the window frame. With her hands pressed to the warm glass, she looked for the source of the interruption.

The roar assaulted her ears, but the sight of the man pushing a lawn mower hit like a sucker punch. Low-slung denim hugged a pair of trim hips. He moved away from her at a steady gait, sending grass spitting to the right in a trail of fresh clippings. The softball-sized biceps and muscles in the broad tan shoulders had found a new maturity she didn't remember, but there was no mistaking—it was Garrett.

Jill yanked the shade down to the sill. She turned her back on the window, stuffed her feet into Pearl's raggedy pink slippers, and stomped out to the living room to check the time on her cell phone.

"Seven thirty?" She activated the sound from where she'd muted it last night, then considered her options. Plan A, ignore him, or Plan B, go out and give Garrett Malloy a piece of her mind.

He knows I'm here. Who else would park a car with a Georgia plate in front of this house?

She rubbed the sleep out of the corners of her eyes, scrubbed her fingers through her hair, and stormed out onto the front porch.

The screen door slammed behind her, but Garrett didn't flinch.

She crossed her arms and rocked her weight to one hip, waiting and getting angrier by the second.

When he finally spun the mower around, he spotted her and waved.

"Mornin'," he shouted, lifting his chin in her direction.

"What is wrong with you?" She marched toward him.

He let go of the lever and the motor choked to a stop. "Couldn't hear you over the mower. Good morning," he said with an easy smile. "How are you holding up?"

She gritted her teeth. Where did he get off being so chipper at the crack of dawn? And what possessed him to do it in her front yard? OK, technically, it was Pearl's yard, but it would be hers. Heck, she was the only *family* left in the family.

"I'm not, and you being here isn't helping. What do you think you're doing?"

"Mowing the lawn," he answered in a sarcastic tone.

"I can see you're mowing the lawn. I'm not an idiot. I just don't know why you are mowing *this* lawn *this* morning?"

"I mow *this lawn* every Friday."

Her temper flared in response to his mocking tone. "No one asked you to do that."

"Pearl didn't have to ask. I offered. I'd do a few chores for her, and she'd cook supper for me in return. I called it even. Pearl called it Friday date night."

"Bet that cramped your style."

"Not at all. I liked helping Pearl, and *she* enjoyed my company." His voice softened. "I'll miss that." Garrett shook his head. "You know, she was really lonely after you left."

The words stung like a hundred angry bees. He knew exactly how to get under her skin. That's why she'd made all her visits to see Pearl quick one-nighters—so she could avoid him.

She strode toward the porch, but he was right on her heels. "There are no free meals here anymore, and I'm not your Friday-night date."

"Look, I'm just trying to help here. Can we call a truce? If not for us, then for Pearl?" He stepped in closer. "I'll miss her, too, you know."

"I know," she whispered. There it was again. The crushing black pain made it nearly impossible to breathe or swallow. Losing Pearl seemed worse than losing her parents, but then, she'd been so young when they'd died, and they'd spent so much time away. This was different. She kicked her toe in and out of the pink slipper, wishing she could disappear or revert to Plan A.

"Come on, Jill."

She closed her eyes and cocked her head to one side. It was just like him to play the Pearl card. He knew her too well.

"I'm sorry." Garrett touched her sleeve. "It's good to see you. It's been a while. You look…good."

She flinched at his touch. "Oh yeah, right. In Pearl's housecoat? I'm a regular hotty." She rolled her eyes, avoiding his.

"Got a little something sweet for me?" Garrett raised his eyebrows in a flirty way.

"Excuse me?" Jill took a step back, eager to put a little space between them.

He pointed to the blue smock with a knowing look. "I bet there's a coffee candy or two in that pocket there."

She dug into the deep pocket. Sure enough, there were two pieces. She extended her open hand toward him. "And just how often were you visiting Pearl in her housecoat while I've been away?"

"Often enough." He snagged one of the coffee drops from her outstretched hand and untwisted the wrapper. "I know a good thing when I see it." He popped the candy in his mouth. "But then you walked out on me. Hadn't counted on that."

She glared at him. "That's not exactly how it was."

He didn't respond, but his eyes spoke for him.

"You threw me away." She drew in a deep breath.

Garrett shook his head and looked to the sky, not saying anything for a long moment. "However it happened, it's in the past. Let's leave it there," he muttered, shoving the candy wrapper in his pocket. "Let's start over. How've you been?"

"Great." She straightened. *Don't let him fluster you.* "Perfect, in fact."

"So the job is all you thought it would be?"

She eyed him curiously. "Even more. It's a great cause, and we've been extremely successful in raising funds to expand the program."

He looked skeptical. "Sounds like a company brochure. Did you write that in your new fancy job?"

"Whatever. You don't care."

"I cared about you." He shrugged. "But I guess you're happy with the choices you made."

"So it seems. How are you?"

"I'm good. Not as good as you, but good." Garrett pulled his wallet from his back pocket and handed her a business card.

She read it aloud. "*Malloy Country Design and Builders. Make Your Dream Come True.*" She traced her thumb across the raised letters. No more Malloy's & Sons. Her eyes met his. "You made it happen," she said. *Without me.* "Pearl didn't tell me."

"Just like we'd planned. You and me." His eyes locked on hers. "Dad stepped down over the holidays. Said he was ready to start doing all the things he'd always wanted to do. You should see the workshop he built. I swear he's working harder now than when we were in business together. He and Mom seem to be loving the free time, though."

She'd thought Mr. Malloy would insist on that partnership until the day he died. Nervous excitement rushed through her, or maybe it was jealousy. It wasn't *just* like they'd planned. They'd planned a whole future around using their combined talents to sustain the lifestyle and agriculture of Adams Grove. Together.

"It's been hard work."

"Anything worth doing is," Jill said with quiet emphasis.

"You sound just like Pearl."

Tears welled, stinging her already tender eyes. For the first time in over a year, she took a good look at the house in the daylight. The flower beds had Pearl's special touch. No color theme, but rather a splash of every color imaginable. Pearl enjoyed spending days on end planting to achieve just the right level of color chaos, and somehow the crazy mix always ended up blending into something beautiful. A fresh coat of paint in a historic shade of sage green gave the house she grew up in a completely different look than the muddy white it used to be. Manicured shrubs provided a rich green backdrop for clumps of bright gerbera daisies that danced like the Rockettes in the light summer breeze, reflecting bright yellow, orange, and red against the long country porch.

Amazing what a little paint and early-summer blooms could do for a place.

"I need you to leave," Jill said. Her bottom lip trembled. "I'm tired. I'm sad. I can't..."

Garrett pulled her into his arms as she broke down into heaving sobs. "I know."

She cried into his shoulder. Feeling lost. Alone.

He held her, his touch soothing the raw pain as he stroked her back and held her close.

Garrett pressed his lips to her forehead.

She looked up and his mouth moved to hers.

His lips touched her like a whisper. For a moment, there was nothing else but that kiss.

Then the butterflies in her gut dimmed to shades of gray and the familiar excitement turned to panic.

She pulled back and shoved him away.

Garrett went airborne off the step and into the flower bed, landing on his butt with a thud.

"What?" She sucked in a breath trying to recover. "What do you think you're doing?"

"I'm…I—" Garrett gasped. He tried to catch the breath that his diaphragm just squeezed out like a dirty sponge. He looked up at Jill and studied her. *She responded. I felt it. All the warmth of a year ago.* "What the…?" He sat in the middle of the flower bed trying to focus on her and not the kiss. "Why'd you do that?"

She dragged the back of her forearm across her lips.

Garrett cringed. *I know that look. That's not good.*

"You need to leave. I don't want you here." Jill's voice trembled.

She's pissed. Why'd I do that?

"Bad timing. I'm sorry." He shook his leg, checking to be sure he hadn't broken anything in the fall. "Look, I know you're hurting, but you're not the only one who cared about Pearl. And you. I still care about you, too. I'm just trying to help."

Her expression didn't soften any.

"Don't. I'm her family." Jill avoided his stare.

"Pearl was special to everyone in this town. Family or not, no one has seen you for nearly a year. You were in and out, visiting Pearl in stealth mode. What? Are you too good for the folks in this town now?"

"I was here to see Pearl. I didn't have time to hang around. I've been busy."

He brushed cut grass from the top of his shoe. "No one's that busy," he muttered half under his breath.

"Just leave." Her lips held a tight line. "You ruined everything. You betrayed me."

Are we still rehashing this old script? She's never going to let it go. "I never did anything to betray you. Bradley Kase brainwashed you into believing that I'd cheat on you. You should've known me better. I don't know why you'd believe him over me. You don't even know him." The old argument made his stomach churn.

"Bradley had nothing to do with my decision."

"Right, I hear ya. Who are you trying to convince of that?"

"You broke our trust. You broke us!"

"No. You were the one who didn't trust *me*."

"Rightly so, I'd say, since you proved untrustworthy. And besides, Bradley didn't have a thing to do with you bebopping around with that blonde whoever-the-heck-she-was."

"She was just some chick at the track. Why do you keep bringing it up if you're not going to believe me. I'd never even seen her before."

"Why would Bradley lie? He had nothing to gain."

"Don't be a fool. He had everything to gain. He got you, didn't he?" Garrett's jaw pulsed. "If you're so happy, then why are you still so upset with me?" Looking up from the flower bed, he watched for a reaction.

"Whatever." Jill stared off toward the trees. "I can't argue with you. I'm tired. I didn't even get four hours of sleep, thanks to you."

She couldn't have missed the old spark in that kiss. "Admit it. You've missed me," he said. "At least a little."

She shook her hair away from her face. "You are so arrogant. You think it's always about you. Just…" She muttered "jerk" under her breath; then she faced him square on. "Doggone it, you're just…"

"Got it. I'm a jerk. I'm annoying, and you don't want my help." Garrett lifted himself out of the flower bed and brushed the mulch from his jeans. "I have to finish the lawn." He righted a tousled daisy with the tip of his shoe and headed back to the mower.

"I'll finish the lawn," she yelled after him.

"No. You won't. It's going to be over ninety degrees today. You don't have any business out here pushing a mower in this humidity."

"Afraid I'm so sweet I'll melt?"

"Not by a long shot. But I know you, and you'll be burnt slam up."

"There you go again, trying to tell me what I can and can't do."

Garrett stared at her. She was already sweating. Long tendrils clung to her neck. She could sure be a pain, but he couldn't help how he felt about her. "Like it would matter." He turned away from her, pulled to start the mower, and revved the throttle. Without having to look, he knew she was heading his way.

"You can't make decisions around here," she shouted. "Please. Just leave."

Garrett ignored the tantrum and started mowing again.

"I hate you!"

The words cut deep. Garrett spun around. Jill stood in the middle of the yard with both fists clenched at her sides like she was about to snap.

He turned back, released the mower handle, and threw both hands in the air. *Why the hell am I putting myself through this?* Standing there for a long moment, he shook his head and pushed the lawn mower toward his truck.

He looked heavenward. *Pearl, she's going to throw an all-out hissy fit when she finds out about the will. I sure wish you'd had a chance to tell her yourself.*

He heaved the mower into the back of the big four-wheel-drive GMC truck in one motion, slammed the tailgate, and hopped in the cab, spinning dirt as he wheeled down the lane.

❖ Chapter Four ❖

Jill touched her mouth where Garrett had landed the unexpected kiss. *Why does he still get under my skin?*

"Good riddance," she murmured, but an unexpected guilt nagged at her. She let the screen door slam behind her as she went back inside and dialed Aunt Milly.

"How are you, dear?" Aunt Milly asked.

"Sad, plus I just had a run-in with Garrett. Did you know he mowed Pearl's grass every week?"

"Yes. That man is such a jewel. I swear they don't make many like him."

Jill was sorry she'd mentioned it.

"I was just getting ready to call you. I just talked to them down at the funeral home. You know Pearl didn't want nobody staring at her all dead and gone, but I thought you might want to spend a little time with her. They said you could see her after twelve today."

Jill tensed at the thought of seeing Pearl that way—lifeless. "Is there anything you need me to do?" Jill fidgeted with the corner of one of the yarn lap-weave place mats on the kitchen table. She and Pearl had made them for the annual Christmas bazaar a few years ago.

Milly didn't even hesitate. "Everything's under control for now. Anything I can do for you? Do you need me to go with you this afternoon?"

"No, ma'am." *I'm not sure I can even do that. With or without you.*

"Well, you run over and visit with Pearl this afternoon. It'll make you feel better. You can check in with me tonight. Love you, sweetie." Aunt Milly made a kiss sound and hung up.

Jill stacked the place mats in a pile in front of her and leaned forward, resting her cheek on the soft yarn. *How is visiting Pearl now supposed to make me feel better?* The back of her throat tightened.

Pearl would hate for her to be such a prisoner to this sadness.

I have to fight this. Think good thoughts. Happy memories. But the mantra wasn't powerful enough to push the gray from her day.

She had to focus on something else. Nose stuffed up, lips swollen, and eyes feeling puffy, she headed to the bathroom to wash her face.

❖

At one o'clock, after circling the block three times and almost changing her mind, Jill stepped into a private room with the funeral director at her elbow. An icy fear wrapped around her heart. She slowed as she looked everywhere but toward the coffin in the middle of the room. Flowers, lots of them, lined every inch of the perimeter. A flash of loneliness chilled her further as she moved slowly toward the inevitable.

She held her breath, closed her eyes, and took that last step. When she opened her eyes, her clamped lips stifled a sigh.

Seeing Pearl laying there made Jill's heart break a little more with every breath. A quick look over her shoulder confirmed that the funeral director had left her to be alone with Pearl.

Jill laid her hand on top of Pearl's.

"Oh, Pearl, I miss you already." She leaned forward, closer to Pearl. A peaceful feeling came over her, warming the iciness that had taken over just moments ago.

"I didn't get to tell you about the Kase Foundation event. It went off without a hitch. Just like you said it would."

Her voice broke. "I can't believe you're not here for me to tell you about it."

Hot tears slid down her face. Jill blew her nose into a lace-edged hankie she'd taken from Pearl's drawer. "Paula Deen showed up, just like you said she would. I told her about your blue-ribbon pie. She was really impressed."

Jill leaned over the edge of the bronze casket, hoping somehow Pearl could hear her or know how she was feeling right now. *Help me, Pearl. I still need you.*

Between sniffles, she continued. "You should have said you were lonely." She drew in a stuttered breath. "You're the most important thing to me—family." Jill kissed Pearl on the cheek. "I'd have come home in a hot minute."

Pearl's voice rang clear in Jill's mind. So clear that it seemed like Pearl was speaking to her. Right here. Right now.

I didn't want to worry you. I was fine, honey, Jill heard, and the voice sounded so much like Pearl that Jill turned around and then touched Pearl again to be sure she hadn't fooled death and was still alive.

Jill smiled at the thought of her grandmother fooling death. If anyone could do it, it would've been Pearl. "I love you. How I hope you know that."

Age—death—was something even Pearl Clemmons couldn't avoid.

"I thought you'd be here forever." Jill clung to her memories like she would a life raft in the ocean. "You will always be here in my heart."

She lowered herself to the floor and sat there unable to leave for the longest time. Finally, she got up and slipped out the back door so she wouldn't have to talk to anyone while she embraced Pearl's memory tighter than ever.

As she drove, Jill's own life seemed to flash before her eyes.

Is this what it's like right before you die? She saw a vivid recollection of time with Pearl. Baking. Knitting. Dancing around while cleaning house. Gardening. Enjoying the simple pleasures of life. *My life will never be the same.*

She pulled over to the side of the road until she could pull herself together. A glance in the rearview mirror told her what she already knew. Her eyes were swollen and red. Pearl's wisdom flooded her thoughts. She took a couple deep breaths, then pulled back onto the road to meet Carolanne.

Chapter Five

As soon as Jill turned into the parking lot of the hotel, she caught a glimpse of Carolanne's fiery red hair. She swung her car into the first open parking spot. Carolanne must've spotted her, too, because she was already jogging toward her when Jill got out of the car.

"I'm so glad to see you. Thank you for coming." Jill and Carolanne hugged, with tears streaming down both their faces.

"I can't believe she's gone. She always seemed so invincible," Carolanne said.

They clung to one another, searching for the strength that only true friends bring to situations like this.

Carolanne stepped back. "I have to head back to New York right after the funeral, but I'll come back and forth as often as you need me."

"Thank you for rearranging everything to be here with me."

"We've got each other. We'll get through this." Carolanne swept at her own tears and then brushed away those streaming down Jill's face.

Jill just nodded. There weren't any other words for what they were feeling.

Carolanne broke the silence. "We better get out of the middle of this parking lot." She led Jill toward the sidewalk. "Have you eaten?"

"I can't eat."

"That might be true, but you need to eat something." Carolanne took charge just like she always did. "Have you been to the house yet?"

"I spent the night there last night, and this morning." Jill's chest tightened as she recalled how empty it had felt. Empty. And lonely. "It's weird without Pearl there. I kept feeling like she was going to scuff down the hall any minute." Another hot tear slid down Jill's cheek.

Carolanne reached across and brushed it away. "I wish we were getting together for anything but this."

"Me too." Jill wished she had a little advice from Pearl about how to get through all of this.

"Do you want to stay at Pearl's tonight or here?"

Jill nodded. "Home. Let's go home."

"That's my rental right there. Let me grab my suitcase, then we'll buy some munchies and veg out at the house."

"This is why you're my best friend. You always have the best ideas. I'll drive."

Jill got in the car while Carolanne retrieved her things and put them in the backseat; then she slid into the passenger seat and buckled up. "Nice ride." She ran her hand across the soft leather. "Looks like Bradley is treating you pretty good. Speaking of which, where is he?"

"That topic is off-limits until another time. I can't even talk about it yet."

"I'm guessing he didn't have a good excuse for not passing on Milly's message." Carolanne caught the look on Jill's face. "No, no. Don't say anything. I'm not asking, but I'm here when you're ready."

"Thanks for not asking." Jill pulled the car out of the parking lot and headed back into town.

"You're welcome, but it's only a reprieve. I want details later."

"Of course you do."

Carolanne repositioned in the seat to face Jill. "I'm just going to say this once. You know he's no Garrett, right?"

"You're going to say that more than once. I know you."

"Probably. So we'll change the subject for now." Carolanne hugged her purse in front of her. "Remember how when we were little and Pearl let us do sleepovers under the dining room table?"

"She'd pack treats in those big bandannas—red for me, blue for you. Those knots she tied were like a *Survivor* challenge."

"I'd forgotten about that part. You sucked at untying them. Kept us busy and out of her hair for a while though."

"That's why I had to keep you as my best friend. I'd have starved without you."

"Remember the time Pearl taught us how to hold our hands over the flashlights so we could see through them."

"Yep. I still can't turn on a flashlight without doing that. You know, to be sure I'm still human."

"I forgot about that part." Jill made a spooky accent. "If the light shines blue purple instead of bloodred, you're not human!"

A serious look crossed Carolanne's face. "Hey, I've dated a few guys in New York who I probably should've tested that on."

"The flashlights were fun."

Carolanne clicked her fingers. "Until the time you made me lick that battery. I had no idea that was going to shock me."

Jill rolled her lips into a tight line and tried to look angelic. "Science class. You should've paid attention."

"You knew I never paid attention in that class."

"Too bad. So sad." Jill tapped the steering wheel. "Remember pretending the dining room table was our castle?"

"And how Pearl would sing and do all those funny things. We thought she didn't know we could hear and see her?"

Jill smiled. "She really went all out to be sure we had fun."

"How about when we started that ant farm and I took them to my house. Dad went nuts over the ant problem that year. I never told him that I was the reason we had them. It never occurred to me that those ants could crawl right out of those air holes we'd punched in the box."

"You were better off keeping that secret. He was so unpredictable back then."

Carolanne sighed. "That was Dad's mean year. The first year after Momma died. No telling what he'd have done if he'd known."

That had been a bad year for Carolanne. She'd spent most of her time at Pearl's while her dad fought emotions that swung from anger to depression to just downright drunk over the loss of his wife to breast cancer. "Last time I talked to Pearl, she said he's been doing good."

"Dad? Yeah, I don't talk to him much. There's a lot of water under that bridge. Enough to damn near drown me over the years."

"I know." Jill held the words that were going to come out of her mouth. It wasn't the time to give Carolanne a speech about forgiving her dad, but the fresh wounds of losing Pearl made her worry about Carolanne's relationship with him.

"We're here," Jill said as she pulled in front of Spratt's Market. They could've saved a few bucks by going to the big chain store, but hometown was hometown and folks supported each other that way. Besides, what was better than the smell of those curing hams that hung from the rafters at Spratt's Market?

As soon as they stepped inside, Carolanne said, "I'll probably gain three pounds in water weight just walking into the salty air of this old store."

Jill nodded. “And so worth it.” She grabbed one of the small shopping carts, and they made a quick spin through the store.

Reggie Spratt checked them out at the register. “Sorry to hear about Pearl. Everybody’s broke up about it.”

“Thanks.” Jill’s voice shook. Carolanne stepped closer and put her arm around Jill.

When they got back in the car, Carolanne said, “Everyone who knew her loved her.” They remained quiet the whole ride back to Pearl’s house.

Home.

With a Spratt’s Market paper shopping bag on one hip and her suitcase rolling behind her, Carolanne bumped the car door closed and headed to the porch.

Jill carried the other bag and unlocked the door, holding it open for Carolanne.

“This place never changes.” Carolanne scooted past Jill and put the grocery bag on the counter in the kitchen.

“Some things have changed. Pearl sleeps downstairs now, and she gave away most of the furniture that was upstairs to the Millers. They lost just about everything they had in that fire last year.”

“At Christmas. I remember.”

“There’s a bad fire every year at the holidays. I’m beginning to wonder just how smart it is to use all the same lights year after year.”

“I’d love to have a few of those old glass ornaments Pearl had. They were so pretty. I loved spending Christmas with the two of you.”

Jill nodded. “You can have some of them. I’m sure they’re all up in the attic.”

Carolanne’s face lit up. “I bet there’s a ton of great stuff in the attic.”

“Are you serious?”

"Yes. Aren't you curious what might be up there after all these years?"

Jill cringed a little. "Not really. I've always been a little creeped out by the attic."

"Well, you're going to have to go up there eventually. Especially if you're thinking about selling or renting out the place."

"With my job being in Savannah, it doesn't make sense to keep it. I don't know. That's something I'm going to have to figure out this week."

"Then you may as well go up in the attic while I'm here." Carolanne unzipped her suitcase. "First things first."

"What's first?"

Carolanne smiled. "We change into our jammies, and I open the wine." She lifted out a bottle of their favorite.

"Where did you get that?"

"Picked it up on my way in from the airport this afternoon. Go change. I'll pour us two glasses, and not those sissy, proper kind. We're going for the ice tea glasses, filled to the improper rim! Because we can."

When Jill came back out in her pajamas, Carolanne was already in a pair of yellow-and-white toile print ones and was holding two big ice tea glasses full of wine as promised.

Jill took a glass and they headed to the living room.

Carolanne sat at the end of the couch and pulled her feet up underneath her. Jill sat in Pearl's favorite chair. The worn cushion sank beneath her.

"Look how threadbare the arms of this chair are. I never even noticed that before," Jill said.

"That chair has got to be as old as you are."

"Are you saying I'm looking worn out?"

"Today doesn't count."

Jill shot Carolanne a look that made them both laugh. "Thanks for being here. You make everything better."

"We're best friends. It's what we do." Carolanne raised a glass in the air. "To Pearl and the kazillion memories she gave us."

"To Pearl." Jill took a long sip from the glass, then reached to the right of the chair. As expected, a work-in-progress was nestled in the top of Pearl's knitting basket. She lifted the half-finished blanket and yarn into her lap.

Jill's fingers lingered in the soft yarn. "I just gave Pearl this yarn at the birthday party."

"How was that? I can't believe I missed it. Especially now. Did you surprise her."

"No! What made us think we could surprise her?" Jill brought Carolanne up to date on every single detail of that day.

Carolanne poured more wine in both of their glasses.

"This blanket is going to be beautiful. There's an *M* in the corner here," Jill said as she examined the pattern. "I wonder who she was making it for?" Though Pearl's eyes were not as sharp as they'd once been, and arthritis had taken the better days from her hands, the beginning of this blanket was flawless.

Carolanne took a sip from her glass. "I loved it when Pearl referred to her arthritis as Arthur, like a pesky guest who had overstayed a visit. Remember how's she'd say, 'Arthur's givin' me a fit today. I wish I could make him a sweater and send him packin' forever.' That always made me laugh."

Jill pulled the handiwork close. With a couple of free afternoons, she could finish this project. "Losing Pearl isn't ever going to get easy." She tucked the blanket and the pattern into the top of the basket, but then something caught her eye. Scribbled on the back of the stationery was a note: *Tell Jill about JC*, underlined with a scroll. Jill ran down her mental list of townspeople with the initials JC, but no one came to mind. "Do you know anyone in town with the initials JC?"

Carolanne thought for a moment. "No. Not offhand. Why?"

"On the back of this pattern, there's a note says, 'Tell Jill about JC.' "

"Ask Aunt Milly. She'll know."

"Good idea." Jill promised herself she'd finish the blanket for Pearl. It was the least she could do.

The sound of a cell phone rang from the other room. "I think that's yours," Carolanne said.

Jill leaped from the chair and raced to dig her phone out from the side pouch of her purse and answered. "Hello."

"How's my girl?"

She dropped her head back. She mouthed the word *Bradley* to Carolanne and made a face. "Sad." She wished she'd let the call go to voice mail.

"How'd you hear?" he asked.

"How I heard is really not the point, is it?" Her chest tightened, and she started to sweat. "There's no good reason for you to have kept that from me."

Carolanne got up and headed to the bathroom. She mouthed, *You got that right*, as she walked by, and they exchanged a look.

"I'm sorry," he said.

"I agree."

"Aw, come on, Jill. Work with me here. I'm trying to apologize. I made a bad decision not telling you right away."

She swallowed back tears. "There wasn't a decision to make. What you did was just plain cruel."

"I tried. I swear I did. But you were so happy, zipping around handling all the last-minute details for the fund-raiser. It was your night to shine, and you did, baby. You were awesome. Pearl was already gone. There wasn't anything we could do to change that."

"That's no excuse." Jill couldn't fathom his line of thinking. She had a suspicion he'd been less concerned about her feelings and more so on throwing a successful event. "I don't expect you to understand." Her grief spilled. "I know your childhood was hard, and you don't have a relationship with your family, but mine is—was—everything to me."

"I made a terrible mistake. I wish I could take it back."

"Well, you can't." Was there anything he could say that would make it OK? She couldn't think of a thing.

"At least Pearl had a good, long life," Bradley said.

"She was only eighty-four. A young eighty-four." Jill clutched her fist to her stomach. "I should have been here."

"I said I was sorry, baby. You *are* going to forgive me, aren't you?"

"I can't have that discussion right now, Bradley. I'm sad. Really sad. And I'm hurt. I feel so…alone."

"You wouldn't be alone if you hadn't left without talking to me," he said. "Is there a lot to do?"

"Pearl had the whole thing preplanned and prepaid. No surprise there."

"Sounds like someone else I know. When's the funeral?"

"Saturday. Aunt Milly has been a huge help." Jill pulled the phone away from her ear for a second. "What's all the noise in the background?"

"Palm Beach ring a bell? I'm at the Everglades Club. We had plans. With the Whitneys, remember?"

"You flew down there this morning?" That struck a nerve. *He's just moving right along like nothing's happened.*

"Yes, but it's not going so well. I can't do this without you. Now that you've made certain that things are being taken care of, I booked a ticket for you—first class. We'll spend a day here, then fly back to Virginia together for the funeral Saturday morning."

Jill plopped down in the chair. Was he completely ignorant of what she was going through? "I'm not going anywhere"—her voice rose as she leaned forward in her chair—"in any class."

"This is important."

"And what I'm going through isn't?" She closed her eyes and took in a deep breath. When she spoke, her voice was just above a whisper. "I just lost my grandmother."

"I know, and I can hear how sad you are. I hate to hear you like that. You said Milly is handling the details. You'll be back so fast no one will know you were gone."

"I'd know, and I'm not leaving."

"I need to close this deal. It's the perfect time, and they love you." Bradley's tone became impatient.

"It's business, not a popularity contest." Jill's voice caught on the words as her emotions surged to the surface. "And I'm using my vacation time."

"It'll lift your mood."

"I don't want to lift my mood, and how about what I'd like? I'd like for *you* to be *here*. I need you, and that's personal. What's more important? Personal or business?"

"Come on, Jill." His tone had turned smooth and gentle. "Don't make me answer that."

"Well, it's not going to happen. I'm where I need to be." Jill sat straighter in the chair, feeling a renewed strength from standing her ground. Why couldn't he set business aside when she needed him most? The Bradley from this week acted nothing like the Bradley she'd met a year ago. Or maybe he did. She'd never pushed him to meet her needs before.

"I'll be there for the funeral Saturday, then."

"It's not just the funeral. It's deciding what to do with the house, her things." *Everything that I've ever known.* "I wish you'd come now. This is breaking my heart. I could use some support."

"I'll be there when I get done here."

"I love you," she said.

"Hang in there, kiddo." He hung up before she could say another word.

She flipped the phone closed, with her heart aching. He hadn't said he missed her or loved her.

When was the last time he had?

Jill dropped her hands to her side. "Did you hear all that?"

Carolanne came back in the room and sat across from Jill. "Enough of it. It's been a long day. Are you tired?"

"Beat, but I can't sleep."

"Let's go check out the attic." Carolanne grinned. "I already tried the string in the hall. That sucker won't budge. Come on, we can use the access in the second bedroom. You won't even have to climb the ladder."

Jill nodded and motioned for Carolanne to follow her. She wasn't eager about going to the attic, but she knew she couldn't sleep and Carolanne would be relentless until she got to snoop around that old stuff. Jill tossed her phone into her purse as she led the way upstairs.

Carolanne paused on the landing, looking between the two upstairs bedrooms. "Boy. You weren't kidding about Pearl getting rid of some things. It's practically empty up here."

"I told you." Jill went to the closet in the far corner of the second bedroom. "I don't know why I let you talk me into stuff. It's creepy to be poking around an attic. Especially at night."

"It'll be fine. Follow me." Carolanne pushed passed her.

The scary closet was practically empty, and not nearly as ominous as Jill had remembered it. She stepped toward the short, angled door, staying close behind Carolanne.

Carolanne tried the dead bolt, but it didn't budge.

Maybe I'm off the hook.

A couple of good wiggles and the metal gave way and slid over. Carolanne grinned and pushed the door open. "Is there a light switch?"

"No, just a string you pull. It should be right there as you walk in."

Following a single click, a stream of golden light swung back and forth like one of those big sale spotlights in the sky, illuminating the dusty space. "It sure is organized," Carolanne remarked as she forged ahead.

Holiday boxes were piled high against the far wall, deep to one side. Everything clearly marked with big letters. Pearl was organized like that.

Feeling much braver, Jill stepped into the dusty attic space and lifted the top off the first box she came to. "Here are those ornaments you love so much." She unwrapped one from yellowed tissue paper that had seen better days. "There should be six of the turquoise ones in here somewhere."

"The turquoise were my favorite. You hung the red; I hung the turquoise." Carolanne set aside two glass ornaments as she continued to search for her favorites. "These old ornaments kind of break the rules. Not just plain old red and green. Kind of like Pearl. Unexpected. Unforgettable."

"You're right." It was actually comforting to be among all these things that had made up so many happy memories. "Pick out which ones you'd like to have. I know Pearl would love that you have some of them."

Jill slapped the dust from the back of her pants and eased toward the middle of the attic. At least a dozen hangers hung over a two-by-four rafter. Each held a flag by the corners with wooden clothespins. "How am I supposed to pack this kind of stuff up? Each one of these things is filled with memories."

"I don't know. I don't want to say the wrong thing, and I'm bound to sooner or later, but I just can't imagine anyone but you and Pearl ever living in this house."

"I know what you mean. I hadn't really realized it before, but now..." She looked around. "All this stuff—I can't let it go."

Carolanne walked deeper into the attic, ducking to clear the lower eaves in the corner near the dormer window. The attic floor squeaked beneath her feet. "Is this the trunk that Pearl used to have at the end of her bed?"

Jill slowly crossed the room, waving her arms to sweep the spiderwebs away almost as if she were swimming across the space toward Carolanne. "I think it is. I have no idea what's in it. I never went into Pearl's things. It's not like she ever told me I couldn't. I just…didn't."

Several smaller boxes, secured with gray duct tape, were stacked on top of it. Jill lifted the first box. The tape had lost its sticky in the heat and pulled back easily. Inside, a layer of tissue paper and cedar blocks protected the contents. "Oh. My. Goodness. Look at this. It's so tiny." She lifted a white christening gown gently out of the box and held it up.

"Do you think it was yours?"

"I don't think so. This looks vintage."

Carolanne shifted the tissue paper in the box. "This ought to tell us." She carried a white book underneath the lightbulb and flipped through the pages. "It's a baby book." The pages held brittle black-and-white photos. "You've got to see this. It's your dad."

Jill started laughing and rushed to Carolanne's side. "Let me see that."

"I told you this was going to be fun."

"Well, you were right. You're always right, so what's new?"

Carolanne squealed. "He's naked." She held up the page for Jill to see.

Pearl's dark hair was fastidiously styled in finger curls. She held a laughing infant. Daddy.

"These days they'd throw you in jail for pictures like these," Jill said. It had been a safer time back then—people thought pictures like these were cute and innocent, and they were.

Jill closed the book and put it back in the box. "I'm suddenly beat. Let's go to bed."

Carolanne crossed the cardboard flaps to hold the box closed and then followed Jill downstairs to Pearl's room.

They crawled into bed, and Jill turned onto her stomach, scrunching the pillow up under her chin. "I can't stop thinking about the phone call from Bradley. I don't know what's going on with him. Just last night, while we were dancing at the fund-raiser, he was aching to say something. I think he was going to propose."

"Marriage? Sorry. He just doesn't seem the marrying kind to me. Besides, y'all haven't really been together all that long. I mean, it was just work for a long time."

"I was pretty excited about the thought of it before, but after this...How do you forgive something like that?"

Carolanne didn't say anything.

"I know you don't like him, but you really don't know him. Pearl was the one who introduced me to Bradley, if you remember. Doesn't that count for something?"

"That's true. I remember how he charmed the support stockings off her with his perfect manners and charisma. He was always just a little too smooth acting for me. Besides, he sounded like a complete ass just then on the phone. That didn't earn any points with me."

"That's the lawyer in you. You're always suspicious."

"Maybe what Bradley was aching to tell you last night was about Pearl. I guess it's possible he just couldn't bring himself to tell you."

"Maybe," Jill said. "That's not a good excuse, either."

"That's because there isn't one. You like the job, though, right?"

"It's great. I miss Adams Grove. It'd been way better had he kept the business in Adams Grove like everyone thought when I took the job. I can't tell you how much I regret being away from Pearl now."

"If you and Garrett hadn't had that falling out, would you still have moved to Savannah for that job?"

"No." She didn't even have to think about it. "I'd never dreamed of leaving this town."

"I didn't think so. I wish you'd give Garrett another chance. He loves you so much. You know I'm not the only one who thinks that you should be with him. Pearl was devastated over y'alls' breakup. To Pearl, that pinky swear under the monkey bars in elementary school was a sign that the two of you were soul mates. Plus, he gave you that ring. So, technically, there was consideration, so it was a contract."

"That ring was hardly worth the quarter he dropped to get it out of the gum machine at Spratt's, and it was a long time ago. He can sue me, but I think he's over it too by now."

"Not that long ago, and who says he's over you?"

Jill flopped over onto her back.

"I'm sorry. Forget I said anything. I love you, Jill." Carolanne reached her hand out across the covers. "As long as you're happy, I'm happy."

Jill grabbed her hand and squeezed. "Love you, too."

A small noise escaped from Jill; then she sniffled back the tears that seemed to come and go as they pleased today. "I love you, Pearl," Jill whispered into the dark.

Chapter Six

That morning, the temperature had already hit ninety degrees with humidity so high that going outside was like walking into a wet sweater. Both Jill and Carolanne were dressed in simple black dresses and had been for quite a while as the morning drug on and the inevitable neared. Every time Jill ran to the front door, she'd expected it to be Bradley, only to be met by a delivery or another neighbor checking in.

By late afternoon, the heat hadn't given up its grip, but that didn't stop anyone from dressing in their Sunday finest on this Saturday to pay their respects to Pearl Clemmons.

When the dark-blue limousine pulled in front of the house, Jill thought she'd faint. Nausea swelled and she began to sweat.

"Are you OK?" Carolanne asked as she rushed to her side. "You look pale. Here, let's take off your jacket." She slipped the jacket off of Jill's shoulders. "Better?"

"I don't know." Jill began to sob, and Carolanne led her to the couch to sit back down. Milly knocked on the open door as she let herself inside. "You ready?"

Carolanne waved toward Milly. "I think Jill's going to need a minute."

Aunt Milly sat next to Jill and wrapped her in her arms. "It's OK, sweetie. You take all the time you need. Izzy Markham is driving us to the church. She's back in town. Ugly divorce. She'll be happy to wait as long as we need."

"I'll let Izzy know and wait for y'all in the car," Carolanne said.

"Before you go, here, take this." Milly handed Carolanne an envelope. "It's for Jill, from Pearl. Connor gave it to me yesterday. She can read it when she's ready."

"Connor Buckham? I thought he was up in Chicago practicing law."

"Oh well, he was, but when his mamma took ill, he came back. She's got the arthritis so bad she can hardly do a thing. Don't know if him bein' back is permanent, though. I think he's still seeing that woman up in Chicago, the one whose daddy owns the law firm or something. Very rich, and boy, could you tell she wasn't too impressed with *us* when she came to town."

"I know the type." Carolanne tucked the envelope in her purse. "Is this a legal document?"

"I don't know. Perhaps. He is handling Pearl's estate." Milly gave Carolanne's hand a squeeze, and then Carolanne went outside.

A few minutes later, Milly walked out with Jill at her side.

Just as Milly and Jill slid into the backseat, a truck pulled in front of the house. Carolanne jumped out. "I'll take care of it. One sec, Izzy."

Just a moment later, Carolanne jumped back in the car. "Someone delivered a flowering pink dogwood for Pearl. They're going to just put it on the porch."

The car pulled out of the driveway with not a sound except that of the engine.

Jill watched as a burly man carried a four-foot tree up to the porch and dropped it right in front of the door. She stared silently out the window as Izzy Markham's limo drove down the lane and then swung wide onto Horseshoe Run Road. Jill pressed the button to lower the window and inhaled the scent of honeysuckle and mimosa that filled this stretch of road every summer. When the wind blew downriver, even the Young farm's smelly pigs couldn't drown out the fragrance. She pulled her jacket around her, feeling chilled even in the summer heat.

Just around the curve, the church steeple came into view. Stately oaks lined the road and colorful wreaths dotted headstones between the mighty trunks that framed the old cemetery next to the church. The thought of Pearl being there, so final, seemed to stop her airflow.

Bradley hadn't shown up. She, Milly, and Carolanne were led inside and seated in the front pew.

Jill tried to concentrate on the light that streamed through the stained-glass windows across the floor. It was easier than dealing with reality. A breeze moved the trees outside, throwing shadows across the bands of colorful light that made them appear to dance.

The congregation hummed with muffled chatter between friends and families. The old church was full, forcing new arrivals to line the back wall. A few latecomers cozied into the remaining space as the strong sound of the organ filled the room.

Milly rambled in a loud whisper to the people seated behind them. "The whole town is in shock. Pearl made the dessert for the buffet dinner after choir practice just the night before—you know. It was lovely, so lovely. But then, you know Pearl. She never did do anything halfway." Milly turned back around and patted Jill's leg.

Jill nodded, unable to say a word. She relived her own last conversation with Pearl. Pearl had shared the latest gossip, right down to the Hooters girl who Ricky Owens brought home when he showed up announcing he'd dropped out of college. Pearl and Ricky Owens's grandmother had been members of this church for years, and it was no secret how competitive the two of them were. Whether it was bragging rights on grandchildren or bake-offs, Pearl always came out ahead. That drove Mrs. Owens nuts.

Aunt Milly wrapped her bony fingers around Jill's balled fist. "You're a strong girl, Jill, just like your grandmother."

I don't feel strong.

"She's very proud of you, dear."

Jill could barely swallow. She held her hand to her chest, willing herself to breathe.

Reverend Burke brought the group to order with a prayer. All heads bowed. His commanding voice reverberated, one single voice, one big message until the amen that seemed to echo forever. The organ struck a chord, bringing everyone's attention to the front, where young Allison Lynn Craddock began to sing "How Great Thou Art" in a voice so pure it lifted Jill's spirit.

The reverend shared his own stories about Pearl's many contributions to the small community and this church. "There was a lesson for each of us in how Pearl lived her life. She was the voice of reason when things got hectic, and she could simplify the most complicated situations. Pearl was the first to give of herself, and nobody made better sweet tea than she did.

"Sweet tea. She told me to say it like it was one word. 'Can't have tea without the sweet,' she'd say." Reverend Burke smiled wide. Deep lines etched his face, and his eyes glistened.

"Pearl said I was officially a surrogate Southerner once I learned how to say that right. 'Sweet tea' and 'y'all.' "

Everyone in the church chuckled.

He invited the congregation to share their own memories. Person after person took his or her turn at the podium. Pearl had helped so many folks find their way. Not because she set out to do so. It had just been in her nature to be there, to share advice, and to never pass judgment. OK, maybe she did her share of talking smack, but even then, it was never without the intent of helping in some way.

These memories people shared were special ones meant to comfort, but they only ripped the hole in Jill's heart wider—if that were possible. *I wonder how many people realize today is the day before Pearl's birthday?*

The moan of the organ vibrated the wooden pew beneath her. Carolanne guided Jill to her feet and toward the church doors. Garrett rested a reassuring hand on Jill's shoulder as he and Milly followed them out. The others filed out behind them.

Pearl had left her mark.

Graveside, the flowers wrapped the area so deeply it was like standing in a meadow. The outpouring of love and respect was overwhelming as everyone settled around Pearl's final resting place.

They waited as the long line of people made the short walk to the church cemetery. Jill stood in the sunlight, shivering. Someone draped his sport coat over her shoulders. She was powerless to move, but thankful for the comfort. People filled in around the tented area four and five deep.

Jill clenched her fist. Her nails dug into her own flesh, and her other hand wrapped tightly around it—as if opening her hand might let the last memories of Pearl escape.

Not even one contrail slashed through the blue sky today. Too perfect a day for such a sad affair. *You'd have loved the sky today, Pearl.* With trembling fingers, Jill tugged her black sunglasses down. Squeezing her eyes shut behind the dark lenses had caused the tears to puddle. She swept the tears from her cheek and from her chin where they'd spilled.

Her line of sight narrowed, as did her throat, and though she was just feet from Reverend Burke, she could barely hear his words as he began to speak.

"Ashes to ashes, dust to dust..."

She clutched her handkerchief to her heart. Someone wrapped his arms around her from behind and then eased her back. Black onyx-and-pearl cuff links secured the crisp white cuff that rested on her arm. Not Bradley's arms. Pearl had given those cuff links to Garrett on the day he graduated from college. As if it had been yesterday, Jill remembered the look on Pearl's face as she watched Garrett open the gift. Pearl had given Jill the matching pearl necklace that day. Jill reached up and slid the pendant on its chain.

Blinking away tears, each bat of her eyes became a blackout. Just the other day, she'd fought with Garrett over mowing the lawn. Now she felt a sense of surrender in his arms as he rescued her—again—like he had so many times over the years. She reached back to brace herself, thankful for the safety Garrett offered. There was no room for anger today. That emotion was temporarily out of order.

As was tradition at this church for decades, the casket lowered. Jill's knees did, too. She fought the urge to jump into the hole that was swallowing her grandmother's last moments on this earth.

Garrett turned her toward his chest, away from the sight. She cried into her hands, her head resting on his chest. Through the final words, he gently rubbed the back of her neck with his fingertips, tangling in the light-brown curls that fell across her shoulders. After several minutes, Jill recovered and pulled away from Garrett, giving him a look of gratitude. Friends approached her and murmured words of comfort as they walked by on their way back to the church. Jill nodded, accepting the kind words and the occasional hug.

"Are you ready to go inside?" asked Carolanne.

"You go on. I'll be along in a minute." She wrapped her hands around Garrett's arm. "You'll stay?" she asked him.

He nodded.

Carolanne excused herself to help the ladies in the reception hall kitchen. Folks began to gather for a feast of home-cooked foods and snacks. They'd fellowship and share memories about the one who just left them for a better place in God's good grace.

Garrett and Jill walked among the flowers that surrounded Pearl's resting spot. Wide ribbons in white, pink, and magenta glittered with the words *In loving memory, Loving Friend, Always Remembered.* Jill read each one.

Garrett plucked a bright-pink gerbera daisy from a wreath and handed it to Jill.

My favorite, but then, you know that. She accepted the flower, lowering her head to sniff it, though she knew it wouldn't be fragrant.

"I'm sorry about yesterday. I had every intention of us having an amicable reunion. I'm not sure how we got off on the wrong foot," Garrett said.

"I carried my share of that." She twirled the pretty flower between her fingers.

He patted his hip and snickered. "Yeah, I have a bruise to prove it."

She winced, but smiled. "I was a maniac."

"At the risk of landing on my ass in a field of flowers again, I have to mention that, while your guard was down, for just those couple seconds, it felt like old times."

She eyed him cautiously, then shook her bangs from her face. "Well, it was probably Pearl. She always was a matchmaker."

"And we're the only match she wasn't right about. Not that she'd given up."

"She was still hounding you, too?" *Pearl's eyes always danced with mischief when she spoke of you, Garrett.*

"Hey, don't make it sound like a death sentence."

The words ignited more memories. "I didn't mean it like that." She shrugged. "It's just that we already tried. It didn't work." She plucked a fringy petal from the flower. *He loves me.* Another petal found its destiny in the wind. *He loves me not.* "Thank you for being here for me after I was so ugly to you." *He loves me.* "I don't know that I'd have been so kind if I were you." *He loves me not.* The wind sent the single petal right back into her face. She sputtered and brushed it from her mouth.

"Yes, you would. We've got history. That doesn't just go away." Garrett pulled one of the petals free, pointed to himself, then let the petal fall to the ground. "He loved you," Garrett said to Jill.

She snapped her head up, her gaze meeting his.

He raised a brow, then took the flower from her fingers.

She chewed on her bottom lip. *You always did know what I was thinking.*

Garrett stepped toward her, then straightened, clearing his throat. "You have a visitor." He motioned toward the parking lot over her shoulder. "Bradley's here."

❖ Chapter Seven ❖

Bradley sauntered across the cemetery lawn, flipping his keys in his hand.

How could he act so nonchalant at such a sad time? She dabbed at her eyes with her handkerchief, wishing she didn't feel like she had to explain Bradley's behavior.

Garrett took a step back just as Bradley came up, laying a territorial hand on Jill's shoulder.

"How's my girl?" Bradley never took his eyes off Garrett.

"Hi, Bradley." Garrett reached out to shake his hand.

Instead of extending his, Bradley gave Garrett a dismissive nod.

Garrett stuffed the unaccepted hand into his suit pocket.

Bradley reached out to stroke Jill's shoulder. "Sorry I'm late."

She stepped out of Bradley's range. She felt her face flush with humiliation, but she managed to give Garrett a sign that she'd be OK.

He backed off and reluctantly headed to join the others inside.

Bradley watched until Garrett cleared the doors of the reception hall. "He sure didn't waste any time moving in, did he?"

"What?" Her voice cracked.

"You two looked chummy. That's all."

Jill could almost feel Pearl's strength rising in her body.

She turned to face him head-on, raised a finger, and pointed it right at him. "Don't…you…dare." She ran her hand through her hair and swallowed back tears. "If you'd been here on time this morning, or to be precise, two days ago like you should've…No, wait. If you hadn't kept the whole doggone thing from me from the beginning, I probably wouldn't even have been standing here talking to Garrett."

"What are you saying? You playing all cozy with your ex is my fault?"

"Don't you turn this into something it's not. I just lost the most important person in my life."

"*Most* important? More important than me?"

"Yes, and don't you mince words with me. I needed you. You weren't here." She spun her back to him. Her breathing was heavy, her black dress lifting and dropping with each intake of air.

"Looks like you did just fine without me. No harm. No foul."

"No harm?" She turned back and glared at him. The fury almost choked her. "You don't even get it, do you? What's wrong with you?"

He reached for her hand. "Come on, baby. You're upset. You're blowing things out of proportion. It's OK. I understand."

"No. You really don't. You know what? I don't want you to stay. I don't even know why you came. Garrett's a part of this community, and we're all feeling the loss. There was nothing seedy about him comforting me, so back off." She pushed Bradley aside and headed for the reception hall under power she hadn't known she had.

Bradley didn't follow her. "Jill. Come back."

She waved an arm dismissively and continued down the slope.

"Are you staying all week?" he called after her.

"Doggone right I am," she shouted over her shoulder as she marched toward the back door to the church's kitchen.

"Don't forget about Friday," he yelled. "That's business."

"Tell me he didn't just say that," she mumbled. She knew that next Friday was the big Independence Day Ball, but what made him so sure she'd forgive him by then?

Unfortunately, she had only so many vacation days, and unless he fired her, she did have to go back to work.

❖

The smell of home cooking wafted out of the screen door of the church kitchen. Jill caught the door midswing to keep it from slamming and slipped into the corner of the room. She hadn't expected this many people to still be milling around in the kitchen.

Even though she'd known most of these women her whole life, panic welled in her throat. She tried to slow her racing heart as she stood in the back of the room. They moved around noisily, shifting pots and unwrapping dishes. There was more Tupperware on the sideboard than most dealers stocked for a good year of sales. The women chattered about who'd made what, took turns heating their special recipes, then couriered them to the tables in the reception hall.

Mrs. Owens leaned over one of the many dishes on the counter, Mrs. Brown's cobbler. "Ooooh. That's a little soupy, isn't it?"

Jill covered her mouth to keep from snickering aloud. Mrs. Owens was shameless. The woman swore that, for years, Mrs. Brown had been passing off store-bought peaches as her own home-canned. She couldn't prove the rumor, but she did have everybody wondering.

"My cobbler is perfectly fine," Mrs. Brown said in defense of her dish. "That oven isn't true to temp." She marched out of the room, miffed. She had to know the other women had been talking about her. Gossip like that had a way of getting back to people.

That's the thing about small towns—if you don't remember how you're doing, don't worry; everyone else already knows.

A younger brunette, with her back to Jill, said to Mrs. Owens, "Oh my goodness. Why would anyone make peach now when blackberries are at their prime?"

Mrs. Owens patted the brunette on the hand. "Exactly. Ricky will appreciate it, too. You know blackberry cobbler is his favorite, right?"

Jill's jaw dropped. The brunette must be the girl from Atlanta who Ricky Owens brought home from spring break when he quit college.

Mrs. Huckaby came into the kitchen. "Who made the chocolate pecan pie?"

No one owned up to it. "Don't know why they'd bother," said Mrs. Huckaby. "Nobody could make that pie as good as Pearl."

"Oh, honey, I tried a piece, and it's perfect. I'm telling you, I think Pearl may have sent it herself," claimed Mrs. Grizzard, the mail carrier's wife. "Be just like Pearl to do that, you know."

The two women exchanged a knowing look.

Jill's lips relaxed into an unexpected smile. It filled her heart to hear them talk about her grandmother. But who else had Pearl's famous chocolate pecan pie recipe?

Now that the kitchen was mostly empty, Jill braved herself to join the others in the main hall. Flower arrangements adorned every table in an explosion of bright colors that Pearl would have adored.

A large portrait on an easel was the focal point at the far end of the room. Drawn to the picture, Jill moved through the crowd, not hearing one word that folks uttered as she passed by.

When Jill got closer, she immediately recognized the signature on the bottom right of the portrait. Mary Claire Spratt had even captured the twinkle in her grandmother's eyes. Mary Claire was Carolanne's cousin and the same age as she and Jill, but Mary

Claire had been born with Down syndrome. Last year, her parents had moved her into the apartment above the store. It gave Mary Claire the chance to have her own space, but was close to Mom and Dad when she needed them. They'd turned the loft into a studio since Mary Claire was becoming quite known in local circles for her sketches and watercolors. She had an incredible ability to translate a memory into a keepsake through pen and ink and paper. Her God-given talent touched everyone who had the chance to see her work.

Though this portrait was done in shades of black and gray pen and ink, the steel blue of Pearl's eyes was still obvious. The way the right corner of Pearl's mouth turned up, almost a smirk, was perfect. She'd probably just said something sassy. Pearl was known to dish out a hard time in good fun.

A warm feeling came over Jill, like Pearl was standing there with her. She turned to look, but it was Carolanne who was at her side.

"Garrett said Bradley's here." Carolanne scanned the room. "Where is he?"

"He left," Jill said.

"Already?"

"Yep."

"I never even saw him. Are you OK?"

"I am." Jill nodded. She reached for Carolanne's hands. "I really am."

"I was planning to leave tonight, but I can stay," Carolanne offered.

"No. I'm fine," Jill said.

"If you need me, just call. I'll hop right back on a plane."

Jill reached for Carolanne's hand. "You've done enough just being here. I don't know how I could have gotten through today without you."

"I loved Pearl, too." Carolanne looked worried. She gave Jill's hand a squeeze. "As awful as today was, this is the easy part. It's what follows that'll suck the life out of you. Call me."

"I will." Jill took Carolanne by the shoulders and turned her toward the door. "Now go."

"Oh wait. I almost forgot." Carolanne dug into her purse and pulled out an envelope. "Milly said this was for you. Read it when you're ready."

Jill took the envelope, holding it with the tips of her fingers.

"I know this is hard. I'll call you in a couple days, but you call me before that if you want to talk."

Jill folded the envelope and tucked it into the pocket of her blazer. "Go, go, go, and drive careful. I'm going to be OK. I promise." The two girls hugged one last time, then Carolanne left. Jill stood in the room, surrounded by the people who loved Pearl. She'd known most of them her whole life. Becky Markham worked her way through the crowd to Jill's side. Becky had always been a solid second to Jill through all of their school years. Cheerleading, student council, Pork Festival Queen, everything except the Miss Fourth of July title their senior year. Of course, Jill'd had the flu that year. The competitiveness had left their friendship more than a little strained. It was no secret Becky had been making plays for Garrett's attention since Jill left town. Not that she hadn't tried to steal him a hundred times while they were together, but that was Becky. Like a goat, she always wanted what she couldn't quite get to.

Becky gave Jill an air hug. "I know how close you two were. You know, people think it's easier when you lose someone old. It's not. In fact, I think it's harder because we have to deal with so many more memories."

"Thank you," Jill stammered. Becky's kindness had caught her off guard.

"Now I hope you don't plan to stick around." Becky crossed her arms.

"What?"

"Garrett, of course. You know we've been going out, right?"

Now this was the Becky she expected. Jill felt a rogue pang of jealousy. "Oh well…No, I didn't. But then, it's none of my business."

"He's mine now. So don't you go getting any ideas." Becky waved to someone across the hall. "You just have a good old trip back there to Atlanta or wherever." She was already walking away as if she could care less what Jill had to add.

"Savannah," Jill answered. "I was in Savannah." *Some people never change.*

After that, Jill needed air. If one more person hugged and kissed her, she'd bruise from the attention. The courtyard would be the perfect place to escape. She headed that way and took a seat on one of the cement benches. Pearl used to sit there and wait until Jill pulled the car around to pick her up. The temperature was always cooler under those big trees. They must have been at least a hundred years old.

Feeling her past wrap around her, she remembered when her parents died. On that last trip, her parents had been searching for Spanish treasure where the Amazon intersects the borders of Ecuador. The culture there was so primitive they'd been missing for weeks before word got back to the States about their deaths. No bodies to bury, just a memorial service. Jill was embarrassed to admit it, but at times, she had to remind herself that they'd existed at all. When they never returned from that trip, she'd felt as if someone had just snatched them off the earth, memories and all, in that one day.

But Pearl, she'd always been there.

❖

Garrett stepped his long, lean leg over the bench. He bumped his shoulder to hers playfully.

"I didn't hear you come up."

A year ago, you'd have bumped my shoulder back. "I heard Bradley already left," he said.

"Yep."

"He didn't stay long."

"Nope."

"You OK?"

"Yep. Fine as I can be." She folded her hands in her lap. "Thank you." She paused, like she was searching for the right words. "For the jacket, the support. Just for being there for me today...and checking on me now."

"You're welcome."

"I wanted to jump right into that hole with her." Jill shook her head and let out a long breath.

I could tell. It broke my heart. He nodded.

"I'm sorry," she said.

"For what?" Garrett leaned back, studying her face.

"Everything. I've treated you awful since you were back. You didn't deserve it."

"You were upset."

"Can you forgive me?"

Will you ever forgive me? He shrugged like he just might not be able to, but then laughed and said, "Of course. Done. Anything for you."

"Don't tell Becky that. She already staked her claim on you. She said—let me get her words right—'He's mine now.' "

He rolled his eyes. "You should know better than that."

"I don't believe I know anything about you anymore. A lot's happened while I've been away."

"Yeah." He stripped a leaf from the tree branch that dipped low above their heads. "Are you ready to go home? I can give you a lift if you need one."

"Izzy'll give me a ride."

"You more the limo kind of girl these days?"

"No, it's not that. I just…"

It's just a ride. Come on. Lower those forty-foot walls you've built to keep me out. "Izzy just took Old Man Piper and Miss Holly back to the seniors home; she'll be a while. I'd be happy to take you back now." *Look at me. I want to help.* He held her gaze.

She smiled a little. "You know what, I think I'll take you up on that ride," she finally agreed.

"Great. Let's go." They walked in silence to Garrett's truck; then he held the door as she climbed up into the cab.

Garrett turned on the radio to avoid any awkward conversation. Maybe that way they could spend more than ten minutes together without a fight.

As they turned down the driveway that led to Pearl's house, even the lane felt quiet, like it was missing Pearl, too.

Jill grabbed for Garrett's arm. "Stop!"

He slammed on the brakes, then pried her fingernails from his arm. "What was that for?"

She strained against the seat belt as she lunged forward in the seat, staring at the front of the house. "Something's wrong."

Chapter Eight

Garrett patted Jill's leg. "Calm down. It's been a hectic day." He'd never seen her so on edge.

"Stop the truck. Please."

"It's not moving." He knew this wasn't the time to argue with her. He pulled the key from the ignition. "See. Totally stopped. It's going to be OK."

"Look. The window by the front door is pushed partway up. I closed every single window in the house this morning when we got up, and as we left this morning, a man was delivering that tree. See it?"

"I see it. It's next to the door."

"It was in *front* of the door."

"OK. Calm down. I'll check it out." He dropped open the glove compartment and grabbed a gun. "Wait here."

Her stomach did a somersault. "You have a handgun? Since when do you carry pistols around?"

"Since I got a concealed weapons permit. Don't panic. I'll be right back." He hit the door lock, stuffed the gun into the back of his pants, and sprinted the hundred and fifty feet to the front door.

Just as he paused to open the front door, he heard Jill step up behind him.

He swung around to meet her eye to eye. “You don’t listen very well.”

“And you’re surprised?”

“I shouldn’t be.” He shook his head. “Some things never change.”

“I was scared.”

He pointed out the window screen lying on the porch.

Jill’s eyes got wide. She grabbed the back of his shirt with her two hands, tucking behind him like a shadow.

The front door was slightly ajar. Garrett pushed it open and stood back for a moment. He crouched, moving slowly, listening for any hint someone might still be there.

Hiccup.

Garrett spun around. Jill slapped her hands over her mouth.

“I told you to wait in the truck.” He straightened and walked on in. “Well, if anyone was here, they know we’re onto them.”

“Sorry. You know I can’t—*hiccup*—help it.”

“How could I forget that?” Garrett took a step forward, then tugged Jill behind him.

“What?” She peeked around him.

“Shh.” Papers spilled into the hallway from Pearl’s office. Garrett checked the office and the other rooms carefully, then turned and relaxed a bit. “Whoever was here is gone now.”

Jill lifted her knees high to clear the mounds of books and papers. “Why would someone do this?” *Hiccup.*

Garrett hesitated, measuring her and the situation for a moment. “I don’t know.”

“I’m calling the sheriff.” Jill got some water for her hiccups, then called the sheriff’s office. When she came back in the room, Garrett had righted a chair and was stacking the mess into piles.

"They're on the way. I'm going to change clothes. You don't have to hang around."

"No. I'll wait. Go change."

Jill came back in the room dressed in jeans and her Virginia Tech T-shirt.

"I like the shirt. Anything missing back there?"

"My suitcase isn't where I left it." Jill walked toward the hearth in the living room. Garrett was at her side when she noticed the broken picture on the hearth. The glass in tiny pieces. The frame held a picture of Jill and Garrett from last summer's Pork Festival.

A car door slammed out front. She looked out the window to see their high school buddy Scott Calvin walking toward the house.

"It's Scott. I haven't seen him in forever." Jill and Garrett met him on the porch.

"You're the sheriff now?"

Scott smiled. "Thank goodness I didn't need your vote. I'd been counting on it, and you were gone." He reached forward and gave her a hug. "So sorry to hear about Pearl."

"Congratulations." Jill reached up and hugged him. "I bet Ruth was thrilled."

He shrugged.

"Oh, don't play modest with me." She smacked his shoulder playfully. "I know how proud she was when you became a man of the law and all." Jill caught the odd look between Scott and Garrett. "What?" She looked back toward Scott. "Did I miss something? What now?"

Garrett cleared his throat and interjected, "They aren't seeing each other anymore."

Jill took a step back. "No way. You were the perfect couple."

Scott nodded. "Yeah, well, I always thought you and Malloy were, too. I guess we were all wrong."

She snapped her mouth shut.

Garrett snickered. It was nice to see Jill Clemmons at a loss for words. That didn't happen often.

Scott got the details from Jill and Garrett and then surveyed the damage.

"Was the door locked?" Scott asked.

"Yes. The windows were closed, and I locked the front door when Milly and I left for the church."

"It's pretty obvious they came in through the window." Scott ran his hand up and down the jamb and twisted the knob. "There doesn't appear to be any sign of forced entry to the door. They must have just not closed it tight when they left."

"I didn't notice anything, either," Garrett said.

Sheriff Calvin lifted his chin toward Jill. "Do you have a hide-a-key?"

"Of course," Garrett chimed in again.

"Let me guess, the planter box next to the door," Scott said, leaning out the front door, still examining it for any other telling signs.

"Guilty," she said.

"Move the key." He jotted a note in a tiny notebook. "No sense making it easy. Especially if the place is going to be empty at all. Nothing of value missing?"

"Just my suitcase, but I didn't have anything of value in it," Jill said. "It's not as bad as it looked at first. It's like a giant picked up the room and gave it one good shake like a snow globe."

"Probably kids causing mischief while everyone was at Pearl's funeral, but I don't like it. Where are you going to be staying?"

Jill shrugged. "Here."

Scott shook his head. "Not a good idea."

"You said it was probably just kids."

Scott and Garrett exchanged a glance.

"I saw that look," Jill said.

"I'll write up a report in case you find anything of value missing and need it for the insurance," Scott said. "I'll send someone over to dust for prints, if you don't mind. It'll be good practice."

"You can stay at my place"—Garrett cleared his throat—"in the guest room."

"That won't be necessary." She shifted her attention to Scott. "Seriously? Nothing ever happens in this town."

"Which is exactly why you need to take the precaution." Scott didn't waver.

"Fine. I'll call Milly. I can stay with her tonight."

Scott nodded and turned to leave. "Good."

Garrett and Jill walked him out to the porch. Scott waved as he got back in the car and drove off.

Jill turned to Garrett. "I'm sure you didn't expect a simple ride home to take your whole day."

"Why don't you give Milly a quick call, and I'll drop you off over there."

"I can drive myself. Why are you hovering? I'll call her later. Right now, I'm just going to get started on cleaning this mess up."

"I'll stay and help, then."

"No, thank you. Really. I've got this."

"I'm not doing it for you. I'm doing it for Pearl," said Garrett.

Jill opened the front door wide. "You know, I've been trying to be nice, but if you tell me one more time how you're doing things for Pearl, I swear I'm going to scream. She's my family. I'll handle it. I'm quite capable, if you've so quickly forgotten."

Garrett waited, hoping she'd realize the tantrum she was throwing was ridiculous and take it back, but she didn't.

"Go!" she ordered from the doorway.

Garrett walked right past her and out the door. *Pearl, you sure did raise a spirited one. Only you and God know why I'm so damn crazy about her that I'd put up with this in hopes of getting her back.*

❖

Jill stood in the doorway until Garrett's truck cleared the path. Satisfied that he was long gone, she shut the front door and went into the kitchen to get a trash bag and the dustpan.

She stooped to pick up the pieces of a ceramic bowl. Her childhood artwork was in a dozen pieces now. She swept the remains into a pile and then scooped it into the dustpan. Broken pieces, like her heart. Like her life.

Sitting back on her heels, she pushed the bag and its contents away.

"Why?" she whispered and bowed her head. It wasn't just a bowl. It was everything falling apart. Things she counted on being safe forever were suddenly gone or had been shaken. She drew in a staggered breath, then forced herself to keep moving.

Jill righted each precious framed photo on the mantel, one at a time. She lifted the one she'd made in Vacation Bible School out of crisscrossed Popsicle sticks. Globs of glue were the only telltale sign that it had once had shells in each corner.

The picture of her and Garrett on graduation day at Virginia Tech seemed so long ago. It felt like a lifetime since they'd planned Bridle Path Estates together. He'd handle the architecture and building it. She'd take care of the artisan center showcasing Virginia artists, especially their local ones. Being right here on Route 58 and close to I-95 would mean plenty of tourist traffic to draw revenue to Adams Grove. Making those plans seemed like another lifetime.

She picked up the next framed picture and held it close. Pearl beamed with pride holding a huge royal-blue rosette at the

Festival Days Pie Bake-off. Grand Champion. Who would win this summer?

Tucked in the corner of one of the frames in back, a small photo in sienna tones of a much younger Pearl arm in arm with a handsome man whom Jill had never seen before caught her attention. Pearl had been so beautiful back then. The young man's dark, disheveled hair and sharply contoured face was in stark contrast to her grandmother's soft features.

Dad's father? Only once had Jill broached the subject of the man in Pearl's life, and the sadness that dimmed Pearl's blues eyes kept her from ever asking again.

Jill froze at the sound of a vehicle approaching. She jumped off the hearth and ran to the front door and locked it. Her heart pounded out an alarm, reminding her how vulnerable and stupid she was for staying.

She stood near the door, trying to decide what to do. Hide? Call Scott? Then the horn honked twice. Burglars weren't likely to honk a horn, and Garrett used to do that when he came to pick her up.

The sound of boots on the porch were followed by a knock. His knock. She wasn't sure if she was relieved it was him or mad that he'd scared her, and why was he back, anyway? Hadn't she made herself clear?

She swung open the door, ready to have her say, but before she could even utter a word, Garrett shoved a blue leash in her direction.

"Since you want to do everything that needs doing for Pearl, here...meet Clyde."

Jill stared at the massive black, white, and tan dog panting at Garrett's side wondering just how big that dog was under all that hair. "He's huge. You've got to be kidding. That beast could eat me for lunch. I'm not taking that leash."

"He won't bite."

She reached her hand to Clyde. He gave her two big sniffs and then licked the top of her hand.

"See, he loves women. Took me months to get him to warm up to me, but he loves the girls, don't ya, Clyde?" Garrett held the leash out to Jill a second time.

"You don't really expect me to believe that's Pearl's dog, do you?"

"Why not?"

"We never had a dog the whole time I was growing up. Why would she get one now?" Jill shook her head in disbelief. "What kind of dog is he?"

"He's a Bernese mountain dog. Clyde was good company. He even pulled her garden cart for her."

"This is not my grandmother's dog." She cocked her head. "He was never here when I came to visit."

"You sure about that?"

She eyed him curiously. Her visits had been quick. It was possible.

"He's drooling." She distanced herself from the slimy string that hung from Clyde's mouth.

"Yeah. He does that." Garrett took a hand towel out of his back pocket and tossed it her way. "Pearl kept one slung over her shoulder."

Jill caught the towel midair. "Oh…my…God. This is just gross." She reached toward the big dog's chin to wipe the string of drool. "Ewww, nasty." Clyde nuzzled his face against the hip of Jill's jeans, taking care of the drool on his own.

"Lovely." She rubbed the towel against the shiny spot on her hip.

"You'll get used to it." Garrett nodded. "Maybe she didn't want to worry you."

"She sounded fine every time I called."

"I'm sure the paperwork is in Pearl's desk. You know how meticulous she was about paperwork. Since you insist on handling everything, I knew you'd want to take care of Clyde, too." He patted her hand. "Besides, I know you're not planning to call Milly."

"Don't pretend to know me so well."

"I'm not pretending. It hasn't been that long."

Clyde took that moment to walk right between the two of them, jump up onto the edge of the couch, and put his chin on the arm like he'd done it a million times.

She stood wide-eyed and motionless as Clyde made himself at home. "I can't take care of this dog." *And Bradley will never go for this.*

"Sure you can."

Jill turned her attention back to Clyde. "What am I supposed to feed him?"

"I've got you covered." Garrett jogged out to his truck, opened the tailgate, and hoisted a bag of dog food up onto his shoulder. He took the fifty-pound bag to the front porch and dropped it with a thud. "This should hold him for a week or so."

"A week? My God, how much does he eat?"

"That size dog? As much as he damn well pleases."

"I guess so," Jill said. The heavy dose of sarcasm in Garrett's voice hadn't gone unnoticed. He was enjoying this way too much. "I must have asked for a dog a hundred times growing up. Do you know how many stray hunting dogs I tried to talk her into? I can't believe Pearl got one after I moved out."

"Believe it. At least you'll be safe with him around." Garrett headed down the steps. "Got to go." He waved from the rolled-down window as he drove off.

Jill wrestled the monster bag of food from the porch through the front door. Once inside, the bag slid easily on the hardwood floors to the kitchen. She ripped open the top, and Clyde came running into the kitchen. She opened the door and let him out while she dished out a bowl of kibble. Clyde ran around the far end of the yard. She'd almost swear she could feel his heavy footsteps.

Not wasting a moment, she slipped the huge bowl of food and another of water out on the patio and closed the door quickly. In an instant, Clyde ran for the door and began gobbling the food, wagging his huge, feathery tail.

"I'd better keep you well fed." She watched him chow down. "You *are* a pretty thing, aren't you?"

She wondered if she'd find anything about this dog in Pearl's files. If it was true that this was her dog, Pearl would have record of it. That lady had detailed records on everything, but it would be just like Garrett to pull her leg for a good laugh at her expense. She went to the library where Pearl paid her bills and kept her records.

To her chagrin, she found a whole file on Clyde, at least an inch thick.

"Great." Jill flipped through the vet records and pictures. Apparently, Clyde was an accomplished companion dog. He had several awards of achievement in the file to prove it, and Pearl was his owner.

Jill leaned back in the chair and slapped the folder closed. *Why didn't you tell me?*

She'd focused on her career since she moved to Savannah, but Pearl never seemed to need anything, and Jill certainly never thought Pearl'd be gone.

Maybe Jill hadn't asked the right questions. Now she needed answers.

Chapter Nine

Thanks to Scott and Garrett's ridiculous warnings, Jill hadn't been able to even close her eyes and finally had to resolve herself to a night at the hotel. That hadn't turned out to be a great solution, either. The couple in the neighboring room were up for anything but sleep, and that kept her awake all night, but at least she'd been safe. Finally, when daylight broke, she drove back home and crawled into bed for some rest.

She stretched and slowly opened her eyes. Then shrieked, scooching backward at the sight of Clyde's huge tricolored head staring at her from the side of the bed until her mind put all the pieces together.

"Clyde," she yelled as her mind connected all the dots, "you scared me."

He retreated to the doorway with his head low and tail slung between his legs.

"I'm sorry. I didn't mean to scare you, but you scared me first." *Hiccup.* The quilt was damp from his hot breath and slobber. "Why do you always have to be so drooly?"

His mouth dropped open, and his tongue hung long as he panted. He looked downright amused.

"That wasn't a compliment." She patted the bed twice. "Fine. Come on."

Clyde made the easy leap to the bed and edged close to her. She snuggled against Clyde, rubbing his soft ears.

She didn't feel like getting up, and why should she? She didn't have anyone to answer to today. But every time she'd start to drift off, the phone rang. The sound was driving her nuts. She dragged herself out from under the covers and answered the phone, just to silence the darn thing.

"Hello," she said, way too loud.

"I thought I'd hear from you last night."

"Bradley?" Jill rolled her eyes and let out a sigh. "Why are you calling me on Pearl's number?"

"I've been trying your cell. Did your battery die?"

"Probably. The last twenty-four hours have been grueling." Jill carried the old princess phone from the hall to the edge of the living room like she had for all the years she'd lived there. Why hadn't she ever thought to buy Pearl a cordless phone? The twenty-foot cord was a hazard.

"I'm sorry," Bradley said. "I didn't help things, either."

"You got that right." Too tired to even get into this conversation right now, she regretted saying the words as soon as they slipped from her mouth.

"I don't know what got into me. I guess I let jealousy cloud my judgment. I wish I'd reacted differently. I wish I'd been there for you."

Jill leaned against the door jamb. "I wish you had, too. It was a horrible day. The worst in my life." She pushed her hair behind her ear, then balanced the phone between her shoulder and chin so she could pet Clyde who'd decided to get up, too.

"I'm sorry, baby doll. Really. I'll make it up to you," he said.

"The truth is, you didn't help me any, but nothing in the world could make me feel better right now short of bringing Pearl back. Think you can do that?"

"No. I guess I can't. How is everything else?"

"I had a special surprise when I got back here yesterday."

"You mean something besides a lifetime supply of fat-laden homemade casseroles?"

"Yeah. This wasn't a welcome gift. Someone broke into the house."

His voice rose with concern. "You're OK, right? Was anything taken?"

"I'm fine. Whoever broke in was already gone when I got here. They made a huge mess."

"Who knows what would've happened had you walked in on them. You should come on home. Is there something of value there you think they were looking for?"

"No. Not really." Jill didn't see any point in mentioning that Garrett had been the one taking all the risk. "Anyway, the sheriff came out. They dusted for prints but said that the break-in was probably the result of kids with nothing better to do while everyone in the county was at Pearl's funeral."

"They dusted for prints? I'm surprised that podunk sheriff's department has the skill. But seriously, I don't like the sound of this one bit. I want you to come home before you get hurt. I don't want anything to happen to my girl."

"I need to be here." Too exhausted to keep soothing his insecurities when she felt so low herself, she wanted to end the call. "I've got to go. I'll call you later." She hung up, unplugged the phone from the wall, and wrapped the long cord around the handset.

She tousled the top of Clyde's head as she walked by him toward the bedroom, but when she caught sight of her black blazer, she remembered the note that Carolanne had given her. She grabbed the letter and called Clyde to follow her to the bedroom.

Clyde was quickly becoming her kind of guy. He was perfectly happy to lounge around all day. No questions, no lectures, just a warm body to snuggle. He clomped into the room and sprawled out on the cool wooden floor as Jill plumped the pillows and climbed into bed. Her name in Pearl's writing was all that was on the plain white envelope.

She slipped her nail under the sealed edge and opened it.

Dear Jill,

If you're reading this, then my time has come to an end here. Dry those tears, and embrace all the good things we shared. I've had a wonderful life. You were one of the best parts of it. Don't mourn my exit, instead take what I've taught you and pass that along. It's what we Clemmons girls were meant to do.

I don't know if you and Garrett will ever get it right and be the couple that I know you could be, but I know that you will both do wonderful things. I hope the legacy I've left with you will help in some way to make all that happen. It's complicated. Get with Connor Buckham. He should've passed this note along so you may have already spoken to him in detail, but if not, set up that meeting and he'll explain everything.

You've grown into such a beautiful woman inside and out. I couldn't be more proud of you.

With love,

Pearl

"Complicated?"

Jill reread the letter, tugging her knees up under her chin. "What's so complicated?" She missed Pearl, and although the memories were wonderful, it didn't make missing her any easier. She pulled the covers up over her head and prayed that she'd find the strength to find her way again. Everything seemed to be off-kilter now that Pearl was gone, and without Pearl to talk to about it just made it seem worse.

Clyde jumped up on the bed and rested his heavy chin on her tummy. Jill lifted her hand out from under the covers and patted his head. She'd have to get up and feed him sometime today else he might resort to gnawing off her foot or something. She rolled over into the pillow, promising herself she'd feed him the next time she woke up.

The sun was starting to set when she opened her eyes again. Clyde's tail wagged like crazy. She wondered how long he'd been watching her. She sat on the edge of the bed. Clyde stuck his nose in her crotch, then ran toward the bedroom door, waiting.

"I know. I promised."

He tilted his head. When she didn't move, he came back over and laid his head on her knee. His huge golden eyes looked sad, like he was begging her to feed him.

She rubbed his big lips and muzzle, then slid off the side of the bed. When her feet hit the floor, the "oh shit" mantra came to mind, but she'd just have to make up for that another day.

Clyde beat her to the kitchen. He looked pitiful until she filled his bowl with food. *Did he just smile and wink at me?* She turned her cell phone on and deleted the seven messages from Bradley without listening to them. Sitting at the kitchen table, staring off at nothing in particular, was about all she had the energy to do.

Clyde stopped his munching and looked at her.

"No, I don't feel like eating. You go ahead." Her cell phone rang. "I just talked to the dog. Great."

He seemed to raise a brow and give her "the look." Jill looked at the caller ID on her cell. Carolanne. Safe to answer. "Hey, gal."

"Hey. I called the house earlier; you didn't answer," Carolanne said.

"I was here. I just wasn't answering. That phone has been ringing off the hook."

Carolanne laughed. "You know how Adams Grove folks are. Everyone will be checking on you for at least a week."

"I know," she said. "I'll think twice before I call during that first week to pay condolences in the future. I'd rather just be left alone right now."

"You doing OK?"

"Clyde and I successfully slept away the day. One down."

"You still have that dog? I figured you'd pawn him back off on Garrett."

"We've found a peaceful coexistence."

"With Clyde or Garrett?"

"I kind of like having old Clyde around," Jill admitted. "He doesn't mind sleeping most of the day away, and he likes to spoon."

"You avoided my question."

"Don't start," Jill said and then changed the subject. "So it seems that note that Milly gave you to give to me was instructions to get with Connor Buckham about Pearl's estate."

"Her estate? I wonder why she used him and didn't call me?"

Jill hadn't considered that. Carolanne's feelings were probably hurt. "Gosh, I don't know, but maybe just because he was here. You know how Pearl was about supporting folks in town."

"Yeah. I guess that makes sense."

"She said it's complicated. I don't how it could be complicated, but now she's got me curious."

"Isn't it just the house?"

"I always assumed she used everything she had to send me to college. We lived pretty lean."

"When are you going to call Connor?"

"Tomorrow." Jill hung up, more curious about the note, and why hadn't Pearl just talked to Carolanne instead of paying Connor? There was only one way to know that.

Before Jill headed upstairs, she decided to call and leave a message for Connor. She'd never known Connor all that well. He was more Carolanne's friend. They'd both attended UVA to earn their law degrees. In Pearl's standard filing technique, Jill found the number under *C* for Connor. Jill dialed the phone and waited.

"Connor Buckham here."

"Hi, Connor. This is Jill Clemmons. I was calling to leave you a message. I didn't expect you to be in tonight at this hour."

"Sorry to hear about Pearl."

"Thank you," she said, shaking the wayward thought of him with a society girl in his arms. "Milly passed along that note." Jill heard a squeak on the other end of the phone. She could picture Connor leaning back in his chair.

"Good. How about you and Garrett come in the morning? Say about nine?"

"Garrett and I? Why does Garrett need to come with me?"

"Details. It'll make sense when we go through it all."

Jill grimaced, but the truth was Pearl loved Garrett and it really wouldn't be surprising if she'd left him a little something. She pushed her discomfort aside.

Connor continued to speak. "Everything will be clear when we discuss the conditions of the will. I also have a video Pearl made for the two of you."

"A video?"

"Yeah. After fifteen takes, she was quite the actress."

"You can't be serious."

"These are Pearl's last wishes, Jill."

"Fine. I'll contact Garrett. We'll be there." Jill had no idea how she was going to control Garrett's schedule, but she'd find a way so they could get this settled. Garrett's cell phone number was on Pearl's short list by the hall phone. She punched in the number but breathed a sigh of relief when her call went to voice mail. She left him a message about their appointment the next morning.

The text message sound played on her phone. She clicked to the message. *I guess I'm not the only one screening calls.* It was from Garrett. All it said was, *I'll pick you up at eight forty-five. G.*

Her first inclination was to text him back and say she'd meet him there; then she realized if she pushed her luck, he might not go at all.

❖ Chapter Ten ❖

The next morning, the short ride with Garrett to Connor's office in town felt like a cross-country road trip. Jill practically leaped out of the truck as soon as it was parked, anxious to put some space between them.

The colorful awnings above the windows on the front of the old bank building looked like playful eyebrows. It was a great piece of old architecture. Tall Corinthian columns graced either side of the wood-and-glass doors, all the way to the top of the three-story building. Pearl had worked hard over the years to preserve these old buildings.

Jill and Garrett kept a safe distance as they walked up the sidewalk together. He held the door for her, and she stepped into Connor's office just as he was walking up the hallway.

"Hi, Jill. It's been a long time. You look great." He slapped Garrett on the back, then led the two of them down the narrow hall toward his office. "Good to see you both."

Connor had slimmed down and neatened up quite a bit since college.

"I sure wish we were meeting under different circumstances." Connor placed a consoling arm around her shoulder.

"I know." She reached up to touch his hand. "Me too."

Connor offered them a seat and then stepped behind his large wooden desk. "That Pearl's a character, isn't she? Wills are usually easy money. Fill in the blank—put the money in the bank. But your grandmother, she made me earn every penny on this one. Oh, and then she talked me into a discount on top of that."

Jill glanced over at Garrett. He had a determined look on his face.

Connor spun his chair toward the ornate bookcase that lined the wall behind him. "Before I walk you through the details, I have a message here from Pearl for the two of you." He shuffled through some files and turned around, holding a DVD in his hand. He opened the center doors and slid the DVD into the player on the shelf below a flat-screen television. He handed Jill the remote. "Just press *play* when you're ready. I'll be back in a bit."

Jill sat staring at the remote.

"When did she make this?" Jill asked.

"The DVD? Just a few weeks ago." Connor dimmed the lights and closed the door firmly behind him.

Her palms began to sweat. "You do it," she said, handing the remote to Garrett.

"You ready?" Garrett asked.

She licked her lips and tried to swallow. "I guess so."

Garrett pushed the button. The screen came to life and there was Pearl.

Jill gasped at the sight of her grandmother on the screen.

Pearl's eyes danced, but her skin hung and her eyes lacked their usual sparkle. She spoke slowly and clearly and assured them that she was of sound mind when she created the terms of her will. "That was all that legal mumbo jumbo Connor said I had to say. Darn near need one of those TV news teleprompters to get through this much red tape. This seemed like a good idea when I saw it on *Montel* years ago, but it's turned out to be a lot of work."

Same old Pearl, Jill thought. Garrett winked at her with a lop-sided grin. He probably had the identical thought.

"Connor will handle the will. I trust him, and Lord knows, I'm paying him enough for it," Pearl continued, "but I need to explain a couple things to you myself. I wanted a clause that made the two of you marry to get the property, but Connor said I couldn't do that. So I found a loophole. I can strongly encourage you."

Pearl leaned into the camera so close Jill could see her pores. "Those were Connor's words, you know—*encourage you* to spend some time together. I'm hoping you two will finally come back to your senses. I love you both. Jill, my dear sweet granddaughter, you are a wonderful young lady. Your father would have been so proud of you. Garrett, a better man doesn't exist. You two were made for each other. If you weren't so doggone pigheaded, you'd be together without my help."

Jill felt a smile on her lips. Seeing Pearl, hearing her voice, was such a comfort. Garrett snickered and then rested his hand on her leg. Her skin tingled beneath his touch.

"So here I am, helping. It's what I do best, you know." Pearl smiled and crossed her hands in front of her, leaning forward on the desk. "I can feel my time coming to an end, my dears. Rely on each other. Take care of each other. For me."

Jill grabbed the arm of the chair and leaned forward, trying to take a breath.

Garrett hit the pause button and laid a hand on her back. "Are you OK?"

She pressed her hands to her face and cried.

"It's OK. I'm here." He squatted in front of her and took her hands into his. "We don't have to do this right now if you're not ready." He held her as she sobbed against his shoulder.

Her tears choked her.

"Do you need some water?"

She shook her head.

He handed her a tissue from the box on Connor's desk. "Here."

She dabbed her eyes.

"Do you want to leave?"

"No." She shook her head. "No. Keep going."

Garrett hit *play* to restart the video.

Pearl came back to life on the screen. "I'd like to ask the two of you to live in the house for thirty consecutive days. If, after those days, you do not find your way back into each other's hearts, I'll admit I was wrong." She leaned into the camera and winked. "But you know I never am." The chair shifted as she repositioned. "No, you don't have to. I said I was just askin' because I'd like that." Pearl turned her attention to someone out of frame. "I said they didn't have to. Stop it, you worrywart. This is my message." She was giving Connor the devil, and that was typical Pearl.

She came back into frame. "So here's the deal. When Connor comes back in, he'll show you the plat. The property is much bigger than you think. Garrett, you're going to want to fuss at me for not telling you sooner, but anyway…" Pearl pushed her glasses up on her nose and continued. "Jill, our home sat on just a small piece of the land John Carlo Pacini set aside for me when he had to leave. I know you're thinkin', *Who was that?* You've never heard of him, I know, but he was a good man. The love of my life. My husband. Your grandfather, and you would have loved him. He built that house for me, and I've always been safe there. I'd be so happy to know the two of you are safe there. I was lucky to not only have had the great fortune to raise our son there, your father, but also to have you so close to me when your father was gone."

Pearl steepled her fingers to her lips and leaned back. "My special Jill and Garrett. I once knew real love. It's precious. I truly believe there's only one true love for each person. My John Carlo was the only man I ever loved. He loved me, too. Jill, you will appreciate this, honey. John Carlo had long dark hair."

Pearl leaned close into the camera again. "He was even foxier than Yanni. That's why I liked Yanni so much. He reminded me of my John Carlo." Pearl smiled and giggled like a schoolgirl for a moment. "Fate kept us apart, but he was with me, protecting me, loving me, every day I lived. Don't let your pride keep you from embracing what you both deserve. Jill, get the frown off your face, girl. You'll get wrinkles."

Pearl paused.

"Now you two kiss," she ordered, waving her bony hands in a merging motion in front of the camera.

Jill slowly turned to Garrett, but neither made the move.

"What? You can't give an old woman a simple thing like this? One kiss. Go on now," Pearl insisted.

Jill grunted and rolled her eyes. Garrett leaned her way.

"Just a little smooch." Pearl was nothing if not audacious.

Garrett leaned over and kissed Jill.

Her lips tingled and other parts danced too as his hands found their way to the back of her neck and then her cheek, holding her at a breath's distance. She blinked. Their faces so close, her lips feeling full, she wished she didn't want him to kiss her again.

"Oh. All right," Pearl said to someone out of frame. "Oh, wait. Connor says I can't make you do that. I think he just called me a pimp-granny. I guess I can only en-co-u-r-age," she exaggerated, making the word sound about five syllables long, "you to kiss and enjoy it, and about the being together thing and thirty days in the house. Can't really do that, either, but I wish you would give it a try for me."

Pearl had just won the first round. She was a slick old bird, that gal.

"I love the two of you. Make it work. I'll be with you in your heart every day, doing what God will let me while I hang out up there with him. No telling what jobs he's got for me."

Pearl blew a little kiss and the video seemed to end, but then came right back into focus. She fussed with whoever was taping the session, probably Connor. "I just have one more thing to say," she said, then turned primly back to the camera. "Jill, dear, tell sweet Carolanne that she needs to get her butt back to Adams Grove. She doesn't need to let that daddy of hers keep her from getting her a good man right here in town. Fact is, he's been doing pretty good staying on the wagon." Pearl hunched forward, leaning on her elbows. "I know she and Connor would make a great couple." Pearl's attention moved off camera. "No, you cannot take that off. This is my last wish to my granddaughter. You just roll that 'til I'm done." Turning back to the camera, she smiled. "I know Carolanne can wrangle this one. They're just alike. He's got that girl in Chicago or California, some big city somewhere, but God knows, if she ain't here yet, she never will be. I love you, dear. You and Garrett find your happiness. The rest will all fall into place." She blew a final kiss into the camera. "Now I'm done, damn it. It's not like I was paying you by the inch of tape. You can shut it—"

The screen went blank in midsentence.

Garrett laid his callused hand over hers, stroking the top with his thumb. She welcomed the gesture at first, then tugged away.

Pearl, the hopeless romantic, had her reasons.

Connor stepped back in the office and turned up the lights. "Any questions?" he asked as he edged around the big desk.

They both nodded.

"Only a million," Jill said, only half kidding.

Connor reset the lights and popped the DVD from the machine. "Sorry about that last part, but there was no stopping Pearl when she had her mind set on something." Connor unfolded a blueprint of a plat across his desk in front of them.

"You're telling us?" Jill said. "I could watch that a million times."

"You can. I'll give it to you. So, in simple terms, Jill, the house and this piece of the property belong to you." With his thick fingers, Connor traced the portion of the property that edged the back road.

She nodded, understanding that what he'd marked was bigger than what she thought all of Pearl's land was to begin with.

Connor turned toward Garrett. "Your property is this section, and Clyde goes to you, too."

"I can take care of him," Jill piped up.

"Her decisions. Not mine." Connor shrugged and continued. "Couple of other things. Jill, you must keep the property, not sell it, for at least five years. Garrett, she wants you to use it only for the Bridle Path Estates project, and you have to break ground within that same five years. If either of you decides to forego the offer, the whole thing will be turned over to Grayson Auction. If that happens, the funds from the auction will be split three ways. One third will go to the county for a new animal shelter and boarding kennel that will take care of Clyde; the rest gets split between the two of you."

Garrett said, "I'll take care of Clyde either way."

Connor raised his hands. "It's not written up that way. Let's see how it all plays out."

Jill stood and folded her arms as she leaned over the drawing. Disquieting thoughts raced through her mind. "This gets more complicated by the minute." She recognized the faint hint of hysteria in her own voice. *Can I hold it together?*

"It's quite a nice spread. See." Connor unrolled a larger image of the plat on the desk and gestured them to move in to view the documents with him. "Even if you choose the auction route, it'll bring a nice chunk of change. Do you know what land around here is going for these days? And that property is full of mature hardwoods."

"All of that is Pearl's?" Garrett shook his head in disbelief. "Wow. Can't believe we never knew that."

"Yours now, but yes. The land and the house were gifted to her by her husband, John Carlo Pacini."

"Pearl was never married," Jill said.

"Oh, but she was," Connor said. "Their marriage was recorded back in nineteen forty-four, but they never lived together. I'm not sure what happened. I don't know any more about that than what was in the video."

Jill flinched, then tugged on Garrett's shirtsleeve. "I thought Pearl had never been married."

"No one in town ever spoke of a man in her life," Garrett said.

"John Carlo? There was a note by her knitting basket that had *Tell Jill about JC* written on it. I thought the message had something to do with the blanket she was working on. I bet she was going to tell me about him."

Connor flipped through a folder, then handed a manila envelope to Garrett. "Pearl wanted me to be sure you had these. Being an architect, she thought you'd find them interesting. They are the original drawings for the house."

Garrett took the envelope. "Thanks."

"Can I assume both of you intend to accept the property?"

Jill noticed Garrett watching her for a reaction. "Can I get a couple days to think this through? I'll probably talk to Carolanne about it, too."

Connor nodded. "Sure. That's fine. Send Carolanne my best. It's been too long since I've seen her. Oh, but don't tell her all that mess Pearl said. I was so tempted to delete that part."

Jill smiled. "Hey. Her last request. I can't just ignore her." She enjoyed tossing the line back at him.

Connor gathered the papers together on his desk. "There's plenty of time. Just let me know when you decide so I can wrap things up. Garrett, I'm assuming you're OK with the deal."

"You bet. It's a dream come true for me." He rose to his feet and shook Connor's hand.

They filed into the hall and headed toward the door.

"I guess I'll see you on the Fourth at the fireworks." Connor cuffed Garrett's shoulder.

"I'll be there around four to set up," Garrett said.

"I've got parking lot duty. How come I always get stuck with parking duty?" Connor complained.

"You look good in that fluorescent vest," Garrett said, mocking him.

Connor shifted his attention to Jill. "Come to the gate by the pond and I'll give you a good parking spot for the fireworks."

The whole town would shut down at noon that day, and the picnickers would start filing into the fairgrounds shortly after that. So many people would show up at the fairgrounds that it would take over an hour to empty the lot when it was all said and done. That steady stream of blinking brake lights would be like another show.

Jill and Carolanne used to sit with Aunt Milly and Pearl in their spot under the big oak tree and wait until Garrett and the rest of the pyro team came by. Pearl always baked her famous cookies for the guys. They'd meet up afterward to munch on the special treats and share all the mishaps and bloopers that they'd experienced during the day.

Connor clicked his fingers in front of her face. "Earth to Jill."

"Huh?"

"Where were you just then?" Connor asked.

"Nowhere, sorry. I'm not going this year," Jill said.

"All the oohing and aahing. How can you miss it?" Connor asked.

"I have some commitments for work in Savannah I need to take care of, but if I change my mind, I'll keep your offer in mind. The gate by the pond, right?"

Garrett nodded. "It just isn't Fourth of July without the hunt club barbecue and fireworks."

Connor winked at Jill. "Are you turning into a city girl on us?"

"No way. You can't take the country out of this girl."

"I don't know about that," Garrett muttered under his breath.

Jill spun toward Garrett. "What did you say?"

"I said I'm running late." Garrett turned and walked toward the truck.

She eyed him, not quite believing what she'd heard.

"He's my ride. Thanks, Connor." She jogged to catch up and fell in step behind Garrett.

Jill hiked herself up into the big truck and slammed the door shut before Garrett got in. She put her purse between them on the seat, feeling the need for a barrier.

❖ Chapter Eleven ❖

Garrett twisted the key in the ignition and dropped the truck into gear. "Think you'll come to the Fourth of July picnic?"

"I doubt it."

"When will you decide?" Garrett asked as they sped through a yellow light.

"About the property?" she asked.

"I wasn't talking about the fireworks. Yeah, about the property. What else?"

"I'll let you know something within five days."

"Pearl's rule of five. If in doubt, wait five days," he recited. Pearl's famous five-day rule was no secret in these parts. She swore that five days was the perfect cooling-off period. Time enough to look at an issue without clouding a decision with emotions, and not so long that it was impolite.

"You know me too well," Jill said.

Garrett slowed at the town square stoplight. Railroad crossing arms blocked the intersection as a freight train rumbled down the tracks. Garrett put the truck in park. He looked over, knowing full well that Jill would have her eyes closed, keeping count of those trains. Even is good; odd is bad. He watched for a moment. Her lips moved slightly with each number. He reached his arm across the back of the seat and dropped two kisses on her unsuspecting lips.

"What are you doing?" She twisted away.

"You used to say that you could count better when we kissed at the train crossing."

"That was just lovey-dovey bull." She unclicked her seat belt. "Didn't you get the message last week?" She opened the door and slammed it behind her as her feet hit the pavement. "This"—she waved a hand between the two of them—"this is not going to happen. I need time."

"Why are you still mad at me?"

Thunder roared from the sky, and nickel-sized raindrops splattered against the sidewalk. She tucked her chin and marched down the street.

Garrett rolled down the window and hollered her way. "Hey, lady, you want a lift?"

She glared at him.

"Stop, Jill. I'm sorry." He edged the truck forward, keeping pace with her. "What are you doing? C'mon, I said I was sorry."

She threw up her hand and kept right on walking.

"I won't let it happen again. Get in. It's too far for you to walk. Look, you're getting wet."

"I'm fine." She squinted through the raindrops dripping from her bangs. *Hiccup.*

"Don't be so hardheaded." Garrett idled alongside her.

"Look who's talking." She edged closer to the buildings.

A car honked behind Garrett. He waved them around. "You're going to catch pneumonia. You're hiccupping. I know what that means. You're mad. I'm sorry. Really."

"Leave me alone."

Garrett tossed something bright orange her way from the truck.

She instinctively snagged the object out of the air. “A ball cap?”

“At least it’ll keep your head dry,” he explained.

She tugged the hat down over her head and dipped her head forward to get the rain out of her face.

“Please let me take you home.”

“Go!” She picked up her pace.

He finally gave up and drove off.

❖

Another truck drove by, kicking a spray of muddy street water up onto her already damp clothes. “Great.”

The sound of a horn startled her. She resisted turning around. *Why can’t he just leave me alone?* The vehicle slowed. She turned to give him a real piece of her mind, but it wasn’t Garrett’s truck. It was Izzy Markham. The limo swerved to the shoulder just ahead of her. Izzy jumped out of the driver’s seat in her black polka-dotted raincoat and rounded the front of the vehicle to swing the back door open.

“Heard you needed a ride,” Izzy shouted over the rain. “Come on.”

Jill stepped up to Izzy, shivering. “I can’t get in your car. I’m soaking wet.”

“Give me some credit. I’m prepared.” Izzy motioned to the inside of the car.

A quilt covered the fine leather seats. “My hero. Thanks, Izzy.” Jill slid into the backseat. She’d heard Izzy had come back home sans her mortician husband, who’d been less than faithful. Lucky he hadn’t ended up dead himself when Izzy found out. Izzy showed him. She took the best limo they had and hauled butt back home. That girl could make a business out of anything. Jill smiled at the thought of the Mary Kay parties Izzy had hosted right out of high school. All the girls had glopped on the goods to be more like her.

Izzy shut the door and jogged back to the driver's seat.

"Garrett called you, didn't he?"

Izzy snickered. "I don't care where I get my customers. No need to explain. You sit back and relax." She raised the privacy window between them.

Jill clung to the blue-and-white quilt. The Jacob's ladder pattern was supposed to represent a path or direction, just like the one that had been on her bed when she was a young girl. She closed her eyes and cried softly into the quilt. "God knows, I need some direction right now."

There'd been too many unexpected changes lately, and that was making her feel off balance. The size of Pearl's property and how she wanted to distribute everything was almost too much to take. Hearing that her grandmother had been married had been the tipping point. Garrett was the last thing she needed to deal with today. She touched her lips where he'd just kissed her. *Why did he keep doing that? And why hadn't she stopped him before he did? She'd known what he was about to do.*

By the time Izzy and Jill got to the house, the sun had come back out. Chilled from her damp clothes, Jill went straight inside and escaped the shivers in a hot bath. While soaking, she decided she didn't want to deal with Bradley while she made her decision about the property. It wasn't his decision to make. She decided to spend at least another week here in Adams Grove. He wasn't going to be pleased, but that was just too bad.

She got dressed and headed to Roanoke Rapids to shop. On the way, she called Carolanne and asked her to walk through all the details with Connor for her. With Carolanne taking care of the real business at hand, Jill turned her focus to shopping. Thank goodness there'd be no more granny panties in her near future. Underwear, a couple tops, and a decent pair of jeans were a necessity. Three pairs of pajamas found their way into her keeper pile, too, mostly because she couldn't decide which she liked best. The shopping had lifted her mood to match the now-sunny day.

In the car, the bags fluttered noisily against the breeze coming through the driver-side window as she belted out the latest Toby Keith song, off-key.

She got home and got started on the bedroom. Jill pushed Pearl's hanging clothes tight to one end of the closet to make room for her new ones. She went ahead and boxed up all the contents of the dresser drawers, except for Pearl's housecoats. She couldn't part with those. The church would make sure the other things were put to good use.

Seeing Pearl on the DVD had been strange, but comforting—in an odd way. Jill stripped the sheets from the bed and got a fresh set from the closet. Pearl had always refused to buy anything but white sheets, so the choice was easy. Jill pulled the fitted sheet tight and then fluffed the top one like a parachute above the bed, finishing with perfect hospital corners, just the way Pearl had taught her. After tossing the pillows back on the bed, she held a small rectangular one with tasseled fringe to her chest. Pearl had embroidered it years ago. Colorful needlepoint flowers framed the phrase:

Too many tears of sorrow
Precious memories tucked safely away
Your love helps me get to each tomorrow
Until we meet again someday.

Jill wept aloud, clinging to the pillow. She'd never asked whom or what Pearl had been thinking of when she stitched the delicate pillow, but the poem echoed Jill's feelings today. *Were these memories of John Carlo Pearl had embroidered?* She plucked two tissues from the box on the nightstand. The mascara she had carefully reapplied after being out in the rain was making a mess of the tissues as she dabbed at the tears. She huddled on the bed against the pile of pillows.

All of her memories of Pearl were joyful ones. She'd been blessed to have a happy life filled with love. Losing Pearl would be the first hard thing she'd have to go through without her. Memories pushed and crowded to the front, making it hard to quiet her mind even though she was exhausted. Finally, she squished the damp tissues in her hand into a ball and forced herself to get up and pull herself together.

She went outside. The welcome scent of the flowering mimosa trees was like cotton candy at the county fair. Their soft pink pompoms flagged in the breeze as hummingbirds dipped in and out, buzzing like electric weed whackers. She and Pearl had always called them hummers, but after Bradley spoiled that by telling her that word meant something else where he came from, she'd resisted using that nickname anymore.

The conversation with Bradley last night still nagged at her. What was it about him that had made her trust him more than the people she'd known and trusted her whole life? He'd been so convincing at the time. Things didn't look as cut-and-dried a year later.

She felt closed in by the memories, so she forced herself to get dressed and headed outside to get some air. Twigs and gumballs, crisp from the summer sun, snapped under her feet.

The old swing still hung from heavy chains beneath the sweet gum tree. That swing had been her safe place through many a crisis over the years. She swished pine needles from the worn seat, then sat down and pushed off, letting the swing whisk her and her worries away. The rusty chains groaned. She pumped her legs until the leaves rustled against the moving links, dropping small pieces of bark and dirt into her lap.

When the swing settled into a steady sway, she ran her fingers over the deep lines of the initials that scarred the silvery, weathered seat. The seat was just wide enough for two people if you squished. Daddy had carved her initials there on the day they'd hung the swing. She'd been only six at the time. Years later, Garrett had carved his initials above hers and added the letters *TLA. True Love Always.* She, too, had thought they would always be together.

She laid her palm flat to cover his initials, then spread her fingers to cover the *A* in TLA.

That was more like it.

TL. *Too late.*

Jill dragged her feet to stop the swing and then walked over to the pecan tree. It was already heavy with new growth, loaded with the treasures that would rock her world in Pearl's famous chocolate pecan pie this fall.

"Time to go inside, Clyde." She held the door open and Clyde ran right past her into the kitchen without slowing down, finally sliding to a stop at the kitchen sink. She locked up and headed back to bed. Clyde was just a step behind her. When she got in bed, she hung her hand over the side. Clyde pushed his wet nose under her hand, begging for attention, but gave up easily and stretched out on the floor beside the bed, facing the door.

❖

She hopped out of the bed and headed to Pearl's desk to begin sifting through the papers the intruders had tossed. What better way to work off some guilt than to throw herself into a project? Sorting the hanging folders out of the mess, she started placing them back in the drawers. Then, one by one, she filed the items back where they made sense because there was no way anyone would've ever figured out Pearl's filing system. Maybe she'd even find a copy of Pearl's will. Among the mess, she found two boxes of thank-you cards. They'd come in handy right about now, so she set them aside.

By lunchtime, the room was in better shape, but still far from put back together. She swept the remaining papers into piles and put them on the desk to sort through later.

Thank-you cards in hand, Jill went to the kitchen and began writing notes to the people who had sent flowers. Carolanne, God bless her, had made sure everyone signed the guestbook and collected the florist cards the staff at the church had gathered. With the personal thank-you notes done, Jill drafted a short thank-you for the *County Gazette* classifieds. That thank-you would run in the Sunday edition to let the community know that she appreciated their support. She'd drop off the note on her way to get stamps at the post office.

She grabbed her stuff and headed for town. The *County Gazette* office had closed for the lunch hour, so Jill dropped the note through the slot in the door, along with a twenty-dollar bill.

She walked around the corner to the post office. Aunt Milly stood just inside the door, holding a large package. Of course, everything looked large next to Milly. She wasn't quite five foot tall, although she'd tell you she'd been five three before she started shrinking. It was rare that Jill had ever seen Aunt Milly without Pearl. Just one more reminder that Pearl was gone. Everywhere she turned, there was another reminder.

"Hi, Aunt Milly. How're you doing?"

Aunt Milly leaned in and gave Jill a half-hug around the box. "I'm doing just fine, dear. I'm just picking up a package."

The heavy wood-and-glass door closed behind Jill. "What do you have there? Treasures?"

Milly patted the top of the box, nodding with pride. "Yarn. The softest yarn ever. Softer than cashmere, but as durable as wool."

"Sounds nice."

"Softer than anything Pearl ever laid her hands on. Alpaca yarn." She balanced the package as she talked, which was hard for Milly to do without her hands.

"Alpaca, huh?" Jill raised a brow, impressed. "I've seen them on a television ad recently. They're cute. I bet they're not so cute naked, though."

Aunt Milly gave Jill a wink. "I'm sure they're happy to sacrifice a bad hair day or two for a nice sweater, dear."

Aunt Milly was so much like Pearl that it hurt.

"Pearl was mighty proud of that peach handspun cashmere you gave her for her birthday. Can't believe she won't ever see this." The old woman leaned in closer to Jill. "She'd have died of envy if she weren't already gone."

"Milly…" Jill gave the old woman a *How dare you?* look while holding back a laugh.

"Oh, honey. At our age, people die." She patted Jill's arm tenderly. "Trust me. Pearl's tapping her toe in heaven, anxious for me to open this box." She looked heavenward and winked. "Ain't ya', Pearl?"

"You're shameless." Jill couldn't help but laugh. "Hey, that reminds me. There's a blanket by Pearl's chair. I thought I'd finish that project for her. Who's that for?"

"Why, honey, that was for you."

"Me?"

"For your wedding, dear," explained Milly.

"You must be confused. I'm not even engaged," Jill said.

"No. I remember. Pearl said that blanket was going to be the most special blanket she ever made in her life. She was working at a feverish pace. Said it was for your wedding." Milly wagged a crooked-jointed finger toward Jill. "Maybe Pearl knew something you don't. It was like she knew it would be her last blanket she knitted. I don't know. But I know what she said." She tapped the side of her head with her finger, nodding.

"Hmmm. Well, I guess I'll finish the blanket and figure it out later."

"Pearl's rarely wrong, so you'll be glad you have it done when Garrett proposes." Milly patted Jill's shoulder. "Enjoy it, sweetie. I've got to go so I can get started with my own project. My grandniece, Elsie—you remember her, don't you? She's gettin' married, too."

Too? Jill resisted the urge to correct her. "I can't believe Elsie is old enough to get married."

"Don't get me started on that. I told her she's too darn young, but you know how she is. Headstrong like her mother." Milly turned to leave, then swung back around. "And a lot of other Adams Grove girls."

"Good luck with your project. Love you," Jill called after her, then hurried to catch back up to her. "Milly. I have a question for you."

"What's that?"

Jill hesitated. "Why do you think Pearl never told me about John Carlo?"

Her eyebrows shot straight up. "Never thought I'd hear that name uttered out loud again."

"You knew? About John Carlo Pacini and Pearl?"

Milly folded her arms across her tiny body. "I know he was the love of Pearl's life. Your grandmother was so torn up over that man. She loved him more than her own life. She swore me to never utter his name. That was a long, long time ago. I'm her best friend. I saw what she went through. You can't imagine how hard it was to be a woman alone back then. I *am* relieved to know that she told you. I didn't know she was going to."

"I can't believe I never knew about him. Pacini. Exotic name. I'd remember if I'd ever heard it."

"No one around here 'cept me knew about him. Pearl found her peace with it. There was nothin' to say."

"What happened?"

"Honey, even I don't know the details. She was a young and tough gal just like you. And beautiful." Milly's voice grew serious. "But, you know, there are some things that you tuck away. They're too painful to share or deal with. I think that's how Pearl dealt with John Carlo."

"I guess I can understand that."

"You don't worry yourself over it. Pearl had a good life. She loved you. Now get on with your life and make her proud. She's still watchin' over you." Milly squeezed Jill's hand and gave her a quick peck on the cheek before heading to her car.

Jill watched Milly climb behind the wheel of her 1989 LeBaron and back out of the post office parking lot. The odometer probably hadn't even turned twenty thousand miles yet. She went to the counter, bought stamps, and dropped her mail in the slot. Milly had a good three- or four-minute head start, but Jill ended up right behind her. She couldn't even see Milly in the driver seat. She resisted the urge to pass her and was thankful when Milly turned to head home. Jill kept straight toward the center of town to finish the tasks on her list.

❖

Back home and now cross-legged in Pearl's chair, Jill ate dinner while watching the news. As she pushed the old metal TV tray away, the blanket sitting in the top of Pearl's knitting basket caught her eye. The scalloped edging and the diamond shapes sculpted in the body were intricate. She held the soft fiber to her cheek. People always thought cashmere came from rabbits, but this had come from Kashmir goats.

She ran her fingers across the sweeping monogram in the diagonal of the corner.

Clyde got up from the hall and plodded to the side of the chair, curious to see what she had.

"This isn't food, fat boy."

He laid his chin on the blanket. "Oh, no you don't." She lifted his drooly wet chin from the fine work and dabbed the wet spot with her shirt. "What am I going to do with you? You drool on everything." Jill fished around in the basket next to the chair for something to wipe his face. She pulled out a pink hand towel that had a crocheted hem and buttoned tab top to hang over the oven handle. Pearl must have made this one for the church bazaar. They were always popular.

"Come here, boy." Jill dipped the pink towel under the dog's neck, then slipped a piece of yarn between the bottom and the top to secure the towel around his neck. "There. That should help keep you from sliming stuff up all the time."

Clyde shook his head and lifted a huge paw in the air, trying to reach the material around his neck. He wasn't that limber.

"Sorry, buddy."

He lay down, realizing defeat. He was smart, she'd give him that.

Jill leaned back in the chair and turned her attention back to the corner of the blanket. An *M*? If this blanket was for her wedding, then Pearl must have thought she would marry Garrett. He was the only M that had ever been in her life, except for M&M's, but then, they brought her back to Malloy, too—at least the green ones, anyway. He loved them.

❖ Chapter Twelve ❖

It was a new day and things seemed a little brighter even though the tasks of the day were daunting. Jill stretched and took the last sip of her coffee. She checked off the first item on her to-do list. She'd just left the message for Bradley. Next was to start cleaning the house as she started making decisions about what to do with the place now that Pearl was gone.

Her phone chirped. Clyde started barking at her purse like it was a wild intruder.

"It's OK, boy. It's just my phone." She scrubbed his ears as she ran past him to grab her phone from her purse and answer it.

"How are things in the country?" Bradley asked.

"As good as can be expected."

"I know you're hurting. I was thinking—have you even started packing yet?"

"Hardly."

"I thought we agreed that you'd head home." Bradley's voice grew tight.

"No. I believe that's what you said. I'm not in a hurry. I've got another week's vacation coming to me."

"What's gotten into you?"

"Me?" The word stabbed the air. She was so furious it took a moment to continue to speak. "What's gotten into *you*? I've got decisions to make. I don't know if I'm going to sell or rent out this place, but either way means I have to pack up Pearl's things, and I don't think I'm ready to pack anything yet, maybe never. Quite honestly, it's been kind of nice being home again. Cooking, baking, things I haven't done in Savannah. Those things used to be part of who I am. Lately, I'm only what you want me to be." With the business of the Kase Foundation keeping her so busy, battling Annie over the rights to the kitchen was a battle she'd chosen not to fight. Those days were over.

"I've already been thinking about all that. I talked to a real estate agent, but I'm not sure I trust those small-town folks. I might just sell the property myself to be sure you get a fair price."

"Didn't you hear a word I said? I'm not sure I want to sell this place. A month ago, maybe, but now? I'm not so sure. And speaking of unsure, I'm beginning to wonder what direction our relationship is going. I need some time."

"This is about Malloy, isn't it?"

"It's not Garrett. It's you. I've just experienced a terrible loss. I needed you and you weren't there for me. All you ever think about is you, you, you."

An awkward silence settled between them. She hadn't meant to start a fight, but she'd gone and had her say now.

"My other line is ringing," Jill lied. She chewed on her bottom lip—she was a terrible liar. "Bradley, I'll give you a call later."

"Come home, baby."

"Talk to ya later." As she hung up, she noticed the voice mail envelope lit on her phone. She petted Clyde on the head. "Don't look at me like that. It was just a little white lie. I could tell you wanted to go outside soon. Besides, you owe me. I've taken good care of you." She grabbed his chin with both hands and kissed him on the nose.

Clyde flapped his ears as if he didn't agree.

Jill dialed in to retrieve the message. Josh, her assistant at the Kase Foundation, had left the voice mail. He left his condolences and then gave her the final numbers for the fund-raiser, which were awesome, and confirmed he'd deposited all proceeds into the special holding account she'd set up until she could get back and verify all the balancing he'd done. He was leaving for a week on the vacation she'd promised him in appreciation for all the hard work he'd done helping her get ready for the big event.

Just thinking about work made her anxious; she knew she had decisions to make and time was zipping by. She headed to the bathroom to run a bath in the big cast-iron tub. She'd never appreciated how deep the tub was until she'd bathed in one of those updated fiberglass models in hotels that were barely deep enough to cover your parts.

As she walked down the hall to get something to wear from Pearl's dresser, she swung her hand high in the air, sending the attic pull-down string swinging back and forth. She swept her hair back in a ponytail and went back into the bathroom, where Clyde lapped up the warm water from the tub. She swatted him with the panties and he trotted out. Slowly, she sank into the tub, trying to shake off the last of the nagging doubts that kept surfacing about her life. She soaked so long her skin turned as wrinkly as a shar-pei.

After the water had turned tepid, Jill toweled off and dressed.

Clyde filled the hall in front of the bathroom door, sprawled from one end to the other on his belly. She'd learned to leave the doors open because he whimpered when he couldn't see her. How could anything that big be such a sissy?

A vehicle crunched down the driveway into the yard. Clyde ran to the door, shaking the tables and jiggling everything on them as he passed.

She stepped on the front porch.

Garrett stepped out of his truck and leaned on the door. "Thought I'd stop by to see if you needed anything while I was in town this morning?"

"Nope. I think we're fine. Anything else?"

"Nope. Just checking in." He dipped his hat in a cowboy sort of way and gave her a wink.

He knew that would make me smile. "Want to come in for a cup of coffee?" *Where did that come from? Too late to take it back now.*

"No time. I need to run by my office before a meeting in town. Maybe I could stop by later this afternoon. Would that be OK?"

"Sure." *Sure? No. It's an easy word, just use it. Pearl are you pulling my strings from up there?*

Garrett smiled and hopped back in his truck.

Jill closed the door and locked it, then headed upstairs with Clyde right behind her. She opened the door to the second bedroom and then headed for the attic door. As she began to step through the doorway, Clyde rushed to her side and pushed his nose next to her to slide through first.

"No. You wait for me here. You'll just make mud out of all the dust with your drool, even with your fancy pink bib."

Clyde spread out on the floor. His tan eyebrows wiggled with a don't-leave-me-this-way expression. If she didn't know better, she'd swear he took exception to the pink towel comment.

"You're a player, Clyde." She turned her back on his sad eyes and stepped into the attic. Swishing her hand in the air, she finally caught the string and tugged. The single bulb came to life. Jill blinked as her eyes adjusted.

She walked over to the chest and moved the cardboard boxes from the top. Years of dust had accumulated, and there were cardboard pieces scattered around, probably from mice. She swept away the dust. The smell of cedar hit her as soon as she pushed back the heavy lid of the huge chest. The contents were lean, only three white stationery boxes. A delicate ribbon, probably blue at one time, secured each box.

Jill lifted the three boxes out of the trunk. She closed the trunk and sat on top of it, forgetting all about the dust and dirt accumulated there. In the light, she could better see that the ribbon had surely once been blue. She tugged the bow. It unfolded easily. She gently lifted the top and set it aside.

Letters. Lots of them.

She flipped through the stack. The letters spanned a two-year period, in order, starting in 1943. The same masculine print addressed each letter, but the postmarks were from all over the world, including exotic places like Tahiti, the Cook Islands, Japan, and others she couldn't decipher. No return address.

She did the math in her head. These letters dated back to just a couple years before her dad was born.

Jill opened the top envelope and slid out the contents. The paper was thick, considered fine even by today's standards. The letter was short, but the longing of lovers separated by distance was clear. The letter was signed, *With all my love, John Carlo.* John Carlo had beautiful penmanship, but the forties were a more formal time.

Jill had taken a handwriting-analysis class right after college. No one in Adams Grove had been safe from her analysis that year. She'd examined the handwriting of just about everyone in town, and it was almost scary how dead-on the readings were.

She held the letter and tried to recall the old skill. The tall upper strokes of the letter *L* and *H* in John Carlo's words meant he would reach for his goals. The narrow spacing between words meant that he wanted to be close to her—well, Pearl, in this case. Jill hadn't thought about those handwriting theories in a long while. Her skills were rusty, but she was pretty sure those old handwriting-analysis books were still on the bookshelf downstairs.

Jill felt a little guilty dipping into Pearl's most private moments, but she couldn't bring herself to put the letters away. Recollections of weekends that her grandmother had spent with John Carlo were filled with sentiments of their ecstasy while together and the heartache of being apart.

I still feel the warmth of your embrace, your mouth on mine, every detail of your face, and the curve of your hip, John Carlo had written. *The mere thought of you sends a warm shiver through me. I yearn to be near you. Will you wait for me?*

Jill picked out the next one off the stack to read. The closing on this short note from John Carlo to Pearl read, *Inez. You are my pearl, my treasure, my world.*

She knew her grandmother's birth name was Inez, but she'd never thought to ask how they'd come to call her Pearl. After about a dozen letters, John Carlo had begun addressing the love letters to her as Pearl.

Then the series of notes changed. Next in the stack were letters that Pearl had sent to John Carlo with his responses in the margins. Jill leaned in toward the letter, wanting to feel closer to Pearl, to John Carlo, to their endearing love. These letters were the best because she got both sides of the story. It was in these letters that her grandmother began signing her notes *Pearl.*

I love you, Pearl had written.

More than life, my dear, he'd written in the margin.

I'm set to meet you off the cape as we planned on the 19th, Pearl had continued.

I'm counting the moments until I have you in my arms. I'll be waiting. I have a special gift for you, he'd written.

I pray for your safe arrival. I will wait as long as it takes for you to get there, wrote Pearl.

I'll never let you down, my love. He'd signed it *JCP* with a heart next to it.

Jill held the note close to her heart, happy to know that Pearl had known such a true love.

"The love story of all love stories," she'd said that day at her surprise party. This had to be it. No wonder Pearl was such a romantic. Jill swept away a tear and tucked the letter back in the stack.

It got hotter as the sun rose higher in the sky. Jill mopped her forehead with the bottom of her T-shirt, then carried the box of baby stuff to put it with the others she'd already explored.

The attic door slammed.

Jill yelped, dropping the box.

Clyde whined, and she realized his tail had slammed the door shut. "Clyde, you crazy dog. You scared the puddin' out of me. That tail of yours is a dangerous nuisance. It should have to be registered as a weapon."

She put the box away, then went to prop the door back open to get a little air.

When she tried the door, it didn't budge.

She pushed and then pulled.

Clyde whimpered on the other side.

A swift kick didn't do anything but jam her big toe. She jiggled and shook the handle, trying not to panic.

The hinges were on the other side, so that was no help. Leaning against one of the support beams, she looked around for options. The stairs used to unfold to the hallway. They hadn't opened when she tugged on the string from downstairs earlier, but maybe if she pushed from here, they would. She stepped carefully on top of the door and pushed it with one foot, then held onto one of the rafters and jumped, dropping her full weight on it. Still not so much as a creak of hope. Kneeling beside the door, she ran her fingers across the dusty boards that framed the opening. Screws secured the old access closed.

Jill took off her shirt and dried her damp skin with it. She couldn't stay up here in this heat. Clyde whined and scratched at the door, but no matter how much she jiggled, lifted, or pushed, the door still didn't budge.

She scanned the attic for tools—a screwdriver, hammer, or anything that might help set her free. Slim pickings up here, but there was a tall metal floor lamp in the corner. She spun the lamp on its round base toward the stairs. The heavy metal prongs might work like a screwdriver, but removing the screws that held the hall attic access in place didn't prove effective. She moved the lamp closer to the door, then heaved its heavy base and rammed it against the door as hard as she could. But this wasn't a cheap luan door. Heck no, she couldn't be that lucky. The door was solid wood, and the lamp barely marred it.

Jill sat with her back against the door. She could smash the octagon window at the end of the attic, but she wasn't sure she could fit through the opening. Even if she could, it would be a second-story jump to the ground. Definitely a last resort.

She carried the lamp to where the floor of the attic wasn't finished—over Pearl's bedroom. She hated to tear up the house, but she was running out of options.

As she swept the blown insulation aside to reveal the joists, the nasty recycled fibers clung to her sweaty body like Velcro. She managed to clear a space, then swung the lamp toward that spot. The angle of the roof prevented her from getting momentum to make an impact. *This might not work, either.* She took a deep breath and pounded the lamp against the floor again, crying out a karate kia for extra power. It cracked. Another thrust with all her might and light poured through the hole from Pearl's bedroom below.

"Yes!"

The ceiling plaster speckled the blue handmade quilt on Pearl's bed below. Clyde barked as she slammed the ceiling one last time to make the opening big enough for her to scooch through.

She put her shirt back on and eased through the opening. The plaster and splintered wood scraped her skin through the thin material.

All she wanted was fresh air.

She put her arms in front of her face, took a deep breath, and let go, falling to the mattress. The air-conditioning chilled her sweat-soaked skin.

She lay there panting.

Chapter Thirteen

Clyde continued to bark upstairs.

"I'm down here, boy. Come on." Jill tried to catch her breath. After a moment, she forced herself to get up to get some much-needed water. When she got up, she felt dizzy but steadied herself until the woozy feeling passed. In the kitchen, she rinsed the insulation and plaster the best she could from her clammy arms and face with cool water, then filled an aluminum tumbler to the top with ice and tap water. She gulped the water down and refilled her cup again before going to check on Clyde. She'd have to take a shower before she started itching from the exposure to all that old insulation.

Sometimes he doesn't seem like such an award-winning dog. Shouldn't he come when I call? That's pretty basic stuff.

"Enough already, Clyde," she yelled as she stomped up the stairs. Jill stopped and stared at the door.

Strange and disquieting thoughts raced through her mind.

The door to the bedroom, which she'd left wide open, was shut tight, and Clyde couldn't have done that the way that door was hinged. She opened the door and Clyde nearly knocked her over as he ran by her at full speed. He didn't even pause on the landing before running down the stairs. She followed behind him all the way down and straight to the back door. She let him out and he went speeding through the backyard barking. He came back after a few minutes of sniffing and more barking. Jill settled him down with a piece of ice that he tossed in the air and rolled around.

Jill went back up to check out the attic door. Not only was it closed, but the dead bolt was thrown. Clyde couldn't have done that.

No accident—someone had locked the attic door and then closed the hall door behind them. But Clyde hadn't barked until after the door slammed shut. Surely he would have barked if a stranger had come into the house.

Jill's hands still shook as she dialed the sheriff's office to report the incident. Scott Calvin would come by to check on things in about twenty minutes.

Showered and changed, she was tugging her damp hair into a quick French braid just as Scott knocked on the door.

She twisted the elastic in place as she ran to the door to let him in.

He stood there in khaki shorts, a Hawaiian shirt, and an Atlanta Braves baseball cap. "Please tell me it's your day off and this is not your attempt to revive the *Magnum, P.I.* look."

He stepped inside. "It's my day off, and don't worry, I know this shirt isn't fashionable. Ruth pounded that into my head every time I wore it, but it's comfortable."

She raised her hands. "You won't get any lectures from me."

"Good. So what trouble are you stirring up this time?"

"Hey, it's not me. I don't know what's going on." She relayed the story to him, play by play, right down to the fact that Clyde hadn't made a sound.

"Would anybody be unhappy that you're back? Anything going on I don't know about?"

She became instantly aware of her surroundings and the fact she might be in real danger. "Gosh. I hope not. I don't know. Maybe Becky? At the funeral, she made sure I knew she had her sights on Garrett, but I'm no threat to her on that. There's only one person who doesn't like me that I know of, and she's a housekeeper currently in Georgia, so I think that clears her."

His brows wrinkled. "You mentioned the other day that Clyde doesn't take to men, except Garrett. If it's not Becky or that Georgia girl, what about Garrett?"

She folded her arms and sighed. "Well, we did just find out that Pearl owns all this land all the way to the big curve, and Pearl left it to us both—together. I suppose he could want it all." *Would Garrett stoop that low?* She started laughing. "Garrett may have broken my heart, but I doubt he'd ever hurt me. You know how silly that sounds, right?"

"Could be motive."

Had he read her mind? She could tell by the way Scott was looking at her that he didn't think that Garrett as a suspect was a possibility, and in her heart, she kind of knew it, too.

Jill put her hands on her hips. "You're the expert. You tell me."

"We won't take anything off the list. I'll see what Becky's been up to this morning. How can we check to make sure your Georgia person isn't around these parts?"

"She's not. I was talking about Annie. You know Bradley. She's his housekeeper. Annie's probably happy as all get out that I'm not there."

"All righty, but I'm pretty sure I saw Becky's car over at the nail salon this morning, so that's not leaving us with much to go on. There doesn't appear to be any sign of forced entry or any difference from when I was here last time."

Jill had checked it out herself earlier. She hadn't noticed anything, either.

"It wouldn't be a bad idea if you stayed with friends until we figure out what's going on with all this mischief."

"I know you're right. I'll see if Carolanne can come stay with me; if not, I'll stay with Milly or get a room over at the Markham House for a couple days."

He took a card from his wallet and scribbled his cell and home phone numbers on the back. "Here, call me if anything happens or you think of something. Anytime. You hear me?"

She held the card tight. It gave her a sense of power, although she prayed she wouldn't need it. "Got it." She walked him out to his pickup truck. "On a brighter note, how many personal cars do you have these days? Every time I see you you're driving something different."

"After Ruth and I broke up, I had to find something to fill up all my spare time. I turned a few wrenches on some old junkers for quick money, but I couldn't part with all of them."

"That's one way to get through a heartbreak. After Garrett and I, well, I threw myself into my work. That's a little harder to do when you're sheriff of a town that has hardly any crime."

"You coming back has been pretty good for business. Where were you back then when I needed a diversion?"

Jill waved good-bye to Scott and went back inside.

She turned her attention to Clyde. "What? Did you take the day off?" She sat down on the couch and Clyde plopped down in front of her. "Some watchdog you are."

Her mind wandered to the small picture of Pearl and the man on the mantel. She walked over to the fireplace and stepped up on the hearth. She pushed the hardware on the back of the frame to the side and removed the picture. The familiar penmanship wasn't a surprise. In faded ink, it read:

Inez—
If the world is my oyster, you are my Pearl.
Keep all that is the foundation of our love safe, forever.

You are the love of my heart. My one real find among all the treasures.
John Carlo

Why didn't you ever tell me about him, Pearl? How did you meet?

Jill returned the picture to the mantel, snatched her keys from the hall table, and headed toward the door to do a quick ride-by. Garrett's office was only a couple of miles from the house, but if he'd gone into town, that was a good twenty-minute drive. He couldn't have made it to town and back yet. If he was at his office, though, then there was a possibility the he *was* the person who left her trapped in the attic.

"Stop it," she admonished herself. "This is nuts." But the self-admonishments didn't stop her from wanting to check it out to just be sure.

Revving the engine of her BMW, Jill sped down the lane. Out of habit, she used the blinker as she turned left out onto the single-lane road. A few new homes dotted what used to be Mr. Miller's crop fields. He'd passed away last summer. His kids had probably sold the land for a huge profit. Too bad. Once the open land was gone, it was gone for good.

As Jill sped down the road, she wondered what she'd say to Garrett if she did find him at his office. She didn't want to sound like she was accusing him. Although he *had* broken her heart, she couldn't believe he'd do anything to harm her. Maybe she should let Scott handle the situation. Even if Scott and Garrett went way back, it was Scott's job to find out who locked her in the attic. Protect and serve and all that.

She lifted her foot from the accelerator to slow the car through the tight curve that twisted back toward Route 58. At the stop sign, she drummed her fingers on the steering wheel, waiting for a break in the traffic so she could pull across and head west. On a summer day like today, there was even more traffic as people traveled to the mountains and south to Florida via I-95 on vacation.

This intersection used to be nothing but fields. Now a gas station sold lottery tickets on one corner, and a new auto repair business looked to be doing a pretty booming business on the other. Next to that was a small building with a peppermint-striped awning—Penny's Candy & Soda Shoppe.

Jill almost drove right past Garrett's office. A large new building stood right next to the little white house that used to be Malloy's & Sons.

"No. Way." She veered to the edge of the road to get a better look.

The sign she'd had Mary Claire paint for Garrett as a Christmas gift a few years ago was gone. A professionally sandblasted sign with Malloy Country Design and Builders in shiny burgundy script now marked the location. An inky-black, freshly paved driveway led to the front door. No gravel drive here. The building was beautiful—a perfect blend of country style and utility. The landscaping assured her that Garrett hadn't overlooked even the smallest detail. No surprise there.

Jill drove up the emergency lane and turned in front of the building. A light-blue Toyota was parked out front. Two white trucks and a work trailer were parked on the side of the building. A tall wooden fence partitioned the front from the back. Inventory and equipment were probably stored behind it for future projects. By the look of things, Garrett had modestly understated the growth of his business over the past year, but his truck was not here.

She got out of her car and caught the door before it slammed, clicking it closed. *Why am I sneaking? So I can change my mind. Great. Now I'm talking to myself.* Garrett's truck wasn't here, but now that she was, she was finding it hard to resist checking out the place.

Custom railing of black iron and chunky wood flanked the steps to the front door. The railing was warm from the sun. She paused with her hand on the handle of the heavy mahogany carved door. Holding her breath, she pushed the door open and stepped into the front office.

As soon as she cleared the threshold, a young dark-haired beauty shot out from behind the large desk and threw her arms around Jill's neck, catching her completely off guard.

"Jill, I heard you were in town."

Jill couldn't place the face in the quick glance she got, but the bundle of energy disguised as a girl definitely recognized her. Jill tried to smile as she feigned recognition. She scanned the room for a hint at who was greeting her. No nameplate on the desk. Darn.

"You look as great as Garrett said. Aunt Milly said you were too thin, but you still look like the prettiest Pork Fest Queen we ever had."

Milly? Then it fell into place—Milly's grandniece. "Elsie?"

"Yeah. I bet you didn't recognize me with the dark hair." She twisted a curl toward her face.

"Last time I saw you, you had bleached-blonde hair—short, spiky, bleached-blonde hair."

"That didn't last long. Billy likes natural girls," she explained. "Did Aunt Milly tell you about my wedding? Look at this ring. Isn't it to die for?" She flipped her hand up in front of her face, wiggling her fingers to flash the tiny stone in the princess setting.

"Congratulations. Aunt Milly told me about you getting married. So who's this Billy guy?"

"Billy Privet."

Jill recalled Pearl telling her about the Privet boy going off to the service. "I didn't know he was back. I thought he joined the Marines. Wasn't he in San Diego or somewhere out west?"

"He was. He did his four years and came back. Hey, it's kind of funny that I'm getting married before you, isn't it?"

Thanks for making me feel like an old maid, Jill thought. "Well, timing is everything."

"I guess." Elsie stroked her ring finger. The newness of the engagement obviously hadn't worn off yet.

"Is Garrett around?"

"No, he left earlier this morning. He wasn't here long, grabbed some paperwork and left around nine."

Right after I saw him. Maybe he'd been telling the truth, after all, but then, she'd never known him to be a liar.

"When should he be back?" Jill asked, but her mind was filled with the big question: *If it wasn't Garrett who locked her in the attic, then who was it?*

"Not sure. He called a while ago. Some problem at the courthouse. One of his permits is hung up." Elsie paused. "You OK? You look kinda pale all of a sudden."

"No. Yeah, I'm fine," Jill answered, only half paying attention to Elsie as her mind raced back to the attic and what could've happened.

"Can you stick around? I'll show you my engagement party and shower pictures. It was the best shower ever."

"I'd love that." Elsie had been a pest when they were kids. She'd wanted to do anything and everything that Jill did. Since Aunt Milly and Pearl were best friends, Elsie usually got her way.

"Cool. I've got them in my car." Elsie raced for the front door, thrilled to share her big plans with her hometown idol.

Jill took in the grandeur of the front office. The room had a floor-to-twelve-foot-ceiling fireplace that would warm the space with no problem at all, with room for fifty guests, easy. The furniture was high quality. She ran her fingers across the soft leather. Sturdy, thick leather hide, too, not the cheap, thin stuff that smushes under your fingers.

Curious, she peeked into the corner office.

Her breath caught. Mary Claire's hand-painted sign hung on the wall. It looked a lot bigger on an interior wall than it did outside. The heavy wooden sign took up nearly the whole space next to the bookcase, but that wasn't all. The pine-needle basket Jill had woven around the antlers from one of the bucks Garrett shot the winter of 2002 took the honor of the center shelf. The buck had been a twelve-pointer and Garrett had been so proud of that trophy deer.

The strong smell of leather and furniture polish didn't hide the spicy smell of his aftershave. Not the fancy high-dollar stuff that Bradley splurged on, but the same scent Garrett's dad, and probably his dad's dad, had worn over the years. The kind you could still buy at the drugstore. Like Garrett, the scent was spicy and manly, fresh and familiar. She inhaled the welcome scent as she looked at the sketches tacked on a bulletin board next to photographs of homes in various states of completion.

He was a remarkable architect and builder, no denying that. A large easel held a thick board with color drawings of a neighborhood. Garrett was living the dreams they'd once shared, without her. She grabbed the back of the desk chair, trying to saddle the emotions kicking up. *Why did I think his life would stand still after I left?*

The walls closed in on her a bit. She sat in the big chair behind his desk. She spun toward the desk and laid her forearms on the cool wood. *In through the nose, out through the mouth*, she repeated as she tried to convince her body to relax.

When she lifted her head, her own image stared back at her from the corner of his desk. In a frame was the picture of her with Garrett at the Pork Festival. The same one Pearl had on her mantel. She grabbed the picture and held it to her chest. *He hasn't moved on.*

Jill heard Elsie come back into the building, then call from the front room.

She stiffened momentarily, then scrambled to get the picture back in its place.

"In here." Jill lifted her eyes toward the door, trying to look relaxed.

Elsie practically skipped into the office. "Here you are."

"You said to make myself at home, right?" How embarrassing to be caught in Garrett's office.

"Sure." Elsie opened the photo album on the desk. "Here are the pictures from the shower. Look, there's Pearl and Aunt Milly." Her smile waned. "Oh dear, you know me. I can get so wrapped up in myself. I'm sorry about Pearl."

Jill slid a sisterly arm around Elsie. "It's OK. Trust me. I need the escape."

Elsie rambled on about the bridal shower, flipping through picture after picture of the gathering. Pearl had frozen mint leaves and raspberries into ice cubes, and Milly made her famous sugared fruit to adorn the table. Nobody ever ate the beautiful fruit decorations. They were just too pretty to eat.

"What do you think? Am I doing all this right? I don't want to screw this up. I can't tell you how many hours I spent in the library trying to get all the rules down."

"It's your wedding, Elsie. You can do things however you like," Jill reminded her.

"I know. I just want it to be perfect. I don't want it to be one of those horrible *Country-Fried Weddings* on CMT that everybody laughs about."

Jill had caught an episode of that show. Visions of brides in camouflage gowns riding off on four-wheelers came to mind. She'd been to a few here in Adams Grove that had been close seconds to those fiascos. The unfortunate red-hoop-skirted bridesmaid from the day of Pearl's surprise party came to mind. Jill took that moment as her opportunity to get the heck out of there before

Garrett got back. "I gotta run Elsie. Thanks for sharing all of this with me. You've already made some great memories."

"I'll let Garrett know you came by."

"No." Jill spun back around. "No need to do that. I'd rather surprise him." Jill hoped Elsie would keep the secret. How would she explain her visit? She wasn't a good liar, and that wasn't a talent she cared to start practicing now.

"Oh yeah, he would totally love that. He misses you, ya know. Still keeps your picture right there." She pointed.

Jill glanced back toward the picture on Garrett's desk. She hugged Elsie, promising to come back and visit before she went back to Savannah.

Her mind reeled the whole way home.

If Garrett wasn't responsible for the incident in the attic, then who else could get past Clyde without a sound?

❖ Chapter Fourteen ❖

Jill marched up the steps, feeling rotten for having doubted Garrett. Clyde's nails tapped out a hello on the other side of the door on the hardwood floors as she unlocked and pushed it open.

Doink, doink-doink. The hollow sound of the rolled paper tube echoed as it bounced to the floor when Jill opened Pearl's front door. Clyde ran toward her and picked up the tube, wagging his tail for a game.

"No, boy. I don't think that's for you. Drop it." He did. He was smart. "Thanks, buddy." She tugged a note from behind a red rubber band around the rolled papers.

J -

You were supposed to put the hide-a-key somewhere else. Hope you don't mind me dropping these by. I thought you'd get a kick out of them. I'll check in later.

G

She must've just missed him. The rubber band sounded like a banjo as she rolled the elastic to the end while walking toward the dining room. She unrolled the stack of paper across the table, placing the centerpiece on the right end to hold them open.

Impressive. There were six blueprints detailing the neighborhood of country homes with metal roofs and long covered porches. She'd seen these sketches in his office just moments ago, but had only caught a glimpse. Of course, he didn't know that. When she'd suggested colored metal roofing two years ago, he had pooh-poohed the idea, saying tin roofs were cliché.

"Aha, you did like my idea." At least one of her ideas had gotten in. The old sketches they'd drawn out on legal pads were now transformed into real blueprints. Their dream had been to build a sustainable agriculture community of homes where no property would be less than five acres. The development was the perfect way to satisfy the city slickers who wanted to come to their tiny town and keep the small-town feel that was such a big part of its charm. The best of both worlds.

The only thing missing from these plans was the artisan center that was supposed to be her pet project. With road frontage on busy Route 58, the artisan center would provide a barrier between the homes and the traffic, while generating business and a few jobs and more revenue to the town.

She scrolled the top blueprint back and scanned the others below. The designs were large and breezy, but the homes had purpose, not just square feet to add up to big spaces.

The last one in the stack was the plat showing about 250 acres with road frontage on US-58 and Bridle Path Way. One edge snugged right up against the Meherrin River. A nice piece of land and nearby, if she was looking at the survey right. The last of the large papers swirled back into a big loop.

The main reason she left Adams Grove was to be away from Garrett, but she had to admit that since she moved to Savannah with Bradley, there'd been an amazing string of extravagant parties, fancy clothes, shoes that cost more than a paycheck, and trips to exotic places she'd never heard of. But the kids who went to the Kase Foundation youth camps would benefit from her travels, because she collected special items in each of those swanky locations for the charity auctions. It was a great cause, and it had been rewarding to see the things she'd brought back bring top dollar.

My life is good. Why is it bugging me so much that Garrett's living the dream I left behind?

A knock at the door brought her back from the daydream. She headed to the door, and Clyde loped along behind her, his nails clicking.

When she opened the door and saw Garrett, she felt a twist of emotion. Sentiment and sarcasm both floated among her thoughts.

"Hey. How was your day?" Garrett stepped inside.

"Funny you should ask."

"Why?"

"Let me show you something." She motioned for him to follow her.

Clyde greeted him, nudging his nose under his hand.

"What is around your neck, ol' boy?" Garrett bent on one knee. "A big manly dog like this can't wear a pink towel." He scrubbed the dog's ears. "What's she doin' to you, boy?"

"Hey, he was slobbering on everything. The bib was a compromise."

"It's emasculating," Garrett said.

Clyde barked in agreement.

"See." Garrett rubbed Clyde's ears. "Women just don't get it, do they, Clyde?"

"What kind of dog name is Clyde, anyway? It's not all that masculine, ya know."

"Pearl named him that because she said he had feet the size of a Clydesdale. Be glad she didn't name him after the king of beers. That was her first choice."

"Pearl did enjoy a cold beer," Jill said.

"For kidney stones," Garrett reminded her.

"I never knew Pearl to have kidney stones. Not once."

Garrett nodded. "It must've worked."

"Do you want to see what I was going to show you or not?"

Garrett nodded and followed her down the hall, muttering words of support to Clyde the whole way about the sissy crocheted towel hanging damp around the dog's neck.

When they reached Pearl's bedroom, she stepped to the side so he could see the bed full of plaster. "Any questions?"

"How about what the hell happened here?" He examined the gaping hole in the ceiling, then looked at her. "Are you OK?"

"I had to break my way through the ceiling from the attic."

"So I see." He picked up a handful of plaster from the comforter. "You're nothin' but trouble since you came back."

"Someone closed and locked the door while I was up there. It got so hot I could barely breathe."

"Who? What happened?"

"I'm not sure, but whoever it was, Clyde didn't even bark at them." She waited for a reaction but didn't get one. "I know you think Clyde is the smartest thing since Lassie, but even Clyde can't dead bolt a door."

She saw the shock register on his face.

"You don't think *I* locked you in the attic?"

"You tell *me* who could get by Sherlock, here." She patted Clyde's head. She regretted slamming him, because she'd grown to love the huge dog already. He always reacted like he understood exactly what she was saying, and he always listened.

"Maybe he did it as payback for the pink towel?"

Jill shifted her weight and put her hand on her hip.

"OK, not funny. But seriously, you've got to know I'd be the last person on earth to ever hurt you."

"I just don't know what to think anymore. It's been a wild few days. Who stole my safe and predictable hometown?" She sat on the edge of the bed, plaster falling from the quilt to the hardwood floor. "That attic door did not lock itself."

"You *are* turning out to be pretty high maintenance this week," he agreed.

"Not by choice." Absentmindedly, she brushed plaster in a pile next to her on the bed. "So why are you here? To rescue me again?"

"Can we talk about this attic thing first? We need to call Scott."

"I already did. Do you think I'm an idiot? He didn't see anything, either."

"Are you sure you were locked in? Maybe the door swelled in the heat."

She shook her head. "And the swelling threw the dead bolt? Not likely. After I crashed through Pearl's bedroom ceiling, I went upstairs. The bedroom door was shut, which Clyde couldn't have done and still been *in* the room, and the attic door dead bolt was latched. That doesn't happen by accident."

"Clyde never barked?"

"Not until I started banging through the ceiling trying to get out."

"That's weird."

"Exactly."

"Maybe Pearl is haunting you because you were mean to me," he teased.

She knew he was only half teasing because everyone knew how Pearl was when she set her mind to something. "That's a more comforting option than thinking someone was trying to roast me."

"Joking aside, I'm staying here with you until we figure this out."

"No, you're not."

"Don't argue with me. Pearl would haunt *me* if I let anything happen to you."

"I don't need protecting, and there's not another bed in this place." She brushed her bangs away from her face. "So why did you come by in the first place?"

"I came to see if you had a chance to look at the blueprints I left."

"I did. They're awesome." Her lips eased into a grin. "You're living your dream."

"With a few of your ideas."

"That didn't go unnoticed." She gave herself a little pat on the back.

"You and I once shared that dream."

Jill really didn't want to go there with him. She'd already thought about those dreams enough for one day. "So-oo"—she eased back on the bed and pointed toward the hole in the ceiling—"do you think you could repair that?" She raised a brow, hoping he'd go along with the change in subject.

"It wouldn't be good for you to be sleeping under that hole."

"My job is in Savannah, so I don't think I'll be sleeping here regularly, but it does need to be fixed." All of the sudden, realization flashed. Jill pushed past Garrett and dashed to the blueprints on the dining room table. She flipped straight to the last sheet, the one with the plat. "It is." She slammed her hand in the middle of the plat and spun around to face him. "You're planning to build your great neighborhood on this property, aren't you?"

"Not phase one. I already own that property. I bought that last year."

"You already knew about the property and the will. Admit it."

"Pearl liked the idea of being a part of our dream."

"Well, then she was demented. No wonder you were so helpful around here. You were manipulating her."

"You know that's not true."

Her anger spiked, and her heart picked up pace. "I know no such thing. Who did you sweet talk the rest of the land out of?"

He stood silent.

"I was so impressed with you making your dreams come true. I had no idea you'd stooped to stealing from elderly women."

He snatched his plans off the table and twisted them back into a tight roll. "I'm out of here. I'll be back, though. No matter what you think, I'm not letting you stay in this house alone, if for no other reason than to protect this place."

Grabbing the edge of the front door, he leaned back inside to get the last word in. "You know, the way I see it, if you can live with Bradley Kase, you can live with anybody. And what's so damn bad about the thought of living on property next door to mine. It's not like you have to live *with* me. We had a pretty good thing once. You'd think we could at least be friends."

"Eeaarrgh," she growled, hurling a silk flower arrangement in his direction. "You arrogant—" *Hiccup.*

The arrangement bounced off his chest before he could turn and head to his truck.

She raced toward the door and slammed it behind him.

Clyde let out a loud woof.

"Now you speak up." She swatted his tail as he wagged it excitedly, and retrieved the dusty silk flowers.

Jill grabbed her cell phone off the table and dialed Carolanne's number, but the call ended up going to voice mail. Between hiccups, she left a message.

What else could she do? Contest the will. She'd look spoiled and unappreciative after all Pearl had done for her. People would talk that up like no tomorrow. She paced the kitchen, hotter than a hornet, before settling on taking Clyde out back for some air. She sat in the swing and rubbed Clyde's back with her foot with each rocking motion. It was a wonder the dog had any fur at all with as much petting as he demanded.

A breeze kicked up and it smelled like rain. As the clouds rolled in, she and Clyde went back inside. A wave of fear crept inside her thoughts; she rushed to locked the front door and pushed a chair in front of it.

❖ Chapter Fifteen ❖

"In New York City, we'd just consider that a normal day," Carolanne said. "But that kind of stuff never happens in Adams Grove."

Jill could hear the concern in Carolanne's voice. "Scott did say the biggest crime he'd had to deal with in the past eighteen months was some guys from Tidewater hunting on posted land, which is really the game warden's gig, anyway. Guess he'll earn his paycheck this year," she said, hoping to lighten the mood.

"Don't tease. It's getting scary."

"I'm not taking this lightly, I promise. If I don't joke, I'm liable to just crawl in a hole somewhere. I'm trying not to think about it. I'm so freaked out about the attic incident, and with Garrett knowing about the will. Do you think he could have done that to me?"

"No way. You could've died up there in this heat. I'd find behavior like that from him hard to believe, but you never know."

"What about Pearl's will? Can she leave the property to Garrett and me jointly? Because that's definitely not going to work."

"She can pretty much do what she wants. The way she's got it written, you can't even buy out the other. It's both, or it goes to auction."

"So what Connor said was true."

"I told you he was a good lawyer. I didn't doubt him. It was great talking to him after so long. So what are you going to do?"

"I don't know. I was going to see if you wanted to come stay for a couple days. I can't stay here by myself after what happened with the attic, and Garrett is threatening to come stay here. If he's going to stay, I might as well stay here, too. But, then again, if it's even a little possibility that Garrett was behind that incident, him being here could be worse."

"If he was trying to harm you, he certainly wouldn't be offering to stay and protect you."

"I want my safe home again"—Jill let out a sigh—"my simple, safe, know-your-neighbor home."

"You're thinking about moving back, aren't you?"

"The longer I'm here, the more I miss it. Even with all the recent drama. I'd be lying if I said the thought hadn't crossed my mind. But don't breathe a word. You know how stuff spreads around here."

"I won't say a word. Keep those doors locked," Carolanne warned.

"Don't worry, I've got a list of options—Milly, Markham House, even Garrett offered me his guest room at one point. That won't be happening, so don't put your money on that one."

Jill said her good-byes and started dinner. There were things in Pearl's fridge she needed to use else they'd go bad, and Pearl hated waste.

She loaded up a sauté pan with leftovers and fresh veggies for a stir-fry. The food began to sizzle as she gave it a good stir with a wooden spoon, then hit speed dial on her cell to call Bradley to check in and let him know she wouldn't be back until Friday night, in time for the Independence Ball. He answered on the first ring.

"Hey, baby doll. Things aren't the same without you around. Forgive me yet?"

She ignored the question because, quite frankly, she didn't think she could. "I know this sounds stupid, but I never imagined I'd be without Pearl. I guess I thought she'd live forever, or at least outlive me."

"I thought that old gal would outlive us all, too. Are you on your way back?"

"Not yet. I've got decisions to still make about the property and all."

"Is there something of value you haven't told me about?"

"No. It's been an odd couple of days, really. I thought I knew everything about Pearl, and suddenly, it's like I didn't know her at all."

"I told you families were nothing but trouble. Secrets and backstabbing."

"No, not like that. It's not bad. I mean, I thought Pearl had always been single. Turns out, she had a whole secret romance with this guy John Carlo that I've never heard of."

"With who?"

"John Carlo Pacini." Jill dished the veggies onto a dinner plate.

"You never heard of him before?"

"I found stacks of love letters they'd written to each other. They were so beautiful."

"You're a hopeless romantic. We both know that."

"I am not. Well, maybe a little. Anyway, it's been neat, and it all makes me miss her so much more."

"Did you check to see if Pearl had a safe deposit box?"

"A safe deposit box? I doubt it. Why would she need something like that?"

"Important papers, things. I don't know. Don't you have one?"

"No." *We're a simple family. He's just making this way too complicated. Why do I let him get me so spun up? I've about had it with his mocking tone.*

"Well, she might have had some valuables. Just something to consider before you leave town. I was just trying to help. Look, I can send a truck to get you and the contents of that house in the morning. We don't need to wait around to see what's ours."

Suddenly it's we and ours? "Settle down, Bradley. No one is out to cheat anyone. People aren't like that around here." Her jaw tensed. "And honestly, I'm not ready to pack up Pearl's things yet. I walked around for two hours with a box in my hands yesterday trying to do just that, and all I ended up with were two brass tea light candleholders and a silk plant that probably should be tossed and not packed, anyway. It's hard."

"Hang on a second." Bradley covered the phone with his hand, but she could hear him barking orders to someone. "I'm back. OK, I've got this worked out. My people will be there in the morning to pack up for you. You won't even have to lift a finger. The truck will be on the road by midday."

Her temper flared. "Stop. Back up the freakin' truck. I'm not packing, and neither is anyone else. I'll be the one to decide when, if, and where. When. Whatever."

Bradley's voice steadied. "Fine. I'm trying to help. If we get the contents out of there, no way anyone is going to ask for it back. Trust me. I know what I'm doing."

"I don't need that kind of help."

"Well, then why the hell did you call if you didn't want me to do anything to help?"

"You mean besides the fact that you're my boss?"

"What do I need to know as your boss?"

"I won't be back until Friday night."

"We've got the Independence Ball. You're not just a guest. That's a work event. You know that."

"I know. I'll be there."

"Fine. I'm more than your boss. Where's the line?"

Jill twisted a lock of hair around her forefinger. Good question. "I don't know. I guess I wanted to commiserate with someone."

"I thought that's what I was doing," he said. "What is it that you want from me, Jill?"

He was frustrated, that was easy to hear. This was the first time her life had trumped his plans, and it was clear he was not used to not getting his way. "Support. Not as a boss, but as a friend, a boyfriend, whatever we are. I'm not sure I even know what that is anymore."

"I don't think you know what you want. And I think we're past the point of keeping personal and business separate. Tell you what, when you figure it out, you let me know."

She started to respond, but he'd already disconnected.

She clicked the phone closed. *This is so over. Why am I letting it drag on?* Their discussion had stolen her appetite. She called the hotel and booked a room for two nights. She'd stay there until they got all this figured out. Once she ate and fed Clyde, she'd head that way. She carried her dinner plate to the living room and nibbled, feeding half of her food to Clyde while they watched TV.

The sound of a vehicle in front of the house sent a tingle up her spine. Clyde didn't react, but his track record as a guard dog wasn't getting big points with her so far. She waited for a knock, but nothing happened.

All the warnings sounded like alarms in her mind. A tense silence cloaked the room. The only sound coming through was the pounding of her heart.

She dropped to the floor and slithered in a low crouch to avoid casting a shadow until she made her way to the hall. Clyde thought she was playing a new game. He bounded alongside of her, kneeling on his front haunches and then running and wagging his tail. Under the safe cover of the dark hallway, she jumped to her feet and ran to the back bedroom.

In her haste, she caught her hip on the edge of the dresser.

"Ow. That'll leave a bruise." She tiptoed to the window and looked outside through the crack between the shade and the window frame.

It was Garrett's truck. He'd parked at the edge of the woods out in front of the house.

Jill let out the breath she hadn't realized she was holding. He said he was coming back. She was much more on edge than she'd realized.

She dropped the shade and walked back into the living room, cursing herself for her spy-girl reaction. Trying to act nonchalant, she flipped through the channels, but after ten minutes, Garrett still hadn't come to the door. She peeked out front again. He was still out there, sitting in his truck.

She dialed his cell phone.

"At your service," he answered.

"What are you doing?"

"I think you already know."

"Why are you doing it, then?"

"I told you I was going to make sure you're safe."

"Do you plan to sit out there all night?"

"Yep."

Jill pulled the curtain to the side and peered out the front window. "This is ridiculous."

"So you've said."

"Are you leaving?"

"Nope. Are you?"

"I was, but I won't have to if you're staying out there."

"Then it's settled."

"I hope you get a crick in your neck."

"Love you, too, angel."

The words struck a familiar emotion, but she wasn't going to give in. "You're a complete whack job." She opened the curtain wide and circled a finger around and around at the side of her head.

He flipped his headlights off and on twice.

"Does that mean you're leaving?" she asked.

"Nope. Morse code for 'takes one to know one.'"

"Oh, that's mature. You can't sleep in your truck. It's muggy. You'll be miserable."

"Are you inviting me in?"

"Hardly."

"Then I'll be here every night."

"I'll be out of your hair on Friday. I have to go back to Savannah."

"Then I'll be here every night until Friday, and Friday morning, I'll pick up Clyde. Things are not as complicated as you're making them."

"Don't—"

"I know. Don't tell you what to do. Just say good night, Jill." The line went dead.

Good night, Jill, she mocked and tugged the curtain closed. Who the heck did he think he was? She called and canceled her room reservation, then picked up the remote and surfed channels to get her mind off him. Finally, she gave in and went to bed. She laid there for a moment, but then got up.

Kneeling on the floor, she folded her hands in front of her and bowed her head. She prayed for help, direction, and strength, then climbed back into bed. Through the night, she woke up several times and checked to see if Garrett was still there. She was obviously the only one losing sleep tonight.

It was daylight when the sound of Garrett's truck engine woke her. The low rumble faded as he idled off the property.

Unable to get back to sleep, she busied herself through another day.

Garrett showed up the next night, too. The third night, Jill thought he'd finally given up. But later that evening, she saw his headlights cut a path through the darkness after she was already in bed. Shortly after he arrived, a summer storm pushed through. She tugged the covers up around her as the rolling thunder vibrated the house and lightning lit every crevice of the dark night. She wondered if Garrett was safe in his truck and had to resist the temptation to call and tell him to come inside. He was a grown man. If he wanted to act like a crazy person, that was his right, but he had to be miserable out there.

Chapter Sixteen

Friday morning, Garrett sat on the edge of the bed watching Jill sleep. She'd cried again last night. He could see the mascara on the pillowcase. It killed him to see her so sad.

He'd knocked, and when she didn't answer, he'd let himself in. Even now, as he sat there watching her sleep, his heart pounded from the worry that had rushed through him when she hadn't answered the door. He rested his hand on her hip.

Her eyelashes fluttered, and then she opened her eyes. "What are you doing in my bedroom?"

"I knocked. You didn't answer. I was worried." He pushed her bangs to the side. "You've been crying."

She closed her eyes and turned her face into the pillow.

"I know. I miss her, too." He rubbed his thumb across her cheek. "Pearl loved you. She will always be a part of our lives."

"She's always been there for me."

"She always will be"—he tapped his fingers just above her heart—"in here."

Jill leaned up on her elbow. "Are you sure Pearl came up with this plan on her own?"

"No one could manipulate Pearl. You know that." *All I ever wanted was to be with you. Please let me in.*

She relaxed a little.

Garrett tucked a wild curl behind her ear. He loved it when her hair curled. She spent so much time trying to straighten it, but she looked beautiful just like she was right now. "Pearl put all her chips—or in this case, all her acres—on us. It's not like she's trying to force us to be a couple—"

Jill's brows shot up.

"OK. She is, but why should that surprise us? She can't do that, but we could at least be friends."

"It's just all so confusing," she said softly. "There's so much I didn't know."

"Me either." Silence built between them. "I didn't mean to bug you. I just came to pick up Clyde before you left," he said, standing up.

She shook her head. "I'm not sure I'm leaving today."

He felt his hopes raise. "Really?"

"I need to figure this out. I don't think I can do that from Savannah."

"Seeing you lying there on a tearstained pillow is killing me. I don't want you to ever be this sad again." He let out a loud breath. "I miss you, Jill. I'm having a hard time believing that what we had for all those years wasn't something special. Couldn't we at least give us another shot, for Pearl?"

"For Pearl?" Jill arched a brow.

His palms began to sweat. "OK, and for me. I'm not going to lie. I've never stopped loving you. You have to know that when you left town, it hurt like hell. I've missed you every single day. Every day without you for the past year has been like wasted time."

She wrapped the sheet tighter around herself. "Things are confusing right now. I can't think straight."

"I should have said this a year ago. I should've fought for you then, but I was pissed. You believed him over me. You didn't trust me. That hurt." He tried to stay calm, but that bastard fired him up. "It'll all work out. No matter what you decide."

"Bradley's not going to be happy about this. He's been so generous, and he *is* my boss. I may not have a job after I make this decision." Jill covered her face with her hands.

"Forget Bradley."

She uncovered her face and shook her head.

"That's not how I meant it. It's you who matters. Forget Bradley. Forget me. Do what's in your heart. I'll respect whatever you decide. I promise. And if Bradley loves you, he will, too. I wouldn't worry about the job. You're a bright girl. You can get another job."

"You'd better go," Jill said.

"Don't make me go," Garrett said.

She glanced away. "Please. I need some time."

Don't slip further away from me. "I'll worry." *What can I do? Give me a hint, a sign. Something.* He stood next to the bed. "I'll give you the time, but please don't shut me out. I love you."

"And the property?"

"The property is secondary. Seriously." *That land and that project are nothing without you being a part of it. Don't you know that?* He held her gaze, then stepped away. "OK, I'm leaving." He backed out of the room, never taking his eyes off her until he turned to go down the hall.

Garrett's boots clicked a steady rhythm down the hallway.

Clyde tilted his head and stared at her. In Clyde's eyes, it was almost like Pearl was asking her what the heck she was doing letting that man leave. Pearl had never steered her wrong. As Jill heard the front door open and close, she bolted from the bed. She ran down the hall, her socks sliding the last three feet to the door as she yelled, "Wait!"

Clyde was right behind her. He didn't stop any quicker than Jill had. He plowed into the hall table, sending the lamp toppling to the floor.

She quickly righted the lamp so Clyde wouldn't tromp on it a second time, then swung open the door.

"Wait," she hollered again, but Garrett didn't hear her over the truck engine. She stepped on the porch and waved her arms to get his attention, but he never looked back.

She sat on the step and propped her forearms on her knees. Clyde sat beside her and licked her ear.

"Thanks, Clyde." She rubbed his chest as she stared out into the yard. How had things become so complicated so quickly?

A year ago today, she'd been sitting in one of the finest salons in Savannah getting a manicure and pedicure at the same time, a surprise from Bradley. Her hair had been up in a towel, steeped with an aromatherapy conditioner that was custom blended just for her. Robert—pronounced *Row-bear,* he'd chided—had his people working magic on her, from toenails to root tips and everything in between. Robert had finished up by sweeping her long brown hair up into a diamond-encrusted claw clip. Sprigs of shiny soft hair tumbled from the top like fireworks. She'd never felt prettier or more special, until later that evening. When she'd gotten home, a beaded gown lay across the toile comforter of the antique four-poster bed. The gown was midnight blue and fell from rhinestone-encrusted straps. The deep blue made her icy-blue eyes look even bluer.

She'd nearly fainted at the sight of the enormity of the mansion when she and Bradley arrived at the Independence Ball via black stretch limousine. It had been her first time in a limo, and the whole night felt like the celebrity treatment. They'd stepped out of the car and flowed into a sea of black-tied men and women of Savannah in an array of red, white, or blue gowns. The women sparkled brighter than the fireworks at the Independence Ball that night.

Guests had filled glasses of champagne from a fountain that must have been twelve feet high. When Bradley had led her out to the dance floor, she'd been so nervous, but he'd been a strong lead, and soon she was waltzing, moving like a real lady in her strappy heels and beaded gown. It had been a fairy-tale night. Only one of so many to follow.

That might have been magical, but today, an Adams Grove Fourth of July seemed more appealing.

Jill took out the ingredients from the pantry and fridge so she could fill in for Pearl tonight. She went to work on batches of chocolate–chocolate chip cookies. Tonight, she'd carry on Pearl's tradition for the guys.

Pouring, stirring, and shaping the secret recipe into two-inch balls shifted her mood. The whole house smelled sweet. Pan after pan, she baked and moved cookie after cookie off the large baking sheets to the cooling grids on the long kitchen counter until she was satisfied she had enough to fill Pearl's largest Tupperware container.

While the cookies cooled, she glanced at the clock. She'd have to let Bradley know she wasn't coming, and that probably meant she'd be fired. Not sure what to say, she started to get dressed instead. But her nerves were making her feel so sick to her stomach she took a deep breath and made the call.

Bradley's cell phone rang once, twice, and then straight to voice mail.

Thank you, God, Jill mouthed toward heaven. She left the message that she needed an extended leave of absence, and if that was a problem, they could discuss it on Monday. "At least that should buy me some peace through the weekend to get things straight."

She felt like she had wings as the relief lifted the stress she'd been carrying around. She hummed as she dressed in one of her new outfits and fixed her hair up in a clip, similar to last year, just for fun. Satisfied with the look, she headed to the kitchen to package up the goodies and call Aunt Milly.

"Hello," said Milly.

"Did I wake you?"

"It's OK, honey. I can take a nap anytime. Are you OK? I thought you were on your way back to Georgia today."

Jill tucked the phone under her chin and stacked the cookies into the container. "No, ma'am. I'm considering staying." Just saying it out loud made it feel more right.

"Pearl would love that more than anything."

"I think you're right," Jill said. "I'm going to go to the fireworks. I was calling to see if you'd like me to pick you up?"

"No, thank you. You go on and have fun. It gets too hot for me these days. You keep me posted about you moving back, though, OK?"

"Count on it," Jill said. "I love you, Aunt Milly."

"Love you, too. Oh, and give my love to Garrett."

Jill smiled as she hung up the phone. Aunt Milly was Pearl's best friend. It should be no surprise that she'd pick up right where Pearl had left off.

She grabbed her things, jumped into her car, and headed for the gate near the pond.

Connor's face lit up when he recognized her behind the wheel of the BMW. He waved his orange flag, gesturing her to the front row.

Now, that's service. She parked and gathered her blanket and balanced the large container of goodies against her hip as she scanned the grounds for a spot. Not just any place, but the one she and Pearl had claimed for so many years in a row. Thankfully, no one else had taken the spot under the oak tree. Jill spread out the blanket and settled in. Tears threatened as she watched all the folks enjoying this annual family event. Children dressed in reds, whites, and blues ran through the crowd. Dads tossed balls and threw Frisbees while moms relaxed nearby.

A whistle blew, signaling it was time for teams to deliver their prize barbecue to the judging tent. Jill recognized most of the judges. Scott Calvin was at the end of the table, and good ol' Chaz Huckaby sat next to him.

Chaz owned Huckaby House, a real estate company, renovation/redecorating company, and rifle range all in one, on what used to be his daddy's cattle ranch. Most of the locals just called it the "Triple R." Chaz had never met a stranger in his life, and he was the source for info on everything that went on in this town. There was never a concern about him playing favorites, because everyone was his favorite.

Old Man Piper sat at the other end of the table. He'd been a judge as long as she could remember. He had to be ninety if he was a day. Even Pearl used to call him an old man.

Jill surrendered to her growling stomach and bought a hot dog and a big cup of sweet tea from one of the 4-H tents. Juggling everything carefully as she walked, she settled back under the tree to read a novel on her Kindle and wait for it to get dark enough for the fireworks.

A few people stopped by, but most gave her some space. She was thankful for that. It was a hot, hot day, like every Fourth of July, but the tree provided just enough shade to make the heat bearable.

Just as she got settled, her cell phone rang. Caller ID showed it was Bradley. He must have picked up the message. He'd be fit to be tied, but this time she'd followed her instincts, and her heart told her she was in the right place today. She let the call go to voice mail.

Her phone boinged. *How many messages would he leave before Monday?*

She turned off the phone and pushed it deep to the bottom of her purse. Out of sight. Out of mind. Leaning against the tree, she took her Kindle from her purse. She read and crunched on soft ice until someone kicked the bottom of her tennis shoe.

Jill looked up to see Connor. She lowered the e-reader and set it aside. "Hey."

"Glad you came," Connor said.

"You can take the girl out of the country, but—"

"You can't take the country out of the girl. I see. I stand corrected," he said.

"Is your shift over?"

He held the orange vest up in one hand. "All done for the day."

"Thanks for the premium parking spot. I appreciate it."

He bowed. "My pleasure, Miss Fourth of July."

"Not me. Didn't Becky win that crown?"

"Yeah. But you should've won." He squatted down next to her and took a swallow of his beer. "Seen Garrett?"

She shook her head. "No. I'm sure he's over there lining up rockets. You can't tear those guys away from that pyro stuff."

"Does he know you're here?"

"Nope."

"Won't he be surprised when he walks by here tonight? It'll be like old times."

"I figured I'd carry on Pearl's tradition." She nodded toward the container to her right. "I brought cookies."

"Chocolate-chocolate chip?" Connor slid back the foil.

"Is there any other kind?"

"Well, then I do have the best seat in the house." He flipped his wrist to check his watch.

"Shouldn't be much longer now. Want anything before the fireworks start? I'm going to go grab another beer."

"Tea would be great. No, you know what? Bring me a cold beer, too."

"I'll be right back."

Jill tucked her Kindle in her purse. Folks picked their spots for the fireworks, and parents quieted impatient children with sparklers. Some children ran aimlessly in circles; others swept the sparklers in the sky, writing their names or making loop-de-loops.

The sun dipped lower.

In the next fifteen minutes or so, it would be dark.

Connor walked back up just as the park lights began to shine.

Everyone cheered and whistled. The sound grew louder by the second, and for a full minute, the cheering continued. Then, with a thunk, the lights went off, and the crowd fell silent. Anticipation filled the air, and except for nervous giggles, everything was quiet.

A moment later, the *ssphhhhp* of the first rocket soared high into the sky over the lake. Then nothing for a two-count before the silence was broken with a series of aerial repeaters. *Pop, pop-pop-pop, snap, pop,* followed by a huge glowing red chrysanthemum that illuminated the starry summer night. As the fire began to fade, hundreds of sparkling flickers streamed down like a waterfall, and that was just the beginning.

"Oooooh." *Whizz, ssphhhhp, shwoosh.* The next three fireworks went up together and exploded into the sky. They dazzled the crowd in red, white, and blue.

"Aaah." A loud whistler followed by a bright white bouquet of flowering lights drifted so slow it left behind a smoky fog in its trail. From there, the show got bigger, faster, and higher. A loud series of Roman candles burst in the sky, one after the other, over and over. The reports echoed, jolting everyone by surprise. Locals knew the extravaganza was getting close to the end of the bright display when the high school band began playing "God Bless America." Everyone sang along, thankful for the day, the community, and the country they were so lucky to live in. The finale began to burst and pop in the sky above them in time with the music. The last flicker faded with the last note.

Smoke hung heavy in the humid night air. Like magic, the park lights came back on. Everyone was still in awe of the beautiful sight and tired from the events of the day. But, like an army of ants, families poured into the parking lot to sit in traffic to get home.

Bugs gathered near the bright lights, starring in a show all their own. Small bats soared through the middle of the bugs, swallowing them up.

Jill stood, trying to burn off the nervous energy building up inside her. What seemed like a perfect plan earlier now left her sad. Pearl should be here. So many things would never be the same.

She half listened to Chaz and Connor as they talked with people they recognized and shared town gossip. Whoever started the rumor that women loved to gossip must've been a man, because it was clear the men in this town didn't miss much.

Jill's eyes were set on the roped-off pyrotechnicians area. Only the fire team was allowed back there, and Garrett had been a part of that elite group for years. Two fire trucks sat in the secure area to ensure their safety. Two guys wound up the caution tape. They reused that same roll each year. Wasting it wasn't an option.

She hadn't spotted Garrett yet. What were the chances he might not notice her standing here and leave?

A high-pitched squeal came from Jill's left.

"I thought you left for Georgia." Elsie bounded up with her fiancé in tow. Both wore matching stars-and-stripes golf shirts. "I knew that was you. Do you remember Billy?"

Jill nodded. "Billy Privet. It's great to see you." That short stint in the military had obviously cleaned up his act, and he sure didn't look like a boy anymore. "You're all grown up."

He blushed, shifting his weight.

"Congratulations on the engagement," Jill said.

Elsie snuggled against Billy's arm. He looked proud to have Elsie at his side.

"I hope you'll be around to come to the wedding," Billy said. "Elsie has been working on every detail nonstop."

"I wouldn't miss it," Jill said.

Elsie bounced and waved beyond Jill. "Hey there."

Jill caught a whiff of smoke, black powder, and the hint of spicy cologne. Her heart fluttered in anticipation.

"Jill?"

She turned to face Garrett. "Surprised?"

"Very," he said.

She scooped up the container of cookies and handed it to him. The offering spoke louder than words anyway, and the words just weren't coming.

He peeked under the top, then called to the guys with a smile. "Hey, guys, over here."

"You must've been busy this afternoon," Garrett said.

She wrinkled her nose. "A little."

"Thank you." He bit into a cookie. "Chocolate–chocolate chip. Every bit as good as Pearl's."

"That's a compliment. Thanks." Jill stepped aside as the other guys joined them and greeted her.

"No. Thank you." Garrett held out the container and the guys grabbed the cookies like they hadn't had a thing to eat in a week.

"OK, this is awkward. We sound like those polite chipmunks in the cartoons. No, thank you." She took a step closer to him.

Garrett handed off the treats to one of the other guys and wiped the chocolate from his hands on his jeans. "Something wrong?"

"No. I tried to catch you before you left the house today."

His face went hard and he reached for her arm.

"Oh no. It's nothing bad," she added quickly.

His expression immediately softened.

"I think we should do it." Jill chewed on her bottom lip. "OK?"

"Do what?" His brow arched ever so slightly.

"Not that. You have a one-track mind."

He lifted his shoulders, proclaiming innocence. "Hey, you're the one who said we should do it."

"I meant a truce and the property…five-year commitment thing. Put the past behind us. No promises, but we both move forward with Pearl's plan for the property and see what happens."

"You sure?" Garrett eyed her curiously. "What about waiting five days to decide?

"That just means five more days I'll torture myself trying to figure out what to do."

"Did you tell him?" He nodded in the direction where Connor stood talking just a few feet away.

"No. I wanted to talk to you first."

"You're sure?"

"I'm sure." In her heart, she knew this was right. "After being here for a while, I can't let that property go. There are just too many memories there."

"Connor," Garrett yelled, "come here."

Connor walked over, and Jill told him that she'd made her decision. He extended a hand to Jill. "We'll finalize the paperwork immediately."

As they talked, the last of the cars were starting to thin out.

Garrett asked Jill, "Where'd you park?"

Connor answered for her. "VIP Parking. Only the best for our little lady."

"I'll walk you to your car," Garrett said.

She picked up her purse, and Garrett helped her with the rest of her things. They walked through the empty fairgrounds toward her car without a word.

When they reached her car, he opened her door for her.

She tossed her things across the driver's seat to the passenger side before climbing behind the steering wheel.

Garrett stood between her and the open door. "I'm going to follow you home."

"Hop in. I'll give you a ride to your truck."

He jogged around to the passenger side and climbed in. "Nice ride." He ran his hand across the smooth leather upholstery.

"Thanks." Without having to ask where he parked, she drove him over to his usual spot.

Once he climbed into his truck, she drove off with him behind her. It was comforting to see him in her rearview mirror on the way home.

When they pulled in front of the house, the porch light was on and everything was just the way she'd left it. Clyde woofed a greeting over the back fence.

As Jill headed for the porch, Garrett went and opened the gate to let Clyde out. Clyde ran around the yard sniffing and prancing, then joined them on the front porch.

"Got news for you, Clyde." He patted the dog's nose. "She's going to be hanging out for a while."

Clyde jumped and put his paws on Jill's shoulders. She had no defense. He was nearly a head taller than her when he was on his back legs.

"Off, Clyde," Jill half yelled, half laughed as he tickled her ear with wet, slobbery kisses.

"He wants me to be happy, too. He loves me," Garrett said. "He's glad you're going to give Adams Grove another chance."

"Off," she said sharply, reprimanding Clyde with a *tsk-tsk* to a sitting position. That dog whisperer stuff really worked. Bradley's housekeeper, Annie, had been obsessed with that television show. Jill must've picked up a few tips by osmosis over her morning coffee, while Annie mused over the host for hours. It used to irritate Jill to no end, but now it was coming in handy.

"I wanted to talk to you about Bridle Path Estates. I've got to spend the day at the job site tomorrow, but how about I bring dinner by?"

"Lucky for me, tomorrow is Saturday, else I might think you were trying to trick me into carrying on your dinner tradition with Pearl."

"I think I'm clear on your opinion about that," he said, rubbing his rear end.

She laughed, thinking of him sitting in the flower bed. Just a thorn among the roses. Pearl would have loved a picture of that.

"Maybe we're starting our own traditions," he said with a wink and headed for his truck.

She and Clyde walked him as far as the front flower bed. Starting a few new traditions with Garrett didn't sound half bad.

❖ Chapter Seventeen ❖

With the morning sun streaming through the windows, Jill busied herself around the house. She couldn't stop thinking about how mad Bradley must have been at her for not coming back. She hated to let him down, and more than that, she hated to let all those kids down. She'd raised more money this year than all the money Kase had ever raised since they started. If he let her go, she'd just have to figure something else out. She wasn't going to let herself think about that until she talked to him on Monday. By then, hopefully things would be clearer.

Jill felt more relaxed than she had for days. She clipped flowers from the yard and arranged a bouquet in a short vase for the table.

At six o'clock, Garrett drove up in front of the house. Clyde must have recognized the sound of his truck, too, because he took off through the house, sliding to a stop at the front door.

"Hello." Garrett rapped his knuckle on the screen door as he came inside.

"In the kitchen."

Clyde shadowed Garrett all the way to the kitchen, his lips puffing with each whiff of the big paper bag swinging from Garrett's hand.

Garrett slid the bag onto the counter.

Jill swatted Clyde away and took inventory of the contents of the bag. "General Tso chicken, beef and broccoli, sticky white rice, and plenty of extra packets of duck sauce. You remembered everything," she said with a smile.

"It hasn't been that long."

"Feels like a lifetime ago."

"I brought something for you, too, boy." Garrett stooped in front of Clyde, who was drooling even more than usual from the aroma coming from that bag.

"No, not food." Garrett reached into his back pocket, pulled out a navy-blue bandanna, and folded it corner to corner. He whipped the pocket knife from his belt and sliced the yarn to free Clyde from the pink towel around his neck. Garrett flipped the bandanna around Clyde's neck, then tied a knot with the two corners.

"That's more like it." Satisfied, Garrett flipped the blade closed and pushed his knife back into the holder on his belt.

Jill walked up behind him. "What do we have here? Cowboy Clyde?"

"You can't expect him to run around in pink and take care of you, too. It's just not right."

"He does do the cowboy thing pretty well."

"You're welcome," Garrett said. "Both of you."

"Let's eat." Jill handed a couple of the containers to Garrett to carry to the living room.

They ate from the cardboard boxes, sitting Indian style around the coffee table in front of the television.

"That hit the spot." She held the empty pint container toward Clyde, who lapped the sauce from the sides of the cardboard. Then he trotted off with the box to finish. He settled on the floor, hugging the carton between his giant paws like a bear.

"You two are getting along well," Garrett said.

"Men. All the same. You get to their hearts through their tummies, y'know."

"You mean y'all don't just do that to fatten us up so we aren't marketable anymore?"

"Well, yeah, that too. But we mostly do it because you love it."

"Does that mean you'll be doing some baking for me soon?"

She lay back, flat on the floor. "Don't push your luck." She lifted her knees up and groaned. "Lord, my back is aching. I might have moved a few too many boxes in the attic yesterday."

Garrett rolled his shoulders. "You're not the only one with a crick or two."

"No one asked you to sleep in your truck."

"If I didn't, I'd worry all night."

"Nothing has happened."

"Maybe that's because I've been sleeping in your yard?" He lifted a brow.

"Not last night."

"That's what you think. I came late and left early."

"You sneak." How could she be mad?

"You're safe," Garrett said. "And that's what matters."

"Point taken, but this can't go on."

"You *could* invite me to sleep in the house. I could sleep upstairs in your old room."

"There isn't a bed in that room anymore. Pearl gave it to someone in the church."

"Remember me? I love camping," Garrett said. "I could sleep on the floor."

"The whole town probably already thinks you are sleeping here. If they knew what was really going on, they'd think you're a crazy stalker, and people always find out around here."

"Or that I'm protective of you after all that's happened. You know that news has raced like wildfire through the town. Crazy or not, Pearl would haunt me if something happened to you. You heard her on that video. What choice do I have?"

"You can take the bed." Jill hoped she wasn't making a giant mistake.

"I'll sleep on the couch."

"No. You're too tall for the couch. My way or no deal. Deal?"

"Deal. Sit up. I'll rub your shoulders." He inched closer and started kneading her back.

Jill relaxed into his strong hands, rolling her neck from side to side. "Aaaaaaaaaah. You always did give the best back rubs. I'll give you five days to stop that."

"Somehow I don't think Pearl's five-day rule applies to back rubs," Garrett said.

"You haven't lost your touch. Who've you been practicing on?" A flash of Becky popped into her mind.

"Just hush and enjoy." After a good five minutes, he finally stopped and hugged her from behind.

She leaned back into his lap.

"I have to drive up to Pittsburgh tomorrow to meet with the metal roofing manufacturer. I can do it in one day, but it's an easier two-day trip. Want to join me?"

She sat up, ready to accept, but then paused. "I think I'll pass. I'm not sure I can trust you."

"Oh, you can trust me, but that's OK. I'll make the trip in one day, then. Now lie back down." He tapped the floor.

She stretched out on the floor in front of him. "No fair. You know my weakness for back rubs."

"I'll behave, scout's honor."

She relaxed and then lifted her head. "Wait a second. You were never a Boy Scout."

"Well, I was for two meetings."

"I don't think that counts."

"I did get my courtesy badge."

"Well, that makes all the difference."

Under the relaxation from his hands, she was fast asleep in less than ten minutes.

The next morning, Jill opened her eyes to a blur of bright red. She lifted her head, squinting until her eyes focused. A trio of flowers nestled on the pillow beside her on the floor. Gerbera daisies—two red and one vivid yellow—with a note tucked between them.

She shifted up onto her elbow. The note said that Garrett would be back sometime late the next afternoon or sooner.

She rolled over lazily and stretched. Sometime in the evening, he'd covered her with a blanket. She picked up one of the daisies and spun it between her fingers. Clyde came running in from the kitchen, a red daisy pinned to his bandana.

Clyde hovered over her, breathing heavily, his lips flopping out with each pant. He looked huge from this position. She smiled and rubbed his head.

She'd experienced the gamut of emotions, the highs and lows, and now was back to the comfort of old routines with Garrett. *Is there a chance if we tried again, the relationship might work?* She felt as if someone had turned back time and she'd been transported to that happy place she'd thought she lost a year ago. The one she once shared with Garrett. But she did have some responsibilities in Savannah she had to tend to. The Kase Foundation, for one.

She twisted a flower under Clyde's nose.

He sniffed and then sneezed, drenching her.

"Uuuuuugh. You sneeze like a whale. Cover your blowhole." She lifted herself up off the floor and headed for the shower.

After Jill showered and got dressed, she headed out back to get lost in the mundane task of weeding the garden. Still unnerved from the attic incident, she tucked her cell phone in her pocket.

Before long, the temperature soared to an uncomfortable level. She could hear Clyde panting under the shade of a tree clear across the yard.

As soon as she stood up, he was at her side, looking very hopeful that she was going to take him back inside. She patted his head, and he plodded along behind her to escape the heat of the afternoon.

She plopped down in a kitchen chair and took a long sip of the sweet tea she'd left there earlier. The ice had melted, but the cool liquid quenched her thirst.

As she stared off at nothing, suddenly everything became clear. She was fighting for all the wrong things and for the wrong reasons. She needed to wrap up her business with the foundation and end her relationship with Bradley. She'd have to find another job, but she had skills. She did have some money tucked away, and she could stay here at Pearl's. Her heart wasn't in that relationship. If it hadn't been for the big charity event, she'd have left a long time ago. She knew exactly what she needed to do.

Jill rushed down the hall, tossed a couple items in an overnight bag, and swept her purse into her arms without missing a step. She slapped her thigh to get Clyde's attention. "Come on, buddy. You're going on a little trip."

He trotted outside with her but didn't want any part of getting into her car. Twice, he jumped in, then turned around and hopped out before she could close the door. Once, she urged him in. But by the time she got around to the driver's side, Clyde was in her seat behind the wheel, unwilling to move.

"Clyde. This is not a game." She nudged him, but he wouldn't budge.

Finally, she tricked him by putting a cherry lifesaver on the passenger seat. When he lunged for the candy, she jumped behind the steering wheel and headed to the Adams Grove kennel, only a short drive away. They were happy to take Clyde, even without an appointment.

When she got back in the car, she called Carolanne. "You're not going to believe what I'm getting ready to do."

"Please tell me you're giving Garrett another chance."

"Not exactly, but I'm not giving Bradley one."

"That's even better." Carolanne whooped on the other end of the phone so loud that Jill had to pull the phone away from her ear.

"I think I just lost some hearing."

"Small price to pay for making a good decision. I'm so proud of you, Jill. He's just not good enough for you."

"Wish me luck." After wiping the drool off the dashboard and passenger window, Jill jumped on I-95 and gunned the engine, heading toward Savannah. She had business to take care of.

At just after nine that evening, Jill pulled her car in the driveway of Bradley's estate. Funny, she'd never realized before that she thought about this place as Bradley's, not her home. That was telling in and of itself.

A couple of lights were on, but that didn't mean anything. The elaborate security system powered things on and off in intervals to make the house look busy even when they were away.

Bradley's Lexus was in the driveway, though. An odd twinge of disappointment ran through her. She'd hoped he wouldn't be home yet and she could ready herself for what was sure to be an unpleasant conversation. But then again, if all her self-talk on the six-hour drive hadn't readied her, she'd never be ready.

She parked her car behind his and walked up the path to the house. She tapped the code into the keypad next to the front door and pushed the heavy door with her shoulder.

Jill took a steadying breath and set her purse on the front entry table. She looked into Bradley's office on the first floor. He wasn't there. Somewhat relieved, she took her overnight bag up to the bedroom and tossed it on the floor of the huge closet. She sat on the bench at the end of the bed and flipped her shoes across the room, bending to rub her feet. They had swollen during the long drive. The Southern cooking she'd been enjoying since being back in Adams Grove hadn't helped, either.

The thought of food reminded her that she'd been in such a hurry to get back to Savannah before she chickened out she hadn't stopped to eat. She went downstairs to grab a quick snack and to see if Bradley was swimming laps as he often did in the evenings.

Halfway down the long entryway that divided the wings of the house, a noise stopped her in her tracks.

She turned her back to the kitchen. The sound came from the entertainment room—Bradley's man cave with the home theater and full-sized billiard table. Bradley was quite the pool shark, too. It wasn't unusual for him to spend hours practicing.

She walked toward the door, but the sounds weren't the familiar clack of pool stick to ball. Bracing herself to look assertive and ready to face him with her decision, she pushed open the door.

She froze, unable to take her eyes off him or the horror of the scene in front of her.

Bradley was *on top* of the pool table with his back to her. In all his glory. He'd mounted the housekeeper from behind. Wearing nothing but his tie, Bradley smacked Annie's hind parts as if she were a pony.

Across the room, a camera on a tripod projected the whole freaky scene on the eight-foot-wide screen in front of them all.

Jill's hand shot to her mouth as she gagged.

She tried to move her feet and back out of the room before they noticed her, but her legs felt like wet noodles.

The only thing within reach to steady her was a rack of pool sticks that went clattering across the floor when she grabbed for them. She tripped over one and ended up on her hands and knees, scrambling to get back on her feet and out the door.

Bradley and Annie stopped midmotion. Jill ran from the room, still holding one of the pool sticks in her hand.

A naked Bradley ran after her, calling her name.

She ran as fast as she could, but he was closing in, and his tie wasn't the only thing flopping.

Her bare feet slapped against the travertine floor as she fled the horrifying scene. The pool stick clipped a vase on the hall table and sent the crystal shattering across the floor. She leaped into the air to avoid cutting her bare feet.

"Jill, it's not what it looks like. Stop. I'm sorry."

She came to an immediate stop.

"You're sorry?" She spun around and marched right up to Bradley with a finger nearly slapping his nose. "You're not going to talk your way out of this one. Don't you dare apologize."

"I'm sorry, babe. It was a mistake." He reached toward her. "Please. Listen to me."

She took a step back and swung the pool stick. A blue chalky smear marred the bare skin of his shoulder.

He slapped the stick from her hand, sending it sailing to the floor, where it rolled in a half circle.

She smacked his arm as hard as she could, then shook off the sting.

"Oh yeah, it was a mistake, all right," she screamed. "A mistake I ever moved here with you. You are sick, sick, *sick*." She clenched her fist in the air. "Stop saying you're sorry. We both know you don't mean it."

"Don't talk to me that way." He jerked her arm as he spit the words in fury. "If you had been here, this wouldn't have happened."

She tugged her arm from his grasp. "Don't you blame me for that sick scenario." Her words spewed.

"Where do you think you're going to go? Back to that gullible Malloy boy?"

Anger coursed through her. "Don't turn this around and make it about me. It doesn't matter if I was here or not. This sick little scenario sure didn't look like a first time. It so would've happened. It *did* happen. You're not sorry. You're just sorry you got caught. No wonder you would never fire her. Everything makes perfect sense now."

She spun and ran for the door, snagging her purse from the front table as she headed to her car.

Bradley was only a couple of strides behind her. "You can walk your sweet ass wherever it is you think you're going. That car is in my name. I won't let you drive it off this property."

"What are you going to do to stop me?"

"I'll call the cops and report the vehicle stolen. They'll throw your butt in jail."

"Great. Fine. You know what? I don't need anything from you." She swatted at a mosquito buzzing around her head.

"I hope the mosquitoes are having a field day on your pecker." Jill threw her keys at him, then jogged toward the gate. "If they can even find it."

Jill didn't look back until she cleared the entry to the driveway. When she did glance back, Bradley still stood there, bare-ass naked except for that tacky tie, staring at her.

What now? She knew lots of folks in Savannah, but the only real friend she'd made was Melanie Hines. They'd met while walking last year, and she'd been thankful for the friendship. They'd made this two-mile walk dozens of times. Of course, she was usually in a pair of sneakers. She had no idea how late it was or if that scene had swallowed an hour or a minute, but she had limited choices at this point. As embarrassing as it was, Melanie was her best choice.

Jill tried to absorb everything that had happened as she walked the well-known route.

Her bare feet had started to ache by the time she stood in front of Melanie's house. A single light burned in the den. Jill drew in a deep breath and rapped hard on the door, three times.

The curtain moved, and then Melanie opened the door. The long-legged brunette was in her pajamas, but still looked picture perfect enough to step out on the town.

"Did I wake you? I'm sorry. I didn't know where else to go."

"Jill. I thought you were in Virginia burying your grandmother. What are you doing here? Is everything all right, sweetie?" Her deep Southern drawl stretched each word.

Jill opened her mouth to repeat the story as she'd planned on the walk over. Instead, tears sprang out of nowhere and she could barely choke out a syllable.

"What's wrong?" Melanie swung the door wide and hurried Jill inside. "Honey, get in here. What happened? That bastard didn't hurt you, did he?"

She shook her head.

"What has you so shaken up?" Melanie grabbed her friend up by the shoulders and guided her into the kitchen. "Where are your shoes, dahlin'?" Melanie asked as she started a pot of coffee.

When Jill regained her composure, she told Melanie the sick story, play by play. "He wouldn't let me take my car. He said it's in his name, and you know, I don't doubt that it is. I never even bothered to check. I've been such a fool."

"Don't be silly. We see what we want to see. And it looks like you might be seeing Mr. Bradley Kase clearly for the first time."

"What else could go wrong?"

"Now, sweetie, it'll all work out. Always does. I probably shouldn't say it, but maybe this is all for the best. I mean, with the rumors floatin' around about him and all."

"What rumors? About Bradley and Annie? Am I the only one who didn't know?"

"Oh, goodness no. About his business dealin's. I guess a few of those investments he made aren't panning out for folks all that well."

Thank God. If everyone in Savannah knew he was cheating on her, she'd die of embarrassment. "No, the Kase Foundation is doing such great work. I'm sure he'll get those investments turned around. He'd never risk the foundation's reputation."

She patted Jill's hand. "I'm sure you're right."

"I need to get back to Adams Grove. I know this is a huge favor to ask, but could I borrow one of the cars?"

"Of course, anything. The problem is that Vernon is out of town in his, and I need mine to take the girls to their cheerleading competition this weekend. The only vehicle I have to loan you is Lindy's car. She's back at Tech for the semester."

"I'll take it."

"I'm sure it's a mess. I swear that child uses that car as a second dresser most of the time."

"I don't care as long as it will get me back to Virginia."

"Oh, it'll get you there. Vernon wouldn't let Lindy drive it if it weren't in safe running condition. Why don't you stay here tonight and get some rest first? You can head out in the morning. How long a drive is it?"

"About six hours."

"That's a long way. Stay the night," Melanie tried to reason with her.

"I'm wide-awake. I'd never get a wink of sleep even if I tried. Besides, I just want to get out of here."

"Well, let me at least get you some shoes and pack the rest of this coffee for you." Melanie got a thermos out of the pantry and added hot coffee, cream, and sugar.

Jill hugged the thermos to her chest and followed her to the garage.

Melanie took a set of keys from the key rack next to the door and tossed them to Jill.

"A Troll doll keychain," Jill said, "how appropriate. You know, part of the charm of these things is they're so doggone ugly that you can't help but laugh, and if I don't laugh now, I'm sure to start crying. It's perfect."

"Well, I'm glad Lindy's style appeals to someone," Melanie said.

Melanie shared the story about how her daughter had gotten the car with her own money despite her parents telling her to wait until she finished school. "She's an independent one, that girl." Melanie raced back inside. "Oh, I almost forgot. You can't leave barefooted." She came back with a pair of leather flats and a newspaper tucked under her arm.

"How am I ever going to thank you?" asked Jill.

"Don't be silly, it's what friends do." Melanie dropped the shoes in front of Jill. "It'll work out great. You can meet up with Lindy when you're done. She's closer to you there in Adams Grove than she is here."

"That I can do." Jill stepped into the shoes and got in the car.

Melanie handed her the newspaper. "I saved a copy of the story about the foundation party for you."

"Thanks. I haven't seen it."

"Are you sure I can't talk you into resting up and leaving in the morning?" Melanie pushed the button to lift the garage door.

"Nope." Jill started up the old Mustang and slowly pulled out of the drive.

During her drive, she had a hard time keeping her mind off the billiard room scene. The evening replayed itself over and over until she turned into the driveway at Pearl's house.

She sat in the car wondering how everything had become so complicated in such a short time. Here she was with no clothes, no car, no home, and no Pearl. No Bradley, either, and that meant no job. How could she have lived with him all that time and not have had any idea what kind of man he really was? He'd told her that she was the only one for him. He'd said exactly what she'd wanted to hear, and she believed him.

She hoped it would be the last time she'd have to make the drive from Savannah to Adams Grove. Home. She was finally home.

Jill lifted the door mat and used the key to get in the door. Under the mat wasn't a much better place to hide the key than the flower box, but she'd been in a hurry and under the mat had been the best she could do at the time.

Too tired to bother with getting undressed or turning on a light, she pushed the door closed behind her and climbed onto the sofa. In the quiet darkness of the empty room, she said, "Pearl, I need you." She never would have told Pearl all the details of the despicable scene between Bradley and the hired help, but she sure could use Pearl's strength.

She let out a long sigh and drifted off, exhausted and defeated.

Chapter Eighteen

Pounding echoed through the room. Jill sat up, startled. *Am I dreaming?* Her hands reached for anything familiar in the darkness.

"Sheriff's department. Open up!" The deep voice boomed through the night; then the front door slammed against the wall.

Jill squealed and cowered back into the couch.

The blinding glow from a flashlight flooded over her face.

She shielded her eyes. "Clyde," she yelled. But Clyde was still at the kennel. "No."

"On your feet."

"Wait. Who are you? What do you want?" she cried.

"Hands where I can see them," the voice ordered. "What's your name?"

She couldn't see a thing past the bright light.

"What?" Jill reached for the lamp on the end table.

"Freeze."

She threw her arms in the air, eyes wide and darting.

"Anyone else in the house?"

"No." Jill splayed her fingers wider.

The unexpected guest flipped the living room light switch.

Jill squinted, her eyes adjusting as slowly as she was to the situation at hand. "Just me. This is my house. Wh-who are you?"

"What's your name, miss?"

"Jill Clemmons."

"I'm going to need to see some identification."

"What?"

"Identification, ma'am. Where's your ID?"

"I don't know. I'm not sure. You're confusing me."

The officer stepped forward and twisted her arms behind her, cuffing them together at the wrist. "Just until we sort this out, ma'am. This house was broken into earlier in the week. Know anything about that?"

"Where's Scott Calvin?" Jill swung around, trying to understand her predicament. "Am I under arrest?"

The officer snickered. "Know the sheriff, do you? Figures."

"Yes…I mean, no. Not like that. I've never been arrested. That's not how I know him. I live here." Footsteps hurried across the front porch. *How many of them are there? Did they send the whole SWAT team after me? Was Bradley behind this?*

Garrett ran into the room. "Thank God. Jill. I thought that was your voice. Are you OK?"

"What are you doing here? What's going on?" Jill asked.

"Where's your car, and who does that old clunker belong to?"

"Mr. Malloy, please step aside. We asked you to stay outside." The officer gestured him back toward the door.

Garrett hesitated to step back, and the officer gestured him out of the room again as he turned his attention back to Jill.

"Ma'am, is that your car out front?"

Cah? "Car? Oh." *With that Northern accent, he sure isn't from around here.* "No…Yes…"

"Which is it?" the deputy ordered.

"Well, no. The car isn't mine, but I'm driving it."

"Ma'am, who is the car registered to?"

She tried to push her bangs from her face with her shoulder. "I don't know. Melanie and Vernon Hines, or their daughter Lindy, maybe."

The officer eyed her suspiciously. "Anything we should know about in the vehicle, ma'am?"

She shook her head.

"Firearms? Drugs?"

"No, of course not," she said. "Garrett. Help me!"

"How much have you had to drink? You seem kind of woozy there." The deputy clicked his flashlight and danced it back and forth in front of her eyes.

"I was sleeping." *When did the county hire this yahoo?*

He stepped back toward the door to consult with his partner, who had just finished conducting his search of the vehicle. They whispered back and forth, looking serious.

Garrett stepped toward the men again. "Look. I made a mistake. I saw the strange car with out-of-state tags and I freaked. I thought Jill was in trouble, but she's right here. My mistake."

"You? You called the cops on me?" Jill shouted across the room. "Why?"

"I didn't know it was you." Garrett's eyes met hers.

"Well, thanks a lot. I love getting handcuffed and nearly thrown in jail. That's a lot of help. You don't think my week has been bad enough already?"

"I'm sorry. I didn't know they were going to send Dirty Harry." Garrett raised a hand toward the officer, who shot him a less-than-pleased look. "No offense."

"None taken." The officer walked over to Jill and uncuffed her. "Looks like everything is in order, Mrs. Clemmons."

"Miss," Jill corrected him and withdrew her hands. "And what's your name? I take it you're new around here."

He dipped his hat. "Dan Taylor. That's Deputy Dan Taylor. I'm from Boston, just took the job down here a few months ago."

"Oh" was all she could say without launching into a speech about what constituted appropriate behavior in these parts, even for law enforcement officers. She couldn't believe Scott would hire someone like him.

"*Miss* Clemmons, we'll be moving on now," the deputy said, turning on his heel and heading back to his cruiser.

"Thanks," she said halfheartedly.

"I guess my imagination got the best of me," Garrett explained. "You can't know how worried I was. If anything—"

"It's OK," she answered, rubbing her wrists.

"Where's Clyde, and where did you get the beater?" Garrett asked.

"It's a long story. I need coffee." She headed to the kitchen, with Garrett following close behind.

Jill filled a paper filter with coffee grounds and started the coffee.

Garrett sat at the table. "I just got back in town. I had a feeling you were in trouble or something was wrong. I decided to check on you. When I saw the strange car, I panicked. It took everything I had not to come in here myself. I wish I had now. I'm so sorry. I didn't mean to create this fiasco."

"If I weren't so furious, I'd be laughing. What a way to wake up." She ran her hand through her bangs. "But it's OK. Really. I know you were trying to help. But this just proves that I don't need your help."

"How did you happen to trade your new BMW for an old Mustang since yesterday afternoon?"

"I went to Savannah last night, and let's just leave it at it's a long story. I had to borrow my girlfriend's daughter's car to get back."

"OK. Where's Clyde?"

"In the kennel. I didn't know how long I'd be gone."

"You could've let me know you were going somewhere," Garrett said. "I'd have been happy to take care of Clyde for you."

"It was last minute and you were out of town." She didn't feel like dwelling on that. "Hey, Garrett, can I ask you something?"

"Are you changing the subject?"

"You noticed." She cast him a sideways glance.

"Yeah, I did. What do you want to know?"

"Remember that night when you accused me—"

"I didn't accuse you." His tone was cool.

"—when I thought you were accusing me of sleeping with Bradley."

"Yeah. I remember that night…every night." His expression turned dark.

"Why did you ask me about that?" she half whispered.

"You know why."

"Tell me again," she pleaded, her eyes begging him.

"Because someone told me you were and I didn't believe them."

"You never told me who told you that."

"Bradley."

I should have known. She shook her head. "I was so hurt. I'd always been faithful to you. You were my whole life."

"That's why I didn't believe it."

Jill took a deep breath and braced herself. *Do I even want to ask this?* "What about the blonde?"

"I've always been faithful to you, too," he answered, without hesitation.

"The pictures?"

Garrett shrugged. "I don't know. I swear I don't. I've tried to think of a logical explanation. I can't come up with one that doesn't make Bradley a liar or manipulator." He shifted, his voice becoming softer. "Why would I lie now? I've already lost you."

She watched him for any sign of guilt. No mouth shrugs. No twitching. "There were pictures. Hard to dispute that."

"I would never hurt you."

"I used to believe that," she said. "But you did."

"You know what bothers me most? You believed a guy you'd just met over me, who you've known your whole life."

She tilted her head and pursed her lips as she considered. "I guess I expected more from you." Everything had made perfect sense at the time. Not so much now. "It still hurts, even after all this time."

"I don't know how to convince you. I just pray someday you'll at least forgive me, even if you can't believe me."

Jill ran her hand through her hair. "I hadn't planned to go to Savannah today. It just suddenly all got clear for me, and I didn't want you to weigh in on that decision. It needed to be all mine."

"What decision?"

"I broke it off with Bradley. I couldn't do that to him."

"Do what?"

"I'm not in love with him. I know the other night was innocent, but being in your arms…It was the best I've felt in a long time."

"Oh, Jill," he whispered, and stepped in to hold her. "Me too." He stroked her hair. "When I saw that strange car here, it scared the hell out of me. I don't know what I'd do if anything had happened to you."

"Garrett, slow down," Jill said. "I'm not saying we're getting back together. Breaking off with Bradley is a separate issue altogether."

"I hear ya. How did Bradley take the news? Was he surprised?"

I was more surprised than he was. "That's a story I think I'll leave where it is. In the past."

Garrett pulled her into his arms.

She took a step back, putting a little space between them. "I'm serious. Don't jump to any conclusions. This is not all resolved and happily ever after and all that stuff. I might be a romantic, but I'm not fool enough to make the same mistake twice."

"Let's hope not," Garrett said.

She knew what he meant was not what she meant, but that was for her to sort out and no one was going to rush her into that.

"Why don't you come with me today?" Garrett suggested. "It's going to be a scorcher. I need to make a run into Richmond to pick up supplies for one of the building sites."

"I think I need a little alone time."

He looked disappointed, and that tugged at her heart a little, but at the same time, she wasn't going to play to his agenda. She stood her ground.

"I understand, but don't you go running off again without telling me."

"I'm a big girl. I can make adult decisions all by myself."

"I didn't mean it that way. Just until we get all the break-in stuff resolved, OK?"

She raised her fingers. "Scout's honor."

"I'll pick up Clyde and bring him back before I head out this morning. I don't want you here alone."

"Thanks."

"It's the least I could do after getting you handcuffed and almost tossed in the slammer."

"Truly. Pearl would roll over in her grave if I got arrested."

"Sorry about that. I've got to go." He headed out the door. "I'll see you at the other end of the day."

Jill followed behind him. Once the door clicked closed, she went and knelt on the couch with the window sheer pulled to the right.

He gave her a nod as he drove by.

She waved. Her eyes and nose tickled. Happy tears. What a bizarre chain of events. She turned and plopped back onto the couch, resting her head on the arm. She stared at the swirled plaster ceiling, counting circles as she had so many times as a young girl. She prayed to God and pleaded for Pearl, too, to help her untangle this complex situation. She used to have such a simple life. No worries, no hurries.

Suddenly, the adrenaline rush she'd been running on since the sheriff's department burst and took a dive. She headed to the kitchen for coffee. After finishing one cup and pouring the next, she heard the door of the pickup slam. Clyde's heavy paws stomped up the front porch to the house. *Clomp, clomp, clomp.* There was nothing quiet or sneaky about him. He'd starve if he had to hunt for food.

She stared out the window long after he'd driven out of view. Inside, she wished he'd turned around and come back in for just one quick minute.

Chapter Nineteen

Jill picked up the phone and called Carolanne. “You got a few minutes?”

“For you, always. What’s up?”

“I’m going to need your help. I broke up with Bradley, and now I’m not sure how to get all my stuff back, and he said my car—the one I traded Ol’ Red in on—is in his name. He’s pissed, and I’m not sure how this is going to all play out.”

“Don’t you worry about a thing. I’ll pull some paperwork together, and we’ll get a restraining order on him, just in case he decides to get silly on you.”

“A restraining order? I don’t think that’s necessary.”

“Better safe than sorry. Trust me.”

A few minutes later, Carolanne had Jill feeling calmer about things. Talking to her always did make her feel better.

With the worries about Bradley tucked safely in Carolanne’s court, Jill’s thoughts turned to Garrett. They didn’t *have* to cohabitate, although Pearl would just simply love that. Jill laughed as she remembered the video and Pearl’s twinkling eyes when she said, “I encourage you.” Garrett could sleep in the house. Even with no bed, there were options aside from sharing a bed. The couch, even bring the camping stuff over or something. Or should she go back to her original plan for them to lead separate, if linked, lives and learn how to become trusted friends again?

She thought the latter was the right thing to do, but it wasn't what she *wanted* to do. Technically, she was on the rebound from her rebound, had suffered the loss of a close family member, and was moving. Three of the most stressful situations a person could go through. Now was not the time to be making lifelong decisions.

Carolanne had been no help at all. Even when Jill had shared all the sordid details of happening upon Bradley and Annie, she'd busted up laughing. Then of course she steered the conversation right back to Garrett. If Jill didn't know better, she'd swear Pearl had Carolanne on retainer to market Garrett.

Jill spent all day rehearsing the speech she planned to give to Garrett—talking to Clyde, to the mirror, and to the daisies as she weeded the garden. She even tried the speech out on her blow-dryer as she worked her hair into submission before he got home—er, back. She practiced telling him he needed to trust that she would call if she needed help and that he needed to go back to sleeping at his house—all night long.

She thought she was ready until she saw Garrett climb out of his truck. He looked so good in a blue-and-white-striped short-sleeve shirt tucked into Wranglers. He headed toward the house with a Cracker Barrel bag in hand. She felt the old tingle as she watched him walk.

"What's in that bag?" Jill leaned nonchalantly on the doorjamb.

He lifted the bag casually. "Crackers?"

"I don't think so."

"Hmmm?" He peered down into the large brown bag and exaggerated a big whiff. "It smells like…Oh yes, it must be hash brown casserole."

"Man, you play dirty," she said. "You know that's my favorite."

"Yep. And there are a bunch of Cracker Barrels off of I-95 between Richmond and here."

She reached for the bag. "What else do you have in there?"

He snagged it from her reach. "Mmm. I think it's"—he dove his head back in again—"oh yeah, country fried steak."

She feigned wooziness and leaned against the porch column. "Oh no." Whose side were God and Pearl on? They were arming Garrett with every possible type of ammo to take her down, even her favorite food.

He wrapped a friendly arm around her waist and tugged her toward the door. "Dinner's on me."

"Careful. I could get used to this."

He spread the plastic dishes across the dining room table. Jill poured sweet tea into aluminum tumblers and grabbed the napkins, forks, and knives. She could smell the peppery gravy from across the room.

Garrett took a chair and patted the one next to him. "Let's dig in. I'm starved."

She skipped the invitation and took the seat across from him instead.

They ate while Garrett recapped his trip to Richmond. Jill kept trying to find the right moment to interject the speech she'd practiced all day.

After the meal, Garrett scooched his chair back from the table and held his plate to the side for Clyde to clean up. The dog made quick work of it. "Well, I guess I'd better get home and shower."

She jumped at the opening. "And then tuck yourself in your bed for the night."

"You trying to tell me what to do, lady?"

"I can't stand you sleeping out in the truck. It keeps me from getting any rest at all."

He moved behind her chair and pressed his hands on her shoulders. He gripped her muscles and squeezed gently. "So what are we going to do? I can't sleep if I'm not here, and you can't sleep if I am. You have choices. You could go stay with Milly for a while, or I'm sure the Markham's would put you up."

"I can't spend the money on a room at the Markham's. I think I'm probably out of a job now, you know." She raised and dropped her shoulders, then leaned her head back and looked up at him. "And Milly's house is so hot it's like sleeping in a greenhouse. Are there other options?"

He leaned forward and pressed his mouth over hers. The kiss was slow and deep. The legs of the chair screeched against the hardwood floors as he scooted her back from the table.

She grabbed the edge of the seat to keep her balance.

Garrett squatted in front of her. "Jill. This two-step we're doing is driving me crazy. I know you've been through a heck of an emotional week, and the timing probably couldn't be worse, but…"

She looked toward Clyde—anything to not have to face this subject.

He tipped her chin back to face him, his eyes set on hers.

"What?" she said, barely above a whisper.

"Let me stay here. No pressure. You set the pace. I'll sleep on the couch." Garrett pushed his hat back on his head a little. "How can I regain your trust if you never give me the chance?"

"You'll get a chance. Later. After I clean up all this stuff of Pearl's. After I figure out what my future looks like. If it's meant to be, you'll be here."

"Why can't I be here while you do all that. I'm pretty handy. Or go to Milly's and we can avoid this whole debate."

"You don't play fair."

"I know."

She closed her eyes and sat quiet for a long moment. Then she took his hands into hers. "You can stay."

As he started to respond, she kissed him quickly on the lips.

He smiled and grabbed his hat. "I'm going to run home and grab a change of clothes before you change your mind. I'll be back in a shot."

"OK." The practice all afternoon had been a complete waste of time and energy. She'd crumbled like toast. *I better hope this decision is the right one.* It wasn't like she'd agreed to forgive him or spend the rest of her life with him. It was purely from a safety and convenience perspective. She looked heavenward and wondered just whom she was trying to convince with all that.

Pearl, this was your doing, wasn't it?

Jill went to the linen closet. The crisp line-dried sheets smelled faintly of bleach and lavender. She changed the linens on the bed for Garrett and then made up the couch for herself. It sure would have been nice if Pearl had kept the bedroom set that had been in Jill's room growing up, but she was sure the family that Pearl had given it to probably was far more in need than Pearl needed a guest bed.

Garrett knocked and came in the front door as she stood in front of the dresser, trying to decide what to sleep in. The silky pajamas she'd bought the other day would be a little too suggestive for a sleepover. She opted for the bottoms of one set with an oversized T-shirt she found in the bottom of one of the drawers. He couldn't confuse this outfit with sexy lingerie. Proud of her decision, she headed to the shower. When she came back into the living room, Garrett was sitting in front of the television in Pearl's favorite chair, petting Clyde.

She stretched out across the couch and caught herself falling asleep during the eleven o'clock news. She snuggled against the pillow, feeling safe.

❖

When Jill woke up, her body ached. She sat up, rubbing her lower back and stretching to work out the kinks. She'd slept hard and was thankful for it, but there wasn't anything soft or comfortable about this couch. It had never bothered her when she'd slept on it as a teenager. The highfalutin living and fancy hotels of the last year must've spoiled her.

Garrett stepped out of the kitchen with a coffee cup in his hand. "I thought I heard you stirring in here." He plopped down on the couch and pushed one of the steaming mugs her way.

"Mmm, smells good. I slept hard."

"No one said you had to sleep out here."

"We already discussed that. You're too long."

"You could sleep in the bed with me. I don't bite."

She rolled her eyes and took another sip, feeling too grumpy to respond.

❖ Chapter Twenty ❖

Garrett sat on the couch next to Jill. "What are your plans today?"

"Don't have any."

"Good. Get out of those pajamas."

She eyed him suspiciously. "Excuse me?"

"Go get dressed. I want to take you somewhere."

She lifted a brow. "I just got up. You must've gotten up at the crack of dawn."

"I've been up a while. Are you going to argue with me about everything?"

"Well, that depends."

"On what?" he asked.

"I need to take Lindy's car up to Virginia Tech tomorrow. If I go with you today, will you follow me up there tomorrow and bring me back?"

"Absolutely."

Pleased with the deal, she gulped the last of the coffee and handed him the mug. "Cool. Give me five minutes."

"I'll feed Clyde and meet you in the truck."

When she went back to Pearl's bedroom to get dressed, she noticed that Garrett had made a first run on the repair of the ceiling. That man never wasted a minute of a single day. She put on a purple tank top and tucked it into khaki shorts. A quick twist in the mirror and she was ready. By the time she climbed into Garrett's truck, he was already behind the wheel with the air on.

Without a word between them, he headed toward town.

"Where are we going?"

"You'll see." He veered his truck along the curb and parallel-parked in front of Spratt's Market.

"You're taking me grocery shopping? You're a fun date." She went for the door handle, but he stopped her.

"This isn't the final destination, smarty-pants. You wait here. I'll be right back."

He left the truck running while he ducked through the blue door of Spratt's Market. When he came out, he had a tall brown grocery bag in his arms. He opened the back door of the truck and placed it behind his seat.

Jill couldn't see over the seat into the bag. "What are you up to?"

"When did you become such a worrywart? Relax and enjoy the ride."

She leaned back in the seat and let out a huff. He was right; she was acting uptight. Fixing a stare on the puffy clouds, she tried to relax as he pulled the truck back on the road.

Garrett turned down Horseshoe Run Road. The hairs on her arms prickled.

She glanced in his direction. He must have read the terror in her expression, because he reached across and patted her leg.

"I can't do this." She shook her head. "I just can't…yet." Jill pulled her hand to cover her nose and mouth and stared out the window. Little colors began to dance in her line of sight as she realized she was holding her breath.

"It's going to be OK." He slowed the truck near the burial site in the church cemetery, then went around to her door and opened it, offering her his hand.

She hesitated, then put her hand in his and climbed down. “I’m not ready.”

“I’m here. Come on.” He reached past her, scrounged around in the big bag, and lifted out a huge bouquet of daisies.

“They’re beautiful.”

“Her favorite.” He took Jill’s hand and led her into the grass.

They walked slowly toward the spot where Pearl had been buried. One day soon a beautiful marble headstone would mark this spot, but for now, a cement urn served as a temporary marker. CLEMMONS, printed in straight block letters, marked the metal plate affixed to the urn.

Garrett and Jill knelt at the side of the still freshly turned ground. A few of the larger arrangements from the funeral still held a place of honor. Garrett picked a bright-yellow daisy out of the bouquet, tucked it behind Jill’s ear, then arranged the rest in the cement urn, fussing with them until they scattered just right.

“Thank you,” she said as he took a knee beside her.

They held hands quietly for a long time. There was no rush and nothing more important than being right here, right now. A sense of peace washed over her, like Pearl was near. Jill swept away the tears with her free hand and clung to Garrett’s with the other.

“The day of the funeral, I didn’t notice any other markers around here.” A single narrow monument spiked from the ground just to the left of them. Only initials. No dates. “At least she won’t be alone.”

Garrett wrapped his arms around her. “She’s not alone. You know that.”

Jill smiled, her lips quivering. “She’s probably giving God advice right now.” She hugged her arms around herself.

Garrett tucked her hair behind her ear. “Ready to go?”

“Yes,” she whispered as she stood. He took her hand and led her back to the truck. Jill stared out the window toward the burial site as Garrett eased the pickup off the church property and back onto the main road.

"You're so thoughtful. Thank you for doing that with me." *He never misses a beat.*

He took a left at the end of Riverkeeper Road.

"Where are we going now?" she asked.

"You didn't think that's all I had planned, did ya?"

"Yes. Actually, I did. What have I gotten myself into?"

They spent the whole day on the lake and then came home for Jill to cook the huge bass that Garrett caught. It was their old deal. Whoever caught the biggest fish didn't have to gut, clean, or cook. Garrett wrapped his tan arms around her from behind, gently squeezing her midsection. "I had fun today," he whispered into her ear.

She leaned to one side and raised the large chopping knife in her hand. "Don't you know you should never mess with a lady while she's armed and dangerous?"

He dropped a kiss in the crook of her neck that made her squirm. "You're worth the risk. Dinner smells delicious. Of course, it *is* my winning fish that smells so good."

"Quit it." She picked up the tongs and snapped them his way.

"See this, Clyde. She's after my tummy now. We'll never leave if she treats us like this."

Jill stacked plates in his arms and shooed him off to set the table so she could serve dinner. Garrett ate every last bit and took continued delight in his win. Of course, her fish story was getting better and better with every bite, until she'd gotten to the point of trying to land Jaws with her small rod and reel. Garrett poignantly reminded her they were freshwater fishing and in waist-deep water, at that. *Details.*

He insisted on doing the dishes since she'd done the dirty work of gutting the fish, which was fine with her. Cleaning up was her least favorite part of cooking, anyway.

Jill went into the living room and turned on the television while Garrett finished cleaning the kitchen. She tucked her feet under her on the couch and rubbed Clyde's ears. He panted, and she could have sworn Clyde's lips formed a grin.

"Hey, can I wrap up this mess in this newspaper that's on the table?"

"No. I haven't read that yet. In fact, maybe I'll do that while you clean up." She took some old brown paper bags from the pantry and traded Garrett for the Savannah paper.

She went back in the living room and started reading the outdated news.

"Thanks. That was a great meal." Garrett rubbed his stomach as he leaned against the doorway.

"You're welcome," she answered, distracted.

"Something wrong?" he asked as he wiped his hands on a dish towel and leaned in the doorway.

"There's an article about the Kase Foundation fund-raiser, but they reported the foundation numbers wrong again. It's happened before. I'll get Josh to have them print a correction." She stretched and tossed the paper on the coffee table.

Chapter Twenty-One

The next morning, the ninety-degree highway breeze whipped Jill's ponytail against her face during the hot and sticky drive. By the time they got to Blacksburg, her hair had curled in a hundred different directions. Jill pulled the Mustang to the curb in front of the bookstore.

"Hi." Lindy bounced off the curb and came to the side of the car.

Jill peeled herself out, her sweaty legs sticking to the vinyl seat. "Hey, girl."

Lindy looked disgusted. "I was going to give you a hug, but you're kind of sweaty."

"You've got to get that air fixed. How do you stand it?"

"Oh man. I guess Mom should have told you. You have to turn it to heat for the AC to work. It's, like, all backward," Lindy explained.

"You're kidding me."

Garrett stepped up behind Jill, laughing. "Nice hair."

"Shut up." Jill swatted him and turned her attention back to Lindy. "This is my...This is Garrett Malloy."

Lindy smiled a perfect over-bleached smile and extended her hand. "Nice to meet you."

"I really appreciate using your car," Jill said. "Even without the air. I filled the tank for you."

"Oh, you're welcome. It actually saved me a trip home to get it. This is perfect. Oh yeah, Mom sent this for you." Lindy handed Jill an envelope. "Some news clipping or something. She didn't have your address."

"Thanks. Can we buy you lunch?"

Lindy bit her lip and wrinkled her nose. "Do you mind if we don't? I sorta have other plans."

"I'm suddenly feeling very old," Jill said to Garrett.

"No. I didn't mean that—"

"Too late now. You already hurt my feelings."

"Mine too," Garrett said with a smile. "I used to be a hot guy on this campus."

Jill laughed. "He might be hurt, but I'm fine. Garrett, why don't you grab us a table for two? I'll be right there."

"Sounds good. Nice meeting you, Lindy."

Lindy's eyes followed Garrett until he crossed through the door of the restaurant. "Oh…my…God. He is, like, so hot," Lindy squealed.

"He's a friend."

Lindy rolled her eyes. "Yeah. Right. Whatever."

"You sure you won't have lunch? It's my treat."

"No, thanks. I gotta run." Lindy grabbed the troll keychain from Jill's outstretched palm and jumped in the driver seat and gunned the engine. "See"—she twisted the knob and pointed the air vent toward the driver's window—"cool air."

Jill reached inside. Sure enough, cool air poured from the vents.

Lindy put the window up and sped off.

Jill waved as she headed to join Garrett. "Can you believe that car had air-conditioning? I sacrificed a perfectly good hair day for nothing."

"You look adorable," Garrett said. "I already ordered."

She slid into the seat, wondering if Garrett had forgotten even one fact about her over the past year. Then she wondered if Pearl had ever forgotten anything about John Carlo.

The waitress walked up and placed the heaping plates in front of them.

Jill took a bite of her taco. Cilantro sauce dripped down the side of her pinky. "Man, that's good." She licked the sauce from her hand. "Lindy thought you were hot."

"I do still have it with the college girls, huh?"

"Guess so, old fart."

"What about you?"

"I don't think she thought I was hot," Jill teased, trying to hold back a smile.

"Funny. You're just not going to give me a break today, are you?"

"Have I ever?" she teased, taking a long sip from her second tall glass of ice water. "Thought that's what you loved about me."

"That and about a hundred other things."

Thankful her mouth was full, she didn't respond. She wiped her hands and ran a finger under the fold of the envelope from Melanie. Inside, she found a short note from Melanie asking her to give her a call and reminding her to stay in touch, three articles about the success of the foundation event, and one not-so-nice article about Bradley and some supposedly dodgy business deals.

"Melanie sent these to me through Lindy. She didn't have my Adams Grove address." Jill scanned the articles, scowling.

"What's wrong?" Garrett asked.

"This article. It has a corrected total from the event I told you about, and it's even farther off the true total than the other one. About a hundred thousand off, in fact."

"Let me see." He reached for the articles and looked them over. "Impressive. Nice work, Jill."

"Thanks. I just wish they'd gotten the numbers right. All three of these articles state a different amount. Great. That looks bad." She stuffed the newspaper clippings back into the envelope. "I'll have to call Josh. He's my right hand on the money stuff. I wonder if he's heard anything about the other article."

"What other article?"

"Some of the investments folks made with Bradley haven't panned out. They're questioning Bradley's track record and planning to look more closely at those deals."

"Told you Kase was bad news." Garrett slid the envelope to his side of the table and pulled out the articles.

Jill leaned back in her chair. "I just pray they don't drag the Kase Foundation through the mud. That could really mess up all the groundwork I laid over the past year to bring in funds. I'd hate to see those kids suffer just because someone was unhappy with the way an investment played out. I mean, none of them are failureproof."

"That's true. I hope the Kase Foundation is clean. People who do sketchy business are just that way."

She plucked the articles from Garrett. "It's just speculation. I'm sure things will get straightened out." *I hope.*

After lunch, they checked out the new shops along the strip. Blacksburg was still a bustling college town. They couldn't help but get swept back to when they had been a part of that buzz, even if the area had undergone a major facelift since their days there.

Feeling nostalgic, Jill was quiet the whole ride back to Adams Grove. She had no idea why she felt so relaxed, under the circumstances. She didn't have a car, and she'd just caught her boyfriend cheating on her—live and in color on an eight-foot screen. If Pearl hadn't left her the house, she wouldn't even have a place to live. *At least I'm not homeless.* She should feel like a shook-up mess, completely out of options, but she didn't. Maybe she was too tired to feel anything, or maybe the day trip had been just what she needed. She settled back in the seat and nodded off to the hum of the truck and the overzealous banter of the AM sports radio show that Garrett listened to.

The rumble under the truck tires changed. Jill recognized the familiar sound of the crunch of shell, sand, and gravel at Pearl's. She stretched and opened her eyes.

"Hey, sleepyhead."

"I was, wasn't I?"

"I could barely hear my radio show over the snoring."

She slapped him playfully. "I do not snore."

"How would you know?"

"I'd know. Quit picking on me." Jill hoped she didn't snore. How awful would that be? "I needed the rest since I'm back on the couch tonight."

"Well. Since we're on a truce here, you should sleep in the bed." He lifted a finger and added, "No hanky-panky, I promise."

"You'd promised to love me and always be faithful. See where that got me?" She was only half joking, but the look on Garrett's face was full-on hurt.

"You're never going to believe me, are you?"

"I'm sorry. That wasn't fair. I guess I'm still hurt by it more than I thought."

"Jill, I promise you, I will never hurt you. You're making me pay penance for something I didn't do. I don't know what it's going to take to make you believe that I didn't. Hell, if I just say I did, would it be easier to forgive me? If so, that's what I'll do. At this point, I'm just about out of ideas."

"I'm trying. I swear I am."

"Then come on. Let's just call it a night." He took her hand and they walked inside without another word between them.

❖

Jill slipped out of bed at sunrise and eased the door shut quietly behind her to let Garrett sleep in. Her relationship with him was getting more complicated instead of easier. Part of it felt so right. But maybe it wasn't. Did she really want to make another mistake? The romantic in her juggled the options and, instead of resolving the issue at hand, drifted right back to what was most romantic of all—Pearl and John Carlo.

She let Clyde out, then poured a cup of coffee before going back to the attic to take a look at the last box of letters. Those letters had been on her mind all weekend.

The attic floor creaked under her socked feet, and she hoped the noise wouldn't wake Garrett. She made her way over to the boxes of letters and carried the last box to the corner of the room. After sitting on the floor, she became swept away to another time as she read letter after letter between Pearl and John Carlo Pacini.

He'd been a treasure hunter and lived his life chasing dreams. Her dad had been the same way. Funny that even though they'd never met—that she knew of—they had that same sense of adventure. It must have been something they were born with.

Not long after they'd married in a small town up north, John Carlo had gotten tangled in a scandal that had put him and Pearl in danger. Just weeks later, Pearl had realized she was pregnant. The stakes had become even higher with a child on the way. John Carlo had left in order to keep Pearl safe, and she'd moved back to Adams Grove. *I wonder if that's why she kept her maiden name?*

Their story was better than any romance novel Jill had ever read. Two completely committed hearts and souls torn apart by fate. A tear slid down her cheek.

Though he referred to it often, the scandal itself wasn't clear. Of course, by today's standards, it might not have even been a scandal. Times were different back then.

Pearl and John Carlo had shared a common language. Not so unlike she and Garrett. Familiar sayings popped up again and again. John Carlo may have been an adventurer, a treasure hunter, but his letters proved he had a poetic soul.

> *Honesty, trust, and patience will outlast all rivals.*
>
> *The* key *to happiness is in the* foundation *we build. Nothing will break us. Like a willow, our love will lean and bend. Our love,* our treasure*—today and enough forever—will never end.*

Jill found each letter to be as urgent and honest as the next. After she read the last letter, an odd twinge of disappointment came over her. She didn't want the love story to come to an end. She placed the letters back in the box, then noticed a piece of tissue paper lining the bottom of the box. She lifted the delicate tissue paper. A single piece of yellow legal paper, folded in half lengthwise, lay in the bottom. Nothing else in the boxes had appeared to be touched in years, but this piece of paper was relatively new.

Her hand shook as she unfolded it. The writing was different from that in the letters, and jagged. *My dearest Jill and Garrett,* the note began.

Jill dragged in a deep breath. This note was for her. She clutched the paper to her heart at the realization. She closed her eyes. It was almost too hard to move on.

Her fingertips trembled. She laid the paper on the floor to steady it so she could read.

> *My dearest Jill and Garrett,*
>
> *You've found the one treasure, the one legacy, I have to share.*
>
> *I hope you are together as you read this, and you have finally acknowledged what I knew you two had the first time I saw you exchange a sideways glance and giggle.*
>
> *I couldn't be more proud of you, Jill. I hope the detours you have made in your life have made you realize the beauty and*

honesty in the man that loves you with all his heart, Garrett Malloy. He is a good man. Don't ever doubt that.

You are good people, God's people, and I am proud to have been part of your lives. Thank you both for the precious memories you shared with me and the meaning you gave this old widow's life.

I, too, encountered difficult learning experiences in life. They all add up to who we ultimately become. My dear husband, John Carlo, meant more than my own life to me. When he happened into the wrong circle and I was with child, we couldn't honor the promises we made in marriage for fear of retaliation. He left me this. I've held it secret, and treasured it my whole life. I hope it brings you the wealth to follow your dreams and the faith to trust each other forever. My nickname, Pearl, came from my dear John Carlo.

Let the world be your oyster and these pearls help make life an easy path.

All my love,

Pearl

"Are you in the attic again?" Garrett called up the stairs.

His voice startled her.

"Yes. Come here. Hurry." She flipped the paper back and forth and reread the note.

His footsteps pounded the steps. "Are you OK?"

She looked up. He had a horrified look on his face. "Yes. I'm fine. Sorry. I found a note from Pearl to us."

"Don't scare me like that."

"I said I was sorry." She handed him the letter. "See if you can figure this out. I don't understand it. Maybe you will."

She watched him as he read it.

He shrugged. "I told you we should be together. This proves it."

She snatched the note back from him. "Not that. The treasure."

"What do you think she means by that?"

"The property? We didn't know how big it was."

"Maybe." Jill flipped the paper again looking for something that wasn't there. "I don't think that's what it means, though." She lifted the tissue paper out of the bottom of the box where she'd found the note and turned the box upside down. Something hit the floor with a clang, and a small piece of paper fluttered after it.

"A key?"

"An old key," she said, picking it up and twisting it in the air.

He stooped to pick up the slip of paper and scanned it as he stood over her. "It's a news clipping from nineteen forty-four. Listen to this." He squatted next to her and read it out loud.

An American man accused of receiving a priceless collection of pearls has fled Australia. John Carlo Pacini, well-known pearl diver and treasure hunter, is charged with receiving the gems after they had been stolen from a remote pearl farm. The pearls disappeared following a dispute concerning ownership of the collection between the farm and Pacini. The theft from the company, Motu Poe Elite Pearls, has been described as the biggest pearl heist in history. Pacini fled the country before sentencing. The pearls have not been recovered.

Jill rubbed the key between her fingers, then handed it to Garrett.

"You thinking what I'm thinking?"

"That he was a thief?" Jill said.

"No, that we know where they might be!"

"Pearl's safe?" Jill squealed. "It's exciting. This treasure hunting thing must be in my blood, too. Come on." She sprang to her feet and grabbed his belt loop, nearly dragging him to the attic entry.

He tugged the string for the light as she rushed him toward the safe.

She grabbed his bicep and snuggled up to him. "Open it. Quick. What do you think it is?"

He moved his chin toward hers, teasing, "How bad do you want it?"

She licked her lips in anticipation. "Badly."

"Mmm," he groaned. He took a pause, looking into her eyes. He shook his head and smiled. *I'm so glad you haven't changed.*

She leaned closer to the safe, almost nuzzling his shoulder. "Now open that doggone safe before I die of excitement. Then you'll really miss me."

He worked the key at the lock, but it didn't fit.

"Quit playing, Garrett. Open it."

"It doesn't fit."

"It has to. Are you kidding?"

"No. It doesn't fit." Garrett jiggled the key.

"Give it here. Let me try," she said.

Garrett handed her the key, and she tried to work it in the lock. "It doesn't fit," she said, disappointed.

"Isn't that what I just said?" He put his hands on his hips.

She tossed the key back to him.

He caught the unusual key midair and shoved it in his pocket.

"Can you get the safe open without a key?"

"I don't think so. It's not like a filing cabinet. This thing is heavy duty, probably even fireproof." He tipped the safe over. "No key taped underneath, either."

"I don't remember seeing any keys in her desk when I cleaned up that mess after the break-in," Jill said.

Garrett stood. "I remember a bunch of keys just inside the pantry, next to the panel box."

"Get 'em," she squealed, perking up and nearly pushing him down the stairs in the excitement. Garrett seemed as curious as she was about what was in the safe.

He ran downstairs, and Jill could hear him jingle all the way back upstairs. He held up the keys as he went to her side. "There are only a couple that look small enough to fit."

"Cool. I'm feeling lucky." She rubbed her hands together and scooched closer to the safe.

The first key slid right into the lock.

Jill clapped frantically as he twisted it and the lock clicked.

He opened the door. "Bingo."

"What's inside?"

"I'm looking. Not much. A few papers." Garrett handed the papers to Jill.

"This one looks like their marriage license." Jill glanced over the yellowed document, then dropped it into her lap. "I still can't believe she never told us. I wonder if my father ever knew."

"Probably not, if she never told you."

"I guess I'll never know if he became obsessed with treasure hunting because of his father or that they just shared that instinct. Unanswered questions." Next in the stack was a photo. "Look." Jill passed the photo his way. "It's so faded. Can you make it out?"

He held the crisp yellowed photo as if it were spun glass. "No"—Garrett shook his head—"I can't make it out, either. Look how brittle the paper is."

Jill glanced into the safe. "There's something else in there." She pointed toward the back corner of the safe.

Garrett reached inside until his fingers made contact with the contents. He lifted a small gray-velvet box the size of a ring box from the safe. The front of the box had an ornate pearl-button clasp.

"It's beautiful." Jill ran her fingers across the delicate velvet.

He held it toward her.

"No." She held her hands tightly to her chest. "You open it," she said, breathless, sitting on the closed trunk near the window.

He slid next to her and lifted the top open on its hinge. There, nestled in a deep-burgundy velvet tray, was the most exquisite ring. A perfect black, almost purple, pearl set deep in the middle of golden filigree that spun up and around the sides of the pearl, protecting the precious and unusual jewel. Small gems sparkled, maybe sapphires and diamonds, encrusting the entire rim of the filigree.

"It's magnificent." The ring sparkled even in the dim light.

"As beautiful as you." He took the ring from the box and lifted it to the light.

"Is there an inscription?"

He lifted the ring to the light, squinting at the inside of its band. "No." Garrett reached for her left hand.

She stiffened, realizing his intentions.

"Just try it," he said.

She took in a nervous breath.

He slid the ring onto her finger.

She raised her hand in front of her. "Breathtaking," she whispered.

"Perfect fit."

"It is." Jill began to take the ring off her finger, but Garrett stopped her.

"Just wear it. Pearl would want you to."

"Really?" Jill wrinkled her nose. "I don't know. What if something happens to it?"

"She wanted you to have it. This ring was meant to be worn."

"Do you think it was her wedding ring?" Jill fluttered her fingers, admiring the ring. It even made her short fingers look delicate.

"Yeah, and a secret all of these years. Time to let it be seen and enjoyed, don't you think?" Garrett asked, thoughtfully.

She held her hand to her heart, then reached for Garrett and hugged him close. "This is such a precious treasure."

He nodded in agreement. "Very special."

She wasn't sure if he meant her or the ring.

❖ Chapter Twenty-Two ❖

Jill spent the first hour of her morning sitting at the kitchen table searching through Pearl's recipe box, determined to find something to fix for Garrett that would be special enough to show him how she felt today.

Pearl's ring sparkled on her finger as she flipped through the recipe cards. Every time Jill saw the ring on her finger, it caused her to pause. Somehow wearing the ring felt like a direct connection to Pearl, and that had a comforting effect.

She came across a recipe that she thought would be perfect.

"Yes." She pulled the recipe out. Pearl's famous FryPan Meat Loaf was always one of Garrett's favorites. Homemade mashed potatoes, gravy, and the last few summer squash from the garden would definitely be a winner.

She scanned through the ingredients and steps, then picked up her ringing phone with a cheerful hello.

"I didn't expect you to sound so cheerful."

Her stomach lurched. Bradley was the last person she'd expected to hear from. "What do you want?"

"I want to know when you're coming home."

"You've got to be kidding."

"I made a mistake, Jill."

"You're telling me. The biggest mistake was that I didn't figure everything out sooner."

"Nothing like that ever happened before. I swear, baby doll. I regret hurting you. Please, you have to come back."

She had no intention of falling under his spell. The sound of his voice made her uneasy. "I don't *have* to do anything. All I want is what's rightfully mine. My clothes, car, and the wages you owe me."

"Your lawyer friend called me. You don't need a restraining order."

Jill was surprised at how fast Carolanne had moved. She knew that Bradley was going to be mad when he got served, but Carolanne had insisted she get the restraining order as a matter of record in case the breakup got ugly. Since Bradley held possession of everything she owned and her job, Jill had finally agreed. "Our relationship is over. It's a precaution. What does it matter to you?"

"Then we don't need a lawyer. You could have just called me."

"I'd rather not."

"We can work this out. And what about the foundation? I need you; the foundation needs you."

"About that. I got a copy of the newspaper article. How did the newspaper get the wrong numbers?"

"See, we need you. You can't just walk out on all that hard work. We're not done here. I am going to come and get you."

"I'll press charges if you do. Just leave me alone." She did hate to let down the foundation, but she'd completed her commitment. "You're ruining a perfectly good day for me. Is there anything else you want? If not, I'm hanging up."

"Don't hang up on me. Listen to me carefully. I have no intention of losing what I want to Malloy or anyone else. I said we're not done, and until I say we are, you will listen to what I have to say. Besides, I still own you nine to five."

"Then I quit."

"You can quit a job, but you can't quit me. So listen up."

Jill's breath caught. "Are you threatening me?"

"No." Bradley laughed and then there was a brief pause. "I don't think you'd care one bit if I threatened you."

"You're right. You won't bully me. I won't stand for it."

"I have no intention of it. You can tell Malloy to quit putting crazy thoughts in your head, or I'll fix it so he can't put crazy thoughts into anyone's head ever again."

Jill could only imagine how much madder he'd be if he knew Garrett had been spending the better part of the last week around the house. Thank goodness she hadn't gotten around to telling him about that before the night in Savannah.

"Leave us alone," she yelled into the phone. "Go play with Annie—she's more your type, anyway."

"Don't push me, Jill—"

Jill snapped her phone shut. She wasn't about to listen to his threats. Carolanne was right to encourage her to get the protection order. He was nuts.

She went to the back door and watched Clyde sniffing along the fence in excitement, probably after a bunny or a mouse, maybe even just a cricket. All was fair game, and in spite of his size, he was still very much a puppy.

She dialed Carolanne's cell. "Bradley's really ticked about the restraining order. He threatened to hurt Garrett if I don't come back to Savannah."

"I pushed a few of his buttons. That's why we have the restraining order, and I took the liberty of calling Scott Calvin to give him a heads up, too."

"Thanks, Carolanne. I can just imagine how mad he'd be if he knew how much time Garrett's been spending around here. He'd come completely unglued."

"Not your problem."

"Well, it will be my problem if he does anything crazy. Although, if there's one thing I know it's that he'd rather wear Armani than jailhouse orange, so the risk is probably low. But then again, there's a lot about him I don't know, like all that kinky sex stuff he's into. I'll never get that image out of my head."

"Enough about Kase, I want to hear more about you and Garrett. Are you finally getting everything all worked out? You know what? Hold that thought. I'm coming back down. You can tell me every little detail when I get there."

"Don't waste all your vacation time babysitting me."

"I'm not wasting anything. I want to be there. I'll be there tomorrow night. Like it or not."

"I like it."

"Good. I'll see you then," Carolanne said. "Besides, I could use some good home cooking."

"I know just the gal to do that." Jill smiled at the thought of having Carolanne around for a few days. She felt better already.

She spent the rest of the afternoon mixing, chopping, slicing, and then frying until Garrett came home.

"What smells so good?" Garrett called into the kitchen as soon as he pushed open the door.

Jill poked her head around the corner from the kitchen. "It's a surprise. Hope you're hungry."

"I'm awake, aren't I?" Garrett rubbed his stomach, following the smells toward the kitchen. The kitchen table was set for two. He peered over her shoulder as she worked her spatula in the hot grease of the electric skillet. "Please tell me that's FryPan Meat Loaf."

"You're right. It's FryPan Meat Loaf."

"I've died and gone to heaven, and you," he said, "are my angel."

Clyde lifted a paw to Jill's leg.

"And Clyde's angel, too, apparently."

"You two are easy as long as there is food around. Sit. It's almost ready."

She put Clyde out with his dinner, served up the meal, then sat across from Garrett.

This was exactly how she'd envisioned cooking for a man, and neither Garrett nor Clyde let her down. Garrett went back for seconds, and Clyde was thrilled when Garrett let him back inside to clean up the last fried tidbits and barbecue glaze from the plates.

Like any young boy, Clyde twisted away when Jill tried to clean his gravy-laden muzzle with the kitchen towel. "Come on, boy, cooperate."

Garrett pretended to pant with his hands up like paws. "Do me next."

"You're impossible." She swirled the dish towel and snapped it in his direction.

"Whoa"—he flinched back—"looks like you think you're still the towel-snapping champion of the county." He reached back and pulled the towel from the oven handle.

"Ohh-hhh, no you don't." She swirled her towel overhead and popped it toward him, nipping him on the elbow as he twisted away. She backed toward the kitchen door and then lunged forward. *Snap!* She tagged him right on the hip. "Take that, puddin' boy."

"Them's fightin' words, country girl." He snapped the towel toward her butt.

"Yow!" she squealed.

"Easy target," he snickered.

"Talk about fightin' words!" She snapped her towel toward him twice but didn't connect.

He chased her around the dining room table and into the living room.

"Good golly, you're whacko. OK, I give," she shouted, jumping to the floor. "Whew. We're too old for that kind of action."

"Speak for yourself, girl," he said, panting.

"Come on, we need to finish cleaning up the kitchen." She tried to catch her breath.

He held her close. "Let's just call it a night." He kissed her softly on the neck, and she relaxed against him.

"It's a night," she agreed. The adrenaline and spunky battle had burned off the edgy anxiety that had niggled constantly at her since she got the news about Pearl. "Oh, and before I fall asleep, Carolanne is going to come back for a few days. She'll be here tomorrow night."

The next morning, Jill had already cleaned the house and made a meat loaf sandwich for his lunch by the time Garrett got up and started reading the paper. With Carolanne on the way, he wondered when she was going to kick him out. He was kind of getting used to being around her every day, even if she was keeping a barrier up. *Maybe I can talk her into letting Carolanne stay at my place.* That wasn't going to happen. Not as long as she was scared he would hurt her again.

"I'm going to run to the store to get a few things. You OK if I use your truck?"

"Sure." Jill hadn't been gone ten minutes when Garrett heard the sound of a vehicle coming up the lane. Figuring she'd forgotten something, he headed for the door to meet her, but instead of Jill, it was Izzy getting out of the limo carrying a huge basket wrapped in colorful cellophane.

Garrett stepped out onto the porch. "Now, that's a delivery in style."

"Well, well, look who's here. Word around town is that y'all are getting back together. Must be true," Izzy said as she walked up to the house.

I sure hope so. "She wants to take it slow."

Izzy rolled her eyes. "We always say that. That's her head talkin', not her heart. Hang in there. She'll come around."

"Keep your fingers crossed for me." He could just barely see Izzy behind the huge basket.

"I will as soon as I can get to them. This thing is huge. How much fruit do they think one little girl can eat?" Izzy shoved the basket in his direction.

Garrett took it from her and she was down the steps before he could maneuver around the face full of cellophane. "This sucker is heavy. What is it? Full of coconuts?"

"They didn't say. Enjoy, and hang in there. The whole town has their fingers crossed for the two of you."

"Hey, should I tip you?" Garrett called out to her.

"Nope. I'm covered."

"Thanks, Izzy." Garrett carried the basket inside and set it on the dining room table. The cellophane crinkled as he slid it back to reveal apples in all colors, oranges, grapes, and bananas. He plucked one of the perfect red apples from the pile and, out of habit, rubbed it on his shirt. It didn't need shining. The apple was already so glossy that he could almost see his reflection in it. It was way too early in the season to be a locally grown apple. He bit into it, and Clyde ran up to Garrett looking for a handout.

Garrett tossed the half-eaten apple into the air. The intent was to tease Clyde, but the joke was on Garrett because the big dog jumped and caught the apple in midair, then ran off with it in his mouth, his tail wagging.

"Fine. There's plenty to go around." Garrett put the basket on the kitchen table. He grabbed a banana and a bunch of grapes and tucked them into the bag with the sandwich Jill had made for him.

They'd made great progress. The year apart had only made him more aware of how much he loved Jill and how real the dreams they'd made together could be. He wanted that future. Pearl had been his lifeline as he waited and prayed she'd come to the same conclusion. Now he was on his own, and he knew it'd be harder without Pearl here on his side. *I won't give up.* He plucked one grape off and tossed it in the air, catching it in his mouth. "I still got it."

Chapter Twenty-Three

Jill parked Garrett's truck in front of the house and started pulling bags out of the truck.

"What all did you get?" he asked her as he headed to the truck to help her carry them in.

"A little bit of this, a little bit of that, and a big bottle of Carolanne's favorite wine."

"Here, let me get that." He took the bags from Jill's arms and followed her into the house.

She stopped in front of the dining room table. "Lordy goodness, that's the biggest basket of fruit I've ever seen."

"I know, right? You could open your own fruit stand with that much fruit. I stole some of it to go with my sandwich."

She smiled. "You saw that, did you?"

"First thing I noticed when I came into the kitchen this morning. To be honest, it took all I had not to eat it for breakfast. I figured you wouldn't miss any of that fruit."

"Who is the basket from?" Jill pulled the colorful cellophane back, searching for a card.

"I didn't look." Garrett grabbed the lunch bag off the counter. "I'm going to get to the office." He flipped the keys in his hand. "Don't you and Carolanne have too much fun without me."

"I can't make that kind of promise." She finally located the card. "Hang on, I'll walk you out." Jill tucked the card in the back pocket of her jeans.

"So, are you kickin' me out?"

"Well..."

Garrett put his arm across Jill's shoulder. "You know how Carolanne stays up to all hours of the night. Y'all could hang out here, but then she could sleep over at my place. She'd be more comfortable at my place, not tippy-toeing around you sleeping."

Jill turned around and picked up the giant fruit basket. "Here, drop this off at your place when you go to change the sheets."

"So you're *not* kicking me out."

"Guess not." She scratched Clyde's hot head. "Carolanne and I will be together all day, and you're right. She does like her alone time. Maybe she'll realize how much she loves this town and move back. I hate having her so far off in New York."

"I'll run it over to the house, change the sheets as instructed. Then I have to pick up the paint sprayer and get it back over to the shop for the guys. They'll need it in the morning. Then I'll stop by and pick you up. We'll go out for supper tonight."

"Sounds good. I'll be ready."

He left, and she got ready, then called the office to straighten out the misprints from the articles on the foundation event. Josh answered after the second ring.

"Josh. It's Jill. I'm so glad you answered the phone. Is Bradley around?"

"Hey. He hasn't been around since I got back from vacation, but he did just call, and boy, was he in a mood. It's been like a tomb around here until this morning. When will you be back?"

She loved that job, and Josh had been such a trooper over the past year. She'd miss them both, but not Bradley. "I won't be coming back. Long story, and I'm not sure if I quit or got fired, but there were a couple things I wanted to be sure to straighten out."

"No wonder Bradley was in a mood. You're the only reason I stay on here. You can consider me gone if you're not coming back. No offense, but your boyfriend is an ass."

Now *you say something. I must've been the only one who hadn't noticed before.* "Oh, Josh, don't do something hasty. It's a good job. That aside, the kids benefit from our dedication. It's work to be proud of."

"Bradley was totally pissed about the account you set up. That's what he called about earlier. He was at the bank, and he didn't know we couldn't move that money without your signature."

"I told him I was setting up that account, since those funds were earmarked for certain projects in our campaign. Sorry if he blasted you."

"Yeah, yeah. Don't sweat it. I'm here for the paycheck. So, what did you need?"

"The newspaper misprinted our numbers."

"I know. Tried to take care of that the other day. Got the slam down from your boyfriend on that, too."

"He's not my boyfriend anymore, either."

"Sorry. Got the slam down from Bradley. He gave the newspaper those numbers. He said it had nothing to do with balancing the books. That the misreported numbers were all about marketing. Saying we didn't meet our goal may bring in more donations."

A feeling of dread swirled in the pit of her stomach. Melanie's mention of dodgy business deals came to mind. Jill sure hoped he wasn't going to put the Kase Foundation's good work at risk.

Clyde barked from the backyard, but his bark sounded different this time. More urgent. Instinct drew her toward the back door. The heavy smell of smoke seeped into the room.

Smoke poured out of the woods.

"Oh my God! Josh, I've got to go. I'll call you later." She threw open the door and screamed for Clyde. "Come here, boy."

She dialed 911, but Clyde ignored her and continued running along the back fence, barking.

On the third ring, she reached the dispatcher and gave him her address.

The smoke thickened, and Jill struggled to catch a clean breath. Soot and ash wafted in the air. She ran back inside and watched from the window over the kitchen sink.

A loud whoosh seemed to shake the house, and the first flame tickled the sky. The woods were dense, and the leaves, crispy from the summer sun, coupled with lack of rain, would fuel the fire. She prayed the fire truck would get there fast.

She grabbed her phone and punched in Garrett's cell number. No answer. Jill opened the back door, put her fingers in her mouth, and whistled. She hadn't tried that in forever, but it worked.

Clyde limped her way and sat on his haunches, anxiously shifting his weight from paw to paw.

She stooped next to him and lifted his left paw. He whimpered when she touched it. The pad was red and oozing.

Jill urged Clyde to the front yard, where they could get farther from the danger of the fire and wait for the fire truck. Time slinked by as she waited for assistance, watching helplessly as the fire gained strength. She checked her watch. Barely two minutes had passed.

She dialed Garrett's number again. Still no answer.

A siren wailed, getting louder as it got closer. Clyde howled.

"It's OK, Clyde." Jill stroked the dog's back to keep him calm. Drool ran down her arm and soaked her shoulder, but it didn't bother her right now. She wiped the rope of drool from his chin, then brushed her hand in the grass.

A convoy of four volunteer firemen raced up the driveway in their pickups. The tanker truck rumbled up and parked near the edge of the woods. She heard the heavy echo of another one on the road side of the fire, blocked from her view by the trees.

Jill sat in the grass out front to stay out of the way. The smoke hung in the humid air. The burn ban had been in place for weeks, and people in these parts weren't fool enough to burn this time of the year, anyway. Everything was too dry and the winds too unpredictable. A recipe for disaster. There'd been times when the county had delayed hunting season until rain because the risk of fire was too high when the underbrush was extra dry. A simple spark from a vehicle, gunshot, or cigarette could touch off an inferno.

An ambulance pulled up. A female medic jogged over to check on Jill. She dropped a medical kit to the ground and took a knee next to Jill.

"I'm fine," she told her. "Clyde got burned, though."

"Was he in the woods?"

"No, he was in the backyard. I'm not sure how it happened. He was barking. That's when I went out and saw the smoke."

"Let's take a look." The medic took Clyde's big paw into her hands. "That's got to hurt like the dickens, big boy." She took out scissors and swiftly clipped the hair surrounding the burn. Clyde pulled his paw back hesitantly as she dabbed salve with pain reliever on the fresh wound and then dressed it with burn bandages so they wouldn't stick. "This should keep him from licking it for a little while, but Dr. Tinker will probably give you an Elizabethan collar to keep him from aggravating it."

Jill wrapped her arms around his fluffy neck. "Thank you."

"He should be OK. I'd run him over to Dr. Tinker tomorrow and let him check it out."

"We'll do that, won't we, Clyde?" At least she wouldn't have the problem getting him into the car, since she didn't have one anymore. He seemed to love riding in Garrett's truck. Where was Garrett, anyway? Had he been called into fight the fire?

The sun had sunk low behind the tall trees. Jill shifted her watch to check the time. Already eight o'clock. The air sizzled with the loud snap and pop of twigs. The underbrush continued to fuel hot flames.

Firefighters from the next county came to help with another fire truck. Volunteers traded places at intervals. The incredible heat combined with the already sweltering summer temperatures were a dangerous duo.

After a while, the wind shifted and the smoke began blowing away from the house. Good news for Jill, but not good for the firefighters. The fire gained ground as it lapped greedily over fresh territory. The firefighters wielded noisy chainsaws and took down small trees, trying to slow the progress.

Jill headed to the house to see if Garrett had called. When she opened the screen door, something fell to the ground at her feet. She stooped to pick it up.

A matchbook?

No one she knew even smoked these days. She turned the matchbook over in her hand. In black marker, someone had scribbled *YOU LOSE* over the logo of one of the restaurants in town.

Jill squeezed the matches in her fist, then tucked the matchbook into her back pocket. Instead of dialing Garrett, she dialed the sheriff's department.

Just as the phone began to ring, call waiting beeped. She hit the flash key. "Garrett?"

"Jill?"

The female voice caught her off guard. "Yes?"

"It's me, Patsy. Garrett's mom. I'm calling about Garrett."

"He was supposed to come pick me up, and he's not answering his cell phone. I've been trying to call him. The woods next to the house are on fire."

"Jill, we just took him to Regional."

The words stunned her. "The hospital? Why?"

"He stopped at the house on his way home. He was having chest pains and vomiting. He couldn't even make it to his place."

A shiver of panic shot through her. "Oh my God." His parents' house was at the front of the lane to his house. If he couldn't make it home, it had to be bad.

"They're trying to stabilize him."

The phone slipped in Jill's sweaty hand, and her other hand balled into a fist. "I've got to get there." *I can't lose him again.*

"He's in the ICU. He's asking for you, but he said you don't have your car. I've sent Elsie to pick you up, dear."

"Thank you." Jill hung up and dialed Carolanne as she ran back outside to wait for Elsie. Thank God Carolanne would be there the next evening. Jill had barely told her about the fire and about Garrett in the hospital when she saw Elsie's car speeding between the trucks parked randomly around the yard, finally skidding to a stop in front of the house. Jill wrapped up the call and shoved her cell phone into her purse as she raced toward Elsie.

"What happened? I saw the smoke earlier. I thought they were burning fields or something—ya know, like planned burning." Elsie talked as fast as she drove.

"The fire started late this afternoon. They've been fighting it for hours."

"These guys won't let your house catch on fire. They're the best."

"They said that once the wind shifted we were OK. I just hope it doesn't shift again," Jill said and prayed silently. She'd done more praying in the last couple of weeks than she had in the last year. She was afraid to ask what else could go wrong.

"I'll take you to the hospital. Clyde can come home with me."

Jill opened the door and Clyde jumped right in. No problem. She slid into the passenger seat, and Elsie punched the accelerator. Elsie took the winding curves of the back roads at a speed that tossed Jill from side to side and had her grabbing for the dashboard. The next curve sent Jill's purse flying and the contents spilled across the floorboard. She righted her purse, put the wayward items back inside, and clamped it between her ankles. But she didn't complain. She needed to get to Garrett's side. The sooner the better.

Thank goodness there were no stoplights between the house and Regional Hospital.

After what seemed a prolonged roller-coaster ride, Elsie braked in front of the emergency room.

As Jill jumped out of the car, Elsie held Clyde's collar. "Call us with an update."

"Thank you, Elsie. I will." Jill raced through the automatic doors, almost slamming into them as they took their sweet time opening. She gave her name to the receptionist at the registration desk, then paced until a nurse came to take her back to Garrett.

"One visitor at a time," the nurse said with a glance toward Garrett's mom.

Patsy got up from the chair and came to the door. "I'm sorry we're seeing each other under bad circumstances again, Jill."

"One at a time," the nurse reminded them.

Jill looked to Garrett's mother, praying for a sign of hope, but she looked as worried as Jill felt.

From where Jill stood, Garrett's skin looked the color of ash. "He was fine this afternoon. What? Do they know what's—"

Patsy shook her head. "No. They haven't given us an update yet. They ran tests to see if he had a heart attack. They're doing blood work now. His blood pressure is off the charts, and he's havin' trouble breathing." Garrett's mother choked back tears and pointed toward the room. "Go. He's been asking for you."

She walked slowly; with Pearl gone and now Garrett hanging on for dear life, she felt as if she were walking in lead boots. She prayed with every step closer to Garrett's bedside.

She pushed her hand slowly under his, careful to not disturb the IV. "Hey."

His eyes fluttered, his movements slow and shaky.

She wouldn't have recognized him. His color was all wrong. "I'm right here, Garrett." *I can't lose you, too*, she thought, but put on a brave face. *No negative thoughts.*

Garrett squeezed her hand. "It hit me…out of…nowhere."

Patsy stepped up behind Jill. "That one-at-a-time crap is for the birds. He needs us."

Jill nodded.

Patsy continued. "He was vomiting like a fountain. Projectile, they called it. I never saw anything like it before. I sent his daddy over to the Swishy Wash to wash out his truck. He was so clammy. Near scared me to death."

"I bet."

"I thought maybe he'd eaten something bad," Patsy said, folding her arms across her chest. "Like food poisoning. The nurse thought so, too."

"No," Garrett shook his head, frustrated.

"We were planning to go out to dinner," Jill said. "He probably hadn't eaten since lunchtime."

"Just one of those…bananas you…love…so much," he tried to joke, but the words were slow and stilted.

"I told you bananas are bad for you." As the words came out of her mouth, her mind raced to the possibility. Her hand touched her back pocket where the note from the fruit basket and the matchbook were tucked. "Garrett, where's the fruit basket?"

Patsy gave her an awkward stare. "Honey, I don't think he's going to be eating anytime soon."

"Garrett, you hear me?" She shook his arm to get him to rouse again. "Where is it? Where's the fruit basket?"

"Truck," Garrett grunted, wincing.

It couldn't. Jill felt the blood drain from her face, and she became light-headed. *No. Bradley?*

"Jill?" Panic crossed Patsy's face.

A nurse stepped between them. "One at a time, ladies. Our patient needs rest."

"You stay, Patsy. I'll be right back," Jill said.

The nurse checked Garrett's blood pressure and spoke to him in a loud voice. "Your EKG looks OK, Mr. Malloy. We're going to check a few more things." She tied a length of rubber around his arm, balled his hand in a fist, and probed for a vein.

Garrett lurched over the side of the bed and puked on the nurse's shoes. He convulsed, then dry heaved uncontrollably. Patsy grabbed a washcloth and held the cold rag to the back of her son's neck.

Jill ran from the room and asked to see Garrett's doctor. She was told to wait, but there was no time for waiting. Jill grabbed the phone book off the nurse's station counter and headed for the visitors' waiting area. She used the courtesy phone to call Scott Calvin at home.

"Hey, Jill. The whole town's over at your place trying to rein in that fire."

"Not the whole town, Scott. Garrett's in the ICU."

"I didn't hear any injuries reported. Was he working the fire? You OK?"

"I'm fine. The fire was under control when I left, but Garrett is in the ICU and the doctors don't know what's wrong. You've got to help me."

"Are you at the hospital?" Scott asked.

"Yes."

"I'm on my way."

"I'll meet you in the lobby. But wait, I need you to get something on the way. There was a fruit basket in the front of Garrett's truck. Garrett's dad just took it to the Swishy Wash on Main. Get that fruit basket."

"What?"

"If I'm right, I think it has to do with Garrett's sickness. The nurses won't even let me talk to the doctors. They told me to wait. I know they won't listen to me, but I know they'll listen to you."

"OK. I'll see you shortly."

Jill covered her face with her hands. *Breathe. God and Pearl, please don't let anything happen to Garrett.* She drew in a deep breath and blew it out. Jill stacked the phone book and the phone on the table, then headed downstairs to wait for Scott.

Patsy was leaning out of the door of Garrett's room in the ICU when Jill walked out.

Jill lifted her finger as if to say *one minute* and stepped into the elevator, pushing the *Close Door* button repeatedly, hoping Patsy wouldn't follow her.

The elevator doors closed.

Alone, Jill found it impossible to control the tears. The doors opened on the ground floor in front of the chapel. She stepped into the dimly lit area and took a seat in the back pew. No one else was there. She cried for Garrett, for Pearl, for Clyde. Everything was unraveling. Pearl had been the glue that kept everything together. Now that she was gone, nothing made sense. The whole darn town was in chaos.

Jill peeled a handful of tissues from the small box sitting on the pew in front of her.

When she stepped out of the chapel, Scott Calvin stood in the lobby, dressed in shorts and a PIG OUT T-shirt, holding the fruit basket.

"Nice shirt." Her mind raced first to Pearl's mantel, then to Garrett's desk. *If the PIG OUT T-shirt is some kind of a sign, Lord, it had better be a good one.*

Scott handed her the handkerchief from his pocket. "Here."

"Thanks."

"Now tell me what's going on and why I needed to bring a puked-on fruit basket to the hospital. I had to dumpster dive, by the way. Garrett's dad had already pitched it."

"Sorry about that. If I'm wrong, you did that for nothin'."

"What is all this about?"

She emptied the contents of her back pocket and sat down.

Scott slid the fruit basket under the chair and took a seat next to her. "What do we have?"

"I'm not sure. I got that fruit basket earlier today, delivered to the house. This is the card that was on it. No signature. I figured it was just an oversight, but maybe not." She snapped the card onto the table in front of them.

"OK." He shrugged, encouraging her to continue.

"And I found this," she said, holding up the matchbook, "between the screen door and the front door when I went to go inside after the fire started this afternoon. Someone wanted me to know that the fire was intentional." She placed the matchbook next to the card, *YOU LOSE* side up.

"Any idea who might be behind these things?"

"Bradley is pretty mad at me. But he's in Georgia. I talked to him this morning, and my assistant said he'd spoken to him from the bank there this morning."

"I've seen people do worse over less. Carolanne told me about the restraining order."

"Yeah, and you heard about the conditions of the will. I haven't told him, but who knows what he's heard. He could still have connections here."

He nodded.

"Bradley says he wants me back in Savannah, but I won't lie to you. He said some pretty threatening things toward Garrett on the phone yesterday."

Scott listened intently.

"Garrett ate some of the fruit from that basket. It's all he's eaten all day."

"You think Bradley Kase might have poisoned the fruit basket?"

"I think it's a possibility." Her bottom lip trembled. "You should see Garrett. He's the color of a rain cloud. He can barely move." Her hands shook. "If I'm right, maybe they can figure a way to make him well."

Scott grabbed the fruit basket. "Who is his doctor?"

"Dr. Banks."

He grabbed her hand and they jogged to the elevator. He pressed the button for the ICU floor. When they stepped off the elevator, Dr. Banks was walking by. Scott stopped him. They spoke low, heads down and nodding, while Jill stood down the hall, just outside Garrett's room.

Patsy came out and hugged her. "You OK?"

"I can't lose him again."

"Tell him that. If that won't cure him, nothing will." Patsy pushed Jill toward Garrett's bed. "He loves you, you know. Never stopped."

She squeezed Patsy's hand.

"Go, honey."

Jill went in and slid the wooden-framed chair close to the bed. She knelt in the seat and leaned over to kiss Garrett on the forehead. "This is my fault. I'm so sorry."

He shook his head and mouthed, *No.*

"I don't think this was an accident. Scott's here. He's checking it out now."

"We'll need to ask you to step outside," a nurse said from behind her.

For the next hour, nurses rushed in and out of Garrett's room. Patsy and Jill sat in the hall outside.

Jill sat silent, unsure of how to tell Patsy what she knew.

After a while, Garrett's father stepped out of the elevator. Worry etched his face.

Jill greeted him, then excused herself to the visitors' lounge to call Carolanne and Elsie with updates. Scott came in with coffee cups in a cardboard tray while she was on the phone.

"Thanks," she whispered, twisting one out. "I've got to go. I'll call you back when we know more." She turned back to Scott.

"You were right," he confided. "When I explained the scenario, Doc said there was a good possibility that Garrett had been poisoned. The lab just confirmed it."

She held the cup to her chest. "Is he going to be OK?"

"Yeah."

Relief flooded every tense muscle in her body, so much so that she thought she might collapse."Thank goodness."

"I'll check with the florist in the morning to see if they can tell us who sent that basket."

"The florist didn't deliver it. Garrett said Izzy dropped it off."

"OK, I'll check with her, then. By the way, I just got word that the fire is out. They've got one truck on standby to ensure nothing flares up overnight. You might want to stay somewhere else tonight."

"I'll probably be here, anyway. Thanks for helping me."

"Don't thank me. I'm just glad you put everything together so quickly. Your fast thinking probably saved Garrett's life."

Her heart swelled. *If anything had happened to him...*"I can't believe any of this. It doesn't even feel real." Jill headed back down the hall, then into Garrett's room. His mother and father stood off to the side. Garrett's color had started to come back already.

Patsy crossed the room and put her arm around Jill's shoulders. "He's going to be OK, dear. They're going to keep him overnight, but they say he's going to be perfectly fine. We're going to head on home. You should do the same. Let us give you a lift."

"Y'all go on home. I'm going to stay here for a while."

Jill watched Garrett's parents walk to the elevator, then pushed the recliner next to Garrett's bed. He didn't stir. His color was good, and he appeared to be resting well. She climbed into the chair with her feet underneath her and leaned her head on the side of the bed, snuggling his arm against her body.

When she woke, he was stroking her hair with his hand.

She lifted her head. He looked better. "Thank goodness you're OK. How do you feel?"

"Like a truck ran over me."

"I'm so sorry, Garrett."

He raised his hand. "No sorries. Let's just put the past behind us."

"But…"

"Sh…" He gave her a half grin. "All in the past."

The nurse came in and checked Garrett's IV while the doctor flipped through his chart. Jill scooted her chair out of the way and excused herself while the nurse took Garrett's vitals.

The elevator dinged and Elsie stepped out. "Hi, Jill. I talked to Patsy. She said you were still here."

Jill tipped her head toward Garrett's room. "The doctor's in with him now, but he's doing so much better."

Elsie hugged her and sat in one of the upholstered chairs outside Garrett's room. Jill took the other.

When the doctor came out of the room, he said that Garrett was now stable and would probably sleep most of the night. He encouraged Jill to go home and get some rest, too.

Jill poked her head in Garrett's room, and he was, as the doctor had said, sleeping. She scribbled a note and left it on the table for him.

Elsie gave her a ride back to Garrett's house since the fire trucks were still at hers. She needed quiet if she was going to rest. Elsie offered to let Clyde stay with her until everything settled down.

Mr. Malloy had dropped Garrett's cleaned-up truck off in front of the house. That gave her a vehicle to drive if she needed to get back to the hospital.

Jill watched Elsie drive off and stood looking at Garrett's house. The covered wraparound porch and steeply pitched rooflines still made this house look as warm and inviting as it had when she and Garrett had worked on the original plans. The first house Garrett ever built. It was meant to be their home as a married couple one day. They had fought for two weeks over the exterior colors. She'd won, though, and the historic color combination still looked great.

The front door was unlocked. She knew it would be. You had to practically drive right through Garrett's folks' front yard to get there. The odds of anyone getting back there unnoticed were slim to none.

It felt a little odd returning to this house after being gone so long. She kicked off her shoes and stretched out on the sofa. After switching sides twice, she gave up. She was exhausted, but couldn't get her body to slow down and rest. Frustrated, she gave in and went into the kitchen to see what she could find. In the cabinet next to the microwave, there was a good selection of her favorite teas that she'd left behind.

While the tea brewed, her phone rang. She ran to answer it, praying Garrett hadn't taken a turn for the worse.

It was Carolanne, checking in. Her flight would be landing around five tomorrow evening. She'd come straight to Pearl's.

She grasped her cup of tea between her hands and prayed. Then she took a sip and wondered how she could have gotten so offtrack. *I've wasted precious time. Time with Pearl. Time with Garrett. Please don't let anything happen to Garrett.*

Following that moment of panic, Jill called to check on Garrett. The nurse said that his status had been upgraded to stable, so he could accept a phone call. She connected Jill's call to the phone in his room.

Garrett was still groggy and told her not to come to sit with him in the hospital. He'd be sleeping, and he didn't need any distractions, not even beautiful ones.

❖ Chapter Twenty-Four ❖

Bright and early, Jill drove Garrett's truck over to Pearl's. Everything looked dull from the layer of soot that had settled. The fire had been contained to the woods, but the acrid smell of smoke hung in the air outside and even inside the house.

At least the house had been spared. Opening windows wouldn't do any good, just cycle in new smoky air, so Jill stuck to wiping everything down inside to get the sooty film off and hopefully freshen the place. She sprayed the inside of a window and wiped it with a piece of newspaper until the smearing mess was clear. Newsprint worked best. No streaks and no lint. Pearl had always sworn by it, and they saved stacks of newspapers just for that purpose.

Elsie tooted her horn as she pulled up with Clyde bobbing his head out of the passenger window.

Jill waved from the living room picture window.

"Anything I can do to help?" Elsie asked when she stepped inside.

"You've done enough already, taking care of Clyde."

"He was a good boy. No problem." Elsie swept a finger across one of the panes and held a black finger up to Jill. "How did so much soot get inside the house?"

"I had these windows open. I guess I didn't get them closed quick enough."

"Man, that's a mess. Sure you don't need any help?"

"Nope. I've got it. It'll be therapeutic to work off some stress until Carolanne gets here."

"OK, have your fun, then." Elsie headed back to her car, waving as she drove off.

Jill put Clyde out back and turned on the CD player. Pearl's favorite Yanni song filled the room. The instrumentals were feel-good music, and she needed to feel good today. She cranked up the volume and danced her way through the chores.

She sprayed the next windowpane and gave it a good scrub. After three attempts, it finally looked clean. Maybe she should've accepted Elsie's offer for help.

Someone knocked at the front door. Carolanne must've caught an early flight. That would be just like her. She hopped down from the step stool.

"Just a sec," she sang out as she headed for the door.

She opened the door to find Sheriff Calvin on her doorstep. "Oh? I thought it was going to be Carolanne," Jill said. "Everything's fine around here for a change. What brings you by?"

"We got some information from the fingerprint work we did after the break-in."

"Well, I'm glad we got something out of it, because it was one heck of a mess to clean up." She stepped out on to the porch toward the deacon's bench. "Have a seat." She noticed the baby-blue Thunderbird in the front yard. "You're still driving that around, huh? Not too good for undercover work, is it?"

"Give me a break." Scott loved that car, and everybody in town knew it. Originally, the car had been a heaping pile of junk they'd dragged out of the woods behind his granddaddy's house. Then he and his dad had restored it to its original glamour, maybe better, working on it night and day the summer after Scott graduated from high school.

"I guess it's true that you never forget your first love," she teased.

"Enough about that." He joined her on the bench. "I came to tell you what I found. One set of fingerprints came back that matched a Kimberly Louann Clatterbuck."

"Never heard of her. Is she local?"

"Nope. She's originally out of the Atlanta area, and she's got a record," Sheriff Calvin explained. "She's done a little time, too."

Another car pulled into the yard. This time, it was Carolanne.

Jill waved her to join them on the porch. Once they all said their hellos, they turned their attention back to the business at hand.

"So, who is this lady?" Jill asked Scott.

"We were able to match a photo to the fingerprints." He handed her a picture from his shirt pocket.

Jill almost choked. "That's not Kimberly Clatter-whatever. That's Annie!"

"So you do know her."

"Well, not under that name. She's Bradley's housekeeper in Savannah." Jill flipped the picture toward Carolanne. "It's a crappy picture, but it's her. I've lived with her for the last year."

Carolanne grabbed the picture. "So this is the microwavin', no-cookin' bitch who's made your life a living hell for the past year?"

Jill nodded and took the picture back from Carolanne.

"Any idea why she'd break into Pearl's house?" Scott took the notepad from his shirt pocket and scribbled something.

"Or possibly fry me in my own attic? No. I mean she doesn't like me. She fawns over Bradley, and she's always misplacing my messages and doing little things to pluck my nerves. She's been

Bradley's housekeeper and cook forever." The image of Bradley and that woman danced in her mind. "He wouldn't fire her no matter what I said to him."

Jill and Carolanne exchanged a knowing look.

Carolanne chimed in. "Nothing would surprise me anymore. You wouldn't believe the cases I've seen where people do crazy stuff because of love, obsession, whatever you want to call it."

Scott nodded. He turned to Jill. "You wanted her fired?"

"Oh yeah. He and I fought about Annie all the time."

"She knew it?"

"I'm sure she did."

"Jealousy, maybe?" Scott's face was serious.

The image of Annie sprawled across the pool table with Bradley made her stomach churn. "Maybe." Fear climbed her spine. "The good news is I know where you can pick her up." Jill grabbed the notebook out of Scott's hands and scribbled down their address in Savannah. "She never goes anywhere. She's all yours."

"So I take it you want to press charges?" Scott asked.

"Absolutely." Annie's arrest would be sweet revenge after a year of harassment. "I kept telling Bradley she was bad news. But, nooo. He always stuck up for her."

"He's a shit," Carolanne said. "Kicking him to the curb was the smartest thing you've ever done."

Jill picked up her phone and hit speed dial.

"Who are you calling?" Carolanne asked.

"Bradley. Who else? I can't wait to tell him I was right." After listening to too many rings and getting dumped into voice mail, Jill flipped the phone closed against her thigh. "No answer. Figures."

"I wouldn't say two words to that jerk," Carolanne said.

"I'll leave you gals to gloat on your own. I wouldn't say too much to Kase, though." Scott headed to his car. "I've got to get some things moving on this."

"Thanks, Scott," Jill called after him.

Carolanne gave Jill a hug. "That was good timing. I'm glad I didn't miss out on that picture of Annie. She isn't anything like I envisioned her."

"It was a mug shot, not a glamour shot. We're about the same age," Jill reminded her.

"Well, you look better than her when you're rolling out of bed after the flu. How's Garrett?"

"Much better. They're releasing him in the morning. Come on, let's go to town and get some supper." Jill was glad to get her mind off illness, crime, death, or anything else bad.

After an early-bird dinner, Carolanne went to visit her dad, and Jill decided to stay at Pearl's with Clyde while it was still daylight. She'd meet up with Carolanne later.

Carolanne hadn't been gone long when Jill's phone rang. She glanced at the caller ID and saw that it was Bradley returning her call. Now she wished she hadn't called him to gloat. At the time, it had seemed like a good thing to rub his nose in Annie's criminal past, but now Jill didn't even want to hear his voice. Begrudgingly, she picked up the phone.

"I saw you called. Did you change your mind? Are you going to give me another chance?"

"No."

"I'm on the road today. Why'd you call, then?"

"I was calling to tell you the fingerprints came back on the break-in from the day of Pearl's funeral."

"What do you know? I guess that small town has some police skills, after all. Anything helpful?"

"Yes. We know who was here. It was Annie." *Not so perfect now, is she?*

"My Annie? No way."

A bitter taste flooded her mouth. *His Annie?* "Yes way. She's using a fake name, too. Her name is Kimberly Louann Clatterbuck. I told you she was bad news."

"What else do you know?"

"That's about it. Isn't that enough?"

Silence hung between them on the line. Jill reveled in the fact he was speechless.

"I can't believe it," he said.

"I saw her mug shot. She's even been in jail. Your saint of all saints isn't all she says she is." Jill enjoyed the smug moment of being right.

His tone softened. "I should have fired her. I never should have second-guessed your intuition."

"I kept telling you she was out to get me." *Finally, he was seeing her side.*

"I bet that's why she seduced me, to get to you. She must be obsessed. I'll fire her today. Please come home."

"Wait a second. You're not off the hook because she's a sleazy felon. You could have said no. Should have said no if you cared about me."

"Please. I can't ask you to forgive me. I know I'll have to earn that, but I'll fire her. I promise. Come home with me today. I'll come get you."

Jill took in a breath. It was invigorating to hear him say she was right and hear him grovel for her attention. A sweet victory, but the truth was that the relationship was never headed anywhere, anyway.

"No. Bradley, our days as a couple are over."

"I need you," he said.

"You don't need me. You just like having me around." She leaned on the rail of the front porch.

"You don't know what I need."

His voice sounded tight. She could hear the shift in it. "You made that pretty darn obvious. I didn't know you needed riding crops and barn noises to turn you on."

The sound of tires crunching on the gravel driveway made Jill look up. The familiar Lexus pulled up right in front of her.

"Bradley? I thought you…" She closed the phone and walked toward his car.

He got out and slammed the door.

She shook the phone his way. "I thought you just said you were on the road."

"I was, and not far away." He stepped toward her. Feather-like laugh lines crinkled around his eyes. "Not happy to see me?"

"Why would I be?"

Wrinkles creased his tan forehead. She hated that disapproving look. It made her feel ten years old. He'd already tried Botoxing them twice before.

"I hope your face sticks like that," she said.

He raised his brows and ran a finger across the lines. "You want to know what I want?" he hissed.

She took a step back. "Is this about the account for the Kase Foundation?"

"No. That's nothing. I can get to that money. It's one signature away."

"You won't get my signature if this isn't on the up and up. I saw that article."

"This isn't about that."

"You need to just leave."

"I've been patient." His voice carried a razor's edge.

"Leave me alone. You're not welcome here." She landed an elbow in his gut, but her angle was poor.

"You're starting to really piss me off. I'm warning you. You and Garrett are way more trouble than I planned for. This whole damn town is more than I bargained for."

"Get out of here," she choked on the words as she screamed them.

"I'll leave when I'm damn well ready."

Clyde must have cleared the fence because all Jill saw was a barking blur of fur come speeding around the corner of the house.

Bradley spun toward Clyde, but instead of retreating, he shoved his hand in his pocket and pulled out a handful of treats. "It's OK. Come, boy."

Jill stood there with her mouth agape as the big dog pushed his nose under Bradley's hand to accept a pat on the head. *Impossible.*

Bradley nodded toward her with a knowing smile.

She should be running into the house, locking the door, and dialing for help, but her legs wouldn't move. She'd seen Clyde bark and scare every man who had come to this house, and yet he didn't seem the least bit worried about the man threatening her now. *Treats? All it took was a couple of treats?*

Jill stood frozen to the spot on the porch. "I don't believe this."

"What? Disappointed in your guard dog? Again?"

"He's a companion dog, not a guardian, but Clyde hates men. He—"

"Not all of us, but then, everyone likes me. You used to be pretty delighted by me, too."

"I don't understand it. I've seen him."

Bradley scrubbed the top of the big dog's head. "He certainly likes me." He dug into his pocket again and held another treat in front of Clyde's shiny nose. "Sit," Bradley said with a hand gesture.

Clyde responded, sitting at full attention.

"Down."

Clyde folded to the ground with his chin between his paws.

The arrogance of his statement was hard to miss. "You broke into Pearl's house?"

"I'm not a petty thief. I don't break into houses." He walked toward her. "I want what's rightfully mine."

She backed up, wanting to keep a distance between the two of them. "You're a piece of work." Her fear turned to anger. "You never cared about me."

"That's where you are wrong. I do care about you. You've been a great asset to my bank account."

She pointed her finger in his face and searched for the words that spun like a tornado in her mind. "I'll tell. I'll have you arrested so fast. I can have you arrested right now. I have a restraining order."

Bradley slammed his fist against the house, causing the globe on the front porch light to fall from the fixture. Bradley grabbed for it instinctively, but that just sent it flying sideways, right into Jill's cheek.

She screamed out in pain.

"That piece of paper doesn't scare me." Bradley grabbed her finger and then her wrist and twisted hard. "Don't you ever—"

Jill screamed.

Clyde's huge jaws clamped around Bradley's forearm and pulled him off balance away from Jill.

Bradley wailed in surprise and lost his footing. Blood soaked through his shirt, turning it dark and shiny.

He shouted commands at Clyde, but he didn't respond to one of them. Finally pulling free from Clyde's jaws, Bradley ran to his car, leaving a trail of blood from the porch to his car.

As he slid behind the wheel clutching his bleeding arm, he yelled back over his shoulder, "This isn't over. Not by a long shot. John Carlo's treasure is mine."

"What treasure?"

"Don't play stupid with me. My mother told me all about that grandmother of yours and John Carlo."

How?

"He was my mother's uncle." Bradley spit the words. "Bastard let us live hand to mouth while he lavished wealth on your grandmother. The Pacini Pearls. They're rightfully mine, and I want them. I know your Pearl has them."

She swallowed, trying to digest the information. "If she did, I don't know where they are."

"Figure it out. I *will* be back." His eyes held hers, intense and dark. "If you need motivation, I can easily handle that. How is Garrett feeling, anyway?"

"Leave!" Emotion swelled inside her; every muscle tensed in her body.

Clyde barked and stomped his front paws on the ground, then charged the vehicle.

Bradley threw an empty water bottle out of the car window at Clyde and left, spinning tires all the way.

Clyde's tongue hung to the ground. Bradley's blood stained one of his paws.

Jill ran to Clyde and hugged the dog's neck. She took a deep breath punctuated with several even gasps. She and Garrett had thought the ring was the treasure, but was there more? Bradley had made a clear threat against Garrett. She couldn't let Bradley hurt him again.

Out of breath and confused, she raced to the attic to search for a clue.

A tumble of thoughts assailed her. All the way up the stairs, she tasted the bitter guilt of putting her trust into that man. He'd used her and everyone she cared about. How would she ever find a way to repay the people he'd swindled with her help? And Garrett? He could have died. She gulped back the sobs. If she hadn't ever met Bradley, she would have been there for Pearl. How could she have been so stupid to fall for his evil ways?

Jill fought to control her swirling emotions. She had to look again for a clue, anything that might lead her to the treasure of pearls.

She still wasn't even sure what the Pacini Pearls consisted of. Was it jewelry, loose pearls, one pearl, a hundred? If Pearl had them, whatever they were, where were they hidden? She'd scoured that attic. *What am I overlooking?*

❖ Chapter Twenty-Five ❖

Frustrated and dirty from the unsuccessful search, Jill began to doubt there was any treasure other than Pearl's ring. As she searched the attic one last time, someone pounded on the door downstairs.

She came to an abrupt stop, her heart jumping in her chest. *Had Bradley come back already?*

Relief washed over her when she heard the visitor yoo-hooing from the porch.

"Carolanne." Jill ran downstairs.

"The door was locked," Carolanne said, stating the obvious. "Good for you. I'm glad you're taking my advice more seriously these days."

"It's been a bad day."

"I bet." Carolanne dropped her purse on the hall table and stepped out of her clogs. "Why are you so filthy, and what happened to your cheek? Is that dirt?" She touched the bruise rising on Jill's cheek.

"Ouch." Jill winced.

Carolanne's eyes flashed with concern. "What happened to you?"

"Bradley was here." She touched her cheek.

"That bastard. We've got a restraining order against him. We'll have him arrested." Carolanne's jaw set and her eyes narrowed. "He hit you?"

"It wasn't like that. It was an accident."

"Yeah, right."

There was no sense trying to convince Carolanne it was an accident, and what did it matter, really? She'd never believe it. "The man Pearl was secretly married to. From the letters. John Carlo. Bradley's mother was his niece. He wants the Pacini Pearls. He thinks Pearl had them." Her eyes bordered with tears. "He's going to hurt Garrett if I don't find them."

"You've got to be kidding me. This sounds straight out of some B movie."

Jill swallowed hard, biting back tears, but then breaking down. "I don't even know what I'm looking for." She held out her shaking hand. "At least I still have this."

Carolanne took Jill's hand into her own. "That's the most beautiful ring I've ever seen."

Carolanne comforted her. "I'm going to call Scott."

Jill grabbed her arm. "No. Don't. Wait, you don't understand. I've been scouring the attic for clues. That's why I'm so dirty. I don't have what he's looking for, but if I don't find it, he's going to hurt Garrett." She blew out a breath.

"Have you Googled it to see if you could get any clues?"

Jill rubbed her hand under her nose and sniffed back the lingering tears. "The pearls? No, Pearl doesn't have an Internet connection. My laptop is at Bradley's, so I guess I've kissed that good-bye."

Carolanne lifted her oversized black leather tote bag. "I never leave home without mine or my air card. You can use it, but first you're calling Scott." She pulled out a wireless device and settled on the edge of the couch, already clicking away on the keyboard.

"He took advantage of your good nature. Don't be so hard on yourself." Carolanne dialed the sheriff's number on her phone. "We have a restraining order on Bradley. They'll arrest him."

Jill sat next to Carolanne on the couch. "We can't call Scott. Not yet."

"Give me one good reason why not."

"You mean besides the fact that it's embarrassing how horrible a judge of character I am?"

"Yes. Better than that." Carolanne lifted her phone and began punching numbers.

Jill grabbed the phone from Carolanne. "Don't. I think I'm in trouble. That's why I haven't called yet."

"Trouble? For what?"

"Bradley said that all those deals, even the fund-raisers, were a big con. Even the Kase Foundation. It's a fraud. No such thing, and I helped him close those deals and make all that money."

"So?"

"So I broke the law, that's what. Or was one heck of an accessory to it all."

"Don't you worry about that. No one is going to fault you for anything except maybe bad judgment. I'll see to that. But you've got to report this," Carolanne said in her lawyer's tone. "We're calling Scott. Bradley can't just slap you around. That's assault. We'll have his ass in jail tonight." Carolanne, always cool in a crisis, started to dial the sheriff's office.

"I'll do it," Jill said, taking the phone from Carolanne. "Sheriff Calvin, please." Jill put her hand over the phone and lowered her voice to speak to Carolanne while she waited. "He didn't hit me. It really was an accident, but he is pissed and he did threaten me."

"If you say so," Carolanne said.

"Scott, it's Jill." She unloaded the whole scenario to Scott. There was a lot of nodding and *yes*ing and *I know*ing and

Carolanne kept making faces trying to figure out the conversation and interjecting comments until Jill finally shushed her out of the room.

Jill walked into the kitchen and sat at the table, relieved to have Carolanne there with her now. "Bradley won't get anywhere near this place without Scott's folks spotting him, and he's let the Savannah police know, too."

"Good. And I'll be here with you, too."

"What if something happens to Garrett?" Jill rubbed her hands up and down her arms, chilled at the thought. "I hope he wouldn't do anything to hurt Garrett to get back at me."

"Garrett's in the hospital. Nothing else will happen to him there. Scott will make sure of that. Go jump in the shower. I brought wine. This is definitely a wine night."

Jill climbed out of the chair. Every muscle and joint in her body ached from her encounter with Bradley and all the searching in the attic. She spent the next thirty minutes Googling "John Carlo Pacini" and "treasures of pearls."

After Jill showered, she and Carolanne finished off the bottle of wine, talking until the wee hours and rereading all the letters between Pearl and John Carlo. They went to bed, but every time one of them almost fell asleep, the other would say something and conversation would start again. Finally, they gave up the idea of getting any rest and got up to go to Garrett's house to get Carolanne settled in before it was time to pick up Garrett from the hospital.

Carolanne followed Jill in her rental car. Once there, Jill took folded sheets and a set of fresh towels from the closet and handed them to Carolanne.

"Aren't you just the regular lady of the house?"

"Weird, huh? If I'd never gone on that job interview, never met Bradley, I'd probably be the lady of this house right now and none of this would've happened."

"You don't know that. Don't do that to yourself." Carolanne followed Jill into the bedroom, and they quickly stripped the bed and remade it.

"You sure you don't mind staying here?"

"Not a bit. Now go get Garrett."

Jill promised to check in with Carolanne later to see what she'd been able to find on the Internet about the treasure. Daydreaming and praying for answers, she arrived at the hospital in no time.

At seven o'clock in the morning, Jill walked through the automatic doors at the hospital. She wasn't surprised to find Garrett already dressed and sitting in the chair, one knee bobbing impatiently, chomping at the bit to get home.

She kissed him three times on the mouth, like they always used to, and then hugged him. "I'm so thankful you're OK."

"I'm fine." His voice was calm and strong.

"Garrett, I'm so sorry."

"It's not your fault. We don't know that Bradley was behind this, you know." He reached for her hand.

"You could have died."

"But I didn't. I'm fine, and I've got you."

"Yes, you do." She'd only been fooling herself since she'd left town. Garrett was everything she'd always thought he was. How she wished now she hadn't believed all the things Bradley had said to make her lose faith. But he'd been so convincing at the time.

The doctor released Garrett with a list of instructions. When the nurse insisted he be taken downstairs in a wheelchair, he was not happy, but the nurse wasn't about to give in.

"Hospital policy," she said, sternly patting the back of the wheelchair. Amazing how much power a blue-haired nurse could wield over a man.

The nurse helped Garrett into the passenger's seat of the truck. Jill jumped behind the wheel and started the engine. "You're a sucker for old ladies, aren't you, Malloy?"

"You can be my old lady?" He winked.

"I'm only a month older than you."

He wiggled his eyebrows playfully. "It counts." Suddenly, he straightened, dropping the playfulness. "What happened to your cheek?" He reached toward her.

She'd done her best to camouflage the purplish swelling, but the sunlight streaming through the windshield blew her cover. "You don't want to know."

"What happened?"

A flicker of apprehension coursed through her. "Bradley came by. He wants the Pacini Pearls."

"He hit you? I'll kill him. Are you OK?" He reached for her cheek again.

"I'm fine. It barely hurts." She brushed his hand away. "The ring isn't the treasure, but apparently that's not the treasure he's looking for."

"That's all we found. If that's not the treasure, what is?" he asked.

"I have no idea. I've gone back through the notes I found in the attic. I can't figure it out, but he's threatened to hurt you if I don't hand over the pearls."

"I'll kick his ass. Let him—"

"Stop it, Garrett. This is no time to be macho. He's dangerous. He all but admitted, almost bragged, that he'd gotten to you once. He was responsible for the break-ins at Pearl's. There's so much to tell you."

"I'll kill him." Garrett balled his fist and punched the dashboard.

"Calm down. Scott doesn't think he'll come back around. He has an alert out for Bradley's car just in case, though."

"You just passed my turn," Garrett said.

"I'm taking you home with me where I can be sure you follow the doctor's orders."

"I knew you wanted me."

"Don't push your luck, Malloy." She tried to hold back the grin as she pulled in front of Pearl's house. She ran to the other side of the car to help Garrett, but he was already out and heading for the porch.

Garrett moved a kitchen chair outside so he could watch as she played with Clyde in the backyard. Clyde limped a little, but his scorched paw wasn't slowing him down much. She tossed the ball, and he took off like a jet to get it. He ran in a circle around the whole perimeter of the backyard before bringing the ball back and setting it at her feet, eager to do it all again.

Jill noticed Garrett fidgeting, getting restless. She tossed the ball one last time and headed over to join him. Garrett stood and gave Jill a friendly peck on the forehead as he grabbed his keys off the counter. "I'm going to run by my office."

"Let Elsie handle things," Jill said. "You just got out of the hospital."

"I've been in bed for two days. I've got a company to run."

"Will you let me drive you?" she asked.

"I can drive. I won't be long. I just can't sit here."

"You should really take it easy."

"I'll be fine. Keep your phone handy, and you call me first, then Scott, if that Kase nut shows up. I'm just a few minutes away."

Garrett was definitely on the road to recovery—the same old hardworking Garrett she'd always known.

As she watched his truck motor down the lane, her heart swelled with a feeling that she'd thought she'd lost for him. But she knew now she'd never lost that love. Being with Garrett was what made her whole. She'd even admitted to Carolanne that there might be an ounce or two of reality to those paperback love stories. Maybe the fairy tale was out there if she didn't interrupt it by trying too hard.

Jill tugged on the old freezer door to see what she could find to whip up for dinner. She decided that she'd bake a couple of

Spratt's pork chops, cut an inch and a quarter thick, like Pearl had always requested. The hard frozen package clonked when she set it on the counter.

Cooking for Garrett was good for her ego. He gobbled up everything she cooked like she was his own personal Paula Deen. Jill picked out a tomato pudding recipe from the recipe box. A perfect choice since Pearl had planted so many tomato bushes and the tomatoes had all ripened at one time. Tomato pudding and some macaroni 'n' cheese would make for a colorful entrée.

For dessert, she decided to whip up one of Pearl's famous chocolate pecan pies.

After a quick run to the store, Jill went to work on the pie. While the pie baked, she worked on the other recipes. Her timing was perfect. Everything was ready to go into the oven when the pie timer buzzed. The crust had browned just right. She took in a big whiff of chocolate as she set it on the counter to cool. Pearl would be proud.

She tossed her apron over one of the kitchen chairs, then put on her tennis shoes to spend some time with Clyde in the yard. Clyde loved it when she weeded. He'd either roll in the discarded greens or grab a mouthful and run around the yard. He had endless energy and was always at her side. Jill and Clyde had built a quick bond, and the huge dog was great company.

After a couple hours of weeding, Jill decided to quit. Tired, but feeling a sense of accomplishment, she hit the shower.

Jill relaxed under the shower stream until she depleted the hot water supply. She shut off the water and grabbed a thick, thirsty towel from the towel bar outside the shower, but paused at the sound of someone humming.

A knot formed in her stomach, until she realized she recognized the tune. "Every Rose Has Its Thorn" had always been one of her favorite songs. She held the towel to cover herself and ripped back the shower curtain.

Garrett stood there with a big old grin, holding out a towel for her. Clyde sat by his side.

"Who do you think you are?" Jill snatched the towel from his hands.

He gave her an exaggerated pout. "We were just tryin' to help."

"You're my thorn, troublemaker." She shooed them both out of the bathroom. "You two get lost. You're in my private space."

"What are you going to do about it, big shot?" Garrett pulled her close.

She squirmed, trying to wriggle from his arms. "That's not fair."

"All's fair in love and pie."

She grinned and settled into his grasp. "You saw the pie."

He kissed her neck. "I did. Chocolate pecan pie, my favorite. Did you make it, or was it left over from Pearl's funeral?"

"Like there'd be any leftovers."

"That's what I thought when I made it," he said.

She arched back to look him in the eye. "You made a chocolate pecan pie for Pearl's funeral?"

He nodded.

She gave him a sidelong glance of disbelief. "Really? You made a pie?"

"Don't look so surprised. I spent a lot of time with Pearl, and she couldn't do everything she used to. There were some benefits to helping her cook. I learned a lot."

"And ate a lot, I bet." She patted his tight tummy.

"Like I said, spending time with Pearl had its benefits."

"Well, I made the pie for tonight, and I'm sure you'll find it scrumptious."

He leaned close and ran his tongue up her neck, then circled her earlobe. "As scrumptious as you?"

Jill shivered in response to the tantalizing chills that melted her like butter in his hands. "Stop that."

I couldn't if I wanted to. Garrett nuzzled closer. "I've got to grab your attention."

"It's working."

"I don't want to give you a chance to change your mind and go back to old what's his name."

She pulled the hand towel off the towel bar and snapped it at him. "You're feeling better."

"That's not fair." Garrett scrambled out of the bathroom. "Come on, Clyde. She's feisty." He and Clyde jogged into the kitchen. Garrett tossed him a treat, smiling at the dinner Jill had prepared. *We're making progress.* He glanced at the dining room table. *I'll surprise her.*

Garrett rushed to set the table, took candles off the dining room hutch and lit them, and had just placed the last dish on the table when he heard Jill's blow-dryer shut off. He went to the kitchen to open a bottle of wine.

Jill stepped into the dining room. "Nice work, Malloy."

"All I did was serve the magical meal you slaved over." He stepped out of the kitchen, trying to look nonchalant with a beer in his hand, and handed her a glass of wine.

She took the wine from him and sipped from the glass, her eyes never leaving his. "Cheers." She lifted her glass to him. "The table looks lovely."

"Clyde did it."

She leaned over and held the big dog's chin in her free hand. "You're a smart boy."

Clyde rewarded her with a single kiss on the cheek.

"He loves me." She took another swig of the wine.

"I hear that's going around." *I love how your cheeks blush when you drink wine.*

She clinked his glass. "Good wine."

"You should like it. You bought it about three years ago when we were at that little vineyard." *One of the best trips of my life. We could have so many more.*

"The one where they bottled by hand?"

"That's the one." They'd gone to a secluded mountain cabin. The fall leaves had put on a colorful show. They'd hiked a trail to a thunderous waterfall that crashed against the rocks so loudly they couldn't even talk over it. Deafening and peaceful at the same time. They'd sat on the rocks until it got nearly too dark to hike back. They'd pitched dozens of coins into the churning water, wishing on every dream they'd ever had.

"We made a lot of good memories there, didn't we?" she said.

He held her chair out for her and she sat. "Here's to many more."

They ate in near silence, until Garrett got up for a second helping of macaroni 'n' cheese. "Is Carolanne coming by tonight?"

Jill shook her head. "Unh-uh, she's going out with Connor."

"Pearl works fast. I thought he was still seeing that Chicago girl."

"Yeah. He is. Carolanne ran into him at Spratt's Market. He's taking her out to dinner. Just friends." Jill air-quoted the *just friends.*

"That's what they think. No one can escape Pearl's power of love." Garrett pointed his fork at Jill. "We know that better than anyone."

"Seems that way, doesn't it?"

I can only hope. "Where are they going?" Garrett asked.

"He's taking her to Roanoke Rapids to the new dinner theater. Have you been yet?"

"No, but I heard it's great."

"I would love to have Carolanne back in Adams Grove."

"Now who's making a bigger deal of the date?" he teased.

She lifted her shoulders sheepishly. “You never know.”

“It doesn’t sound like just a friendly night out to me, either.”

“Stop getting my hopes up. But Pearl’s never wrong, is she?”

Garrett tipped his beer toward Jill, his eyes sparkling in the candlelight. “I hope not.” *I want my future to be with you.*

Chapter Twenty-Six

The next morning, Jill padded into the living room, to find Garrett sitting on the living room floor surrounded by blueprints and notepaper. He balanced a near-empty coffee cup on one knee in the middle of it all.

Jill stooped next to him. "Whatcha doin'?"

"Good morning, sleepyhead. I didn't hear you come in."

"Want more coffee?" Jill asked.

He gulped the last sip and handed his cup to her. "Thanks."

She came back with two steaming mugs and sat on the floor next to him, peering over his shoulder. "Are those the plans for Bridle Path Estates?"

"Yep." His eyebrows drew together.

"Problem?" Jill scooched closer to him.

"No. I was just thinking that maybe we could still do the artisan center—you know, like we'd originally planned."

Are you serious?"

"It was a great idea. I mean, if you want to stick around. Running the artisan center would give you something to do, and it would be great for the community. No pressure."

"Are you kidding me? I'd love that."

"Look at the barn area over here." Garrett pointed to one of the blueprints. "I think we can move the playground to the back side of the pastures, closer to this cul-de-sac." He scribbled on the plans, trying to translate his vision for her. "Then if I turn the barn to face west and run the pastures this way, it would leave this space open, adjacent to the road."

She traced her finger where he'd just pointed. "Right here? Facing north?"

"Instead of pastures at the entrance, we'd have the artisan center." He leaned closer to her. "Do you think it would work?"

His face was so close to hers that she caught her breath. "Would what work?" she said, not wanting to take her eyes from his.

"The plan," he said.

"Yeah." She looked back down at the papers, concentrating on the drawing. "Yes. With the pasture behind it here, right?" Jill swiveled to get a closer look, examining the changes.

"Right. We could build a small livestock area in that space if we wanted to. Better yet, we could have a Four-H meeting area. The county could use a spot for that."

"That would be cool. We could do watercolor and pen-and-ink workshops back there."

"I like the idea." He nodded. "The artisan center would be almost diagonal from Penny's, so it would help her business, too."

"I think it's perfect." She sipped her coffee. "Are you bribing me?"

"Is it working?" He held her gaze for a moment.

She shrugged her shoulders but held his gaze. "Maybe I'm looking for a reason to stay."

He took her hand in his. "I think we should do this no matter what. I don't want to bribe or buy you. The artisan center is good for the community, whether we're a couple or not. If you come back to me, I want it to be because that's where you want to be."

That just made her feel even more confident that she was right where she should be. "Count me in. I even know who I want to be the first artist to display her work in the center."

"Who would that be?"

"Mary Claire. I'll let her know so she can start thinking about what she'd like to show, but I definitely want that portrait of Pearl on display."

"She really captured Pearl's sparkle, didn't she?"

"Yes, she did." They shared a moment of silence thinking about Pearl.

"We have a deal?" Garrett extended his hand for Jill to shake.

She didn't hesitate. "Deal." She started to say something and stopped.

"What?"

"I'm still worried."

"About our deal?"

"No. Not that. I'm worried about Bradley. It scares me to death what he was able to do. He's not like us."

"You got that right."

"He wants that treasure. You didn't see him. He's not going to give up until he gets it."

"I don't know that we'll ever figure out the whole story, but I know we'll find him and put him away for all the trouble he's caused you." Garrett didn't let go of her hand. Instead, he tugged her close, gently dropping a quick kiss on the tip of her nose.

Jill smiled at the familiar gesture. It was one of those little things she used to love about him. She got up from the floor and sat on the couch.

He rolled up the plans, snapping a rubber band around them. "So what are you and Carolanne up to today?" Garrett popped her on the head with the rolled-up tube.

"Don't start something you can't finish, Malloy." She grabbed the other end of the tube and tugged on it.

"Look who's talking," he warned.

Over the years, she and Garrett had battled with watermelon seeds, popcorn, marshmallows—and blueprint tubes were fair game, too. Deciding to avoid the challenge, she answered his question about Carolanne. "We're going to take Aunt Milly to Rocky Mount to check out some yarn and then to Shoney's for an early supper."

"Milly will love that. But if you have any pull with her, would you please make sure she doesn't knit me another sweater vest this year?"

"A sweater vest?" Picturing him in a sweater vest made her laugh.

"Quit laughing. It wasn't funny. For Christmas last year, she knitted me a red sweater vest."

"Get the heck out of here."

"I'm not kidding. Even Pearl joked my ass about it. That thing was redder than a fire truck."

"Did you wear it?"

"Of course I did. Milly worked hard on it. I wore it to the Christmas cantata at the church. She told everyone she'd made that vest for me. It made her day."

"You're a sweet man."

"Don't you forget it, but promise me you won't ever dress me funny, like you did Clyde."

She raised her hand in a scout sign. "I, Jill Clemmons, promise to never dress Garrett Malloy funny on purpose"—she lowered her voice to just above a whisper—"unless he drools a lot."

"A disclaimer. I see how you are." He dropped a quick kiss on her lips.

After a full day with Carolanne and Milly, Jill met Mary Claire at the diner to share the news about the artisan center.

The supper crowd had already cleared out. Jill flipped slowly through a portfolio of some of Mary Claire's latest work while they snacked on a basket of onion rings.

"I like the sketches of Pearl's gardens the best," Mary Claire said.

"Me too." Jill took a picture out of the stack. "This hummingbird in the mimosa tree is probably my favorite. I don't know. The birdbath is nice, too. They're all great."

"Yep," Mary Claire agreed. "Those other ones in the back are local people I sketched."

Jill flipped more quickly through those, paused, then flipped back to one that had caught her eye. The drawing featured a man standing behind a woman with his arms around her waist and leaning against a car.

Jill held the picture closer. She tried to control the concern from showing in her voice. "Mary Claire, when did you sketch this one?"

Mary Claire squinted at the picture, tilted her head, then looked to the ceiling as she tried to remember. "That's the lady who asked Izzy to deliver the fruit basket. See, there's the basket on the ground. That man and woman were behind the store. I saw them from my apartment."

"Had you seen them before?"

Mary Claire nodded. "At the park. I saw them at the park the day of Pearl's funeral. I was there feeding the ducks that morning. I was really sad that day."

"I know. Me too."

"I miss Pearl a lot." Mary Claire's pale-blue eyes watered.

"Me too." Jill looked at the picture again. "Can I borrow this?"

"Sure. You can have it."

"You're the best." Jill went to the counter, paid for their snack, then came back and hugged Mary Claire. Jill picked up her purse and the sketch and ran from the building toward the sheriff's office, just two blocks down Main Street.

After jogging all the way there, Jill pushed through the heavy wooden doors of the sheriff's office, half out of breath.

The dispatcher looked up from her desk.

"Where's Scott Calvin? Is he in?" Jill asked.

The dispatcher nodded toward the back and continued her duties.

Jill walked down the hall and knocked on the glass window of the open door of Scott's office. "Knock, knock," she said.

Scott looked up from the paperwork that was stacked on his battered metal desk. "Hey, Jill. Everything OK?"

"Yep. But I think I just found something that might help."

"What's that?"

"Look." She stepped into his office and laid the sketch on top of his papers.

"What am I looking at?"

"Mary Claire sketched it." Jill tapped the picture. "She saw these people in the parking lot behind the store." She pointed to the basket at the bottom of the photo. "That's the fruit basket, and that's Annie."

"Really?" Scott leaned back in his squeaky chair. "Well, I'll be darned. I hadn't seen any of her recent work. Man, she's even better than I remembered."

"Yeah, but that's not what I wanted you to see. Guess who that is?" Jill pointed to the man in the drawing.

"Is that Bradley Kase?"

"That's why you're the sheriff of this town. You can solve a crime"—she snapped her fingers—"just like that."

Scott gave her a broad smile. "Good work, Jill."

❖ Chapter Twenty-Seven ❖

A week later, Carolanne and Jill sipped coffee on the back patio and watched Clyde run the yard. In a few hours, it would be too hot and humid to sit outside.

"You and Connor have been spending a lot of time together, haven't you?" Jill topped off her cup of coffee and passed the pot to Carolanne.

"It's strictly business."

"I'm not usually one to speculate, but he does have you moving back to Adams Grove. Actions speak louder than words." Jill hoped Pearl was right about them.

"*He* doesn't. Our partnership does. When Connor told me that his practice had grown too large, too quickly, and he was turning away work, I suggested he get a partner. I didn't even think about myself until later."

"So how's this going to work?" Jill tugged on the toy Clyde had brought to her, then tossed it as far as she could throw.

"He's going to focus on the family and estate planning. It's what he does best. I'll pick up the real estate end. We'll just split any other work."

"Do you have a date set for the move yet?" Jill asked.

"I'm going to give my notice next week. So I'll be home before the month is out."

"Home. Sounds good, doesn't it?" Jill had to agree that Adams Grove felt like home to her again, too.

"Connor said that I can stay in one of the apartments over his office until I find a place. You know, I was thinking it would be neat to be the first homeowner in Bridle Path Estates."

"I happen to have an in with the builder," Jill said.

"I've heard. It's all over town, by the way."

"No doubt. Secrets are hard to keep in Adams Grove. I'm praying we can keep the Pacini Pearls under wraps. They probably don't even exist anymore, but they've caused enough trouble already. I think they're cursed. But I'm trying to not obsess about them. Speaking of secrets and under wraps, this deal with Connor, are you sure it's not just a teensy bit pleasure?"

"Stop it. I told you it's all business. Pearl was right, though. We do make a good team, but that's where it ends. Her skills must have been getting rusty there at the end," Carolanne said.

"Did you see Pearl's message from the video? She was very convincing."

"No, besides Connor is still seeing Katherine."

Jill hoped something more would happen between Carolanne and Connor once she moved back to town. Both being redheads, they'd make beautiful babies together. For a moment, her thoughts drifted to little ones, thoughts that hadn't crossed her mind in a long time.

Garrett's truck pulled in front of the house. A brown sheriff's car followed behind him. Scott Calvin got out and began talking to Garrett.

Jill walked over to the gate. "You break the law, Malloy?"

He waved and smiled. Scott waved, too.

Jill and Carolanne walked out to join them.

"What's up?" Jill asked as she got within earshot.

Scott turned toward the girls. "I was just telling Garrett that Izzy and Mary Claire have been very helpful, thanks to that sketch you brought me, Jill."

"My pleasure."

Scott continued. "Turns out the gal working the register that day can place Clatterbuck buying the fruit in Spratt's market, and as you know, Mary Claire saw Clatterbuck and Kase putting the basket together out back."

Scott handed the photo of the woman that Jill had identified as Annie earlier to Garrett. "You ever see this woman before?"

"No," Garrett said after a quick glance, then did a double take. "Wait. I might have seen her around town before. I'm not sure."

Scott took the picture from Garrett. "She's got a record. Clatterbuck and her husband, a Carl Townsend, have a string of warrants out for them."

"Who's Townsend?" Garrett asked.

Jill shook her head. "Don't know him."

"Those two have apparently duped dozens of folks up and down the East Coast over the past few years."

"She was a pain, but I never thought of her as a criminal. Never knew she was married, either," Jill said. "She was a live-in. Maybe they'd split up and she found herself a new partner in crime in Bradley. Sounds like he was perfect for her."

"Maybe." Scott crossed one foot over the other and explained. "That's where it starts to get a little interesting. Your old address in Savannah that you gave me"—Scott held up a finger, pausing—"it's owned by Townsend."

"What?" Jill shook her head and held her hands up in front of her. "I thought that was Bradley's house."

Carolanne stepped in closer to Jill. "What are you trying to say, Scott?"

"They are still investigating leads, but I got word from Savannah about an hour ago. They sent a car to pick up Clatterbuck, but the place has been vacated."

"He moved?" Garrett asked.

Scott jumped back in. "We're trying to get a recent picture of Townsend. I'll bring it by as soon as we get it."

Jill pulled her arms tight across her chest.

Garrett put his hand on Jill's shoulder. "You OK?"

She nodded, and Scott continued with the update. "These two have conned more people than you can imagine out of homes, cash, stocks, you name it. There's a laundry list of outstanding warrants. If we can get our hands on them, they'll be put away for a long time."

"I can't believe I never suspected a thing. Do you think Bradley Kase and Townsend are the same person?"

Scott nodded. "It's possible."

Jill stared at the ground, feeling humiliated and deflated. "Garrett, Bradley was into some shady dealings, too. I might be in trouble."

"You will not be in trouble. You're a victim of their shenanigans, too." Carolanne flipped her red hair over her shoulder. "Don't you worry, Jill. I'll take care of that."

Scott stuffed his notebook into his shirt pocket. "The Savannah police are working with us. I'll keep you posted. They'll want to talk to you, Jill."

Jill turned and headed toward the house without a word.

How could I have been so naive? One lie after another. I gobbled them right up.

❖

Garrett watched Jill leave, then turned back to Scott. "She's really upset."

Carolanne chewed on her cuticle. "Scott, Jill told Bradley about Annie. If they were in it together, if he's Townsend, she tipped them off. You realize that, don't you?"

He nodded. "Yes, I know, and I'm still worried, too, because this fruit basket thing has the feel of a personal attack."

"He better not come back around here if he knows what's good for him." Garrett's jaw pulsed.

Scott said, "We've probably seen the last of him. If he knows we're on to him, he won't want to risk getting caught. But, that being said, if he does come back around, be careful. There's no telling what he's capable of doing now."

Garrett put his arm around Carolanne and gave her a friendly hug. "We have to be careful, but let's not worry Jill more. She's been through too much already."

Carolanne crossed her heart. "She won't hear it from me. I agree."

Scott left, and Garrett and Carolanne stood soaking in the details.

Carolanne pulled her car keys from her pocket. "I'm going to give you and Jill some time alone."

"Yeah, that would be good." He hoped like hell Kase was out of the picture forever.

"Just give her some space, but not too much. You know what I mean. Call me if you need me," Carolanne said, then turned to leave.

"I will." Garrett stood there wondering how to give Jill space without leaving her alone. He walked to the backyard gate. Clyde ran alongside Garrett as he walked over to the swing. It hurt Garrett to see Jill looking like the stuffing had been knocked out of her. She felt betrayed, he could tell. If only he could erase the past year for her.

"Want some company?" Jill broke the silence.

"I didn't hear you walk up." She looked fragile. He slowed the swing and scooted to one side. "You OK?"

"I feel so stupid." She kicked the pine straw, avoiding eye contact, and sat next to him. "I can't believe I didn't see all this coming. Look at all the trouble I've caused for everyone." She laid her head against his chest.

"Don't blame yourself. It's not your fault. It sounds like they've conned a lot of people."

"But why me?" She leaned back in the seat and crossed her arms across her chest. "I was gullible—an easy target."

"You were trusting, and that's good," he said.

"I didn't trust you." She scooted around sideways in the seat. The swing creaked as it rocked backward. "I'm so sorry, Garrett."

"Stop it. You don't need to apologize to me—ever." He took her hands into his own. "It's the past. Let it go."

She leaned forward and kissed his fingers. "How can you ever forgive me?"

"I love you, Jill. I've never stopped."

"I'm very lucky."

Garrett took her hand and opened it, then pressed a kiss into the palm of her hand. "I'm the lucky one." They rocked as the sun slipped behind the trees. The frogs croaked and lightning bugs lit up the shrubs and trees. He pulled her closer and looked up at the heavens—just in time to see the streak of light cross the sky.

"Did you see that?" Jill pointed skyward, eyes wide.

"The shooting star?"

"Yeah. That's lucky, right?" Jill squirmed in the seat, scanning the sky for another.

"Rumor has it," he said.

"Thank goodness. I could use a little good luck." Jill swatted a mosquito. "The mosquitoes are starting to chow down on me."

"Come on, let's head in."

Clyde ran into the kitchen and dropped to the floor with his paws around his empty water dish.

"Is someone out of water?" Jill laughed, and Garrett smiled at the warmth she exuded.

"He's a little dramatic, isn't he?" Garrett picked up the bowl and filled it up from the tap, then set it down.

Clyde lapped loudly from the bowl.

"Oh no," Jill said, "that's ammunition for that drool hound."

Garrett tossed her a towel. "Quick. Better suit up."

As if on cue, Clyde trotted across the kitchen and rubbed his chin on Jill's pants.

"Great." She brushed the wet spot with the towel. "Guess I'll go ahead and jump in the shower and change into my pajamas."

"I'll feed him. How about I throw a couple burgers on the grill. Does that sound OK?"

"Sure. I'll make a salad."

"Your famous chopped salad?" Garrett said, hopeful.

"I think I have everything to make it if you start the hard-boiled eggs while you're in the kitchen."

"Deal. No one makes a chopped salad like yours."

"Hey, before I forget, could you drop Clyde at the kennel in the morning? I made a grooming appointment for him, and Dr. Tinker is going to take a follow-up look at his paw."

"Sure. I have to run over to a job site, anyway. The kennel's on the way. Why don't you come along? You'd love this house. Do you remember the old Miller farm on Nickel Creek?"

Jill nodded. "Isn't that where the old pumpkin farm was that we went to in elementary school?"

"That's the one."

"No one's lived there in years. Who bought it?" she asked.

"Chaz sold it to some goat farmer from Virginia Beach. The guy bought it last year but had a laundry list of remodeling he wanted done. The schedule is tight. He's going to surprise his wife on their anniversary."

"How romantic," she said wistfully.

"I knew you'd say that." He hoped to do something just as romantic for Jill someday.

"Stop teasing me. It is romantic." She faked a pout.

"Come with me. You'll love it."

"Soon. Promise. But I've got to remedy this car situation first. I feel like I'm trapped here without any wheels. I'm going to get Carolanne to take me car shopping." Jill headed down the hall to shower and change.

Garrett watched her walk down the hall. From the familiar curve of her hips to her tiny waist that he could practically encircle with his hands, just the sight of her made him want to protect her, to love her, more than ever.

❖ Chapter Twenty-Eight ❖

Garrett had already left to go to work when Jill woke up. She'd just poured herself a cup of coffee when she heard a knock at the door.

Jill opened the door. Elsie stood on the front porch.

"Garrett asked me to drop this truck off for you." Elsie lobbed the keys toward Jill. "He said you needed some wheels."

Jill caught the keys against her chest. "I do. Thanks."

One of Garrett's smaller work trucks was parked out front. "Come on in."

"Can't. I gotta run."

Billy pulled into the driveway in Elsie's car. "We're going to sample wedding cakes this morning."

"That sounds like fun."

Elsie's smile faded. "It should be, but we're kind of fighting about it." She looked over her shoulder toward Billy sitting in her car, then turned back to Jill and rolled her eyes. "I want almond. He wants chocolate. How can you have a chocolate wedding cake?"

"I went to a wedding last year that had the prettiest cake—white frosting with elegant flowers, but the cake was chocolate. It was to die for. That type of cake is the hottest thing going back in Savannah."

"Really?"

"Oh yeah. All the rage." Jill embellished the story a little, hoping she might soften Elsie's edge. The cake was probably the only part of the whole wedding planning process Billy had an interest in.

"Well, that doesn't sound so bad," she said, looking impressed. "Maybe it could work."

"I wouldn't rule it out." Jill winked.

Elsie skipped down the porch steps and jogged toward the car.

"Thanks for bringing the truck," Jill said as she waved to Billy.

Jill tossed the keys from hand to hand, suddenly feeling as if she had wings. She straightened the house and put in a load of laundry.

The sun was bright, so she hung the laundry out on the line. It would be dry before lunchtime.

By noon, she'd cleaned every nook and cranny in the house. If those pearls were anywhere in this house, she surely would have come across them by now, and as much as she'd like to put that troublesome treasure out of her mind, she just couldn't stop thinking about it. She decided to ride into town and shop for a car of her own since Carolanne was tied up. She knew she couldn't drive Garrett's company truck for long without affecting his business.

As she drove, she kept thinking about the old Miller farm he was working on. At the last second, she turned left on Nickel Creek Road instead of heading toward town.

Tall hardwoods grew tight to the shoulder and shaded narrow Nickel Creek Road. Only a few crop fields interrupted the lush foliage, unlike the road to Pearl's that was beginning to feel the burden of urban sprawl.

Jill slowed as she approached the recently paved driveway to the old Miller farm. She pulled the small truck next to Garrett's.

The house sat back off the road. A single story, which was unusual for a farm house of that era. Rumor had it that one of the young Miller boys had been born with a birth defect that kept him in leg braces. When Mr. Miller built this home, he'd kept it to one story so his son could get around more easily.

Jill had driven by there many, many times over the years on the way to the lake, but she'd never been inside. Back then, the house had been dilapidated. Now the white clapboard was new, as was the bright-red tin roof.

As she approached the house, she heard a radio blaring between the hums of a compressor inside the house.

Jill knocked on the door, but only to be polite, knowing darn well that Garrett wouldn't be able to hear her. She twisted the knob and peeked inside. The rhythm of the nail gun led her to the back corner of the house. Garrett squatted over the molding along the floor, nailing and duckwalking his way around the room.

His face lit up as soon as he saw her.

She wiggled her fingers in a wave. "You made this place sound so great I couldn't resist a visit."

Garrett balanced the nail gun on a sawhorse and turned off the noisy compressor. "I'm glad you did."

He placed his hands on his hips, looking proud. "Did you check out the front of the house?"

"Yeah. It's great. I love it."

"This room is for Nick's wife. She's a famous photographer or something. All this will be work surface and storage," he explained. "That was a small bedroom, but they have me changing it over to a darkroom for her."

Jill crossed the room to the wide span of windows overlooking the backyard. "Look at the view from here. What a great place to work. The light is amazing." She imagined working on a project in this space. "Are you going to put storage under the work surfaces over here?"

"I don't know yet. He left the design up to me. What are you thinking?"

She dropped her purse in the corner and walked the room. With her finger pressed to her lips, she finally stopped in the middle of the room. "I think…"

Garrett rested his hip on one of the sawhorses.

Jill's mind engaged. She loved this part of design, and she was a natural at it. "You could use, like, a French cleat so the shelf looks like it's floating over here on this long wall under these windows and do an angled worktop that hinges on the back. That way she could keep supplies or paper underneath." She walked to the other side of the room. "Then, on this inside wall, I'd run a flat surface and make it deep, at least thirty-two inches deep, for cutting mat board and framing."

"I like it. Not too hard to do, either."

"Five-minute job, right?"

They'd had an inside joke that every project she came up with was just a five-minute job, at least in her mind. She and Pearl had come up with great ideas and inspiration from those DIY shows they watched all the time. The tasks had never been as simple as they appeared, and Garrett always paid the price for her creativity. Not that he'd minded.

"Yeah, right. I've missed those five-minute jobs." He removed his tape measure from the tool belt hanging low on his hips and scribbled some measurements on a scrap piece of wood.

He walked by her, gave her a high five, then penciled a couple of marks on the window wall for the angled work surfaces.

"Perfect." She clapped her hands. "I would love to have a room like this."

"Then I'd say Nick Rolly ought to be pleased with it, too."

"Well, his wife is the one that will love it, but he'll get the benefits, I'm sure," she said with a wink.

"Want to see the rest of my handiwork?"

"Absolutely." She fell in step behind him. "Where's your help?"

"I'm doing this one alone. I get bored just managing the work teams, so I try to keep some of the fun projects for myself."

"It's what you do best," she said.

He gave her a tour of the house, sharing what he knew about the Rolly family from Chaz. "Nick Rolly and his son, Jake, come up when his wife is out of town to check on the progress. Jake entertains himself the whole time they're here. Never gets in the way. Cute one, that boy."

"Your clock tickin'?" she teased.

"Maybe."

Jill ran her hands across the hand-carved bar in the kitchen. "Did you do this?"

He nodded proudly.

"I recognize your work." The craftsmanship was unmistakable. Jill enjoyed hearing him talk about his projects with so much enthusiasm. But she knew he was under a tight deadline, so she didn't stay long.

He walked her out to the truck.

Jill stopped midstep and grabbed his arm. "I can't believe I didn't say thank you for loaning me the truck the first second I saw you. I feel like a teenager with her first set of wheels."

"I figured if I waited for you to ask for help, I'd wait forever."

"You know me, don't you?"

Garrett nodded. "That I do."

Jill opened the truck door and slid behind the wheel. "The house is fabulous, Garrett."

"Thanks. I'm really proud of how it's coming together." He looked toward the house and then back to her. "What are you going to do the rest of the day?"

She hung her elbow out the window. "I'm going to run by the grocery store and then back to the house. I want to get some pruning done."

"Uh-oh," Garrett said.

"What?"

"I know how you are with those pruning shears. I better hurry else the woods will be cut down to knee-high by the time I get there."

"What a comedian."

"Hey, you come by it honestly. Pearl was the same way."

"Yeah. She was." It was getting easier to think about Pearl. The memories were so special. "I'm not going to hold you up any longer. Thanks for the tour."

"Glad you came. I'll be done here in another hour or so. How about I pick you up? We'll go to dinner."

"Deal."

He waved as she backed the truck out of the long driveway.

When Jill got home, she put every other worry aside and settled in to do some research on the Pacini Pearls on Carolanne's laptop. It took a while, but finally she'd run across the right search engine and the right combination of words to find something helpful.

She leaned closer to the screen. "I can't believe it." Excited by the find, she tried to call Carolanne but didn't get an answer. Garrett's phone went right to voice mail, too.

Enlarging the image on the computer screen by another 50 percent, she wondered if there was any way possible that they really still existed.

Too anxious from all the new information, she got her pruning shears and went outside and started clipping her way around the outer edge of the garden. The adrenaline was working to her favor. She pruned the roses that had gotten long and wild already, snipping two perfect blooms for herself. They'd be a cheerful sight to wake up to in a tall bud vase on the bedside table. She held one of the full double-fringed blooms to her nose and inhaled the spicy scent. They'd be even more fragrant early in the day when the dew on the leaves was drying in the bright sun.

She and Pearl had made it a habit to start their morning by smelling the roses. It was clichéd, but it was true that it made them feel good and was a wonderful reminder of God's perfect creations.

"Miss me yet?"

The voice from behind her sent goose bumps climbing up her spine.

Jill spun around to see Bradley and dropped the two perfect roses at her feet. "What are you doing here?" She raised the purple pruning shears in defense. "Go," she said, snipping the air. "Go away."

"What? Am I supposed to be afraid?" Bradley asked. "Are you going to prune me with your little purple scissors?"

"You can't imagine how appealing that sounds." She jabbed the pruners in his direction.

"Mad?"

"Furious. What the hell are you up to, and who are you?" She hated him for making her feel so stupid. "It was all a lie. Everything about you—about us—was a big fat lie."

"Oh, come on, baby. Was it that bad? You had some fun. Admit it." He licked his lips.

"You're a liar and a cheat."

"It's a dirty job, but someone has to do it."

"You've done enough damage around here. Leave."

"I'm not leaving until I get what's rightfully mine."

"I don't have anything that belongs to you."

"You've made a huge mess of this, Jill."

"Me? You're the one—"

"No. I had it all planned out. If you had just packed everything up like I told you, this could already be over. No one would have gotten hurt. I'd have the Pacini Pearls." He took a step closer.

"Now I can't be responsible for what happens. You know way too much, and I won't lose that treasure."

"If that treasure exists—and that's a huge *if*—it doesn't belong to you."

A cloud crossed overhead, dimming the bright sunshine and shadowing Bradley's eyes.

She needed to get to the house and call for help.

"I've got to pee. I'll be right back." She breezed past him and walked to the house, praying he wouldn't follow her.

She didn't look back until she got to the door, but he was already making strides in her direction. She willed herself to move slowly, trying to appear calm, but as soon as she crossed the threshold, she ran as fast as her feet would take her to the phone in the hall. She fat-fingered the number, trying to dial Scott Calvin. Finally, the phone rang on the other end, but went straight to the dispatcher.

"Get a message to Scott Calvin. It's Jill Clemmons. Tell him Bradley's here. There's a warrant out for him. Hurry."

Bradley walked in just as she hung up.

He called down the hall, sounding impatient. "What are you doing?"

She rounded the corner, pretending to wipe damp hands on her jeans. "I told you, I had to pee."

He walked into the living room and took a seat on the couch. "Come sit with me and chat." He patted the seat next to him.

"Don't pretend you really cared for me."

"Oh, I didn't say that."

His smirk made her sick.

"You used me," she fumed.

"I sure did. Meeting you was like striking oil. Your small-town, goody-two-shoes way had people lining up to invest in my deal of the day. I've never taken money from rich people with such ease."

Melanie had said some of his deals were going bad, called them dodgy, and then that article. She'd trusted him. "*I* never took anyone's money. Don't group me in your category."

"Oh, but you did. And all in a good day's work. Now, once I have those pearls, I'll be set for a long stretch. You did all the work. I get all the benefits."

"The charities benefited," she lifted her chin. He wouldn't take that from her.

He looked at her like she was crazy.

"You're kidding, right?" Bradley smirked. "Are you that naive?"

His words didn't register on her dizzying senses.

"You still don't get it, do you?" Bradley threw back his head and laughed. "I'm a con, Jill. It's what I do. I'm the best. There were never any charities. The Kase Foundation goes straight to me. There were no great real estate ventures. I took money from greedy people. Don't feel sorry for them. They had it to spare and wanted more."

"I saw the camps. The foundation does good work," she said, but her head swirled with doubt.

"Those camps have nothing to do with the Kase Foundation. I wove videos from YouTube together to get most of them." He slapped the mail in his hand against his thigh.

"You and Annie were in cahoots when she broke into Pearl's house, weren't you?"

"You know I was out of town."

"So says you. What's your word worth? Nothing? You locked me in the attic, didn't you? No, wait. You called me from out of town."

"Maybe I was at the end of the driveway when I called you that morning," he said smugly. "Just like today."

"You could've killed me. It was the hottest day of the summer."

"But I didn't," he said. "Pearl lived too lean to have cashed in the Pacini Pearls. I figured they'd show up once she died if I was patient. My mother always said I reminded her of her uncle, John Carlo."

"You're nothing like John Carlo Pacini." Jill shot him a cold look.

"How would you know?"

"I've read his letters. He loved my grandmother, and he was sensitive and caring. When his treasures put Pearl in danger, he protected her. He was a good man."

"Believe what you want. He left her. We're both treasure hunters of sorts, and we're both very charming."

"Don't flatter yourself, Bradley."

"When I learned of John Carlo's fortune, I knew I could find it. It was meant to be mine."

"You're just a common thief."

"Nothing common about it, my friend. I don't stalk around in black tights robbing people. I get what I want because people feel compelled to hand it over to me. Only you don't get it, do you?"

"You're a manipulator. You used me."

"And it was my pleasure, babe."

Disgust surged through her. "Screw you."

"And that was my pleasure, too. Believe me. So anyway, that was when I hooked up with you. You and Malloy were easy enough to manipulate, you righteous do-gooders. You think everyone is as honest as you are." Bradley tipped his head back with a smirk. "You Southerners are so gullible."

"We're trusting. Besides, look who's talking. You're from farther south than me."

"No, actually, I'm from Maine."

"Good lord." She gestured in a sweeping motion with her arm. "Where does it end?"

"You were so easy. A digital camera and a little Photoshop touch-up to a picture of a blonde tucked into a picture of your high school sweetheart and you swallowed that bait like a hungry catfish," he said in a mocking Southern tone.

"You're despicable," she spewed. "Garrett swore he'd never seen that blonde. You made me believe there was something going on."

"I didn't *make* you believe anything. I simply made some artful suggestions."

"You're disgusting."

"You don't really appeal to me anymore, either." He stood and approached her.

Please get here, Scott.

He pushed her toward the kitchen. "Walk."

"Stop it. That hurts." She stumbled. When she turned to him, she met his cold stare. She lifted her chin, refusing to falter.

He looked surprised by her resolve. "Go on. Move."

"What are you going to do?" She stepped into the kitchen and turned to face him.

"I'm going to give you one more chance. Hand over the Pacini Pearls."

"Or what?"

"Or I'll burn down the house."

"You won't do that. You want your treasure."

"You said you don't have it," Bradley reminded her. "Either you give them to me and go on with your small-town life or you and the pearls go up in smoke."

Her thoughts flashed to the fire in the woods. He'd do it. *Where are you, Scott?* She wished she'd called Garrett instead. She glanced at the clock on the stove. Garrett would be here to pick her up in just fifteen minutes. *I can stall that long.*

Bradley's voice was calm. His gaze steady. "I'm not going to let you have my treasure. I'd rather let you die with it than to lose it to you. I've waited too long. Those pearls are mine."

She spoke with quiet yet definite firmness. "I don't know what or where they are."

"Don't play games with me." He tapped the face of his gold-and-diamond watch. "Time's a wasting. I've been patient, but I'm over that now." As he admired his expensive timepiece, she mustered all the strength she had and landed her bent knee in his groin.

He doubled over, then stumbled backward.

Jill shoved him as hard as she could and ran.

He recovered quickly and ran after her, grabbing her by her hair and twisting it in his fist, stopping her in her tracks.

Pain ripped through her, clear down her spine. She screamed and lunged toward him to relieve the pressure of his grip.

Bradley forced her against him. "Don't want to play nice?" he choked out, his face red and sweating from the pain. "There are a couple good things about the country, babe. No one is going to hear you way the hell out here. You go right on and scream until your lungs bleed. It just turns me on, anyway."

Bradley shoved her into one of the wooden kitchen chairs.

The woven bottom scraped the back of her thighs as she landed hard. She kicked toward him, trying to land another blow, but her angle was wrong.

He had a tight grip around both of her wrists in one of his large hands. "Quit kicking, damn it," Bradley yelled.

Jill wasn't going to give in. She finally knew what she wanted, and she had every intention of fighting for it. "Leave me alone, you freak," she screamed.

He knocked her to the ground.

The wind rushed from her chest when her back hit the floor.

In one quick move, he knelt on her arms to keep her from moving.

She heard his belt clear loops in three loud snaps.

She continued to kick and thrash against him, landing a few good kicks.

He wrapped the belt around her arms and tightened it to immobilize them. The leather bit into her soft flesh.

Bradley dragged her to the chair and buckled her belted arms through the chair rails at her back.

She squirmed and kicked her heels against the ground, hopping in the chair, frantic to get loose.

Bradley loosened his tie with one hand and pulled it over his head. "Do you remember buying this neck tie?" He pushed her hands through the loop of the silk tie and tugged hard.

She continued to kick and caught him in the back of the knee as he moved in front of her.

"Bet you didn't know at the time that you'd be dying with it tied around your wrists." He opened a drawer and rummaged through the contents before slamming it shut. In the next drawer, he came up with a roll of duct tape. He caught one of her ankles midkick, then wrapped the tape in a quick figure eight around it and the second rung of the chair.

"You're pissin' me off." The force of his seething reply caused her to tense as he grabbed her other ankle and did the same.

She glared at him. "You think I care?"

He backhanded her.

She flinched against the power of the blow that made her eye feel like it had exploded. Warm blood trickled down to her lip.

He'd clearly mastered that move, landing the blow right on top of the already bruised knot he put on her cheek before. She took a big gulp of air, fighting to stay conscious, but unsure if she still was. She blinked against the pain.

She heard his laugh as he moved through the living room.

Thank God, she thought. Maybe he would leave now. Maybe this had just been to "show" her. She heard him moving through the house, his steps echoing loud on the wooden plank floors. Books crashed and glass broke as something hit the floor in the other room.

She caught his reflection in the dining room mirror.

He paced like a wild animal, back and forth through the rooms.

"Where are they? Damn it." He climbed the stairs, clomping from room to room, then back down the stairs, growling out obscenities the whole way.

She heard a familiar sound. The flick of his pipe lighter. "Bradley," she screamed.

"I'm busy," he yelled back.

"Stop this." Fear sliced through her. "Bradley, what are you doing?" Her voice rose in panic as she realized his intentions.

"Smoking. Want one?" He leaned back and gave Jill one last glance. Their gazes held for what seemed like a long time.

Please, she mouthed to him. Her eyes pleaded. *Don't do this to me.*

He moved out of her line of sight.

She heard the unmistakable flick of the lighter again.

Silence.

But only for a moment.

Then a flash of orange followed a loud whoosh as the first flame lit. The heavy drapes that covered the long row of windows in the front room went up quick. Yellow and gold danced in the mirror, and dusty smoke snaked through the air.

Bradley stepped back to the doorway between the living and dining rooms. "I might just miss you a little, after all, babe. What a shame."

"Please, let me go," she begged. "Don't do this to me." She struggled against the binds that held her tight to the chair. She tried to hop, but with her feet up on the rungs, she wasn't able to get any leverage.

"I won't tell," she pleaded, exhausted from the struggle and trying to catch her breath. She gulped smoke and coughed uncontrollably. "I won't tell. I promise."

If she could just scoot the chair to the cabinets, she might be able to get her hands lose with the metal of the handles. She felt a thread of hope as she heaved herself forward, and finally, the chair bumped. But it landed crooked and toppled over to the right, throwing her hard against the floor on her shoulder.

Pain splintered through her body.

She fought to reconnect with the breath that had been knocked out of her in the fall.

I'm OK. I'm OK. She prayed she wouldn't pass out. Her hands wiggled and tugged against the spindles of the chair until one finally gave way.

She heard Bradley snicker.

"You're not going to leave me like this," she said. "Help me."

He knelt on one knee, only feet away.

She didn't let go of his gaze. She wouldn't let him off that easy.

"You lose," he said.

A loud pop came from the living room.

"Don't. Please help me," she said, but she wasn't sure the words were even audible. There was a lethal calmness in his eyes. "How could you?"

He jumped to his feet and ran. The door slammed behind him.

She cried as the heavy black smoke rolled into the kitchen.

Trapped.

She tried to scream even though she knew it was pointless, wasted breath. There were no neighbors to hear her.

As the smoke thickened, sweat dripped from her hair into her eyes. As the fire in the next room popped and crackled, the temperature around her instantly rose.

Chapter Twenty-Nine

The road ahead clouded with dust. Garrett swerved his truck onto the soft shoulder as a car zoomed by from the other direction. The car's speed was reckless, even for locals who were comfortable on these back roads. Garrett's tires spit dust and gravel as they spun, trying to get traction back onto the pavement. Clyde barked from the passenger seat.

An uneasy feeling came over Garrett. He was about a mile from Pearl's house. Jill was there waiting on him, but that car looked an awful lot like Kase's Lexus. *Would that jerk have the balls to come back around here again?*

Garrett jammed on the brakes and turned his truck around to follow Kase, dialing the sheriff as he did.

"Calvin? Malloy here. I think I just passed Kase on Old Pond Road." Garrett mashed the gas pedal, accelerating quickly.

"We're on our way." Sheriff Calvin committed to get help to intercept him.

Garrett glanced in his rearview mirror out of habit.

The dusty road blurred dark gray.

His eyes narrowed as he tried to gain perspective on the image behind him, and then he slammed on his brakes.

"God, no," he said, forgetting he still had the cell phone to his ear.

"I've got someone only about four miles out. If it's him, we've got him this time. Do you still have the vehicle in sight?" Sheriff Calvin asked.

"Yeah." Garrett glanced in his rearview mirror. He slammed on the brakes, sending papers and tools sliding across the floor of the truck. "Shit. That's smoke. I've got to check on Jill."

"What's going on?" Voices on the radio crackled in the background. "Garrett, that was dispatch. Jill called. Kase was there."

"Damn him." Garrett leaned his body forward, willing the truck to go even faster.

"We're on our way," Scott said. "Be careful. He's out of control. No telling where he's going."

"Yeah. Well, I know where he went." Garrett grabbed the wheel with both hands as he pushed his truck to new limits. "I'm heading for Jill. Get that bastard this time, would ya?" He tossed the phone in the seat.

Black smoke billowed over the trees. He prayed that it was only the woods on fire again.

His pulse raced. Sweat beaded on his upper lip. He frowned with fury.

Garrett gasped as he cleared the trees and saw the house in flames. "Jill!"

Ash showered like tiny blistering snowflakes on his windshield.

He jumped from the truck, leaving Clyde barking in alert, safe in the truck. The smoke stung his nose and eyes. He imposed an iron control over himself, trying to keep a clear head.

As he neared the house, the press of the heat was almost unbearable. His skin tightened against it. A gold flame spiked high into the sky, and another pushed through the front wall of the house. He raised his forearm against the blinding inferno.

A loud roar filled the air as the flames pushed through the roof.

Garrett had a hard time distinguishing between the noises he heard. *Is the fire whistling, or is that sirens?* The sound got louder, but he didn't have time to wait.

He sprinted around the side of the house and leaped over the low picket fence, searching for a safe entry point. At the back door, he forced himself to stop long enough to lay a hand on the door to check for heat, although he knew in his heart it wouldn't matter. *She was supposed to be here waiting for me to pick her up.* If there was any chance…

He couldn't leave Jill inside. He had to get her out.

Thankfully, the heat wasn't as intense back there. He twisted the knob, but the door was locked. He balled his hand in a fist and popped out the back glass panel and reached through the shards of glass to unlock it. Blood spilled from the slice in his forearm.

Garrett squinted in the heavy smoke, desperate to find Jill. Hot flames blazed, roasting his skin. He raised an arm to shield his face so he could look for her.

He stumbled in the kitchen, barely able to see through the thickening smoke.

"Jill," he choked out, frantic. If she was upstairs, he'd never get to her. "Where are you?" *I can't lose her now.* "Jill, can you hear me?"

But the fire was snapping up everything in its path, muffling even his own voice.

He tripped and fell to the floor.

As he clambered to get up, he realized it was Jill he'd stumbled over.

Thank you, God.

"Jill!" He shook her, but she seemed lifeless.

She didn't move.

Flames licked from the dining room into the kitchen.

Time was running out, and he knew it.

He tried to lift her, but the chair jammed near the cabinet.

Garrett shook off a dizzy feeling. *Give me a second chance. Please, God. I'll never let her down again.*

He lifted his shirt up over his nose and pulled his knife from his hip to cut her loose, but his eyes were tearing so badly he could barely see. He coughed, choking on the acrid fumes.

Unable to free her from the chair, Garrett heaved the chair and Jill into the air in one swift motion and ran out the back door. He didn't stop running until he was nearly to the woods and away from the heat.

Jill's head hung forward, limp, her hair a tangled mess.

"Talk to me." He reached for her face and tipped her chin up, but she didn't respond.

"Come on," he shouted, "you have to be OK. Hang in there, angel."

Garrett dared to hope when he heard Jill trying to draw in fresh air between raspy coughs. Soot smudged her face.

I'll kill that bastard.

The EMTs dragged Garrett away. He hadn't heard the emergency vehicles arrive. He prayed that they were in time and could save his girl.

The emergency workers began immediate triage. Jill responded to the CPR. They quickly put her on oxygen to quiet her heavy coughing and gagging.

They transferred Jill to a stretcher and put her in the ambulance. Garrett jumped into the back of the ambulance and the medic closed the door behind them.

"Stay with me, Jill. Please. You've got to hang on." He clung to her arm.

Jill's lashes fluttered. A tear cleared a trail down the soot on her face.

The ambulance lurched forward, sirens blaring as they sped toward the hospital.

"How bad is she burned?" Garrett asked the medic.

The large man didn't look to be out of his twenties, but he moved with confidence. "She doesn't appear to have any severe burns."

"Thank God," Garrett said.

"But she's not out of the woods." The medic raised the IV bag to a hook, repositioned the oxygen mask, and took her blood pressure.

Garrett wiped his hands on his jeans and then put his hand on the wall of the ambulance for balance.

"Burns look worse, but more people die of smoke inhalation than from burns." The medic stayed steady at work as he spoke.

Garrett swallowed hard. "Hang in there for me, baby." *Don't leave me.*

The medic pointed to the gash on Garrett's arm. "That doesn't look good. You probably need a couple of stitches."

Garrett tugged his arm away. Blood had coagulated and stiffened against his shirt. "Concentrate on her. I'm fine."

Jill thrashed.

Garrett reached for her arm, trying to comfort her.

The medic talked to the ER on a two-way radio. Through the scratchy speakers, they repeated the vitals and followed the treatment plan the hospital dictated. "Do you know how long she was in there?" the medic asked.

He shook his head. "No. I don't know."

The medic conveyed the message and gave the hospital the update on Jill's condition. It sounded serious. If she had to be intubated, they didn't want to do it in transit.

The medic monitored Jill and tried to keep her comfortable, while reporting status to the hospital via the radio.

Jill flailed and appeared to struggle for air every time she floated into consciousness.

When they got to the hospital, the ER team met them at the doors, ready to move Jill directly to an individual resuscitation bay for immediate care.

The hospital team worked quickly.

"She took in a lot of smoke," said the attending physician, a tall, lanky man. "There are burns in her throat. Even her nose hairs are burned."

He leaned in, placing his stethoscope to her chest.

A nurse fussed with the monitors and they began to beep and spit out data. Another nurse drew blood, then scurried from the area.

"Start hyperbaric oxygen therapy. Her oxygen levels aren't where they need to be," the doctor said. The nurse moved immediately to execute the orders.

Garrett's injuries were minor and treated quickly. The slice in his forearm took over a dozen stitches. Getting the stitches hurt far worse than the cut itself.

After he'd been patched up, he paced the length of the waiting room. He'd spent more time in this hospital this month than he had in his lifetime. If he ever had to be there again, it would be too soon. As much as he'd hated being a patient, it was far worse to have Jill behind those curtains fighting for her life.

The desk nurse called Garrett over. "The doctor will be right out to discuss her condition with you." She pointed toward the green double doors. "There he is now."

Garrett met the doctor in the doorway.

"We're watching her closely. We've started oxygen therapy."

Garrett closed his eyes, his chin quivering. "Thank you, God."

"Depending on how she does overnight, I'd like to do a bronchoscopy in the morning. It's a visual exam done with a fiber-optic tube. That will give us the chance to see how much damage has been done to the lungs and airways."

"She's going to be OK, right?"

"I'm not going to sugarcoat my prognosis. Her condition is serious," the doctor said. "We're monitoring her respiratory rate and other vitals. We'll take good care of her. We're going to move her to ICU as soon as we can get a bed. You've been through a lot yourself. You might want to go home. She won't be allowed visitors."

Garrett hesitated.

"I know it's hard to leave. We've sedated her to keep her comfortable and regulate her breathing. Trust me. We'll call if anything changes." The doctor cuffed Garrett's shoulder and gave him a nod. "Any other questions for me?"

Garrett couldn't think of any. "No, sir. But please, Doc, take good care of her."

The doctor nodded, then turned and walked away.

Garrett stood there alone, not wanting to leave.

The nurse at the desk must have recognized the lost look on his face. "Sir, can I call a friend or a cab to give you a ride home?"

"No, thanks." He walked toward the front of the hospital. He lifted the phone out of the clip on his belt and pushed redial.

Scott Calvin answered. "Is Jill OK?"

Garrett wiped his brow. His arm was stiff from the heavy bandage they'd wrapped from his forearm to his bicep. "She's not out of the woods, but she's going to recover." He swallowed hard. "She has to."

"I'm out here at the house. Garrett, it doesn't look good."

"I know. The place was engulfed in flames when I got there. I can't believe I got her out of there, man."

"Thank God you turned around when you did."

"Did your guys get Kase?"

"No," he admitted, "I'm afraid not."

"Damn it." Garrett pounded his fist into the air. "I thought you said you had a man right in the area."

"We did."

"Then what happened?"

"My deputy had pulled him over just before the APB went out for speeding. Kase talked his way out of it. He had fake FBI credentials and said he was on undercover assignment in hot pursuit of the perp. By the time the call went out, my deputy had already escorted Kase all the way to the county line, blue lights and all. Kase gave him a thumbs-up as he crossed into Carolina."

"I bet he did. Damn Kase." Garrett kicked a trash can over. "FBI? Could that guy stoop any lower?"

"He's a pro."

Garrett dropped his head into his hands. "Kase won't get away with this."

"Trust me. Dan is feeling pretty bad. We haven't given up, Garrett. We'll find Kase."

"He better hope you find him before I do."

"Don't go doing anything crazy that I can't get you out of, old buddy." Scott's warning reminded him of a few times when his temper had flared and gotten in the way of clear thinking.

"I hear ya, man." Garrett picked up the trash can and righted it. "He needs to pay for this."

"We'll get him. Look, there's nothing else I can do here. Need a ride to your place?"

"No. I'll catch a ride from here." Garrett flipped his phone shut, then reopened it to call Carolanne to tell her what had happened.

"Garrett?"

He turned to see Carolanne running toward him.

"I heard the sirens. I went to Pearl's when Jill didn't answer. They said they'd just taken you both to the hospital. My God. Are you OK? Your arm?"

He hugged Carolanne to his chest. "Yeah. I'm fine. Jill's going to be in ICU all night. No visitors."

"But she'll be OK?"

"They said the burns weren't severe, but the smoke…It's bad, Carolanne. I've never been so scared in my life."

"No," Carolanne gasped.

"The smoke got her real bad. It's serious, but they're doing everything they can."

Carolanne held her hand over her mouth for a long moment. "Oh…my…Garrett, if anything happened…"

"Don't even say the words." Garrett lifted his hand in warning.

"I can't see her?"

"Nope. Neither can I." He shrugged.

She tossed her keys to him. "Let's go home and get some rest so we'll be in shape to see her tomorrow when she really needs us."

"The doctor said he didn't know how long they'd have to keep her. It could be a while," Garrett explained as they walked toward the parking lot.

Carolanne pointed out her rental car in the emergency room patient parking area.

"How did the fire start?" Carolanne asked as they got in the car.

He sighed and dropped the keys to his lap. "I'm not sure. I passed Kase on the road just before I saw the smoke. I know he set the fire, but I guess we won't know the whole story until Jill can tell us more."

Carolanne leaned her elbow on the center console and rubbed the side of her face, shaking her head the whole time. Her hands trembled. "I never thought I'd be capable of hurting someone, but I swear if he were here right now…"

"Get in line." Garrett started the car and headed to his house. He knew exactly how Carolanne felt. They stopped at Garrett's parents' house on the way home to tell them the news and ease their concerns. Garrett's mom would pass the information on to whoever else needed to know, and he could count on lots of prayers from the community for Jill.

Garrett stayed right by Jill's side as soon as they'd let him in the room. She'd slept the better part of the first couple of days in the hospital. Permanent internal scarring was still a possibility, but finally, she was showing signs of improvement. She was alert, but Garrett still couldn't shake the fear that had rattled him to the core. He felt the need to protect her from anything. Everything.

The blue-haired nurse who had given him such a hard time had recognized him, and it had become a running joke with the nurses on the floor about how much better a patient Jill was than he'd been. Other than some bruising, her only major injury, aside from the smoke inhalation, was her right shoulder. When the chair had tipped, she landed full weight on her shoulder, dislocating it and causing a fracture.

Jill sat propped in the hospital bed looking pale in the blue-and-white hospital gown. She was weak, but alert. Garrett helped Jill through the breathing exercises. They wouldn't let her leave until she'd reached a certain level, and it was painful for Jill, and that made Garrett's heart clutch. He held the contraption that monitored her progress for her.

Three days later, the doctor finally told Garrett that Jill could go home.

"We'll send her home with an inhaler and pain medication," the doctor said. "You'll want to be sure she doesn't exert herself.

She may notice shortness of breath for a while, even with light activity. We'll want to monitor her closely for an extended period." He handed Garrett a two-page checklist of precautions and conditions to watch for.

Garrett scanned the list. "Anything special on the shoulder?"

"I don't think she'll be overdoing that for a while. I've already talked to her primary care physician. He's expecting a follow-up visit at the end of the week. I've got that information at the bottom of the page." The doctor pointed out the instructions.

"Great. Thank you." Garrett shook hands with the doctor. After the doctor left, Garrett entered Jill's room and stooped next to the chair where Jill was sitting. He handed the doctor's instructions to Carolanne.

"Hey, cutie," Garrett said to Jill.

"Hi, yourself." Even whispering, her voice was hoarse.

"Sexy," he teased.

"If you like girls that sound like frogs," she answered.

"Let's get you home. Milly and Carolanne are bursting at the seams to spend some time with you. I've been hogging all the visitation time. You were asleep when Milly came by."

"Hey, I've been a good sport," Carolanne said from the doorway.

"You sure have," Garrett said. "If we'd been in opposite positions, I would've been complaining."

"Oh yeah, you'd have been a whiner for sure," Carolanne answered playfully.

"Let's go." Jill started to get up out of her chair.

"Oh no," Garrett said, "if they made me go downstairs in a wheelchair, you're going down the same way."

She flopped back in the chair. "Says who? You?"

Right on cue, the blue-haired nurse walked in with the wheelchair. "Says me."

Jill smiled at the nurse's familiar face.

The nurse helped her into the wheelchair, adjusting the sling and leaning in to whisper loud enough for Garrett to hear. "You're a much better patient than he was. I knew you wouldn't give me a hassle."

Jill smiled angelically and poked her tongue out at Garrett as they headed for the hallway.

"I've got some news to share with you," Carolanne said from her side.

"Good news?" Jill looked hopeful.

"I think so."

"You're still moving back, right?" She held her hand to her throat.

Garrett hated to see her still suffering.

The nurse stopped the wheelchair and reached over the nurse's station countertop, grabbing a pen and legal pad. "Here, missy, you don't need to be straining those vocals after what you've been through." She dropped the pen and paper in Jill's lap, then pushed her toward the exit.

Jill scribbled on the paper. *Your laptop.* She held up the sheet to Carolanne and mouthed the word *sorry.*

"Don't you worry about that. I'll use my Kindle Fire for a couple days until I can get a new one. I can get a new laptop. Getting a new you wouldn't be near as easy." Carolanne reached out and gave Jill's hand a squeeze as they wheeled down the hall.

The blue-haired nurse helped Jill into the car.

Jill breathed heavily from just the short few steps to the car. The doctor had told her she'd probably become winded easily, but this was ridiculous. They rode home in silence.

"Can we go to Pearl's?" Jill asked.

"I'll take you there tomorrow," Garrett said. "The house is a complete loss, Jill. You don't want to see it." He tapped on the pad in her lap. "Use this."

"Fine." She scribbled and held up the pad for him to read.

"Everything is gone. There's nothing to see." Garrett noticed the determination on Jill's face. He knew that look. She wouldn't be satisfied until she got her way, but he knew how heartbreaking it would be for her to see the last thing she shared with Pearl, her childhood home, destroyed. And any hope of finding that treasure was now long gone.

Carolanne reached over the seat and squeezed Jill's good shoulder. "Honey, I don't think it's a good idea to go over there until you get a little stronger."

Garrett pulled his truck up to the front steps of his house.

While Carolanne helped Jill inside, Garrett scrambled from room to room gathering pillows and blankets to prop Jill up on the couch so she might be comfortable for the day. He tucked a blanket around her legs and handed over the remote control to the television.

Jill scribbled on the pad. *Am I going to make it?*

Garrett read the note and gave her an odd look.

She held the remote up and pointed at it.

"Don't get used to the royal treatment. I'm just feeling sorry for you right now," he said.

COOL, she wrote and flashed it in his direction before punching buttons and flipping through the satellite channels.

Carolanne brought a big glass of water and placed it on the end table. "The doctor said we should give you lots of fluids. Drink up."

"This is service," Jill croaked. *Where's Clyde?* she wrote.

"He's at the kennel. Garrett didn't want him to knock you around on your first day home," Carolanne said.

Garrett's laptop? she wrote and held up.

"Is your laptop here, Garrett?" Carolanne asked.

"In the bedroom."

"I'll get it." Carolanne disappeared down the hall. She pressed the power button and handed it to Jill.

Jill started to write and then swallowed and spoke in just above a whisper instead. "Scooch over here. Look at what I found out about the Pacini Pearls. You're not going to believe it." Jill typed and then turned the computer screen toward Carolanne to reduce the glare so she could see it.

The computer screen showed a picture of an ornate box. Below that picture was another with the box open and filled with pearls. Pearls of orange, pink, violet, and black. Below the picture was a caption: *The Pacini Pearls.*

Wow, Carolanne mouthed in utter amazement.

"Read this," Jill said to Carolanne. "Out loud."

Carolanne read the article. "It says there were nearly fifty pearls believed to have been in the box, some as large as grapes or bigger."

Jill jotted words on a piece of paper and lifted the tablet. It read, *That's a big-ass pearl.*

"Darn right it is." Carolanne nodded in agreement.

Jill started to write and then dropped her pen and started talking, albeit softly. "The article reiterated what I read in that original clipping. That John Carlo had been accused of heisting them, but look here. He wasn't a thief. He was later cleared and deemed the rightful owner of the treasure."

"Treasure?" Carolanne asked. "They really called them a treasure?"

"Yep, and you won't believe what they say they were worth."

"Try me."

"Yeah, how much?" Garrett leaned on the doorjamb with a soda in his hand.

Jill closed her computer and smiled wide. "Over a million dollars." She paused, enjoying the looks on their faces. "How could Pearl have kept this a secret all these years?"

"I sure couldn't have kept it a secret," said Carolanne.

Garrett shook his head. “I don’t believe they were at the house. We searched everywhere. Even now, knowing what we were supposed to be looking for, I don’t know of anywhere else we could have searched.”

Jill held up her hand, flashing Pearl’s ring. “At least I still have this.”

❖ Chapter Thirty ❖

After breakfast, Garrett drove Jill over to Pearl's, as promised. They parked in the driveway, and Jill surveyed the scene. All the descriptions hadn't prepared her for what she saw. A messy pile of ash, skeletons of furniture, and charred appliances littered what used to be her home. The plants and flowers that used to thrive brightly around its base were all gone, too. Charred, soppy ground spidered out for close to fifty feet in each direction from the footprint where the house once stood.

The blood seemed to rush from her head, leaving her feeling clammy and unsteady. *Devastation like this happens to other people. Not here. Not to the only home I've ever known.* Jill grabbed Garrett's arm. She was overwhelmed to know that she'd been trapped in the middle of the devastating fire. She swallowed hard.

"Maybe this wasn't a good idea." Garrett laid his hand on her knee.

"No. I want to be here." Her hand went to her heart. How much could one person lose in a month? This was the first moment that she fully understood how close to death she'd been and how quickly her life could change. Jill grabbed the door handle, intending to get out of the truck.

"What are you doing?"

"Getting out. I want to see." She pushed the door open.

Garrett hopped out and ran to her side. "Jill, I don't think you should. There's still so much dust and ash flying around. Breathing that stuff can't be good for your lungs."

Her mouth settled into a tight line. "It wouldn't be good for my heart not to be here. I need to do this," she whispered.

He raised his hands. "Fine. Let's take it easy, though." He helped her from the truck and steadied her as she gained her balance.

Jill glanced his way, hoping he didn't notice how unsteady she was. She was much weaker than she realized. If he noticed, he wasn't letting on. He wrapped his arm around her waist and walked with her, closer to the ruin. "Wow. It's hard to take in."

Garrett nodded.

"What do we do?" she asked.

"I don't know. Rebuild?"

"How do you rebuild memories?" She didn't expect an answer; there wasn't one, and she knew it. The dark mess seemed as deep as it was wide. She stepped closer to the debris.

"Jill, the fire chief said there could still be hot spots."

She wandered into the mess, drawn to the memories and what it used to be. So many memories, up in smoke. "I want to see if anything is salvageable."

"We'll come back tomorrow better prepared. Those canvas tennis shoes will just melt if you step into something hot," he warned.

Jill hated to admit that he was right, but he was. She took a step back and nodded. "Yeah. OK. Let's come back tomorrow."

"We will." They turned and walked back to the truck.

Garrett helped Jill buckle her seat belt. "Are you OK?"

"Just give me one more minute," she said quietly. Her voice sounded raw. *Losing Pearl, and now the house. How do I start over from this?* A moment later, she leaned back in the seat. "OK. Let's go."

Back at Garrett's house, Jill called it an early night.

"Good night." She kissed Garrett good night.

"You feeling OK?"

"I'm fine. Just tired," Jill said. She turned and headed to bed, anxious to go to sleep and get to morning sooner.

As soon as the sun broke the horizon, Jill had dressed in heavy denim jeans and a pair of Carolanne's hiking boots before Garrett had finished his second cup of coffee. Unable to tie her boots with her arm in a sling, she crossed the room with her shoestrings flapping. She propped each boot on Garrett's leg for a little help. He was happy to accommodate, taking advantage of the chance to caress her knee, tickling it softly, while she was at his mercy.

"How much longer before you're ready?" She giggled and twisted her knee away from him.

"In a hurry?"

"Anxious."

"I'll get dressed now." He picked up his coffee and headed to the bedroom.

When he came out, Jill stood next to the door, clutching her purse.

"You *are* anxious." They walked outside and Garrett closed the door behind them and followed her out to the truck to take the short ride to Pearl's place.

As they drove up to Pearl's house, a vehicle was driving out. Garrett pulled his truck up next to the red-and-white fire department Yukon and rolled down his window. "Hey."

"Hi. I just wrapped up the final pieces of the investigation," the man said.

"Investigation?"

"We have to investigate all possible arson cases."

Garrett nodded. "We have a witness to this one, you know."

"I heard." The man leaned forward and waved to Jill. "You're a lucky lady." He then leaned back in his seat and hung his arm out the window. "And you, sir, were a hero."

Garrett's jaw tightened.

"We were able to resolve the point of origination and source," the fire investigator explained.

Jill leaned forward. "I told the investigator in the hospital that he lit the drapes in the living room on fire."

"With a lighter," the man added. "We found the lighter just outside the front door. He must have dropped it when he fled the scene."

"Now they just have to find the son of a bitch." Garrett's jaw pulsed.

The man put the Yukon in gear. "Y'all take care, and be careful of hotspots if you're going to poke around." He waved as he headed out the driveway.

"Kase is going to pay for this," Garrett said. "I know it's not Christian to wish ill on someone, but he earned some real punishment." The truck idled alongside the edge of what little was left of her childhood home.

Garrett shut down the motor; then Jill climbed out of the truck. The two of them moved among the rubble, sifting through the debris for any memento that may have escaped ruin.

Jill leaned over and picked up a charred silver picture frame. She stood in the ash of what used to be the living room. Only a few pieces were preserved enough to figure out what they'd once been.

She had difficulty imagining that, just days ago, this had been a house that had withstood time. A house that had held strong against the worst hurricanes the coast had seen. Floyd, Andrew,

Isabelle—all had given these counties a fit, but this house had never shirked its duty to keep them safe.

Jill swatted her hand against her jeans, sending dust flying in all directions. The sun had dried most of the deep ashy mess. She stepped carefully into new territory, wary of finding hot cinders.

Springs from Pearl's favorite chair still sat in front of the brick hearth. The blanket she'd been working on was nothing but a memory now, along with so many other personal things.

Garrett stood in the middle of the kitchen among the charred appliances. They were black with soot, and most of the boards that once held the structure strong were scorched and unstable.

Jill walked over to him and wrapped her good arm around his neck. His palms rested on the small of her back. She felt safe in his arms, even in the middle of the disastrous mess.

He rested his chin on the top of her head and kissed her hair.

"We probably should get going," he said.

"Can we stay just a little while longer?"

"Don't push yourself. We can come back every day if you want," Garrett said. "If you're up to it."

Jill raised her hand and gave him a thumbs-up, but that didn't stop her from continuing to move through what was the only home she'd ever known. She moved slowly, methodically, through the deep mess. She squatted to take a closer look. Part of a photograph peeked up from a pile of ash. She lifted it with two fingers. That little piece of paper felt so fragile. She pulled herself from the draw of her life, all those years reduced to ash.

It was late in the afternoon, and the air was starting to cool a little. The sun dipped lower in the sky, casting orange-and-pink swirls along the bottom of the skyline. Jill continued to kick through the ashes while Garrett walked the perimeter.

Garrett got a blueprint out of his truck and rolled it open across the hood of his truck. After a moment, he twisted the paper into a roll and walked back toward the far end of the house, tapping the twisted tube of paper against his leg with each step.

"Jill?"

She waved. Her voice still too fragile to yell.

He motioned for to come over. "Come here. I think...Well, just come here."

She moved through the uneven mounds of black ash to the outer perimeter and then crossed the yard.

"Look at this." He circled a spot on the plans.

"Is that the old fire box thingy?" she asked.

He shook his head. "No, that's right there." He pointed to a section just a few feet away where they used to store wood from the outside and access it from inside.

She tried to reorient herself. "So what's this?"

"That's what I was trying to figure out." Garrett lifted the rolled papers. "Know what this is?"

"Uh, yeah. A blueprint," Jill said in a sassy tone.

"Smarty-pants." He popped her on the top of the head with the tube. "It's the blueprint that Connor gave us that day we met with him."

He scrolled out the paper on the ground and pointed out the bricked area in front of them. "See how this is blocked in?" He pointed toward the left end of the house. "It's reinforced. Something is different about how that is designed."

"The built-in bookcases are in that corner. Everything on them is a mess, but the shelves are still there." Jill looked toward that part of the house and then back at the blueprint. "You know, this would have been where the decorative metal grate was in the center of the bookshelves."

"Structurally, there's no reason for the foundation to be reinforced here."

Jill's eyes lit up. "That's it!"

"What?" Garrett asked, reacting to the change in her expression.

"The foundation. That's it. In the letters, remember?" Her voice rattled as she forced the words out. She took the bottle of water from where she'd tucked it in her sling and took a sip.

" 'Keep all that is the foundation of our love safe' and then"—she took another sip so she could finish the thought—"something about the strength is in the foundation or something like that. Remember?"

"I do." He jumped to his feet. "Wait here." Garrett ran to the toolbox on the back of his truck. He jogged back carrying a small canvas bag of tools and the big heavy maul he used to split wood for the winter.

She backed out of his way.

Garrett held out his hand protectively, scooting her even farther back. He swung hard, landing the maul squarely on the spot in the foundation of the house that they'd been looking at. The cinder block cracked, and the wood splintered. Several more slams exposed dark metal.

Garrett knelt and scattered the broken pieces to get a closer look. He paused, his eyes meeting hers.

"What?"

"It's a safe, Jill. Pearl had access to it from the grate in the bookcase inside the house."

She clutched her bum arm as she kneeled beside him. "I bet the key we found in the attic fits this safe. Too bad everything is gone," she said wistfully, her eyes sweeping the ashy mess.

He slowly turned toward Jill. "What did you just say?"

"I said—"

Garrett put a hand on her knee. "I heard you. Wait here." He sprinted over to the truck.

Jill watched him rummage in the console.

In just a few quick moments, he sauntered back, holding something in his hand. "It was so unusual I couldn't bring myself to throw it away."

Her mood soared when she realized he had the key. "For once, being a pack rat is coming in handy."

"You haven't forgotten everything about me."

"Trust me, not a thing—and I tried."

"I'm unforgettable." He gave her a wink.

"And so modest," she teased. "Now hush and try it." She shifted nervously.

He slid the key in the lock. "A perfect fit."

One turn and they both heard the click.

"Finally. Thanks, Pearl."

Garrett opened the safe. "There was no chance anything in here was going to get ruined. This thing is indestructible." He lifted another box out of the safe, set it on the cinder block, and lifted the lid.

Jill reached for the roll of deep-blue fabric tucked inside. A ribbon secured it, just like the one that had held the letters.

She nodded toward her sling. "You open it."

He took a handkerchief from his back pocket and laid it on the ground, placing the package in front of her.

Jill tugged on the ribbon, and Garrett flattened it slowly.

She couldn't believe her eyes. A rainbow of colors and shapes spilled out in front of her. Her skin tingled as the vivid colors danced in front of her so bright she couldn't bear to touch them. These were not worthless baubles. The pearls' luminescence radiated a precious story that matched the awe she felt as she'd read the letters between Pearl and John Carlo. "This is more than I'd ever imagined." Her heart felt full as she blinked back the tears of realization of just how precious this treasure must have been to her grandmother.

"No wonder Kase was so hot to find this." Garrett leaned back on his heels.

"Do you think Carolanne was right? Do you think those pearls are really worth a million dollars?"

"I couldn't begin to imagine." He stared in awe at the pile of brightly colored pearls. "Maybe more. I've never seen anything like them."

Pearls of orange, pink, violet, and the shiniest blue black he'd ever seen—the Pacini Pearls.

Jill separated them into piles by color as Garrett counted them. "There are more than fifty loose pearls here."

"What's that?" Jill pointed to the edge of the fabric. A heavy seam outlined the inside edge of the cloth, like a pocket.

Garrett ran his fingers down the seam and reached into a small slit in the hem. He tugged something out of the self-fabric pocket, then held it up in front of her. The icy-blue sapphire was the size of a nickel. The teardrop-shaped gem had been set as a pendant. A thin sliver of that same light-blue ribbon looped through the golden slide, and a paper scrolled tight beneath a man's wedding band hung from the end of the ribbon. He handed the treasure to Jill.

Her eyes locked on the magnificent pendant. "I can't," she whispered. "You."

"You can." He nodded for her to hold out her hand.

When she didn't move, he lifted her hand and dropped the pendant into the center of her palm.

She gasped.

He slid the ring from the scroll and placed it in her hand, too.

"Put it on." She held it up between her fingers.

"You're sure?"

"Positive."

He slipped the ring on his finger, then opened the small scrolled paper. "It says, 'Thank you my dearest Pearl for our perfect son. With Love, JCP.' "

Their son. My dad. Jill mouthed the words.

Jill laid her hand, with Pearl's ring on her finger, across his. "A perfect match."

"The rings look good, too," he answered. "There's something else." He opened a florist-size envelope and flipped the card over. "Listen to what it says." Garrett cleared his throat. " 'The pearls are a treasure, but love—that's the real find. Never let go.' "

"From him to Pearl."

"Are you crying?"

She turned away from him for a moment. "It's romantic. Can you imagine a love so deep? So true?"

He leaned in closer to her. "Yes. I can imagine it completely."

❖ Chapter Thirty-One ❖

Clyde barked in the middle of the night, waking Garrett and Jill. Jill shot straight up in bed, startled.

"Wait here." Garrett sprung from the bed and grabbed his gun from the top dresser drawer. He stalked toward the front of the house in the dark.

Jill followed, grabbing his arm from behind, nearly scaring him out of his skin. "Sorry, I was scared."

Garrett shushed her and stepped forward. Clyde whimpered. When Garrett reached the front door, he leaned against it and listened.

Clyde barked again.

Garrett stepped to the far side of the door, Jill hugging tightly behind him. He opened it wide and backed out of view. Clyde raced through the door and sniffed his way toward the edge of the yard, but didn't bark.

"Oh, God. Garrett, it could be Bradley. Clyde didn't bark at him, remember?" Her breathing became difficult.

"Calm down. These are new surroundings for Clyde." He peeled her fingers from his flesh. "Slow down," he said, trying to keep her from hyperventilating.

She squeezed his arm tight again. “I’m scared.”

“I’m not going to let anything happen to you.”

“Don’t leave me,” she pleaded.

“You’re OK. I’m just going to look,” he said as Jill stooped to the floor.

He started toward the door, then paused to make sure she was where he’d left her.

She huddled on the floor, her knees tight to her chest.

Garrett picked up the flashlight from the table next to the door, stepped out on to the porch, and then called for Clyde.

“Come on, boy,” Garrett called as he crossed the yard.

Clyde lay down and whimpered.

Dew covered the ground. Garrett flashed the light around the yard. There were no footprints except for the path that Clyde had just made toward the trees. Garrett held his gun steady.

When he got close to Clyde, he saw what all the fuss was about and lowered his gun.

A tiny orange kitten huddled between the dog’s large paws. The kitten’s hair spiked from the slobber of Clyde’s greeting like a bad hair day. Garrett lifted the soggy kitten into his arms. Clyde jumped and kept his nose up under Garrett’s arm where he held the kitten. Another scan of the yard proved there was nothing else to worry about.

“It’s OK, Jill,” Garrett called as he walked back into the house with Clyde at his heels. He flipped on the light switch. Jill was still huddled on the floor.

“Look. We have a visitor. A welcome one.” He stooped next to her and transferred the tiny kitten to her hands.

Her heart raced, but she could at least stop holding her breath. She snuggled the tiny kitten to her chin.

“I’ll get a towel,” Garrett said.

Jill dried the kitten with her nightshirt. “You *are* too cute.”

“You like the kitty, kitty, Clyde?”

Clyde dropped to the floor next to Jill and put his chin on her knee next to his new friend. He licked the back of the tiny kitten, soaking it again.

Garrett tossed the towel to Jill and held out his hand to help her up. "Come on, I think we've had enough excitement for tonight."

They walked back to the bedroom and crawled into bed. Jill held the kitten between them. It purred loudly, content.

"What are we going to name the little guy?" Garrett wiggled a finger across the kitten that lay snuggled between him and Jill.

Jill tilted her head as she pondered a name. "How about Pearl? She's about the color of some of those pearls, and it's a special name."

"I like it," he agreed.

The kitten got up, scampered down the comforter to the floor, and snuggled between Clyde's huge paws.

Garrett propped himself on his elbow and looked over the side of the bed. "He looks pretty pleased about the new addition to the family."

Jill sighed in agreement and tried to relax in Garrett's arms. She worried that until Bradley Kase was apprehended, she'd never feel safe. Bradley was angry and willing to kill her over the treasure he believed was rightfully his. She prayed that they could keep the pearls a secret, but keeping that kind of news quiet in this town would be a challenge. Everyone trusted everyone, and word raced through the population like wildfire—especially if it was a secret.

"Quit worrying. I'm not going to let anything happen to you."

She turned in his arms to face him.

He leaned forward and kissed the top of her head. His hands swept over her shoulder and down her back. The warmth of his touch stole her breath.

She lifted her chin and their lips met. Though she'd promised herself they'd take it slow, she was happily powerless against the familiar passion in his kiss.

Garrett swept the covers back, cradling her head as he kissed her again, slower. His cool hands ran over her body, warming her in the heat of his embrace. He slowly worked her nightshirt over her head and tossed it to the floor. Flesh on flesh, he clung to her like he was afraid to let go.

Her instinctive response to his touch rekindled the old feelings. When he whispered her name into the nape of her neck, a tingle soared through every one of her nerve endings. Emotion and fulfillment flowed between them that surpassed anything she'd ever known.

She released all of her worries into his hands and let her own yearnings meet his.

Out of breath, they turned back onto the pillows, still holding hands.

"I'll always keep you safe, Jill," he said between breaths. "Please believe me."

Her breathing began to settle into a more even pace. "I do. I trust you with all my heart."

The little kitten, Pearl, meowed loudly from the side of the bed.

Garrett kissed Jill's tummy as he leaned across her and swept the orphan kitty up onto the bed between them.

❖ Chapter Thirty-Two ❖

There weren't a lot of businesses in Adams Grove, but the town made up for the lack of tax revenue with fines from traffic tickets—mostly out-of-town speeders. Not a speed trap, just a strictly enforced speed limit to keep their residents safe.

Too bad Bradley Kase hadn't remembered that little piece of trivia about Adams Grove, because he was pulled over for speeding on August 8. The eighth day of the eighth month. Eight had always been Jill's lucky number.

At the time, the state trooper writing the simple speeding ticket had no idea that he was getting ready to tie up a whole lot of loose ends with this arrest.

The high-tech equipment in his patrol car spit out a list of several outstanding warrants for the speeder, including the ones that Jill and Garrett had recently filed. If Bradley Kase, aka Carl J. Townsend, thought for a second he was going to slick talk his way out of this one, he was wrong. Today wasn't his lucky day. The trooper glanced at the report printing across his console and called for a backup unit.

An hour later, Sheriff Scott Calvin dialed Garrett. "You won't believe who I just put in a cell."

"Kase?"

"Yep, and let Jill know that Carl J. Townsend is Bradley Kase. That solves the Clatterbuck connection. They were married. Partners in crime. I was sitting here at my desk when the state guys came in to turn Kase over."

"What about Clatterbuck? Was she with him?"

"We haven't located her, and he's not talking," Scott said.

Garrett hung up the phone. "That was Scott."

Jill sat straight up. "What did he say?"

"They've got him," he said.

"Bradley?" she squeaked out.

"Call him Bradley, or call him Carl, whatever. They've got him."

"What about Annie? Do they have her, too?"

"I guess Kase assumes Annie can live on the money they scammed. He's not telling where she is."

"Still protecting her. Figures. Where do they have him?" she asked.

"In town."

"I can't believe he came back here. He thought he'd duped the foundation out of that money, but I messed up that plan. Those dollars needed my signature to be released—of course Bradley said he could get to it, anyway. Add forgery to his list of skills. I don't think that's going to get me off the hook for being a part of his scam, though."

"It'll be OK. You know Carolanne will prove you weren't a part of his lies. Don't even waste any worry over that." Garrett pulled her close. "Do you know what today is?"

"What?"

"The first day of the rest of our lives. A fresh start."

She put her arms around his neck and kissed him on the cheek.

"What are you going to do about the pearls?"

"They've been nothing but trouble. For John Carlo, and Pearl, and now us. They represent the past. Let's leave the Pacini Pearls there, too."

"Maybe we can just tuck them away in the foundation of our new home and leave them to our little ones," Garrett reasoned.

Jill smiled. "I love the sound of that."

"Yeah, but we better get started. We're not getting any younger."

She slapped him playfully. "Hey, speak for your own self, old man. I'm still a hot young babe."

He pulled her close and whispered in her ear, "You won't get an argument from me."

His breath tickled her ear. "I'm sorry I hurt you."

"We're not going to talk about that again. We both know where we've been. I love you, and I don't want you to be hurt or lonely again." Garrett tugged her closer, breathing in her scent. "Jill Clemmons, you are a real find."

His words lit her heart like a sparkler.

"I want you to marry me, and I don't want to wait. We'll break ground on Bridle Path Estates immediately. If we work quickly, we could get the artisan center open before the spring traffic picks up with tourists heading to Virginia Beach on Route Fifty-Eight."

"Was that a proposal?"

"No." He knelt in front of her and took her hands.

Her eyes glistened.

"This is." He held out his pinky. "Jill, will you marry me?"

"Yes." She wrapped her pinky around his, her smile so broad she could barely speak. Nodding, she whispered, "Yes, I'd love to be your bride, Garrett Malloy."

"I guess it's official, then. Come on, let's go tell Pearl."

She smiled and took his hand. They drove in that good kind of quiet all the way to town. Garrett stopped in front of Spratt's and ran in to pick up flowers. Jill held the bag in her lap as they drove to the church.

Garrett turned into the lot, and they headed to the graveside.

Jill reached into the bag and took out the flowers. "There are two bouquets here."

He reached around and turned her to the left. "I thought maybe we should acknowledge JCP over there, too." He pointed out the single monument. No dates. Just initials.

Her lips parted in surprise. "I never made the connection."

"It came to me on the ride over." He took her hand and they knelt between Pearl and John Carlo.

Jill held her hand up for Pearl to see—the one with Pearl's wedding ring on it. Her tears flowed and Garrett's eyes misted, too.

"Don't worry, Pearl. She said yes." Garrett looked heavenward and then took her hand in his. "Pearl had a perfect track record, after all."

"We'll have to wait to see if Connor and Carolanne are together before we bestow that title on Pearl," she said with a slight smile of defiance.

"When are you going to learn?" Garrett turned and looked into Jill's eyes, then leaned in and kissed her neck, whispering in her ear, "Never doubt Pearl's wisdom."

THE END

❖ Recipe Favorites from Adams Grove ❖

Pearl's Sweet Tea

You'll want to make this tea by the gallon, and please keep this recipe our little secret.

Glass jugs make all the difference, and I swear a good one with a spigot is the best way to go. Something about the way the tea splashes in the glass over the ice is just a little miracle all to itself.

The secret is all in the steep, ya see. Like anything that's worthwhile, you have to give it the time to mature, to marry up and merge to its full potential. Love is like that, ya know. Anyway, all tea has a temperature point of perfection, and you really have to get that water boiling if you want to get it right. Here we go!

- Place 3 family-sized tea bags (or 10 regular-sized tea bags) into your glass jug.
- Boil up a pot of water. (Be sure it's less than a gallon of water because you'll need to leave a little room for that cup and a half of sugar you'll be adding!)
- Once the water has come to a full rolling boil, gently pour that bubbling hot water right over your tea bags in the jug.

- Steep for 3–5 minutes depending on how strong you like your tea. Me? I like mine nice and dark like a summer tan. I go for the whole 5 minutes.
- Stir. This is important. Stir in one direction. *You don't want to unstir it, now, do you?*
- Remove the tea bags with a slotted spoon.
- Now swish in 1.5 heaping cups of sugar into the hot tea and stir until dissolved.
- Top off the jug with some cold water or ice cubes.
- Chill on the top shelf of your fridge. The colder the better. Enjoy, y'all!

Pearl's Blue-Ribbon Chocolate Pecan Pie

Butter Crust:

1 cup all purpose flour (refrigerated)
⅛ teaspoon salt
½ cup cold butter
6–8 tablespoons cold water

- The trick is in keeping the dough cold. Combine flour and salt in a bowl.
- Cut in the butter with a pastry blender until mixture becomes pebbly. Stir in enough water with a fork, just until flour is moistened. Don't overwork the mixture.
- Shape dough into a ball and flatten slightly. Wrap in plastic wrap and refrigerate for at least 30 minutes.
- Roll out the dough on a lightly floured surface into a 12-inch circle. Fold into quarters and place in a pie pan. Unfold, pressing dough firmly against the bottom and sides. Crimp edges.
- Prick the crust with a fork. Butter the bottom of a smaller cake pan and set it inside the pie crust in your pie pan. Heat for 8–10 minutes in a 475-degree oven until lightly browned.

Pie Filling:

4 Hershey's chocolate candy bars (1.55 ounce size)
2 tablespoons margarine
3 large brown eggs
⅓ cup sugar
1 cup corn syrup
1 teaspoon vanilla extract
3 handfuls of pecan halves
1 handful of coconut (optional)
Just a tap of cinnamon and a pinch of nutmeg

- Put your butter crust in your favorite pie dish—Pearl was partial to ceramic pie plates.
- Preheat oven to 350 degrees.
- In a double boiler, melt only 3.5 of the chocolate bars and the 2 tablespoons of margarine. Stir until smooth. Let cool slightly while you eat that leftover half of a chocolate bar.
- Whisk eggs lightly in medium bowl. Add sugar, corn syrup, chocolate mixture, and vanilla; stir until well blended. Mix pecans into chocolate mixture and then combine with the egg mixture.
- Set pie shell on heavy-duty baking sheet and pour in filling. Sprinkle the coconut across the top.
- Bake 50–55 minutes. The crust will be golden and a toothpick should come out clean when inserted into the center.
- Cool pie on wire rack to room temperature before cutting. Serve with whipped topping and a few shavings from the last bit of the chocolate bar if you haven't already eaten it.

Garrett's Favorite FryPan Meat Loaf

1 lb of lean ground beef
2 eggs
2 pieces of sliced sandwich bread cut in cubes
2 tablespoons ketchup
1 cup of sharp cheddar cheese, shredded
1 packet of beefy onion dry soup mix
Barbecue sauce to spread on top of the loaf
½ cup of all purpose flour (enough to coat)
1 teaspoon of dried basil
Tiny dash of thyme
Salt and pepper to taste
Oil

- Preheat oven to 350 degrees.
- Mix first 6 ingredients in large bowl. Form into a ball and place in a bread loaf pan, leaving space around all sides. Push the side of your hand down the center of the meat loaf to create a long hollow and pour a generous amount of barbecue sauce down that slot.
- Bake for 50 minutes until the loaf is crusty on top and meat temperature reaches 160 degrees on a meat thermometer.
- When the meat loaf is done, let it cool, then place in the refrigerator to chill and firm.
- Slice the meat loaf in thin slices. Dip in the mixture of flour, salt, pepper, basil on both sides, then fry in the oil, forming a crispy coating and heating the cooked meat loaf to a serving temperature.

Jill's Quickie Chopped Slaw Summer Salad

This quick and easy recipe always gets a lot of compliments. Keep the easy-as-pie steps and ingredients to yourself and you'll be known for this scrumptious salad, too.

1 pkg. of crisp green salad
1 small tub of coleslaw (your favorite brand or homemade)
2 eggs hardboiled, chopped
2 tomatoes, chopped
1 cucumber, cubed
½ cup shredded cheddar cheese
¼ cup Parmesan cheese
Bacon bits
Croutons
Pepper to taste

- Open bag of salad onto a cutting board and cross-cut into bite-sized pieces.
- Combine the rest of the ingredients. Mix well so that the coleslaw is well distributed. Top with bacon bits, croutons, and fresh ground pepper to taste.

Also from Virginia author Nancy Naigle
...another novel with ties to the small town of Adams Grove

Out of Focus

Kasey Phillips thought her biggest problem was photographing Cody Tuggle's honky-tonkin' country music tour and turning it into a family vacation—until shots fired on Route 58 claim her husband Nick's life. Then the photo shoot is the least of her problems. Her son is missing from the car wreckage and Hurricane Ernesto is bearing down on the Eastern Seaboard, forcing them to halt the search.

Her life in turmoil, questions she can't answer haunt her. Who shot her husband and why? And where is her son?

Stay up-to-date with Nancy and her novels by subscribing to her free newsletter at www.NancyNaigle.com

Acknowledgments

The act of writing might be a solitary task, but bringing a book to life is not. I've been so blessed to have a wonderful support system of family and friends along the way. Without them, I could never have done this.

Thank you to Kelli Martin and the incredible team at Amazon Publishing for providing me unwavering support through this process. Kelli, your enthusiasm and belief in the stories I have to tell brought me to thankful tears more often than you'll ever know. I'd be remiss not to call out Brooke Gilbert who I met at Book Expo America and was so impressed with that I knew I wanted to be a part of the Amazon Publishing team. She's the dot that started all these connections! My editor, Krista Stroever, made the revision process an absolute pleasure. For a city gal, she sure tuned right into this Southern girl, and her guidance and touches made this book absolutely sparkle. I've learned so much from all of you. Your talents will shine through in everything I do from here on out. I'm grateful to be a Montlake girl.

To my critique partners and writing friends, thank you for the tireless feedback, promo, and rah-rahs through every dip and lift of the journey. Y'all make even the toughest parts of the ride to publication sweet (even if sometimes that means consuming alarming amounts of chocolate!).

Mom, you're my inspiration, my support system, and how you read this story over a hundred times and still cried at the right parts still blows me away. Dad and Greta, thanks so much for spreading the word about my books and hand-selling my titles everywhere you go. Thank you for believing in me.

Mike, my dear husband, is the best parts of every hero I write. Men with integrity, honor, and good old-fashioned manners just aren't that easy to find. Thank you, Mike, for being a part of my life.

With this book a dream has become a reality, and I'm excited to walk down this new path with such wonderful folks. I can't wait to meet the rest of y'all. Until then, hugs and happy reading!

About the Author

Photograph by Studio 16, 2009

Nancy Naigle was born and raised in Virginia Beach. She balances her career in the financial industry with a lifelong passion for books and storytelling and is co-author of the novel *Inkblot* with Phyllis C. Johnson. When she isn't writing or wrangling goats on the family farm, she enjoys antiquing and cooking. She lives with her husband in Drewryville, Virginia.

Made in the USA
Charleston, SC
12 November 2016